Arctic
Blue
Death

Arctic Blue Death

A Meg Harris Mystery

R. J. Harlick

RendezVous Crime

Toronto, Ontario, Canada

Cover design by Emma Dolan, photo by R. J. Harlick

Le Conseil des Arts | The Canada Council
du Canada | for the Arts

We acknowledge the support of the Canada Council for the Arts
for our publishing program. We acknowledge the financial support
of the Government of Canada through the Book Publishing Industry
Development Program (BPIDP) for our publishing activities.

RendezVous Crime
an imprint of Napoleon & Company
Toronto, Ontario, Canada
www.napoleonandcompany.com

Printed in Canada

13 12 11 10 09   5 4 3 2 1

Library and Archives Canada Cataloguing in Publication

Harlick, R. J., date-
        Arctic blue death / R.J. Harlick.

(A Meg Harris mystery)
ISBN 978-1-894917-87-2

        I. Title. II. Series: Harlick, R. J., date- . Meg Harris mystery.

PS8615.A74A73 2009   C813'.6   C2009-904768-3

To Jim

One

"Meg, you have to go. I can't," my sister Jean said, squinting myopically up at me from the comfort of her Muskoka chair. More concerned about preserving her patrician good looks than being able to see, she wears her glasses only in extremis.

A flock of honking Canada geese were passing high overhead, adding to the calls of the others that had just passed. Several more V formations followed close behind. These geese were flying northward on their annual spring migration to the distant shores of Hudson Bay, easily a couple of thousand kilometres from where we were watching them at my cottage in West Quebec.

We were at the end of the dock, sitting, or rather Jean was sitting, sipping hot tea. I was standing binoculars in hand, afraid to miss even one bird as it flew over Echo Lake and the hills beyond. My sister was futilely wrapping her manicured hands around the thermos mug in an attempt to keep them warm. Although she'd turned down my offer of wool mitts—admittedly they were a tad dirty—she'd deigned to wear my old fleece jacket. But she hadn't been able to resist squinching up her nose when she thrust her cashmere-clad arms into its worn sleeves. And by her feet lay the snakeskin portfolio she'd insisted on bringing down to the dock.

Another flock breasted the ridge of the neighbouring shore. I counted, ten, twenty, thirty…and came up with about sixty. "That makes about nine hundred we've seen so far this morning. Doesn't the sight of them make you feel wonderful to be alive?"

1

"Forget your stupid geese. We're here to talk."

Much to my astonishment, Jean had arrived late last night, unannounced. It had to be easily a dozen years since she'd last visited Three Deer Point, and that was when our great-aunt Agatha was still in residence. She'd certainly never bothered to come since I'd taken over the property. I was amazed she remembered how to navigate the twisting dirt roads, let alone that she would subject her gleaming new Jaguar XKR to the punishing miles of loose gravel.

She must want something badly, very badly.

"I told you we'd talk after the geese had gone by."

I pointed my binoculars at the next flock coming into sight. There looked to be at least a hundred.

Last night I'd stalled her by saying I was too tired. This morning when I'd woken to the cries of the geese, I'd used watching them as another excuse. Although I was itching to know what had forced her to drive seven hours from her home in Toronto, I wanted it told in my time, not hers.

But the fly-by wasn't really an excuse. Every spring, since I'd fled the stress of Toronto for the peace of this northern wilderness, I'd headed down to the dock at the first sounds of their passing with a thermos mug of hot tea and enough clothing to keep out the frigid morning air. Invariably they came through the first week in May, so my ears had been waiting for this morning's dawn sound.

I wasn't going to miss this rite of spring to listen to a long harangue from my sister. Just because she was older —albeit by only eleven months—she thought she could order me around at will. Needless to say, Jean had been a contributing factor in my decision to leave the big city.

"I can't wait any longer. I have to be back in Toronto by three." Jean's voice took on a peremptory tone. She also thought because she was older, that she was smarter. And perhaps she was. After all she was a hot-shot judge of the Ontario Superior Court, whereas I hadn't even finished university.

"Fine, you'd better leave now."

"I'm not kidding, Meg. We have to talk. It's about Father."

The joy of the morning took a sudden downward spiral. I hadn't heard her mention him for a very long time. In fact, I hadn't either.

"What's there to say?" I answered warily. "He's dead. Has been for almost forty years."

"Maybe he's not dead."

"Of course he is. He died in a plane crash."

"We don't know if his plane crashed. We just know it never arrived. Here, read this."

She extracted a brown, document-size envelope from her portfolio as another honking V formation spread across the sky. The envelope was addressed to "Mrs. Sutton Harris".

"This belongs to Mother," I said. "What are you doing with it?"

"She gave it to me."

"Why didn't she call me about it?"

"She did, but you didn't return her calls."

Jean was right. Mother had left several voice messages recently, and I was waiting for the right moment to call her back. She had been another reason why I'd left Toronto.

"Read the letter," Jean ordered as she hastily moved her Gucci loafers clear of a rogue wave.

I pulled out a single sheet of plain white paper. Written in an awkward scrawl were the words

> *Dear Mrs. Harris*
> *Your man okay.*

"It's unsigned. It has to be a joke."

"Look at where it's from."

I turned the envelope over. No return address, but the stamp cancellation indicated it had been sent a little over three weeks ago from Iqaluit, a town in the Canadian Arctic. In fact, as I recalled, it was the capital of Canada's newest territory, Nunavut.

"In case you didn't know, it used to be called Frobisher Bay. Surely that name means something to you."

"Of course it does. So what?"

It did, however, leave me feeling unsettled. Thirty-six years ago on a clear sunny day in April, my father and a pilot had taken off in a chartered plane from the isolated community of James Lake on Baffin Island. Their destination was Frobisher Bay, only a couple of hours away on another part of the island. But they never made it. Neither they nor their plane were ever seen again.

"There is no way Father can be alive, so it has to be a hoax. Besides, this isn't the first time Mother's received such letters," I added.

"True, but that was years ago."

The perfection of Jean's coiffed hair was being challenged by this morning's brisk breeze. She captured several flying strands and shoved them behind her ear.

"But didn't they turn out to be hoaxes? So why should we pay attention to this one?" I countered.

"Because I think there might be something to this. She received another one ten days later. Here."

She passed me another brown envelope also sent from Iqaluit and without a return address. Moreover, the contents contained the same message written in the same almost child-like hand and similarly unsigned. No, not quite. It had been signed, but the signature had been so heavily scratched out that it was impossible to make out any letters, let alone identify a name.

"I still don't see why you think this isn't from someone trying to get money out of mother."

"Because this one came two days ago."

This envelope contained a torn-out page from the *Nunavut News*, dated September 10 of last year.

REMAINS OF PLANE FOUND
Iqaluit, NU

On a recent ice monitoring flight, a submerged plane was sighted in Davis Strait near the mouth of Frobisher Bay. Unfortunately the location iced over shortly afterwards, so the R.C.M.P. will not be able to investigate until after spring breakup.

They believe this is most likely the remains of a chartered plane that went missing last year on a flight between Iqaluit and Nuuk, Greenland. Although an extensive search was conducted at the time, the plane was never found.

Readers may recall that there have been other plane disappearances over the years, most notably that of millionaire philanthropist Joseph Sutton Harris, whose plane disappeared in 1973 on a flight between James Lake and Frobisher Bay, both since renamed to Tasilik and Iqaluit.

I glanced at my sister. "So you think this is the reason for the letters. But if this is his plane then surely his remains will be found in the wreckage. Why write that he's okay?"

Jean nodded in agreement. "That's what we need to find out. That's why we want you to go to Iqaluit."

Two

Unable to fully trust my sister, my suspicions went on high alert. "Why me? You can go just as easily."

Jean was a master at trying to get others to do her bidding.

She shook her head. "Impossible. I have a busy court schedule coming up. Plus Erin and Megan both have important piano recitals that demand my full attention."

"I get it. Just because I don't have a husband, a job or kids, you think I can just drop things and go off on some wild goose chase."

And speaking of geese, another flock passed overhead. I raised my binoculars to focus on the leader of a ragged V formation that was struggling to maintain order. He was having little success in keeping the upstarts in place.

"Well, you do have fewer responsibilities. Besides, you like the wilds. I would've thought a trip to the Arctic would fit right in with your perverse idea of fun."

I had to admit, the thought of travelling to Canada's arctic wilderness did have a certain attraction. Besides, with her manicured nails and smart little designer outfits, she was hardly a candidate for rough northern travelling. Still... "How do we know this will lead anywhere? The article said the plane sighting took place last fall. Why would this anonymous sender wait until now to contact us?"

She shrugged. "It could be for any number of reasons. Perhaps the individual was away, or maybe they didn't think it important to let us know until the search was about to begin."

"What about the police? Have they contacted Mother?

Surely they would if they suspected it was Father's plane."

"No, they haven't, but maybe they don't want to get her hopes up, since, let's face it, it's highly unlikely this is his plane. After all, they conducted a massive search right after it disappeared. Surely if this plane has been so easily spotted now, it could've been just as easily found back then."

"Precisely, so why go?" I persisted.

She finally cast her eyes skywards at another flock of high flying geese, watched them for a few minutes then turned back to me. "Mother wants one of us to go."

"No, let me guess. She wants *you* to go because she feels you would get the job done properly. You in turn want no part of it, so you're pushing it onto me."

She had the honesty to blush. "Please, Meg, this could be important. Don't you want to finally know what happened to our real father?"

Her question took me aback. Of course I did. But his disappearance had been so long ago. I hardly remembered him. After all, I was barely ten at the time. In fact, my mother was hosting a birthday party for me when the police had come to tell her about the missing plane. "I suppose I do. But more importantly, why does Mother want to know? She didn't spend a lot of time agonizing over his death before she linked up with another source of Harris money."

"Don't say anything bad about Dad or Uncle Harold—if you want to call him that. He was a far better father than our real one ever was. Besides, she waited the legal seven years before marrying him."

She sat straighter in the chair, as if to emphasize her judicial disapproval, which I chose to ignore.

"Yes, but you and I both know that it didn't take her long to let him into her bed," I retorted. Although the two of them had pretended nothing was going on, I clearly remembered surprising Uncle Harold sneaking out of my mother's room one morning in the rambling Harris family home in Toronto where we all lived.

"We both know she was going through a very rough time. She just needed some comfort."

"More likely a solid fix on the Harris money," I quipped.

Our father had been the eldest son of John Harris, who'd taken the fortune Great-grandpa Joe had amassed in mining, put it into whiskey and turned it into an even greater fortune. Harold was his younger and only sibling.

"You should talk. Look what you did to get Great-aunt Agatha's money."

"I did nothing other than visit her."

Jean had always resented the fact that I had not only inherited the century-old Victorian cottage from our Aunt Aggie, along with the surrounding fifteen hundred acre wilderness property that made up Three Deer Point, but also what remained of the money our great-aunt had inherited from her father, Great-grandpa Joe.

"But don't blame me," I continued. "You would've got half, if you'd bothered to come visit her. But you never did."

Annoyed by my logic, Jean stood up. "I've got to go. Are you going to go to Iqaluit or not?"

At that moment, my buddy and sometime protector came scrambling over the rocks that ran along the base of the cliffs lining the shore. Sergei, my black standard poodle, sensing the tension between Jean and me, placed himself protectively beside me. Though he didn't growl, he certainly gave my sister a challenging stare.

"Why can't you get yourself a real dog? Like a pit bull. More your type," Jean shot back, and ignoring him, started walking back up the stairs to the cottage.

"Good boy, a very good boy." I gave my buddy a vigorous hug before the two of us followed after her annoyingly slim figure.

Even though we'd both inherited the Harris tendency towards plumpness, Jean did her best to keep it at bay by starving herself. I on the other hand tended to help it along with a love for chocolate-chip cookies, rich creamy cheese

8

and other weight-gaining foods.

"I'll think about it," I said as my sister slid into the soft leather seat of her low-slung Jag. "I'm not sure when ice break-up occurs that far north, but it's got to be weeks away. So we have plenty of time before the police can even begin to try to retrieve the plane. In the meantime, I think we need to gather more info, if we can."

My sister nodded. "I have contacts in the Nunavut court system. I'll give one of them a call to get their take on this plane."

"Even a simple call to the police might do," I suggested. "I'll do that, and I also want to talk to Mother. Perhaps she has some idea who's sending these notes."

"She vows up and down that she doesn't." Jean clicked her door closed, turned on the engine and powered the window down.

"Maybe so, but something has prompted her to act this time, unlike the other times when she received similar letters and did nothing. Maybe she saved some of them?"

Jean shrugged. "I doubt it. I remember seeing one in the garbage."

"Was it like these ones?"

"Can't remember. It was ages ago, when I was in law school. Look, I've got to go." She shifted her car into reverse. "And thanks for taking this on."

But before I had a chance to say I hadn't yet agreed, she'd backed her car around and was speeding down my drive. Maybe when we were growing up, she'd used this tactic to bamboozle me into doing something she herself didn't want to do. Not any more. If I was going to the Arctic, it would be my decision, not hers.

However as I watched her Jag's red brilliance whisk behind the trees of the first bend, I couldn't help but feel myself drawn into whatever tangled web these letters were going to lead to. For I had no doubt that they would. Nothing to do with the Harris family had ever been simple.

Three

A week later I found myself heading into Toronto. It felt surreal driving into the city where I'd been born, grown up, gone to school and married, yet I felt a stranger. In the years since I'd left, it had changed, like all fast growing cities. Faceless housing developments had spread their grasping tentacles along the main Highway 401 corridor over what were once undulating hills of fields and forests. Big box malls filled the spaces in between. And the traffic had increased exponentially.

Accustomed to empty rural roads, I'd doggedly kept my aged Ford pick-up in the highway's slow lane and let those eager to exceed the speed limit, namely the majority including rumbling transport trailers, whiz past me. But so keyed up had I become, whether from the traffic or the uncertainty of returning home, I found myself stopping frequently to fortify my nerves with Tim Hortons coffee and chocolate cream-filled donuts.

I'd set out this morning, around nine o'clock, after safely delivering Sergei into the care of the dog's best buddy, Jid, a boy who'd also become an important part of my life. Another friend, Teht'aa, had promised to check on my house for as long as I would be away, which I hoped would only be for a few days. After some hesitation I'd also asked her to let her father Eric know I was going to visit my mother, just in case he was interested, for he would know the significance of this not-so-simple act.

Eric had once been my best friend, my saviour and my lover, but all that had changed because of my fears and my cowardice. But I didn't want to dwell on that, not now. I had enough on my plate. I was about to tread into a past I had avoided since childhood.

I suppose one could say that I was good at avoiding things that touched too closely, something with which Eric would certainly agree. Until, that is, he had pulled away from me and locked me out with his own version of avoidance.

I wasn't sure why I eventually gave in to my sister's request to go to Iqaluit. I just knew that I had to learn more about my father's long-ago disappearance and break the silence that had always surrounded it.

The anonymous letters implied that he was still alive, yet the newspaper article clearly indicated a submerged plane, which meant death. After the massive land and sea search had turned up nothing, Mother had accepted his death and had had him declared so. Over the years there'd never been any hint, any suggestion that he might have survived. Other than those bogus letters years ago, there'd been no other letters, no calls or sightings...until now.

I supposed in each of our minds, certainly in mine, there had always been a kernel of doubt, of hope. Jean's request had triggered me into wanting finally to put them to rest, one way or the other. Perhaps Mother felt the same way. Why else would she decide this time to pay attention to this new round of letters?

I felt goosebumps creep over my skin as I turned into the very familiar drive of the old Harris family mansion. Although it was years since I'd threaded my way through the labyrinth of the heavily treed streets of Rosedale to reach this cul-de-sac on the edge of a ravine, I found my way easily as the memories kicked in.

Little appeared to have changed. The driveway still followed the same circular path to the overarching stone portico. The flowerbeds with the tulips just bursting into bloom were arranged in the same angular patterns. Even the shrubs and ornamental trees remained at the same height, but then my mother would've made sure the gardeners kept them trimmed to her precise specifications.

The house loomed as massively as it always had. Built by Grandpa John in the early 1920s to survive a millennium, it was made of huge blocks of red sandstone, the same used to build the Ontario Legislative Building. Over the years, ivy had succeeded in softening its harsh lines, which had prompted people to call it the Christmas Mansion. My favourite rooms had always been those occupying the turret with its expansive curved windows overlooking the ravine, which was probably one reason why I'd fallen in love with Three Deer Point. The old Victorian cottage also had a many-windowed turret.

I glided my truck to a stop under the archway and hesitated. Did I really want to go inside? Did I really want to resurrect old memories, ones I'd successfully buried? I glanced at the window beside the front door to see if anyone had noticed my arrival, but the late afternoon sun glinting off the leaded windows prevented me from seeing inside. It wasn't too late. I could always turn around and go back to Three Deer Point and let Jean pursue the letters.

Then the front door eased open and the slim, elegant figure of my mother stepped outside. She was leaning heavily on her cane, more so than the last time I'd seen her. Perhaps with her advancing years, the polio she'd suffered as a child was causing greater weakness.

"Welcome home, dear." For a moment I thought I saw a real smile, as if she had been looking forward to my arrival.

After the prescribed pecks on the check, she ushered me into the hall, but not before suggesting I give my truck keys to Akbar, who would be happy to take it around to the back. Ah, yes. I'd forgotten. Its rusty, bedraggled appearance wouldn't quite conform to neighbourhood standards, would it? It had to be banished to the garage.

Though I would give her this much, she never once commented on or even flinched at my worn but clean jeans, my Zellers-bought T-shirt or my trail shoes, not even when I sat on one of her treasured Louis XV chairs. Mind you, it wasn't as if this antique chair covered in pale yellow silk had been my choice, since I knew how much she prized them. No, Mother had actually offered me the chair, while she sat down on its matching settee. Moreover, when the housekeeper placed the gleaming Harris silver tea service down on the mahogany coffee table separating us, I couldn't help but gape in surprise. She was going to treat me to one of her special English high teas, something she'd never done just for me.

"It's so good to see you, Margaret." Her glistening eyes hinted at a warmth her smile couldn't quite convey. She poured tea into an eggshell-thin porcelain cup. "Milk, no sugar, isn't it, dear?"

"Yes, Mother, your memory hasn't failed you."

I glanced around the large living room, or more correctly, drawing room, for it did speak of an age long dead. It was elegantly furnished with the priceless English and French antiques first Great-grandpa Joe then Grandpa John had imported from Europe. It was a room we children had never been allowed to breathe in, let alone sit in, and only rarely after we became adults. This too was a special honour.

But it was so far from what I'd grown used to that I had the decided feeling I'd taken a wrong turn and landed in the mythical Land of Oz. I could see from the way the cup clattered on the saucer Mother passed to me that she was just as nervous.

"Although it has been awhile, dear, you've hardly changed." She offered me a sampling of neatly arranged finger sandwiches. "Still my sweet Margaret."

I groaned inwardly at the word "sweet" while I helped myself to a cucumber sandwich. "You haven't changed either, Mother. As beautiful as ever."

And she was. One of those classic beauties with the fine features of a porcelain doll, including the sapphire blue eyes and honey blonde hair, although in her later years her blondness depended more on the contents of a bottle than on nature. But who was I to talk, with my attempts to hide the niggling grey hairs sprouting amongst my red ones. But she really hadn't aged much since I'd last seen her. In fact, one would never think that she was in her late seventies.

"But you inherited my genes, dear. You just need to help them along. As I used to tell you when you were a child, an orchid doesn't bloom without a lot of care and patience."

Knowing any reply could lead to one of our inevitable arguments, I held my tongue, and so did Mother. Perhaps she, like me, wanted to keep this meeting as positive as possible.

Nonetheless, I knew she meant well, for I had let myself go. I hadn't seen a decent hairdresser in months, and though my nose was more of the ski-jump variety than her perfectly sculpted one, I did have her blue eyes and fine features. Too much rich food had just blurred some of this fineness.

Great-grandpa Joe's statesmanlike portrait by some famous Canadian artist whose name I'd forgotten stared down at me from its station above the marble fireplace. Although, if Aunt Aggie's stories of his notorious prospecting days were anything to go by, he was as far removed from being a pillar of society as I was a socialite. He seemed to be saying "Go girl" or whatever words of encouragement he felt fit the moment.

His wasn't the only painting. Some of Canada's best artists hung on these walls, including one of Lawren Harris's icy blue Arctic scenes, a fine example of Emily Carr's swirling West Coast rainforest and Riopelle's frenetic paint splatters, this one red, brown and orange. Tucked into a back corner hung a piece of artwork I remembered well, but one I was surprised to see hung in such illustrious company.

"Of all the prints in Father's Inuit art collection, I always liked this one of the *Mystical Owl* the best."

"You do have a good eye, dear. That particular stonecut

print with its Mona Lisa eyes has appreciated considerably since the government put it on a postage stamp."

Hence its place in this room, where only the best of the Harris art collection was displayed. Hanging on one of the narrow walls between the French doors, I spied another Inuit print I'd always admired, although I couldn't remember the name of the artist. The stylized angry bear against a background of blue ice seemed to leap from the page.

"I guess that bear print must've gone up in value too."

Mother turned her head to study the print. "Yes, that is Joly Quliik's *Growling Bear*. After the Art Gallery of Ontario had a retrospective showing of his works a couple of years ago, I had several people contact me about buying it, but for your father's sake I couldn't sell it. It was one he was especially fond of. I'm not exactly sure why, but perhaps it was because he knew the artist."

"I remembered him once telling me about an artist who'd taken him out for a ride over the ice and snow on his dog sled. Maybe this Joly Quliik was the man."

"Perhaps."

"There used to be other Inuit prints hanging in the library. Are they still there?"

"Yes, your step-father liked them too. But much too primitive for my liking." She delicately raised the porcelain cup to her lips and took a tiny sip of tea.

As for me, I found the carefully crafted *Mystical Owl* or the *Growling Bear* no more primitive than Riopelle's flung paint.

"After your stepfather died, I had the other prints stored with the rest of Sutton's collection. It's really quite large, you know. I've recently donated it to the Art Gallery of Ontario. I thought a gallery in Sutton's name would be most appropriate, considering all he did for those people."

"You mean the money he gave to the gallery?" I crunched into another cucumber sandwich. It was quite tasty, and lunch had been several hours ago.

"Heavens no. I mean those Eskimos. That's why you're here, isn't it?"

"I'm not sure what you mean. I'm here because I want to talk to you about the anonymous letters and learn as much as I can about Father's disappearance. I really don't remember much myself."

"It was all because of those Eskimos." She didn't bother to hide the disdain in her voice.

"Please, Mother. I wish you wouldn't use that term. They prefer to be called Inuit. I think it means 'people' in their own language."

"Well, whatever." She waved her hand dismissively. "They caused his death."

At that moment the housekeeper entered the room. "*Madame*, the car is ready."

"Oh dear, I forgot. I have a meeting of the planning committee for the Black and White Arts Gala, which I'm afraid I can't miss, so, Margaret, let us talk later." She got up to leave. "Hannah, could you please show my daughter to her room."

"If it's my old bedroom, I think I can find my way."

"Sorry, darling. I'm not used to having you visit." She gave me a gentle peck on the cheek and squeezed my hand. "I'm glad you've come. I've missed you."

As I watched her neat, slightly stooped figure limp from the room, I couldn't help but think that I'd been away too long. Sure, my lifestyle didn't come close to intersecting hers, nor my values for that matter, but she was my mother. I was finally glad I'd made the decision to come home.

Four

It was only when I entered my old bedroom that I felt I finally was home. Nothing had changed. Even my dusty collection of stuffed animals continued to flop on the top shelf of my bookcase. On the wall hung my Branksome Hall graduation diploma that Mother had insisted on framing beside a faded poster from a Neil Young concert, which I'd ripped from a telephone pole as a dare in Grade Ten.

I had spent a lot of time in this cozy L-shaped room with its slanted ceilings, which stood at the end of the long hall on the third floor, where all Harris children were relegated. Although after my marriage to Gareth Mother had offered me a more spacious, more adult room on the second floor, I had refused to take it. This room had become my oasis, my sanctuary from life's pressures.

Besides, I hadn't wanted to sleep in this house with Gareth, and I never did during our thirteen years of living together. I only returned to this room after I'd run away from him. But Mother's relentless chastising eventually drove me to Three Deer Point. She blamed me for the marriage breakup, insisting it was a wife's duty to stick by her husband's side no matter what. As for the broken arm he'd given me, along with the bruises and black eye, her only comment had been, "these things happen."

I smiled at my old photographs filling up one of the end walls. I used to derive a lot of enjoyment from photography. In fact, in the early years of my marriage, I'd even thought of doing it professionally until Gareth pummelled the desire away with his barrage of criticism. But as I perused

17

these pictures of Canada's great outdoors, I felt they were as good as any I'd seen in travel magazines and calendars.

Maybe I should take it up again. I'd felt a tremendous sense of accomplishment at having captured the ethereal beauty of a wildflower or the magic of a still lake at sunrise. In fact, I recognized a couple of lake and forest scenes taken during my many stays at Three Deer Point when Aunt Aggie still lived there.

But enough of this useless musing. It would get me nowhere. I hadn't come all this way to reminisce. Although I wouldn't be able to learn more about these letters until Mother returned home, I could at least get my call to the Iqaluit police over with.

A week ago, after my sister's car had sped out of sight, I'd phoned but was told to call back in a week's time when the constable in charge of the missing airplane files had returned from leave.

Fortunately, Corporal Reilly was back and in the office when I called this time. After listening to my request for information on the submerged plane, he replied in a brusque, almost impatient voice, "Give me your e-mail, and I'll send you our press release on it."

"I'm afraid I want a little more than a press release," I replied rather testily.

"Why should I provide you with any more information than what's been sent to the other journalists? Besides, the press release pretty well sums up all we know to date."

"Because I'm not a journalist. This plane may very well be my father's that went missing in 1973."

"Whoops. Sorry. I've been getting a lot of calls from the southern press on this. Even had some from Europe. Just assumed you were another one. Who did you say your father was?"

"Sutton Harris. I'm wanting to know if it's possible that this could be his plane."

"Let me see. That's the one that disappeared between

Tasilik and Iqaluit, right?"

"Are you familiar with it?"

"Yeah, I've read the file. I wish I could be more definitive, but at this point in the investigation, we aren't able to establish the plane's identity. Christ, we don't even know if the sighting was accurate. Could've been a rock, even a whale for all we know. Unfortunately, we can't verify until the ice is gone, which won't be for another couple of months."

"Do you think this could be his plane?"

"It's possible. But this sighting has to be at least three hundred kilometres from what would've been its direct flight path between Tasilik and Iqaluit."

"Maybe bad weather, instrument problems, whatever, caused the pilot to stray off course, and he ended up crashing at this spot."

"Anything's possible. But from my experience, it's highly unlikely a pilot would veer that far off course."

"So you're fairly certain it's the Greenland flight mentioned in the newspaper article."

"Yes, ma'am. The purported crash site is only twenty-thirty kilometres off that charter's filed flight plan."

"I guess you're right, but the reason for my call is that someone has been sending my mother letters from Iqaluit that suggest this is my father's plane. In fact, the letters even say that my father is still alive, which is ridiculous."

"That's gotta be someone's idea of a sick joke. Even if he did survive a plane crash, the brutal conditions in that area, hell, anywhere in this godforsaken north, would've killed him. You gotta realize, winter is still going strong in April, which I believe is when your father's flight went missing, eh? And this crash site has gotta be a few hundred kilometres from the nearest community. So there is no way in hell he would've made it."

He paused while I heard him drink something. "But say by some miracle he did, then sometime over the last thirty or more years, his presence would've come to our attention.

Not too many whites up here we don't know about. But his file's still open, which means he's most likely dead—we just haven't found the body."

"And we, his family, would also know if he had survived, because he'd be with us." I felt I had to add the obvious, which he'd forgotten to mention.

"Yeah…of course. Any idea who sent the letters?"

"Unfortunately, they're not signed, and there's no return address."

"Then it's just someone wanting to make trouble. We get a lot of that here."

"You mean anonymous letters."

"No, people making trouble. Not much to do up here. People get bored. The sender probably saw the newspaper article and thought he could make a quick buck out of it."

"They haven't asked for money."

"Not yet. Look, if you want I can look into these letters for you and find out who sent them. Shouldn't be too difficult. We're a pretty small community up here and everyone knows everyone's business."

"Thanks. Since they were addressed to my mother, I'll check with her before I send you copies. You mentioned that you won't be able to check out this plane for another couple of months."

"That's right, not until the ice is mostly gone in Davis Strait, which is usually about mid-July. That's the earliest we'll be able to get a salvage boat out to the site along with the divers. But given this here global warming I suppose it could be sooner."

"When you have a date, could you let me know. I want to be there."

"Don't see why you'd want to go to the expense. Even if it proves to be your father's plane, doubt there would be much to see…" He paused, then cleared his throat as if embarrassed. "By that I mean given the length of time the plane has been in the water, it's highly unlikely there'll be any readily identifiable remains."

"You mean his body."

"Hmpf, yes, ma'am. So no point in you coming up. If it proves to be your father's plane, only way we'll be able to identify the body is through DNA analysis, which is handled by our guys in Ottawa. Just as easy for them to get a comparison sample from you at your home as up here."

I hung up feeling disappointed. Although I'd initially had reservations about flying to Iqaluit, the chance to visit Canada's most northerly capital was starting to intrigue me. But Corporal Reilly had a point. My presence wouldn't add anything to their identification. Besides, I wasn't sure if I really wanted to see my father as a collection of bones, and Reilly was better equipped to find the sender of those letters than I was. No, a trip north made little sense.

I walked back downstairs in search of a cup of tea to tide me over until dinner and to find out when Mother would be returning. When I reached the front foyer, I heard the postman putting the mail in the outside box. Trying to be helpful, I retrieved an assortment of envelopes and magazines and headed down the hall to the kitchen.

While the rest of house appeared to have changed little from my last visit, apart from the odd new art item or two, the kitchen was another matter. Mother had been on a spending spree. Gone were the knotty pine cupboards I'd known since a child, the white Melamine counters and pale yellow appliances. So too the racks of gleaming copper pots and the hanging ceiling lights with their copper shades. Instead the large room, aglow with pot lighting, had been upgraded to the crisp efficient modernity of the twenty-first century.

It now sported what seemed like miles of black granite counters and acres of rich cherry wood cupboards with the appliances discreetly hidden amongst them. Only a six-burner gas stove top was visible. All the other appliances were hidden behind the cherry veneer, so too the pots. I was

21

amazed that Mother would go to such expense when I'd never known her to express any interest in food preparation, let alone spend time in what she considered the cook's domain. But when I saw the fancy Italian espresso machine complete with coffee grinder and an automatic frother, I knew Jean had been the influence. Mother drank only tea.

Hannah was sitting in the wide bay window drinking regular coffee at the one item in the room that hadn't been replaced, an old pine table that dated back to my grandfather's day. Obviously someone had put her foot down. And I had a pretty good idea who.

Hannah stiffened and placed her cup carefully back down on the saucer. She tucked a stray strand of grey-blonde hair into her bun. "Can I help you, Miss Margaret?"

I had the distinct feeling that she wasn't used to her realm being infiltrated. I didn't know Hannah. The last housekeeper I remembered was Caroline, a large buxom grandmotherly type who loved nothing better than to prop her varicose veined legs on a chair at this very same table and watch the soaps on TV. I would sometimes join her. Although a new and larger TV stood on a cherry wood corner stand, it was turned off.

"Sorry, I didn't mean to disturb you. I was just wondering if you knew when my mother would be coming home."

"Akbar is to pick her up at six thirty. Is there anything else I can assist you with?"

"Margaret, is that you come home?" cried out a voice.

I turned around to see the short, wiry figure of Shelley emerge from the pantry, hefting a bag of potatoes in her strong but work-chafed hands. She dropped them onto an inlaid chopping board of a centre island and ran over to me.

"Here let me have a look at you, lass." Her smile added more wrinkles to her beaming face. "A little more meat on those bones, otherwise still the same little Maggie who used to steal my chocolate chip cookies."

I hugged her back. Shelley had been the cook since as

far back as I could remember. She had to be well over sixty but appeared as spry as ever. "It's great to see you. You don't happen to have a batch of those cookies around, do you?"

She chortled, pulling out a tin box from a cupboard and loading the cookies onto a platter. "Fresh made this morning. When your mum told me you'd be coming, I knew you'd be wantin' some. Might as well have a cuppa, too." She poured me a cup from the teapot standing at the other end of the table from Hannah. "Sit yourself down and tell me all about yourself, while I make supper."

It was then I noticed the mail in my hand. "Hannah, here's today's mail." I placed it on the table in front of her. As I did so, a large brown envelope slipped out with the address in a hand I immediately recognized. I snatched it up to confirm the postmark. Iqaluit. Mother had been sent another letter.

Five

"W ell…aren't you going to open it?" I asked, watching with amazement as my mother placed the unopened envelope back down on the coffee table. Her hand, however, shook with more than just age as she set it down.

This time we were sitting considerably more comfortably in the deep, cushioned chairs of the den cocooned in the coziness of its mahogany panelling. In front of us loomed the floor-to-ceiling fieldstone fireplace that Grandpa John had modelled after the one in the front room of Three Deer Point. Though unlike my own, this fireplace still sported one of Grandpa John's kills, a giant moose head with an expansive set of antlers. When I'd moved into the cottage I'd removed all the dusty animal heads shot by my relatives over the years. I preferred to see my animal heads alive and moving.

"No, dear. Let's have a nice dinner and talk about other things. Besides, your sister and her family will be here shortly, and I don't think the children will be the least interested," she replied.

Aching to know what was inside the envelope, I nonetheless acquiesced and said, "Of course. But I do want to discuss these letters with you, so please, let's do it after dinner."

"As you wish, dear. Now tell me about Three Deer Point. I did so enjoy our summer visits there when Aunt Aggie was alive."

Even though I thought those long-ago visits had been more a test of endurance for Mother than an enjoyment, I didn't dispute her comment. Instead I told her about the ups and downs of day-to-day living in the wilds. There was one aspect, however, that I didn't bring up, which was my relationship with Eric and other members of the Migiskan Anishinabeg who lived on the Algonquin First Nations reserve neighbouring my property. Although Mother liked to think she had an open mind, she was nevertheless a snob. I wasn't entirely sure she would understand or accept these friendships which had become an integral part of my life.

Soon Jean whisked in with her husband Leslie and two daughters in tow, much as I remembered Mother doing with us when we were children. I'd always rather liked Leslie and felt a bit sorry for him. The heir to one of Toronto's oldest Establishment families, he was a quiet, self-effacing man who hovered behind the shadow of Jean's boundless energy. I'd always wondered why Jean had married him, since she didn't need his money and they seemed to have few intersecting interests. But the marriage was still going strong, unlike my own, which had started off with much greater promise. Perhaps because underneath Jean's hard edge I sensed an unerring love for this gentle man who in turn felt the same kind of love for her.

Of medium height with a full head of brown curly hair, Leslie was wearing his standard bow tie, this one red. His lips reflected a wisp of a smile. "It's good to see you, Meg. I think you must enjoy your new home. You're smiling again." He blushed as he said these last words, almost as if embarrassed he'd gone too far.

I hugged him. "I'm very glad to see you, too. And you're right, my new life is treating me very well."

Turning to the tall, leggy girl clinging to his side, I said, "You must be Megan. You were this high when I last saw you." I placed my hand about two feet below her current height, which was about the same as her father's. "You must be thirteen or fourteen."

"Thirteen," she whispered and blushed.

"Yeah, she's the pipsqueak in the family," added Erin,

who proceeded to guffaw at her joke. Although the eldest by two years, she was at least a full head shorter. But unlike her shy sister, she displayed all the bold confidence of her mother, despite having inherited her father's head of brown curls and his slightly oversized nose. "So I hear, Aunt Meg, you're going to the Arctic to find out what happened to Granddad."

So much for Mother's attempt at censorship. "Probably not," I replied.

"Hey," Jean cried out, "you promised."

"I didn't. Just said I would consider it. And I have. The Iqaluit police have said there is no need to go. They don't think it's Father's plane."

"But the letters seemed so certain," Mother whispered, her steely demeanour suddenly gone as she clenched her hands to her breast.

Her reaction took me by surprise. I'd always had the impression she'd laid her husband firmly to rest when all hope had gone of finding the missing plane. "I hadn't realized finding him meant so much to you."

"I don't have too many years left, and before I die, I would like to know Sutton's final resting place. And I think you do too, both of you." She glanced from me to Jean.

"I agree," Jean said. "We need to end the mystery of his death once and for all."

"I'm with you," I replied. "But the police are just as certain that this isn't his plane. But if it is, chances are his body will no longer be with it, or if so, what is left of it won't be identifiable other than through DNA, which is done in Ottawa."

"But at least we will know where he passed his final moments. Jean, you'd better go, as I suggested in the first place. You were always closer to your father."

I felt the stab of Mother's censure. "That's not true. I loved him just as much."

In fact, I'd always felt there was a special bond between

us. We both loved staying with Aunt Aggie at Three Deer Point. He always took me and not Jean on his ambles through the woods, canoe paddles on the lake or on his visits with friends at the Migiskan Reserve. We would often stay a week or so longer than Mother and Jean, both desperate to flee back to the city.

Not wanting to prove my mother right, I said, "I'll go, but there is no point in going to Iqaluit until mid-July when the water should be ice-free. Police won't be able to salvage the plane before then."

"Sounds good to me." Jean's face relaxed into a smile. For a few minutes she must've been worried. Perhaps I shouldn't have been so hasty to respond to Mother's rebuke.

"And I'm happy to pay some of your expenses," she added.

"That's terribly kind of you, Jean, but there is no need," Mother interjected. "Since this is a family matter, I'll handle all the expenses."

My initial knee-jerk reaction was to refuse, simply because it felt like a payoff, nor did I want them to have the last word. But I didn't refuse. Although Aunt Aggie's estate provided me with enough income to allow me not to have to work, it was only enough to live modestly at Three Deer Point. It wouldn't cover a costly trip to the Arctic.

"And while we're on this topic, perhaps it's a good time for you to open the letter you got today." I pointed to the envelope in front of her.

"You were sent another anonymous letter?" Jean's high heel shoes clicked on the hardwood floor as she walked over to have a look at the brown envelope lying so innocently against the dark mahogany of the table.

"We don't know if it is or not." Mother retrieved it from the table.

"But it's from Iqaluit," I interjected. "And the writing looks the same. So why not open it now?"

"Our dinner is waiting. Shelley won't want us to eat

it cold. I'll do it after dinner." Clutching it in her hand, Mother headed towards the dinning room, leaving us with little choice but to follow.

While Leslie shepherded his two daughters after his mother-in-law, I held my sister back. "Is it me, or am I getting the impression Mother doesn't want to open it?"

"It seems that way to me too."

"Did she act this way with the others?"

"I've no idea, but I wasn't here when she received them. She only told me about the letters after she received the newspaper clipping."

"Did you ask her why she waited?"

"Yes, she said she didn't think they were important."

"But she didn't throw them away."

"No, she didn't. But let's face it, the letters are worthless. It's absurd to suggest that Father is still alive. I'd go so far as to say it's an insult to Mother and to us. It's only the newspaper article that is credible."

"True, but let's make sure she opens this latest one tonight. I can't help but feel that she's afraid of what she'll discover inside."

Jean nodded and followed her husband and children into the dining room, from which the most delicious aromas were wafting, which drew me after them.

Six

"Mother, you must open the envelope," Jean insisted. "Since this concerns all of us, we have as much right to know what's inside."

The six of us had returned to the den after one of Shelley's signature meals: rosemary chicken stuffed with wild rice, new potatoes, creamed pearl onions and of course the broccoli, al dente, just the way I liked it. She'd topped it off with another of her specialties, maple rice pudding. The scrumptious meal had mellowed me somewhat, so Jean had taken over the badgering.

During the course of the meal, whenever the conversation had veered towards Father or the letters, Mother had deflected it. I'd assumed that once we'd placed our forks on our empty dessert plates, she would finally open the envelope lying in full view next to her place setting, but she flatly refused, insisting it must wait until we finished coffee. So the six of us had straggled out of the dining room and back into the den, where a fire was flickering in the fireplace. Hannah followed us in to take our orders for espresso or latte.

Erin had immediately put the TV on, only to be ordered by her mother to turn it off. She'd then stuck her earplugs into her ears, turned her iPod on and plunked herself down into one of the overstuffed chairs as far away from us as she could get. Jean and I had taken up station in the wing-back chairs flanking the fireplace. Across from us on the chesterfield sat Mother, with Leslie and Megan joining her. And in between, the brown envelope lay enticingly close on the coffee table.

But as much as I wanted to rip it open, I kept myself in check.

"Yes, Mother." My brother-in-law's low voice broke the silence. "It's time to open it. I know this is hard for you, but we are here to support you. It's best to share these things and not keep them to yourself."

Mother gently patted his knee. "You're a good man."

Placing her teacup back on the saucer, she reached for the envelope. It fluttered with her trembling as she tried to peel off the scotch tape sealing it and failed.

"Here let me." Leslie pulled out a small penknife and slit the envelope open. He passed it back to her.

I found myself holding my breath in anticipation and noticed Jean was doing likewise.

Mother slowly inched out what looked to be a thick sheet of paper sandwiched in between a cardboard backing and a piece of tissue paper. Her hands were shaking so much she had difficulty separating them. Leslie took it from her, removed the tissue and placed the paper face-up on the table.

Mother gasped and closed her eyes.

"Cool," Erin said from behind my chair.

I found myself speechless. So too Jean.

On the coffee table lay a drawing, a stylized, one-dimensional drawing in black ink of an Inuit sled with several of what I took to be dogs and a plane falling towards it. Jagged orange flames shot out of the back of the plane. A figure dressed as an Inuit with a fur-trimmed hood and mukluk-like boots stood to one side as if watching this plane fall from the sky. In the upper right hand corner were some odd symbols, inscribed one on top of another, almost like a Chinese chop. The corner of a sheet of thinner paper peeked out from underneath.

I pulled it out.

"Your man okay" read the message in the same square handwriting of the other letters. Again with no signature.

What little colour Mother had drained from her face. "Oh no," she gasped. "Just as I feared."

Leslie moved over to put his arm around his mother-in-law.

"You've seen a picture like this before," I said more as a statement then a question.

She whispered, "Yes."

"Did it come with one of the other letters?"

She nodded.

"But you didn't mention it," Jean said.

"No, I didn't," was her simple answer. The firm line of her clenched lips indicated that she wasn't willing to explain why.

"Where is it?" I asked.

"Upstairs in my desk drawer." She handed me the key.

It took me only a few minutes to retrieve the drawing, or more correctly drawings, for there were two of them, from the walnut desk in her study.

I laid them on the coffee table beside the latest picture in what I thought was their order, for they seemed to depict a progression of events, almost as if a story were being told. Like the one Mother had just received, these drawings had also been drawn on thick almost linen-like paper in the same flat, naïf manner.

The first drawing depicted an Inuk driving a sled with a couple of dogs towards what could be seals lying on ice. The second was more or less the same picture but with the airplane flying normally above them. Like the drawing Mother had just received, these two also had symbols inscribed along the upper right hand edge. In fact these symbols looked to be the same in all three drawings.

"I'd say this is telling us about someone witnessing Father's plane crash, don't you think?" I said.

"I agree," Jean acknowledged. "But this happened in 1973. It seems strange that they would wait until now to send us these pictures."

"It's pretty isolated up there. Maybe they didn't know who to tell."

"I would've thought telling the police would've been obvious," Jean replied.

"But for whatever reason they didn't. Maybe this newspaper article reminded them of the plane crash. And it would've given them Father's name."

"Yes, but the article didn't mention Mother. "

"I'm sure it's information easily garnered," suggested Leslie. "Sutton Harris was a fairly public figure and so is your mother. This person probably came across a newspaper article or found it on the internet."

"Perhaps the more important question to ask," I said, "is why they would go to all this trouble to send these pictures and not identify themselves?"

"Maybe they did," Leslie offered. He picked up one of the drawings and headed out of the den. The rest of us, even Erin, followed him along the hall, past the dining room and library and through the archway into the drawing room. He didn't stop until he reached Father's *Mystical Owl* print hanging on the back wall.

"These look to be the same kind of markings." He pointed to a set that had been made along the lower right hand edge of the print. "Someone once told me that this was the artist's signature in Inuit writing, what they call syllabics."

Although the *Mystical Owl* print symbols were similar to those of the drawings, they weren't the same, further evidence that it might be the artist's name.

"We need to have someone translate them for us. Do you know anyone who could do this for us, Leslie?" I asked.

And then for the first time since I'd brought the drawings down from her study, Mother spoke. "There used to be an art gallery near Bloor Street that Sutton dealt with. The Davis Gallery. They specialized in Eskimo art."

The phonebook quickly told us that the gallery no

longer existed, which wasn't surprising, since it was almost four decades since Father would've dealt with them. "What about a museum? Mother, you must've dealt with some Inuit art expert at the art gallery when you were donating Father's collection."

"Wait a minute. I know someone who's considered quite the expert," Leslie replied. "I'll give her a call to see when she's available." Flipping his cell phone open, he walked out into the hall.

A few minutes later he returned. "She can see us tomorrow about nine a.m. It'll take us an hour or so to get there, so we'll have to leave at about eight. Hope that's not too early for you, Meg?"

"I'm an early bird, but what about your wife? She's the one who hates to get out of bed in the morning."

My sister's immediate response was to stick her tongue out at me, something she'd done frequently when we were growing up. "I can't come," she said. "I have an early morning court case. And for your edification, I'm up every morning at six and off to my personal trainer. How else do you think I keep this perfect bod in shape? Which is more than I can say for you, darling."

I ignored her insult. "Is the early time okay for you, Mother?"

"If you don't mind, dear, I'd just as soon not come. I find these drawings too painful."

It was only then that I realized tears were slowly seeping from her eyes.

"I do hope Sutton didn't feel much pain." She dabbed her eyes with a thin cambric handkerchief.

"Oh, Mother, I'm so sorry," Jean said. "We've been so thoughtless not thinking of the full implications of these drawings."

She placed a comforting arm around Mother, something I should've also done, but overt physical contact was something Mother and I had always shied away from. Call it our cold British roots, whatever. We'd never been able to show each other much physical affection, but Jean, coming from the same roots had never had a problem.

Instead I said, "Mother, remember what the letters say. Maybe he didn't die." Although I didn't believe it for a moment, I felt it might help to alleviate some of Mother's distress. "Is this why you didn't want to show us the drawings?"

"Yes." She took a sip of her coffee. Her hands weren't shaking quite as much now. "I was afraid of what this most recent drawing might depict. And I was right. Poor Sutton, to die so horribly."

I could see she didn't believe the letters either, and the pictures, if they indeed depicted my father's crash, put the lie to them also.

We all remained quiet, lost in our own separate thoughts. There was nothing more any of us could say. The thought of Father dying in a burning plane was just too horrific.

Seven

While my sister and brother-in-law continued to comfort Mother, I poked at the fire, poured myself another cup of coffee and returned to my chair. Erin, her interest no longer tweaked, plugged back into her iPod, while Megan picked at a thread in her skirt as she cast anxious glances at her father.

In a matter of minutes Mother was drying her eyes and brushing Jean and Leslie aside, saying, "I'm okay now."

I waited a few more minutes before asking, "Mother, you received letters like these many years ago. Did they have drawings, too?"

It took such a time for her to answer that I thought she might not have heard my question, but as I was about to repeat it, she said, "I don't remember, it was so long ago."

"Did they also come from Iqaluit?"

She remained quiet for a moment before answering. "I don't recall that name, but it seems to me some of them did come from some place in the far north. I remember being surprised by the location."

"And it wasn't Frobisher Bay, Iqaluit's former name?"

"No, it was a place I wasn't familiar with. When I looked it up on the map, I recall thinking how odd; it was on Hudson's Bay, very far from where your Father used to travel, which was mainly to Baffin Island. At least that's what he told me."

"Can you remember what any of the letters said? Or even how many there were?"

"There weren't many. Maybe two or three in total. The

first came not long after your father's plane disappeared. It asked for money, a lot of money in return for information about your father. I didn't like its tone, so I passed it onto the police, who said the man who'd sent it was dead. How ridiculous using the name of someone who was dead. Obviously the sender wasn't very smart."

"What about the other letters? Did they ask for money?"

"They did, but not enough to bother the police. I just threw them away. They weren't worth my time."

"What about the timing of these letters?"

"As I told you, the first one came one or two years after your father disappeared. The others maybe ten or so years later, say the early 1980s."

"And you didn't receive any more until now?"

"No, dear."

"Is there any possibility that the same person sent both sets of letters?"

"I have been wondering that myself. As I recall, the letters that came in the 1980s were written like these latest ones, in a roundish rather childlike handwriting, the way a person writes when first learning. But apart from that similarity, I couldn't say whether it is the same person."

"Can you remember what the letters said? Or the name of the sender?"

"No, not at all," she replied with a sudden abruptness as she placed her cup back down on its saucer. "Children, it's getting late and I'm tired. I think I will go up to bed. But you continue visiting. You haven't seen each other in such a long time."

She raised herself painfully from the sofa. "I'm afraid I haven't been a very good hostess. Leslie, you know where the liqueurs are. Please help yourselves."

She gave us all a gentle peck on the cheek and shuffled, cane in hand, out of the den towards the elevator that Grandpa John had had installed after a stroke had left him partially paralyzed.

I waited until I heard the elevator's folding brass door clink shut and the motor start up before saying, "I think Mother remembers more than she is letting on. What do you think?"

"I will admit I had a similar impression." Leslie poured himself a snifter of Armagnac and offered us our choice from Mother's eclectic collection of liqueurs.

Although I hadn't had a liqueur since going dry over three years ago, I felt very tempted. All this delving into the past was just a little too nervewracking. Nonetheless, I resisted and poured myself another cup of coffee instead.

As I watched my sister enjoying her blueberry grappa, I said, "It's too bad you didn't read the letter you found in the garbage."

She nodded then paused as if mulling over a thought before saying, "You know, I do remember something. These drawings have reminded me of it."

She ran her eyes over the three pictures lying on the coffee table. "In the same waste basket were bits of paper, as if something had been ripped into shreds. Some of the pieces had parts of a drawing on them. I remember being surprised at the time that mother would tear up a piece of art, given her love of it. I also remember seeing the head of an Eskimo with a hood." She picked up one of the drawings. "Very much like these ones."

"Did you happen to read the letter?"

"No...no I couldn't. It had been ripped too."

She thoughtfully sipped her grappa. She seemed to be savouring it so much, it was all I could do not to rush over to the liquor cabinet and pour myself one.

"And you weren't tempted to try to put it together?"

She started to shake her head, then changed her mind. "You're right. I was about to, but Mother came into the room and grabbed the wastebasket from me. She was really angry. In one of her snippy moods."

"Too bad Caroline doesn't still work here. She might've

seen the letter." I paused. "Shelley was the cook back then, maybe she knows something."

The kitchen was as spotless as only Shelley could make it. In the days when Mother and my stepfather, that is my uncle—I never knew what to call him—had big parties, within an hour of the last guests leaving, Shelley would have it equally spotless. Although Mother would hire extra help for the occasion, Shelley would invariably kick them out after the bulk of the clean-up had been completed and finish the last polishing on her own. It was her realm. She had to put her final stamp on it.

Shelley was resting in her creaking bentwood rocker with her feet up on a small stool.

"Mind if I join you?" I asked. As I child, I would sometimes sneak down after I'd supposedly gone to bed to nestle in the kitchen's welcoming warmth. This was invariably after yet another disagreement with Mother or Jean. Shelley would give me hot chocolate in my special Montreal Olympics mug and of course a chocolate chip cookie. Then she would settle into her rocker and lend a sympathetic ear. It wasn't that she would offer advice, she never did. It was more her quiet rocking back and forth listening to whatever I had to say. Once I'd spilled everything out, I would perk back up and feel ready to take on life's next offering.

"You don't need to ask, lass. Of course you're welcome. Here, have a cuppa." She poured me a cup of tea. "And a wee dram." And before I had a chance to refuse, she poured a good measure from her special bottle of twelve-year-old MacCallan—she only drank the best—into a tumbler and added a bit more to her own.

Not wanting to hurt her feelings, I clinked glasses with her. Although the spreading tingle of the whiskey felt good, really good, I was nonetheless determined to drink only a sip or two.

"This is quite the kitchen," I said, my eyes roaming over the sparkling granite counters and gleaming stainless steel.

"When did this happen?"

"Last year. It was your sister's doing. She thought the old one needed a facelift. But I tell ya, Maggie, I do miss the old charmer. It was a place where a tired old body could sink back and relax and not worry about a wee bit of dust. But this monstrosity with its shiny surfaces drives me crazy. I'm forever removing smudges and the like." And with that, she got out of her chair to shine a spot on the counter where she must've seen a smudge.

I laughed. "But if you shine it up too much, you might rub the surface away."

She eased herself back into her rocking chair and winked. "That's the plan, lass. Then perhaps your mother would give me back my nice white counters. But you're not here to listen to an old woman grumble. Tell me what ails ye."

"Nothing really, I just wanted to sit down for a chat for old times' sake. But before we begin, I do have a question. I think you're probably aware that Mother has recently received some anonymous letters about Father." I took another sip of the whiskey, just one more. It was delicious. I'd forgotten how smooth a single malt could be.

"Aye, so Hannah tells me. Mind you, I knew something was amiss. Your mother's been terribly quiet lately, like something was bothering her."

Since she had known Father and had lived with us through the unsettling time of his long drawn-out death, I figured she had a right to know, so I told her about the letters and the drawings.

When I'd finished, I asked, "Mother received similar letters sometime in the 1980s. I'm wondering if you remember those."

"Aye, I remember." She took a long sip of her whiskey. I joined her. "Caroline told me about them. They upset your Mother, they did. Something terrible. I remember all the door-slamming upstairs. Could hear it clear through the house. She was that angry."

"Funny, I don't remember that part. I just remember the hushed whispers with Uncle Harold. I overheard him telling Caroline that if any more letters came, she was to give them to him instead of Mother. It was Jean who found out what they were about."

"You were probably at school when she opened them up. But it did put Caroline in a bit of a predicament, for she didn't want to lie to your mother. And another one did come."

"It did? Do you know what was in it?"

She shook her head. "Caroline never saw the letter. Your uncle took it from her and hid it away in his desk."

"Damn, I was hoping you could tell me if there were any drawings with the letter. What about the earlier letters? Did you ever learn what was in them?"

The soothing warmth of the whiskey was beginning to make me feel mellow. I relaxed further into the chair.

She shook her head again. "No. Caroline and I just knew it was something hurtful. And figured because they came from the far north, they might be about your father."

"You knew where they came from?"

"Oh yes, Caroline was quite curious when she saw the postmark that said Churchill. She even got out the map to show me where it was on Hudson Bay. Not as far north as where your father's plane got lost, but still a long ways away."

At least Mother's memory hadn't failed her in this aspect. And I agreed with her. Churchill was a very long way from Iqaluit, easily a thousand kilometres or more. And because it was situated in the province of Manitoba, it wasn't even considered real Arctic. It did seem very strange that someone living in that town would know anything about Father's death.

"Curious you should mention drawings," Shelley continued. "I recollect Caroline mentioning a drawing she saw on your uncle's desk not long after she gave him the strange envelope. One of those Eskimo ones, like your

40

father used to collect."

"Do you know what it was about?"

"I think Caroline said it was just some Eskimos standing by an igloo. She couldn't see what all the fuss was about."

"Do you know what happened to it?"

She shook her head again. "Sorry, can't help you there." And she poured both of us another "wee dram", which I didn't for a second think to refuse.

Realizing I'd probably exhausted Shelley's memories, I turned the conversation to her brother's family. Although they lived on the other side of the globe in Scotland, they were Shelley's only family, and she took great interest in their doings.

Eight

The morning traffic was heavy as we drove north on the Don Valley Parkway out of Toronto. Fortunately, most of it was headed downtown in the opposite direction. Leslie's friend, Mary Goresky, was the director of the McConnell Art Gallery in Victoriaville, about an hour's drive northwest of Toronto. Apparently her gallery had one of the largest collections of Inuit art in Canada, specializing in works from Cape Dorset and James Lake, two of the Arctic's renowned art centres.

"In fact," Leslie said as he slid his Mercedes into the passing lane. "I believe Cape Dorset was one of the first settlements to start producing art, at least so Mary has told me. Apparently a man by the name of James Houston introduced print making in Cape Dorset back in the late 1950s."

"James Houston. I recognize that name," I said. "Father had something to do with him. In fact I think he was the man that got Father involved in collecting Inuit art."

"Could very well be. James Houston was a big name in the field. He was really the man that got it going. Back in the late 1940s he brought a number of soapstone carvings down to Montreal to see how they would sell. They took off like wild fire. I remember my mother travelling with a group of friends all the way from Toronto just to buy some. She didn't want to miss out on a chance to discover the next Picasso."

"And did she?"

"Damn!" he muttered as he suddenly braked to avoid hitting a red Miata that cut in front of us.

"Whew, that was close," I said, removing my hands from the leather dashboard.

He smiled apologetically. "Sorry about that. Crazy drivers around here. Let me see, where was I? Oh yes. My mom might not have picked up the next Picasso, but she always had a good eye for artistic merit, and she did pick up one or two carvings that have appreciated considerably in value. One in particular of a kneeling caribou with antlers."

Unfortunately, the traffic going north had slowed to a snarl as we closed in on a major interchange.

The car clock read 8:15. "Think we'll get to Victoriaville on time?"

"Mary said her calendar was open until 10:30, so we should be okay. Besides, once we're on the 407, we should move along like greased lightning." He emitted a nervous laugh almost as if embarrassed by his bold statement.

But he was proved right. Once we passed under the cameras of the toll highway, we breezed across the top of Toronto. In the distance I could see the downtown skyscrapers with Toronto's signature CN tower rising above them. But they were soon lost to view as we approached the western outskirts of the city. A jet on its descent path told us we were passing the airport. And before we knew it, we were back into the westbound traffic of the 401.

"I hope you don't mind taking the scenic route into Victoriaville rather than the expressway." Leslie glanced shyly at me as if looking for my consent, which I readily gave, not liking major highways any more than he did.

We eased off the highway, and for a few kilometres the two lane county road was indeed scenic, complete with rolling pastures, gabled stone farm houses and forests flush with the new green of spring, but before long they were replaced by wall-to-wall Monopoly houses.

"Victoriaville used to be a nice, quiet farming town," Leslie lamented. "Now it's been overrun by commuter suburbs."

Almost as if a line had been drawn, the sardine-packed

houses were suddenly replaced by elegant nineteenth-century merchant homes with overarching maples and expansive lawns. We passed another reminder of Victoriaville's prosperous roots, an imposing stone church with many stained glass windows and a towering bell spire. Just beyond the cemetery, no doubt housed with Victoriaville's finest, we turned into the heavily treed grounds of what was once a stately Edwardian brick home. "McConnell Art Gallery" read the brass sign.

We walked passed a bronze sculpture of a man guzzling what looked to be a bottle of hooch and climbed up the stairs to the large glass front door. It sprang open and out strode a tall angular woman with sculpted white hair. Although her dark brown pantsuit was mannishly conservative, her fuchsia ruffled shirt was anything but, nor were her rhinestone-tipped glasses.

"Leslie, it's great to see you." She thrust out her hand. "And you must be his sister-in-law, Margaret. I knew your father."

"Do you mean Sutton?" She didn't seem old enough to have known my real father. "Or more likely it was Harold, my stepfather?"

"Harold. I never knew Sutton. He died before I became involved in Inuit art, but I remember Harold telling me about the missing plane. Such a tragedy. They were brothers, weren't they?"

I nodded appropriately. "I hadn't realized you knew my uncle."

"Yes, Harold generously provided the funding for the beginnings of the McConnell Gallery's Inuit art collection."

"Amazing. I'd never realized he'd had such an interest in Inuit art."

"He was more a dabbler, but I believe his donation was really in memory of your father. Sutton Harris, as you know, is regarded as one of the visionaries. He recognized the potential artistic value of Inuit Art and helped get it recognized as an art form rather than a native craft."

"I guess I hadn't realized Father had such a reputation. I just knew he collected. In fact, he died during one of his many collecting trips to the Arctic."

"It must've been difficult for you and your sister." She glanced at Leslie as she flicked a sculpted curve of white hair away from her face. "Harold was a wonderful man and would've made a good father." The strident tone of her voice softened. "But it's never easy having one's father replaced, is it?"

"No, no, it isn't," I replied, wondering if she was speaking from personal experience. However, not wanting to dwell any longer on this dangerous ground, I changed the subject. "We have some drawings. We're hoping you can identify the artist."

"Yes, so Leslie has mentioned. However, since my knowledge of Inuktitut is rather limited, I've asked one of my graduate students, an Inuk from James Lake to join us. She should be here shortly. Meanwhile, I'm dying for a smoke. Unfortunately, I can't smoke in the gallery, so must satisfy my vices outside…at least some of them." She laughed. "Come, let me show you our sculpture garden."

She lit up a cigarillo and marched us around to the side of the building where a diverse collection of stone, metal, and even plastic sculptures were scattered throughout the grounds. While I was rather partial to the large bronze feather, Leslie preferred the sickle stabbing a cell phone. Said he'd always wanted to do that to his own phone. By the time the director had finished her cigarillo, her graduate student had arrived, a plump, smiling cherub wearing too short a skirt for her chubby legs and a mischievous glint in her black eyes. Mary introduced her as Ooleepeeka McLeod.

The four of us trooped into the gallery past a small exhibit of, interestingly enough, several Joly Quliik stonecut prints.

"My mother has an Quliik print," I said, eyeing a herd of

caribou prancing across the paper.

"Lucky you. Do you know which one?"

"Yes, the *Growling Bear*."

"How marvellous! *La crème de la crème*. Born in an igloo and raised in the old ways, Joly Quliik had a wonderful talent for capturing the highlights of traditional Inuit life. His drawings were among the first to be carved into soapstone for printing." She paused, glanced at the prints then turned back to me. "I've always wanted to show the *Growling Bear*. Do you think your mother would lend hers to the gallery for a special exhibit?"

"I've no idea. I could ask," I replied, somewhat taken aback by her forwardness. But I supposed like anyone working in the art world, where money was scarce, she had to take advantage of every opportunity to bring the best to her gallery.

"But enough on Joly Quliik, let's go upstairs to my office where we can inspect your drawings."

Nine

Mary's office was an exhibition space in itself. Every wall and surface, other than her desk and a glass coffee table, which were themselves stacked with papers, was covered in works of art, tapestries, paintings or sculptures. She motioned us to sit on a rather hard antique settee, while she sat down on a considerably more comfortable chintz-covered chair, one she clearly spent a lot of time in. Ooleepeeka took a seat on the ergonomically correct desk chair, which looked like it was seldom used.

"Do you have them in there?" Mary pointed to the leather portfolio I'd been lugging around. She brushed aside a pile of documents to clear a space on the coffee table.

I heard a quiet gasp as I laid the drawings down, one after another in their order. For the next several minutes she carefully studied each drawing while Leslie and I sat somewhat bemused by this intense interest. After all, they were just a set of simple drawings. But I could see that Ooleepeeka's interest was also piqued as she too slowly scanned each drawing in turn.

When Mary finally leaned back into her chair, I couldn't help but notice a rather excited glint in her eye.

"Please forgive me," she said. "You both must be dying for a cup of coffee. Cappuccinos? Great."

After passing our orders on to her male admin assistant, who sported a shaved head and a pearl drop nose ring, Mary turned back to us. "First, these aren't drawings. They are soapstone prints."

"Sorry. I just assumed that because the figures are in

outline, they'd been drawn in ink or charcoal."

She dismissed my lack of expertise with a shrug. "Second, something which is quite unique, the artist who drew the pictures also carved the soapstone and did the actual printing on the paper. Rarely does this happen. Usually the artist doesn't have the skill to do the carving, particularly with soapstone, which is both very heavy and quite fragile. One mistake, and you have to start over again. So usually an experienced stone carver is used."

"How can you tell this didn't happen with these prints?" I asked.

Mary pointed to an Inuit print of a fluffed-up owl hanging above her desk. "Both names appear on the print." She pointed to the small square syllabic signature in the upper left hand corner. "Take this print of the *Little Owl*. The first characters denote the artist. In this case 'Pitseolak' and the next set the printer. This last character, the red arch, indicates where the print was made, Cape Dorset."

"Does this mean there is only one name on my prints?" Leslie asked.

"Precisely."

At this point, her admin assistant came in carrying a tray of oversized cups brimming with foaming milk and a plate of shortbread cookies.

"And do you know who the artist is?" I asked.

"I have a fairly good idea, because I recognize the style. Although I am surprised, because he didn't normally make the stonecut." She lifted up one of the prints and scanned it carefully. "But I don't recognize the syllabic signature. However, Ooleepeeka will be able tell us, won't you, dear?"

"Yes. The name is Suula." She beamed proudly as she tugged to pull down her denim skirt, which had ridden up on her chunky thighs.

Mary started. "Suula? Are you sure?"

"Yes, positive." Ooleepeeka beamed back at her. "I had a teacher with this name."

Appearing somewhat baffled, Mary placed the picture back on the table, picked up another one and studied this one just as carefully, then she nodded. "My apologies. I was a little too hasty. Curiously enough, given our previous conversation, I thought they were Joly Quliiks. But although the style is similar to his, I can see now that it doesn't reflect the same level of maturity or refinement of line. Too bad."

"Why do you say that?" I asked, helping myself to one of the shortbread cookies.

"As you know his work has appreciated considerably since he died."

"I hadn't realized he was dead."

"Yes, it happened many years ago. If these uncatalogued prints could be attributed to him, they would command a good price. But since they are by this unknown artist Suula, I'm afraid they won't be worth much. In fact, one could almost accuse this artist of copying his style."

She tossed the rejected picture back onto the table. It caught on the edge and fell to the floor. Leslie hastily bent over to pick it up.

"I don't care about their value," I shot back, annoyed by her high-handed manner. "It's the artist and his whereabouts I'm interested in. You said unknown artist. Does this mean you don't know who this Suula is?"

"I've never heard of him, and I'm *au courant* with most Inuit artists, at least the ones that matter. Perhaps, Ooleepeeka, you know of this artist?"

The graduate student shook her head. "Suula is probably a female name, though with Inuit names you can't always tell. And I'm afraid I don't know the community where these were done either. It's called Naujalik, meaning 'place of seagulls.'"

I turned back to Mary. "I suppose you're not familiar with this town either?"

"It's certainly not a recognized art centre like Cape Dorset or James Lake. By the way, in case you didn't know,

James Lake has been renamed Tasilik. When Nunavut came into being, several towns took on Inuktitut names. In this case, Tasilik means 'place with a lake', isn't that right, Ooleepeeka?"

She patted her grad student patronizingly on the thigh. Ooleepeeka stiffened and moved her leg away.

"You must appreciate that there are only a handful of places in the Arctic which are recognized for their consistently excellent work. And this Naujalik isn't one of them. I'm afraid that these are just someone's amateurish efforts." Mary stopped to sip her foaming coffee.

At this point, I wanted only to leave. Clearly we were going to get no further useful information from this overbearing snob. But Leslie, more tolerant and more forgiving, spoke up. "I realize these drawings aren't something you normally deal with, Mary, but perhaps there is someone who handles this type of amateurish art who might know. As I mentioned on the phone, the whereabouts of this artist is important to us."

"One thing you should be aware of, Leslie, is that these prints are much older than you probably think. At least twenty to thirty years old, if not older, so the artist may no longer be alive."

"How can you tell?" I asked.

"It's the paper, dear." She paused for another sip of coffee while I had to bite my tongue not to shoot back, "I'm not your dear."

"See those tiny brown dots on the paper? Those are mold marks. They develop over time if the artwork has been exposed to cardboard or other inferior paper materials. Plus, this type of paper was generally used in the 1960s and '70s. Today they use a much finer quality, one less prone to deterioration."

"Okay, so the artist may be dead, but someone sent these to my mother, and we want to know who. The only name we have at the moment is this Suula. So please, if you know of someone who could help us find him or her, let us know, and we'll be on our way."

She rested her chin on her tented fingers and peered at me over the frame of her glasses. "Yes, I can understand why you would like to speak to the artist. The scenes depicted in these prints are of your father's plane crash, aren't they?"

"We believe so."

"And you are assuming that the artist witnessed the crash, aren't you?" She didn't wait for my reply but continued speaking. "I find these three prints rather interesting. They tell a story. Now the Inuit, like all indigenous people, are wonderful storytellers. And many of their artworks do tell a story. But usually they depict just one aspect of the event or folktale, or if several events are depicted, they are contained on the same page. Never have I seen a story spanning several drawings. Do you know if there are any more?"

"What? You want to see my father's plane splat on the ground with his body beside it?"

She cast a shocked glance at Leslie then back to me. "Sorry. That was thoughtless of me."

"Look, I don't think we should take up any more of your time." I started to collect the pictures.

"Why don't you let me do some asking around? Some of my colleagues might know of this Suula. Ooleepeeka can also inquire of her friends up north. I'm sure we will find this artist for you. We'll let Leslie know, okay?"

I grudgingly accepted her offer.

As Leslie and I made our way back through the gallery, I stopped at the Joly Quliik exhibit to see if I could tell if the style in my mother's prints was the same as his. With my uneducated eye, I couldn't readily discern any similarities. But then, there weren't any people in those prints.

Ten

I'm not about to sit back and do nothing while we wait for Mary to get back to us," I said to my brother-in-law as we whizzed along the 401 back to Toronto. "I'm going to pursue my own inquiries."

"I don't see how we could do better than Mary."

Leslie braked as the Mercedes glided up to a transport trailer clogging the passing lane, then breezed past as the truck returned to the slow lane.

"I suppose. But I got the distinct impression she didn't want to dirty her fingers on such a mediocre artist, so I'm not sure how much effort she'll put into it."

"I'm sorry you feel that way. But you're right, Mary can be a bit of an art elitist. However, I know from experience that when she agrees to something, she always carries through."

"Maybe, but she's running a gallery. It may be some time before she can make her inquiries. In the meantime I want to see what I can learn on my own."

"What are you suggesting?"

"Mother mentioned the art gallery where Father used to buy his artwork. Although it's no longer in business, there must be other private galleries that specialize in Inuit art?"

"Yes, I suppose. There's also the AGO, to which your mother donated your father's collection. I'm sure she still has the contact information for the people she was dealing with. I would start with them. They're bound to have a more in-depth knowledge of the field than a private gallery would. Here, use my cell."

A quick call to Mother produced two names. She'd been

quite impressed with their knowledge, and since they'd been so helpful during the lengthy negotiations, she felt certain they would be quite willing to extend their help again. Unfortunately, when I called, I learned that both curators were away at a conference in Europe and wouldn't be back until the following week.

"I don't want to wait that long," I said as I snapped the phone shut. "I'll check the phonebook when I get home to see what private galleries might be able to help."

We were passing the looming abutment of the Niagara Escarpment through a break in the mountain-high ridge that extends northward to Georgian Bay. It brought back a memory of a weekend, I think it was the autumn before Father disappeared, when the two of us had hiked a short section of the Bruce Trail that meanders along the top of the escarpment. The fall colours had been glorious, the fallen leaves fun to walk through. We'd laughed and sung as we ambled, only keeping quiet when we thought we saw deer.

I supposed it was one of the last happy memories I had of Dad, particularly since I hadn't had to share him with anybody. Afterwards had come that dreadful Christmas when the shouts of their arguments and Mother's door slammings had rung through the house.

"Meg, Meg, you with me?" Leslie's voice cut through my thoughts. "I said, I'll have my assistant find out for us, okay?"

I shook the conflicting images from my mind as he hit the speed dial on his cell.

Although Leslie didn't have a job per se, having more than sufficient funds from his family's trust to support his own family, he did keep an office to handle a foundation he'd set up many years ago to handle his philanthropic interests, which were oriented around cultural and environmental concerns.

"Just a moment, Claire." He turned to me. "Meg, do you mind grabbing a piece of paper from the glove compartment and writing down this info?"

He recited the names of two galleries and their addresses.

"Punch the first address into the navigator." It pointed to a side street in Yorkville.

Within thirty minutes we were standing in front of expansive windows with Schmitt's Fine Art Gallery emblazoned in gold across the front. But despite the keen interest of the manager, he was unable to provide any more information than Mary had. After thanking him, we set off for the Jasper Izerman Gallery, which was further downtown on Queen Street. Unfortunately, he couldn't help us with the identity of the artist either.

"However, I do know the name of a person who might be able to help you," said the impeccably dressed grey-haired Jasper Izerman. "Carter Davis."

My ears perked up at the name. "Did he own the Davis Gallery on Prince Arthur?"

"Yes, his was one of the first galleries to handle Inuit Art."

"My father used to deal with him. In fact, we'd been hoping it was still in business."

"Sadly, he had a heart attack a few years back and was forced to sell. But given his years of experience with Inuit Art, I'd say he is one of the foremost experts in Canada."

"Great. Do you know how we can get in touch with him?"

"Most assuredly. He comes by my gallery frequently to keep apace with the latest. There has been a tremendous change since the 1990s with some of the younger Inuit artists wanting to break away from the more traditional themes. Take this piece, for instance."

He showed us an Inuit sculpture that was markedly different from the traditional polar bears and seals I was used to seeing. Carved out of whalebone and soapstone, it depicted a head wearily leaning against a hand with a liquor bottle sticking out of the top of the head. The face wore a befuddled expression and sported the large bulbous nose of an alcoholic. It was obviously a comment on the alcoholism that was reported to be rampant in Inuit communities.

While I wrote down Carter Davis's contact information, Leslie continued to stare at the sculpture. Finally he asked the price. By the time we left the gallery, Jasper was lugging to the Mercedes a large wooden box with the carving carefully wrapped inside and a promise to let my brother-in-law know when the next collection of sculptures arrived. Knowing my sister's penchant for ultra-modern minimalist art, I wondered what her reaction would be to her husband's impulsive purchase.

Eleven

Fortunately, Carter Davis was more than happy to meet us once he discovered I was the daughter of Sutton Harris. We agreed to meet at his house in Cabbagetown at four p.m., after his doctor-prescribed nap. He also asked if we would mind bringing a litre of milk for afternoon tea. He was almost out and wouldn't be able to get to the store.

Leslie had other commitments, so I went alone. After parking my truck in the only spot I could find on a nearby street, I tramped up his narrow street, which was lined with Victorian rowhouses with steep gabled roofs and brightly coloured doors. I turned the brass doorbell on his own brilliant yellow door just as a clock from inside his house gonged the agreed hour. In one hand I held the portfolio containing the prints and in the other the bag of milk plus a tin of Shelley's chocolate chip cookies as an extra butter-upper.

A rotund, drowsy-eyed man of about eighty answered the door. After a sleepy "Come in, missie," he led me down a dark hall, the wooden floor of which creaked as we passed over it. Although some modern features had been added, the house appeared much as it would've when it was built a century or more ago. The dark oak trim and doors had been left in their original varnished state, so too the mantle over the tile-rimmed coal fireplace. The hardwood floors appeared as waxy shiny as they would've when first laid. Even the doily-covered velvet and walnut trimmed sofa and chair in the front room could've been the original furniture.

But not the art. As I would've expected, every wall, every surface sported some form of Inuit art that clashed with the fussiness of the room. Victorian excess doesn't go with Inuit simplicity. Still, who was I to judge? I complimented him on his house and the collection as I followed him into the tiny kitchen to help prepare the tea.

"How wonderful that your house is still in its original condition," I said. "Almost as if it has had the same owner since the beginning. You must treasure antiques."

"Wife's doing, not mine," he said succinctly, almost as if wanting to distance himself from it. "Her house. She was born in it, and we've been living here since her parents died in the early 1960s. It was her grandparents' before that."

I glanced around the simple kitchen with its white-painted wooden cupboards and pink doodle design countertop looking for signs of her presence but saw only the clutter of a man living on his own.

"She couldn't bear to make a change, so we kept things as they were. Except of course for my art." His smile, not so sleepy this time, added another layer of wrinkles to his face. "And when she went off to the home, came down with Alzheimer's, I promised myself to keep it ready for her for when she comes home. Here, missie, take the teapot. I find these shaky old hands can't carry much any more. Parkinson's."

We stepped back into the front room. I carried a silver tray holding a very ornate porcelain teapot, complete with a crocheted tea cozy and a couple of equally ornate porcelain cups, while Mr. Davis carried a plate of Shelley's cookies. His lips were already smacking from the one he'd sampled while waiting for the kettle to boil.

"Knew your dad well," he said before I had a chance to find a seat that looked relatively comfortable. He'd already settled into what clearly was his usual chair, a maroon velvet affair sagging from years of usage and draped with lace doilies and a mohair afghan. "He was one of my best customers. Sure knew his stuff."

I lowered myself into a gold velvet chair, being careful

not to disturb the doilies covering the arms. It proved to be considerably softer than my initial impression.

"The Inuit art world lost a great supporter when his plane went missing," Mr. Davis continued. "Do you mind pouring the tea? I'll just slop it onto the saucer."

I poured the tea into the cups, careful to give him a little less to minimize any spillover from his trembling hands. "That's why I'm here. As mentioned on the phone, my mother recently received some Inuit prints. I'm hoping you could provide information on the artist."

I moved several seal and bear stone carvings aside, plus one caribou, and laid the artwork out on the dusty walnut coffee table.

As Mary had done, he sucked in his breath, then slowly let it out. "Intriguing. In all my years of selling Inuit art, I've never come across a series that told a story. Wonderful. This your dad's plane, eh?"

"We assume so. There doesn't seem to be any other reason for sending them."

From his shirt pocket, he removed a magnifying glass and carefully scanned each print. When finished, he replaced the magnifying glass and sat back into his chair. "Boy, if it weren't for the syllabic chop, I'd swear they were Joly Quliik prints. Shame they aren't."

"Yes, that's what the director of the McConnell Art Gallery thought too."

"You went to see Mary, eh? Great gal. Knows her stuff. She probably also told you if they were Quliik's, they'd be worth a fortune. Mind you, not having an edition number would knock down the price."

I waited for him to finish eating another chocolate chip cookie before asking, "What do you mean by edition number?"

"Boy, sure are tasty." He brushed a few crumbs from the corners of his mouth. "With print making, you can print as many copies as you want from a single plate. Only trouble is, the more you make, the lower the price. So to ensure maximum value, an artist will limit the edition or the number printed."

I watched as he carefully brought his cup shakily to his lips. It was all I could do not to reach out and steady the cup for him. But he made it without spilling a single drop and took a long, slow slurp as his reward.

"When printmaking was first introduced in Cape Dorset, they set fifty as the standard edition. Afterwards, the stone print block was to be destroyed. As is standard practice, all copies are marked with an edition number, which indicates their ranking in the print run. Here, let me show you what I mean."

He lifted himself out of the chair with more spryness than I would've expected. Intrigued, I followed him into the dining room, where I was immediately surprised by a familiar print that commanded centre spot over the buffet above another collection of Inuit stone carvings.

"Why, you have a *Mystical Owl*. My mother has one too."

"I know. Your father bought it from me. There's a story to tell with this particular print, but I'll save that for later. See that number."

He pointed to a small pencil notation of 12/50 at the bottom of the print on the same line as the date: 1963; place, Cape Dorset; title, *Mystical Owl*; and artist's name, Lucy Ootoova, had been inscribed in pencil.

"This indicates this was the twelfth copy printed. One thing you need to know, missie, is that each time an impression is made from the plate, in this case a stonecut, an ink residue is left behind that builds up with repeated use. This can cause the pictures of later printings to be not quite as sharp as the first ones, which lowers the value. So as a collector, it's important to pay attention to this and invest only in the low numbered editions. One of the things I taught your father. He didn't know much when he first came to me, but he sure knew a lot at the end, almost as much as me."

"Since my pictures don't have this number, does this mean they are fakes?"

"Nope. Could mean your copies were what we call proofs. The printer usually makes a few copies to make sure everything is working properly before starting the actual run. But these are supposed to be destroyed. Or it could mean the printer didn't know enough or think it important to put this information on. But you mentioned the word fake. Now I want you to take a good look at this *Mystical Owl* print."

I ran my eyes over the Mona-Lisa-eyed owl with its floating black and orange feathers and sharp talons. It looked exactly like my father's print, but then I didn't have the connoisseur's eye or the experience to discern any differences. "Looks okay to me."

"So you would think. Let me tell you a story about this picture. I won't say how it came my way, but let's just say it wasn't through the normal government-controlled channels."

I must've looked blank, for he went on.

"In the early years, the government was very concerned about ensuring legitimacy and retained value for these works of art, plus they didn't want the Inuit taken advantage of, so they established the Canadian Eskimo Arts Council. All Inuit prints had to be approved by this council, which also set the price, and they could only be sold through designated galleries, such as my own. They didn't want them being treated as souvenirs, which would seriously erode their value and reputation as a work of art.

"You see, the Inuit didn't have many sources of income. This was viewed as a possible good source. Up till then, the Inuit had used their stone or bone carvings as barter for supplies from the Hudson Bay Company trading posts."

"In the early Seventies, I was approached by a friend wanting to sell this particular print. He said it came from a private collection. I wasn't suspicious at first. The person was well known in the Inuit art world, and I'd handled other private sales like this for him, but when I examined it, it became fairly obvious to me that the print wasn't quite what it purported to be.

"Here, run this over the picture." He retrieved the magnifying glass from his shirt pocket. "Look at these lines, here and here." He pointed to several spots where the bird's feathers joined the main body.

It took me a while to discern what he was pointing out, then I noticed. "The edges are blurred. The ink seems to run into the paper."

"Precisely. Not what you would expect to see in such a low edition number. But more importantly, what really raised my suspicions was the number itself. You see, I knew where a copy with this same 12/50 edition number was hanging. In the front room of your house. I even checked with your father to ensure it hadn't been stolen."

"Maybe the printer lost track of the numbering?"

"Not possible. Too many people check to make sure only fifty numbered copies are made. At first I suspected that the original stone block hadn't been destroyed and that someone was reprinting it to cash in. You've got to realize the value of a *Mystical Owl* print skyrocketed after it was used as a postage stamp. The last time one came up for sale, it sold for $70,000.

"But then I noticed the owl's eye." He held out the magnifying glass again. "Take a look."

I could just discern an s-shaped squiggle in one corner of the eye, a mark which wasn't readily visible to the naked eye, unless that is you were looking for it.

"That squiggle wasn't in your father's print. So I decided to do some more checking. The first copies of a run always go to designated locations, such as museums, and of course the Artist Co-op, where it's made always keeps the first print, so it was easy enough to locate and check some of these copies. None of them had the tiny nick. I then searched out copies with higher edition numbers in case the nick had been caused by improper handling of the stone block, but none of the three copies I was able to locate had this mark, also the lines weren't as blurred as in this 12/50 edition."

"So what did this mean?"

"Instead of using the original stone block, I think someone carved a copy using one of the original prints and accidentally cut this nick. Maybe the knife slipped. Hard to tell, but soapstone is very soft, so it can happen. And to support my theory, I located another print that looked exactly like this one, including the squiggle in the owl's eye. Unfortunately, I couldn't locate the original with the same edition number, but I'm sure it exists."

"So what did you do?"

"I knew I had to alert my friend, because obviously he'd been taken in. I was concerned what this would do to his reputation if it became public. But sadly, before I could get in touch, he died in a dreadful car accident. So I alerted the Council to the possibility of forged prints being in circulation. Since I didn't want to damage the memory of my friend, I didn't tell them I had this counterfeit print. I would've had to explain how I got it."

"Did they ever discover who was behind it?"

"Not as far as I know, although they did send out notices to all the designated galleries to be on the look out for forgeries, particularly with the *Mystical Owl*."

"Did you ever come across any other forged prints?"

"Only once. A good fifteen years later. A Jacobie Nakasuk. The seller had picked it up in Europe. I had strong suspicions that it was an illegal copy like this one but was never able to prove it. Needless to say I refused to take it on. But prints weren't the only Inuit art being faked. The stone carvings have had their problems, but that's a whole other story. Let's get back to your prints."

We resumed our chairs in the living room. As Mr. Davis sat down, he said, "You know the forgery quite annoyed your dad. He was worried over the harm it could do to the Inuit and their reputation as artists. Remember him saying he was going to check things out on his next trip north. But when he got back, he wouldn't tell me if he found anything. Just said he had his suspicions but needed to do some more checking before he'd say anything. And then a year later, his plane crashed, so I never did find out what, if anything, he had discovered."

Twelve

But you didn't come here to talk about forgeries, did you, missie? You want me to tell you about the artist of your prints." Mr. Davis sank back into his sagging chair. "That's easy. It's Suula."

"I already know the name," I replied. "Mary was able to tell me that much. Unfortunately, she didn't know this particular artist or how I could reach her."

"She wouldn't." He slurped his tea, which by now was cold.

I offered to make more, but he declined and continued, "It's only happenstance I know about Suula, at least if it's the Suula I'm thinking of."

I groaned. Of course there could be more than one artist by that name, if not several more. "Too bad she didn't provide her last name."

"They don't often do, especially if the prints were made thirty or more years ago. You see, Inuit didn't have last names until the authorities forced them to take one. In fact, in the beginning the authorities just gave them numbers. Couldn't make head nor tail of their Inuit names. Numbers made it easier to keep track of them. But southerners started to make a fuss. Thought it likened Inuit to prisoners, so they were allowed to use their own names, but they had to add a last name. Many just used their father's name. Which come to think of it, isn't too different from a lot of cultures around the world, eh?"

He helped himself to another of Shelley's cookies.

"So how am I going to know if I have the right Suula?"

"I wouldn't worry. Unlikely there's more than one artist by the name of Suula. After all, it's a pretty small community. Nope, I'm pretty sure it's the Suula whose work I came across in the late 1970s."

I sank back into my chair with relief. "Super. Where do I find her?"

"First saw her work in 1978. Terrific stuff. Had a lot of depth to it…" He ran his eyes over the prints. "Yeah, just like these. I remember thinking that at the time her style was a lot like Quliik's. In fact, for a moment I even thought it was Quliik. But that was wishful thinking on my part. You see, Joly Quliik was dead, had died a few years earlier. The 1975 James Lake Co-op series included his last print, *The Bear Hunt*. Was a winner. Why last year a copy sold for over $65,000 at Waddington's Inuit Art auction."

"All very interesting, but I'm afraid I need to know about Suula."

"Sorry, missie. Got a little carried away, didn't I? Let me see, where was I?"

"You were going to tell me where you saw Suula's artwork."

"Yes, that's the strangest part. You see I saw her work, three or four prints, hanging for sale in a place where you don't usually come across them. Stone carvings, yes, but rarely prints. It was at the HBC store in Broughton Island. It surprised me because, you see, the quality of the prints and their execution showed a lot of knowledge of print making, something you wouldn't expect to see in a place that didn't have an art centre. Anyway, I bought the prints and resold them for a tidy sum."

"Where is Broughton Island?"

"On Baffin. East coast, north of James Lake. It has a new Inuktitut name. Begins with a 'Q', but a bit too complicated for this old brain to remember."

"Did you come across any more of her work?"

"Not at Broughton Island. I returned a couple of years

later specifically to see if she'd done any more, but the store said they hadn't seen her or her father since she'd sold them the prints. Apparently they didn't live in the community but at one of the many traditional camps along the coast. Like many Inuit living on the land, they probably only came into the community for supplies and medical attention."

"Maybe the place where the print was made was one of these camps. I gather from Mary that it's identified here?" I pointed to the syllabics on one of the prints. "I can't remember the name, but know it begins with an 'N'. Think it means 'place of seagulls'."

"Sorry, missie, I'm not good with syllabics either, but do know a few words in Inuktitut, and seagull is one of them. Joly Quliik had a superb print of flying seagulls. So your place name will have 'naujaq' in it."

"That's it. It was Naujalik. Do you know it?"

The whispy hair on his head barely moved as he slowly shook his head. "Wish I could help you, but it isn't a familiar name to me. You might try a map. Got one around here somewheres." He started to push himself off his chair.

"Please don't bother. I've already checked, and I couldn't find any town by that name anywhere in the Arctic. Not too many towns, are there?"

"Nope, the north is a pretty empty place. You could always try the RCMP in Broughton Island or better yet, Iqaluit. They probably have some record of the community."

"Thanks, I will."

Figuring I'd pretty much reached the extent of his knowledge, I began collecting my prints.

"Her father's name was Nanuqtuaq." He spoke up. "I remember now. Nanuqtuaq. It means 'one who kills bear'. 'Nanuq' means polar bear. You could always try using that as a last name for her."

"Yes, I will. So you suggest it would be best for me to speak to the police in Iqaluit."

"Yeah, that's where most records are kept and if not, they

can tell you where to go. You can also try the nursing station in Broughton Island. Often the nurses know more than the police. Mustn't forget the church either. The churches were right up there with the Hudson Bay Company and RCMP in opening up the Arctic. Anglicans and Catholics. Think Broughton Island had an Anglican church. You can try them."

As I was slipping the prints into the portfolio, he said, "Do you mind leaving one of those with me? I have a friend who owned another gallery. Retired now, like me, but I remember seeing a couple of Suula prints in his gallery a few years back. He might be able to tell you more."

I gave him the first print in the series, the one with the hunter alone without the plane. Somehow the other two showing my father's plane about to crash were just a little too personal. I left with a promise to bring another tin of Shelley's cookies when I returned for the print. He suggested he would search through his old papers to see if he had anything on Suula or her father. I could tell by the bright gleam in his eye and the lightness in his step that my quest had sparked a bit of energy into an otherwise quiet and probably empty life.

I returned home feeling quite pleased with my progress and fully expected Mother to feel likewise. I hastened with my good news to the atrium, where she was tending her orchids. An avid orchid grower since as long as I could remember, her blooms had won many a competition.

But when I mentioned the name "Suula", she dismissed it by saying, "There must be a hundred Eskimo girls by that name. Without a last name, you'll never find her."

"But I do have a possible last name. Nanuq…something, which means 'one who kills bear'," I said, knocking myself for not writing the name down. "I can start in Broughton Island."

She rejected my suggestion with a wave of her hand then continued watering the only variety I knew the name of, a moth orchid. This one sprouted not one spike, but three foot-long spikes of spectacular purple streaked blooms.

She squirted the plant with water from a brass spray can before continuing, "I'm beginning to think we should just let this be. Your father's dead. Those pictures tell us as much. Knowing where he died won't bring him back. We should leave it where it is and do nothing more."

"But Mother, I thought you wanted to know what happened to him."

"I do. And the pictures have told me."

"But, you didn't think that last night."

"Call it an old lady's whim. A right to change my mind. And I have." She snipped off a spent stem.

"Does this mean you don't want me to go to Iqaluit?" I asked, still trying to absorb this sudden about face.

"Let's talk about it in the morning. I have to go out now." She placed her tools on the garden table and removed her gloves. "It's my bridge night, and I know you wouldn't want to spend the evening with a bunch of fussy old ladies, so I've asked Shelley to make you something. I hope that's all right with you, dear?"

She lifted her face for me to give her a peck on the cheek. And I did. Some habits never die.

She left me standing in the atrium's hot, humid air, amidst the pots of tangled green and floating blooms with my mind a whirl of confusion, disappointment and anger. I was confused over her sudden change of mind and disappointed that the search was about to stop before it was fully underway.

What upset me the most was the realization that she'd done it to me again. She'd managed to excite my interest only to later dash it with a flick of a dismissive hand, something she had frequently done as I was growing up. I thought I'd learned to recognize the signs and deflect it. Well, I hadn't.

Thirteen

After tossing and turning most of the night or staring aimlessly out my window at the moonlit tulips below, I decided that I wouldn't let Mother make the decision for me. Maybe she wanted to stop the search. I didn't. I wanted to find out how this mysterious artist by the name of Suula had come to draw the pictures of Father's death. Had she witnessed the crash? Or had the man in the picture told her? Moreover, why did she or the writer of the letter, if not her, contradict the message of the picture by saying he was okay? Did this really mean he still lived?

I had to find the answers even if it proved this was one big hoax. I knew deep down inside that Mother would also want the uncertainty raised by these letters and pictures laid to rest.

So first thing in the morning, I called the RCMP detachment in Iqaluit. Unfortunately, the Corporal Reilly I'd talked to previously was away on a case and would be for several more days, but I was given the phone number of the Broughton Island detachment, which I immediately dialed.

But after explaining who I was and the reason for my call, all I got was a brusque "sorry can't help you", followed by the explanation that there was no detachment in Broughton Island until the mid 1980s. For records of past residents, especially that far back, I would have to speak to the Department of Indian and Northern Affairs in Ottawa, where the most comprehensive records of the Inuit were kept, and for that I would need the individual's identity number or official name.

It was all I could do not to slam the phone down in

frustration. The constable did supply me, however, with the phone number for the nursing station and the church.

The nursing station line was busy, but the church phone was answered by a tired female voice. "Yes…we have some records here, baptismal records, marriages and the like. Unfortunately, the Reverend and I have only been living in Broughton Island since 1998, and I don't recall any parishioners with that name. Nanuqtuaq, you say? Would you like me to check and get back to you?"

"Yes, please."

"I'm really busy this week, and there's a funeral tomorrow. You must realize too, that our records are in a bit of a turmoil, so it might take me a while to find the ones for that time period, but I will get back to you as soon as I can."

I hung up not feeling the least optimistic that I would hear from her any time soon. I hoped the nursing station would be more forthcoming, but when I finally got through, I was told that all their medical records were confidential. Of course, I should've thought of that. But then the man suggested that I speak to Nancy, their head nurse, who'd been at the station the longest.

My hopes were immediately quashed when she informed me that she'd only arrived in 2000, and as far as she could recollect had never dealt with anyone by the name of Suula Nanuqtuaq or any other family member by that name, but she did offer a ray of hope. "You might want to touch base with Sandy Steeves, the head nurse in Tasilik," she suggested. "Although Sandy was on temporary duty from Tasilik when I arrived, I believe she'd spent a good ten years here earlier, during the period you're interested in."

When an expansive, motherly voice answered the Tasilik number, I felt my optimism rising.

"Suula. Hmm…" she replied in response to my query. At least she hadn't turned me down immediately. "Let me think. I've encountered several patients of that name over the years."

"She might've been a patient in the late 1970s in Broughton Island."

"Oh dear, I'm afraid my memory isn't that good. I've cared for so many people over the years."

"As I said, her father's name might be Nanuqtuaq. Perhaps he was once a patient."

"You know, dear, that name is familiar, but I didn't encounter the man in Broughton Island. No, it was here in Tasilik. It happened in the mid 1980s, shortly after I was transferred here from Broughton Island. He was brought in by another hunter and had a bad gunshot wound. He didn't want any part of our white man's medicine. Kept cursing us in Inuktitut and trying to leave, but the poor man was so weak from loss of blood, there wasn't much he could do.

"There wasn't much we could do either. It was a gunshot wound that had turned septic. We knew he wouldn't survive the flight to the hospital in Ottawa, so the most we could do was make him comfortable until he died. But we had a difficult time keeping him still. The morphine didn't seem to do it. Only thing that worked was the *angakkuq*."

"What's that?" I asked. "Some kind of Inuit drug?"

"No. A shaman. Even though most Inuit are Christian converts, many continue to believe in some facets of traditional spirituality, particularly those who've spent their early years on the land. Anyway, the supervisor at the time was quite sympathetic to Inuit culture, so he brought the shaman in against the objections of the Anglican minister, who was a bit of a prig. I can still remember the shouting that went on between the two of them. Don't think they ever spoke another word to each other."

She chuckled. "But it worked. The shaman, an elderly Inuk woman, quieted Nanuqtuaq down and remained with him until he died. There was a bit of a fracas when Reverend Penn wanted to sit with the dying man, but the nursing supervisor insisted he leave. In fact, the minister left Tasilik not long after, to be replaced by a much more open-minded minister. Not long afterwards, I ended up marrying that new man." She chuckled again. "I suppose that's why I'm still here twenty-five years later. We both fell in love with each other and with Tasilik and its people. Wouldn't want to live anywhere else."

I could sense her inner peace flowing over the phone line. I wished I could absorb some of it.

"But you don't want to hear about me. You want to know more about Nanuqtuaq. I'm afraid I can't tell you much more. Because it was a gunshot, the RCMP got involved. I remember them having to go out in a middle of a blizzard to the man's camp. He wasn't a Tasilik resident."

"Do you know where this camp was?"

"Sorry. I had a feeling it was a fair distance away, somewhere along Cumberland Sound. The police were gone for at least a week."

"You mentioned another hunter brought him in. Do you know this man's name?"

"Sorry, can't help you there either. I don't think the man hung around. But there was someone else who came to visit Nanuqtuaq."

My hopes suddenly shot up. "A woman, maybe his daughter Suula?"

"She had a young boy with her, about seven or eight years old. I remember thinking at the time that she was the man's wife not his daughter, although she was easily half his age. She was quite a striking woman. Tall for an Inuk. Seemed to combine the best of Inuit and *qallunaat* features."

"What do you mean by *qallunaat*?"

"Sorry, dear, that's the Inuit term for white man. I suspect she had some European blood in her ancestry. She also spoke English, so she acted as his interpreter."

"Do you know her name?"

"I don't think he called her anything. No…wait a minute, I remember now, he called her *Panikulluk*, which means 'little daughter'. So perhaps she is the Suula you are looking for."

"Do you know what happened to her?"

"She and her son were staying with one of the local families, probably a relative. After her father died, I think they stayed another week or two, then I didn't see them any more. They probably returned to their camp."

"And you never saw her again."

"Now that you mention it, I do remember seeing her from time to time. Probably picking up supplies at the store, which in itself is unusual. Usually the men do the bartering. Living on the land, I doubt she would've had money. Instead she would've traded seal skins and the like for bullets, gasoline and other items necessary for hunting."

"Gasoline?"

"Yes, by that time dogs were no longer in use. Most teams had been killed, which is a whole other story I don't want to get into now. Safe to say the killing of the dogs took away the Inuit nomadic lifestyle by forcing them to remain in the communities such as Tasilik. Since this woman still lived on the land, she must've had a means of travel, most likely a snowmobile and a motorboat."

"And you have no idea where their camp was?"

"Nope, sorry. But the RCMP will have it on file."

"I've talked to them in Broughton Island, and they told me I have to go to the Department of Indian and Northern Affairs for information on Inuit."

"Talk to the Tasilik detachment. They're bound to have the old case file on Nanuqtuaq. But I have a better idea—talk to Dan Bouchard at RCMP Headquarters in Iqaluit. He was the investigating cop at the time. He left Tasilik a number of years ago, but after doing his stint at other northern detachments plus a few in Ottawa, he's come back as the commanding officer. He should be able to help you. Just tell him Sandy Steeves said for you to talk to him."

"Thanks, I will. One last thing. Do you know if Nanuqtuaq

had a last name or an identifying number?"

"How about I check our files and get back to you? If he had one, it will be there."

"Sounds great. And many thanks for all your help."

"Happy to. And if you're ever in Tasilik drop by the nursing station or the parsonage to say hello."

I hung up feeling considerably more optimistic, and this optimism continued despite being told when I called the RCMP Headquarters that Chief Superintendent Bouchard was on leave and wouldn't be back for another two weeks. I had a good feeling that once he returned, he would be able to help me locate Suula.

Mother found me a few hours later chatting in the kitchen with Shelley, who was making Carter Davis his batch of chocolate chip cookies.

"Excuse me, Shelley," she said in that peremptory manner she adopts to forestall any opposition to her request. "I'd like to have a word with my daughter," and turning to me said, "Margaret, can I have a moment with you in my study?"

As I walked up the stairs to the second floor, I prepared myself for what was surely going to be an unpleasant argument over my continuation of the search.

I was completely taken aback when Mother said, "Margaret, I'm sorry I acted the way I did last night." Her officious manner had disappeared. Instead, I could sense a degree of uncertainty as she cast her azure blue gaze up at me. "I acted too hastily," she continued. "Please, if you want to find this Eskimo woman, don't let my foolishness stop you. And if you want to go to Iqaluit, I will pay your travel expenses as promised." She sank back into her yellow armchair by the window. Her face appeared pale in the sun streaming through the window. Her hand trembled ever so slightly as it brushed a strand of pale blonde hair from her face. It looked as if her night had been as sleepless as mine.

I supposed my face must have reflected my astonishment, for she continued, "Please don't look at me that way. I was wrong to tell you to stop."

"I must admit you had me confused," I replied. "I couldn't understand your sudden change of mind, especially since you were the one who had started this venture."

"I was silly, that's all. I was taken offguard by your news that we might indeed locate this Eskimo woman."

"But why would that upset you? I thought you wanted to find her?"

She glanced out the window as a shaft of morning sun suddenly lit up a sculpted bed of red and yellow tulips. "I do...but I suppose I'm somewhat fearful of what she will tell us."

"You mean, about Father's death."

She nodded ever so slightly. "Yes... Now, dear, if you don't mind, I would like to be alone. Could you ask Hannah to bring me up my mid-morning tea and ask her to include some of Shelley's chocolate chip cookies. I do rather like them." A soft smile spread across her thin lips. Her eyes twinkled. "Just as you do."

Fourteen

Don't take it to heart, lass," Shelley said as I resumed my chair in the kitchen.

I felt as if I'd just been taken on a roller coaster blindfolded.

"Your mother's not herself these days," the cook continued.

"Seems her usual self to me. As inconsiderate and uncaring as always."

As I brought my mug to my lips for a healing sip of tea, I watched Hannah slip through the door with my mother's tray.

"Here, give me that." Shelley took the mug from my hand. "It'll be stone cold." She dumped the contents into the sink and poured a steaming stream of tea into the mug, but she didn't offer a wee dram. I'd never known her to top up her tea until after her day's work was done. "Something's worrying her. That much I can tell," she added.

"Yeah. You're right. I've noticed it too. Still, it's no excuse to ignore the fact that this latest business with Father concerns me and Jean just as much as it does her."

I placed my hands around the warm mug and slowly sucked in the hot liquid, feeling its soothing warmth spread through my body. A wee dram, however, would've made it that much more comforting.

"I remember how she handled herself, and you kids for that matter, when your father went missing. She was a rock. Didn't break down once. Not that I saw. 'Course, she had your uncle to lean on."

Shelley placed a ball of chilled pastry on a marble pastry

board sprinkled liberally with flour and began flattening it out with a marble rolling pin. "Still, she was a brave woman and strong, 'specially when all them newspaper folk kept botherin' her. Handled them like the lady she is. Nope, this time, she's actin' differently. Like she's afraid. All the years I've been working for her, and I've never seen her like this."

She flipped the paper-thin pastry into a greased pie plate with a finesse that only comes through a lifetime of pie making and began trimming the excess.

"Making another favourite of yours, rhubarb pie," she said.

"Terrific. Here, let me help." I got up and started chopping the rhubarb lying on the inset chopping block. "I'm sure Mother's bad mood has to do with these pictures of Father's plane crash."

"Perhaps you're right, lass. And speaking of pictures, I had a thought. Remember the Eskimo picture I told you about, the one your stepdad didn't tell your mother about. I think I might know where it is."

"But wouldn't it have been thrown out long ago?"

"Maybe not. After our talk the other day, I got to thinking and remembered seeing a picture like that when Caroline and I packed up your stepdad's things after he died."

"Do you know what happened to his stuff?"

"Surely do. Akbar carried the cartons up to attic. As far as I know, they're still there." Shelley pricked the bottom of the pie shell and stuck it into the oven. Then, brushing me aside, she said, "I can continue with the rhubarb. You go on upstairs and have a look."

After thanking her with a hug, I ran upstairs, but not before dropping by my mother's room to make sure I had her agreement to search through her second husband's belongings. I didn't want her pouncing on me for going where I didn't belong. But she was slumped in her chair sound asleep, an empty teacup on the table beside her and a half-eaten cookie on the saucer. I watched her for a few minutes and wondered if she was indeed troubled by the resurrection of Father's death or could it be, as Shelley suggested, that she was afraid of something. But her porcelain-like face spoke only of a peaceful sleep.

I draped a pale mauve mohair throw over her and continued my journey to the attic. I'd have to deal with her anger when it came, but chances were, she'd never find out.

Like my attic at Three Deer Point, the Harris family attic was filled with the accumulations of generations of Harrises, in fact more so. The mansard roof provided more height to stack the many boxes and trunks, while the larger footprint of the house provided a greater storage area. Fortunately someone, maybe even Mother, had the wherewithal to label everything, so within a relatively short time, I discovered the boxes and trunks belonging to Harold Harris. They were right beside those marked Sutton, which seemed only fitting.

I sarcastically wondered why Mother hadn't identified them as husband numbers one and two. But that was mean. Harold had been there at a time when she needed him. Jean and I had been more than a little upset when it became obvious to us that the relationship between the two was more than that of brother and sister-in-law. In fact, we'd felt Mother was betraying Father's memory by marrying someone else, but as Jean always said, he had ultimately proved to be a good stepfather, and a good husband.

The air in the attic was musty and close, a sign that it had been some time since anyone had trodden on these dusty wooden floors. I opened one of the narrow windows and filled my lungs with the clean air. Since Shelley had used the word "carton", I ignored the two trunks marked "Harold" and pulled the first of his four labelled cardboard boxes into the centre of the room.

It didn't take me long to realize it was business-related correspondence and paraphernalia, so I shoved that box aside and pulled out the second. This was filled with books.

I wondered why Mother hadn't kept them in the library, but a quick skim through a couple of coffee table-sized books provided me with the reason; they were filled with glossy photos of naked women, some artistically done, others just plain pornography. There were even some literary works noted more for their taboo subjects than their artistic merits by such authors as Walt Whitman, Henry Miller, Henry Fielding and the like, all of which had garnered their share of infamy and censorship. And there were quite a few lesser, more blatant works by unknown authors with suggestive names such as Linda Lovelace or Vanilla Lips.

I laughed. Uncle Harold had been into erotica. Who would've thought? Certainly not his nieces. He'd always seemed the epitome of uptight respectability. But then again, weren't people like that often the ones with something to hide? No wonder Mother had taken these books to the attic after he died. They would never fit with her own image of uptight respectability.

The third box showed more promise. I carefully sifted through a biscuit tin containing old postcards collected from his various travels, on the off chance the drawing might be amongst them, but no Inuit print slipped out from the faded images of far-flung places.

An artist's pad of charcoal drawings immediately caught my eye, but a quick flip through its pages revealed no Inuit picture. Still, I was quite impressed with the detailed line drawings, many of which were candid images of my grandparents and my uncle as a child. There was even one of Great-grandpa Joe, who'd died many years before I came on the scene. Amazingly all were signed "Sutton" in the lower right hand corner. Flipping the front cover closed, I now noticed that he'd carefully written his name in calligraphic script with the date 1946, when he would've been in his teens.

While I'd known Father liked to draw, (in fact, I had one of his Echo Lake watercolours hanging in my bedroom at Three Deer Point), I'd never realized what a good artist he had been. Too bad he'd never formally taken it up, but then this artistic bent had probably led to his interest in collecting art. I put the drawing pad aside, intending to take it with me.

At last, in a collection of black and white photo portraits of various family members taken over the years, including one of me in Grade Six, I found the print. It had been inserted into a photo folder containing a family portrait of us from a year or two before Father died.

I took the print over to the window for better viewing and felt a satisfying thrill as I realized almost immediately that it had been drawn by Suula. The two Inuit figures, a man and a woman, were drawn in the same style as the man in Mother's three prints. A couple of the sled dogs were almost exact replicas, and the syllabic chop in the left corner appeared to be the same, although I wouldn't know for sure until I did a side-by-side comparison. Like the others, it was also a stonecut print, a conclusion I could make now that I knew what to look for. The two adults with the head of a baby peaking out from the hood of the woman's coat were outlined in black ink, as were the dogs and the igloo behind them. Like the print of the flaming plane, colour had also been added to this drawing, but in a rather curious manner. Unlike the woman, who was drawn entirely in black, the man's hair was orange. Hardly the colouring of an Inuk, I thought, but then perhaps Suula was toying with artistic license, or she was commenting on a European ancestor in the man's past.

I slipped the print between the pages of my father's pad of drawings and continued sifting through the box in case my uncle had intercepted other prints. I didn't find any in the fourth box. So I carefully repacked all the boxes and stacked them back into place. As I struggled to lift the heavy carton of books onto another box, the carton slipped out of my hands and toppled to the floor with a thud.

Fearing my mother would send Hannah up to investigate, I hastily threw the scattered books back into the box and this time managed to place it on top of the other box. It was only after the last carton was back in its place that I noticed a folded piece of paper on the floor. Before I had a chance to inspect it, I heard footsteps climbing the attic stairs. I jammed the paper into my pocket and walked towards the opening door.

Hannah gingerly poked her head around the door and relaxed when she saw me. "Oh, it's you, Miss Margaret. Your mother heard a noise. She thought it might be a raccoon. We've been having problems with them lately."

"Sorry, I dropped a box. I was going through my father's stuff and found some of his early drawings." I showed her the firmly closed pad with his name boldly written on the front, careful to hold my hand over the jagged white edge of the Inuit print hiding inside. "They're really good. I might frame some."

"I was looking for you anyway." Hannah eyed me suspiciously. I could tell she didn't quite believe me. "You've had a couple of phone calls. The names are on the front hall table."

"Good. I'm finished for now." I walked towards her, hoping to block her view of the restacked cartons. I didn't want her noticing which boxes I'd actually been searching through all afternoon.

Without giving her a chance to step inside the room, I closed the door tightly behind me and followed her down the steep attic stairs to the third floor. We parted on the second floor, with her heading towards my mother's room, while I continued on downstairs to the front hall. There I discovered the two messages, one from Carter Davis and the other from Jid.

Fifteen

My first thought was that something had happened to my dog Sergei. There couldn't be any other reason for Jid's call. I dialed his number only to hear a busy signal. I waited a few minutes and tried again. Still busy. I tried again. No luck. While I waited for the line to disengage, I returned Carter's call.

"Glad you called, missie," he said. "I've got the name of someone who might know how to find Suula. Frankie Ashoona, an artist living in Ottawa."

"That's good to hear. And it'll be easy enough to visit him from my home in West Quebec."

After giving me the man's phone number, Carter continued: "I've got a couple of letters to show you. Found them this morning. Your dad sent them during his last trip north. I'd forgotten about them. Think they might shed some light."

"Can you tell me what they're about?"

"Best you come here and see for yourself."

"I can come now."

"It's getting a bit late for me. How about tomorrow morning?"

"Nine okay?"

"Best make it nine thirty. Takes me a while to get going in the mornings."

"Nine thirty it is, and I'll bring you a fresh batch of Shelley's cookies."

"Sounds good, missie." I could almost hear his lips smacking through the phone line.

"By the way, I've found another Inuit drawing," I said. "I

think Suula is also the artist. There is, however, one curious aspect. She's drawn the man's hair orange. Seems rather unusual colouring for an Inuk."

"You don't often see it, but it does happen. Why, I've seen blond Inuit myself. Could be the genes of Big Red coming through."

"And who is Big Red?"

He chortled. "Big Red McGregor, a nineteenth century Scottish whaler who couldn't keep his pecker in his pants. Left his seed from one end of the Arctic to the other. He was also noted for his flaming red hair. Much like yours, I imagine."

Lucky him, I thought sarcastically—I'd never liked my red hair. "I'll see you in the morning then."

I redialed Jid's number, but this time the phone rang unanswered. I tried to convince myself that I was being overanxious, that Sergei was fine. Jid was only calling to find out when I was coming home. But several more unanswered calls over the course of the evening only served to worry me further. Jid lived with his aunt and uncle and a couple of cousins. It wasn't normal for someone not to be home. I began to worry that perhaps something had happened to the boy.

The young Algonquin boy'd had a rough time. First his mother had died when he was only a baby, then his father had ended up in jail after killing a man. Jid himself had almost died from a drug overdose when he was only eight. Thank god, it had put enough fear into him to keep him away from drugs afterwards. But his beloved Kòkomis, the grandmother who'd brought him up, had died last year, and he now was forced to live with his aunt, a woman he didn't particularly like.

I'd wanted to adopt him myself, but the band had refused, saying he had to be brought up within his cultural heritage. Despite my promising to have him continue attending the Migiskan Reserve school and Anishinebeg cultural classes, they wouldn't accept my request—and his, for that matter, so he'd reluctantly moved in with his aunt. We had maintained our friendship, with him frequently dropping by my place to chat and play with Sergei. They'd become the best of buddies after the dog had kept the unconscious boy warm in a freezing abandoned shack while I'd sought help.

For the last couple of months, he'd started spending the occasional weekend with me when his aunt and uncle were off doing the rounds of bingo halls. Sometimes the three of us would take off to explore the sights of nearby Ottawa or drive the many kilometres to Montreal. But most of the time, we just hung out, enjoying the delights of the surrounding wilderness together. I was very glad of his company, his energy, his laughter. He filled the void left by Eric.

By nine p.m., when there was still no answer on his aunt's phone, I called the Migiskan First Nations Police Station.

"He's gonna be fine," Corporal Sam Whiteduck said after I explained my difficulty in reaching the boy.

"Who? Jid?" My heart sank. "What happened to him?"

"No, your dog. He got run over by a truck."

"Oh no! How badly is he hurt?"

"A broke leg. Teht'aa took Jid and the dog to the vet's in Somerset. Probably not home yet."

"But his aunt should be home."

Sam snorted. "You know Dolores. She'll be at bingo. Can't pass up a chance to win some cigarette money."

An hour later, Teht'aa called. "I just want to set your mind at ease. Sergei's going to be okay."

"Thank goodness. How badly is he hurt?"

"Just a broken leg, his back right one. The vet said it's a simple fracture. They put a cast on, but they're keeping him overnight to make sure no problems develop."

"How did it happen?"

"I guess Jid was chasing the dog along the road when Pete came along in his truck. I think the dog darted out in front. Anyways, Sergei's back end got clipped. But poor Jid, he blames himself. Keeps saying it's all his fault. It was all I could do to drag him from the vet's. Wanted to spend the night with Sergei."

"Oh dear, poor Jid. Is he at his aunt's now?"

"Nope, she wasn't home yet, so I decided to let him sleep here tonight."

"Can I speak to him?"

"Sure thing." The phone clattered against a hard surface. Within a few seconds, Teht'aa returned. "Sorry, Jid's dead to the world. Guess he was all tuckered out, and I hate to wake him."

"Please don't. I'll talk to him in the morning. And please tell him it's not his fault. Accidents happen. The key thing is Sergei's going to get better. What time is the dog to be picked up tomorrow?"

"The vet told me to call around nine thirty, after they've done rounds."

"If you don't mind, I'll call him. And rather than bothering you again, I'll pick up Sergei on my way home. There's no need for me to stay here any longer. And Teht'aa, many thanks for all your help. I really appreciate it."

"It wasn't any bother. Anything to help out a friend. Besides, Sergei is one of my friends too."

I hung up glad to have Eric's daughter as a friend. When we'd first met, it had looked as if we would be lifelong enemies. But events had transpired to allow us to see beneath each other's bristling veneer to the real person underneath. We both had decided we liked what we saw and had become good friends, despite the demise of the relationship between her father and me.

Before heading up to bed, I decided a nightcap was just the thing to get over my rollercoaster of a day. I poured a generous amount of Armagnac into a crystal snifter. Its tingling warmth felt better than good. I added more and trudged up the stairs to my bedroom.

As I passed Mother's closed door, I hesitated. Should I wish her good night? I'd not seen her since the morning. In the afternoon, she'd been off to yet another charity meeting, and upon returning home had complained of tiredness, so Hannah had taken her supper up to her.

I glanced at my watch: 10:22. She'd be sound asleep. Best not to disturb her. Besides, she wouldn't be interested in Sergei's accident. She thought I should be pouring my affection onto children, not dogs. And I certainly couldn't tell her about the drawing her second husband had hidden from her all those years ago. I silently tiptoed past her door to the third floor stairs.

It was only as I started to turn out my light that I remembered the piece of paper I'd stuck in my pocket. But I was too tired to get out of bed, and the Armagnac had done its work. I slept the sleep of the dead until the morning sun fell on my face.

The folded piece of paper slipped out as I removed my jeans from the chair. This time I read it and immediately wished I hadn't.

> *Dear Harry*
>
> *I miss you. Sutton is being so tiresome, I only wish he would go off on one of his trips to the Arctic. At least then you and I can be alone. I hope those Riviera ingénues aren't turning your handsome head. But if they are, please keep a small place in your heart for me.*
>
> *I love you.*

There was no signature, just a squiggle, but it was obvious who the writer was. Only Mother had called my uncle "Harry". His parents and his brother had called him "Hal" and everyone else had used "Harold". He was not a man who easily accepted familiarity. Although there was no date, it was obvious. She had written it before my father went missing.

She must've written it when Uncle Harold was away on holiday in France. I thought I remembered the trip, because there had been talk of all of us joining him at the villa he'd rented somewhere near Nice. But Father had nixed it at the last moment. I must've been eight or nine. I remembered thinking it such a funny name for a city. Instead we'd gone to spend a month at Three Deer Point with Aunt Aggie and Mother had been furious. I could still hear the slamming doors and feel the tense silences that filled the cottage until she had returned home with Jean in tow.

Shit. I didn't want to know this.

Maybe the letter had been written out of anger? But no. I was only trying to push aside what I knew was the truth. Mother had been having an affair with Uncle Harold even before Father had died.

Then I felt the anger rising. How could she? She had betrayed Father, just as Gareth had betrayed me.

I wanted to rush downstairs and confront her. Shout at her. Tell her what a traitor she was, how she had hurt him. But I knew I couldn't—the time was long past. I would have to keep this letter and my knowledge to myself.

Sixteen

I did the only thing I could do. I packed, and I took my anger out on my clothes. I didn't bother to fold them. I just threw them into the suitcase one after the other, until everything was out of the drawers and closet. I slammed the lid down, zipped the suitcase shut, threw on my jeans and yesterday's T-shirt, ran a comb through my hair and tramped downstairs. I left my suitcase by the front door.

I had to leave this house. I knew I couldn't dissimulate and pretend all was well. I needed time to digest what I'd just learned before I would be able to face her. Even though it would be another hour and half before I could learn what Carter had discovered about Father, I couldn't wait here. I would hang out in a coffee shop near his house. But I couldn't sneak out without saying goodbye to Shelley.

I stifled my anger, my hurt as best I could, plastered a smile on my face and went to the kitchen, where I found Shelley sitting at the communal table finishing off the last of her porridge before starting on our breakfast.

Before I had a chance to tell her I was leaving, she said, "You look a wee peckish, lass. Here have a cuppa with a wee dram of my favourite meds."

She poured me a mug of steaming tea then retrieved the now half-empty bottle of MacCallan from a nearby cupboard and added a generous amount to the tea.

I knew I should've told her not too, not this early in the morning, but didn't have the strength to say no. As I felt the first tingle of its emboldening heat, I was glad I'd given in. It felt so good.

"Thanks, Shelley. That hit the spot." I put the almost empty mug on the counter. "I've come to say goodbye. I'm heading back home."

"Bit sudden, isn't it, lass?" Her dark blue eyes hardened with suspicion.

"It has to do with my dog. He was run over yesterday. I have to get back home to look after him," I said and left it at that.

"I'm sorry, lass. I know how much your curly Sergei means to you. Hope it wasn't too bad. Here, have another one for the road and sit yourself down. You're making my neck hurt looking up at you."

She refilled my mug with tea and a larger dollop of whiskey while I took the chair next to her.

"It was wonderful seeing you again, Shelley," I said. "On your next holiday, you should think of coming for a visit. I'd love to see you at Three Deer Point."

"And so I would, but ach lass, me and them wilds don't mix. It's the bugs and the snakes and all the lurkin' critters. Can't bear them. No, I'm city folk. Best I stay in the city. But thank you for asking."

I supposed I must've remained quiet for too long, lost in my swirling thoughts about Mother, for I jumped at Shelley's touch as she patted my hand affectionately.

"Cheer up, Maggie," she said. "Things have a way of working themselves out for the better."

The suddenness of this unsought sympathy must've taken me by surprise, for I found myself unleashing a flood of dammed-up tears, and before I knew it, I was telling Shelley about the letter.

"It can be hard on a child to discover a parent is only human. But there's something you should keep in mind. It takes two to tango. Perhaps your mother had her reasons."

"But nothing can excuse betraying your lawfully wedded spouse," I shot back with more force than I intended.

"I know you're still smarting from your own unfortunate

marriage, lass. Best you talk with your mother."

"I know Father used to be away a lot. Are you saying that's why Mother turned to Uncle Harold? She was lonely?"

"Talk to your Mother." Shelley eased herself from the chair, placed her hands on her hips and stretched backwards. "Ach, these creaky old bones. I've been restin' long enough. Time to make breakfast." She walked over to the fridge. "I've some fresh asparagus and ripe Camembert. How about a nice omelette?"

"Sounds delicious, but I'd better get on my way. I have a long drive ahead of me." Although Shelley might think it a good idea to talk to Mother, and maybe it was, I wasn't in the mood to consider it, let alone stay around long enough to make it a possibility.

"Could you make sure Mother gets this?" I left an envelope on the counter containing a note hastily written to explain my sudden departure. Needless to say, I blamed it on my dog. "I'll call her later, when I get home." By then distance and time should have done their work, and I would be able to keep my emotions in check.

"You take care of yourself, lass," Shelley said as we hugged. "And don't wait so long to come visit us again. Your Mother isn't getting any younger, you know. She needs you, Maggie."

Maybe she did, but she sure hadn't acted like she needed me on this visit. I picked up my bag and silently closed the front door behind me. As I drove down the long drive, I gave the silent house one last glance. As the trees closed around it, I couldn't help but think that I'd moved so far beyond this place, where I'd lived, loved, laughed and cried, that it seemed almost unreal. Unfortunately, it was a place that still held me in its clutches.

I found a quiet corner in a Second Cup café a few blocks away from Carter's house and had a much less tasty breakfast than the omelette Shelley had been prepared to feed me. While I waited for the appointed time to arrive,

I spoke to the veterinarian and found out that Sergei was coming along nicely, with no ill effects from his accident. Although the cast on his leg would need to be on for at least six weeks, he should be able to move around fairly easily. The technician had already taken him out for his morning walk with no difficulty.

After making a promise to pick Sergei up before the vet closed at six, I called Jid at Eric's place. I knew Eric was away, otherwise it would've been awkward. We'd had little to do with each other, except for the occasional non-committal pleasantry, since that awful night less than a year ago when things went so terribly wrong between us, when one misunderstanding had led to another and another...

Between pig-headed male stubbornness on one part and outright fear on another, we'd never had what we needed most, a calm and collected conversation to sort out the misconceptions. As time passed, my fear increased, as did my unwillingness to grapple with my demons. It was probably best that we left it where it lay. Besides, he'd made no attempt on his side to reconcile. Why should I? But oh... I missed him.

Jid's voice was still groggy from sleep. He seemed hesitant to talk to me, as though afraid of what I might do to him.

"Please, Jid, it's not your fault," I hastened to say.

"But I shouldn't oughta let Sergei run along the road."

"But you've walked him along that road plenty of times before, haven't you?"

"Yeah..."

"And nothing's happened before, has it?"

"No..."

"And you know how he likes to chase other animals. Maybe he saw a squirrel or a deer?"

"Yeah, it was a squirrel. I saw it too. And when he started to run, I tried to grab him, but he got away, and Pete was just driving by, and oh it was terrible. I thought Sergei was gonna die." The tears began to flow.

"But Sergei's going to be okay, isn't he?"

"Yeah. The vet says he can get the cast off in a month."

"And he'll be running around as good as new. In the meantime, maybe there's something you can do for me and Sergei?"

"What...?"

"Well, you know how Sergei isn't very good with cars. This isn't the first time he's run in front of one."

"Yeah, you gotta be real careful with him."

"Well, I think some special training might be in order. What do you think?"

"You mean like teach him not to run in front of cars?"

"Exactly. You've been pretty good at teaching him to shake a paw, roll over and other tricks. I bet you could teach him how to behave with cars. What do you say? Do we have a deal?"

"Yeah, you bet. When can I start?" By now the enthusiasm I knew so well had returned to his voice. The tears had vanished.

When we hung up a few minutes later, Jid was laughing freely, the last vestiges of guilt gone. He bubbled over with excitement at the prospect of giving his buddy a big hug and vowed he'd be waiting on my doorstep with a big moose bone.

I gave Carter an extra ten minutes to get himself ready then walked to his house along the tree-shrouded street. Many of the street's nineteenth century rowhouses had been rejigged into twenty-first century luxury, while others retained the tiredness of their years. Although some had been converted to law or accountancy offices, most were still residences. Above the relative quiet of the street I could hear the approaching siren of an emergency vehicle.

As I neared Carter's house, I noticed a heavy-set man standing on the front stoop. He wore a grey hoodie that barely covered his jutting paunch. Carter's front door was wide open. The man was watching my approach.

No. He was looking beyond me at the ambulance coming up behind me. It screeched past and stopped in front of Carter's house, just as I reached it.

"What's wrong?" I shouted to the man, whose face was twisted with worry. "Is Carter okay?"

But he ignored me and hastened towards the ambulance. Fearing the worst, I raced up the stairs into the house and began shouting Carter's name. My only answer was a deathly silence that sent shivers down my spine. *Please, let him be okay.*

I raced through the living room, dining room to the kitchen and stopped when I came face-to-face with the open door to the basement. An ominous light glowed from below.

"Carter, you down there?" I cried out and gingerly stepped down the steep uneven stairs. He lay crumpled on the damp earthen floor as if he were resting, but I knew from the awkward angle of his neck that it was a sleep from which he'd never awaken.

"Oh, Carter, I'm so sorry." I started to kneel down by his side but was brushed away by two paramedics, who had followed me down.

They went through the motions of checking his vitals and examining his body, but within minutes the woman craned her neck up at me and said, "I'm sorry, but it appears he suffered a broken neck in his fall and died almost immediately. Our condolences."

Feeling somewhat embarrassed at being treated like family, I looked around for the man in the hoodie and found him standing off to one side. Tears dribbled down his freckled cheeks.

"I'm sorry, miss. Given the accidental nature of his death," the paramedic continued, "I'm afraid we have to call in the police."

While she called, her colleague covered Carter with a sheet.

The ginger-haired man, who appeared to be in his early

thirties, nodded mutely.

I found myself wanting to comfort him. "It happened quickly. I'm sure he didn't feel any pain."

He turned grief-ravaged eyes towards me. "But I told him to stay away from the stairs. They're way too dangerous. If he needed something from the basement, I would get it."

"It's not your fault. He probably felt confident he could do it. He was pretty spry for his age. Besides like most old people, he probably didn't want to admit that he was too old to go down them."

The man smiled wanly. "Yeah, he was a stubborn old coot."

"But a nice one."

"Yeah, and he was my only family."

For the first time the man looked at me with query in his faded blue eyes. "I'm afraid I don't know you. Are you a friend of his?"

"Yes, you could call me that. He knew my father many years ago, although I only met him recently. I was supposed to pick up some old letters up from him this morning. That's why I'm here. By the way, my name's Meg Harris."

"Mine's Lynwood Greenberg. He was my uncle. He and my mother were brother and sister." He thrust out his hand. "But she died a few years back. He and Aunt Sarah are all I've got. And now I've just got Aunt Sarah, and well, you know, she's…." More tears seeped down his cheeks. "I guess I'm looking after her now."

He seemed such a lost soul that I felt I should take charge, so I said, "I don't think there's anything more you can do here. Let's go upstairs and I'll make you some tea or coffee or something stronger if your uncle has it."

"Beer," came back the quick reply.

Feeling I couldn't leave him alone, not yet, I sat with him while he waited for the police to arrive. As I sipped tea, he guzzled a bottle of beer and rambled on about his uncle and how like a father he'd been to him, especially after his own father died when he was only a kid.

As he told his story, I couldn't help but draw parallels to my own situation. Except in my case, the uncle had become the actual father. But only after he'd become the mother's lover, I thought bitterly.

While Lynwood talked, I glanced around the kitchen to see if I could find the letters. Even though the kitchen held the kind of clutter one would expect from an old man living alone, I didn't see them.

When the doorbell rang announcing the arrival of the police, I said, "If you don't mind, Lynwood, I'd like to look around to see if I can find these letters."

"Sure, whatever." He shrugged indifferently as he lumbered out of the chair to answer the door.

As the police tramped down the basement stairs, I escaped to the dining room, where I scanned the table and buffet searching for pieces of paper, even envelopes lying amidst Mrs. Davis's Victorian kitsch or Carter's Inuit simplicity. I saw nothing that wasn't a porcelain figurine, a cut-glass bowl or a soapstone carving.

The living room appeared much as it had on my first visit, all tidy neatness except in the immediate area of Carter's favourite chair. I riffled through the magazines and yesterday's newspaper but didn't discover anything remotely connected to Father. When I saw his porcelain teacup with a small amount of cold tea lying on top of an opened copy of *Maclean's*, I realized he'd been reading when he'd decided to go downstairs.

I glanced at the open page of the magazine, trying to ascertain if there was anything in the article that would've prompted him to go to the basement, but it was an article on the latest goings-on of elected officials, a topic more likely to elicit sleep than action.

However, as I laid the magazine back down on the table, I saw a pale grey envelope addressed to Carter that had been hidden underneath it. I recognized my father's handwriting immediately. The cancellation stamp indicated he had mailed it from Frobisher Bay on March 31, 1973, a date I realized with a sudden chill was only two weeks before his flight went missing. Underneath lay another pale grey envelope. This had been sent just two days prior to that.

At the sound of footsteps coming back upstairs, I snatched both letters up and put them in my jacket pocket. At the same time I glanced quickly around for the print I'd loaned Carter. With him dead, I might have difficulty proving that it belonged to me and not to him. Better to take it with me now. My search, however, failed to unearth it.

I retraced my steps to the kitchen. As I passed through the dining room, I suddenly realized that something else was missing. Where two days before, Carter had been pointing out the flaws in his fraudulent copy of the *Mystical Owl*, an empty wall now faced me. Only the darker rectangle of the original rose-coloured paint revealed where it had hung. Although Carter could've removed it, I doubted it. Instead I had a sneaking feeling it was somehow related to his fall.

"Excuse me," I called out to the policeman who'd come back upstairs. "I think there has been a robbery."

Seventeen

Unfortunately, I knew the moment I opened my mouth to summon the police, I'd be delaying my departure. I hadn't, however, anticipated that it would be a good couple of hours before they would allow me to leave. As a stranger, I had immediately become a person of interest in whatever crime, if any, had been committed.

And Lynwood concurred that one had been committed with his confirmation that the *Mystical Owl* print had been hanging on the wall during his previous day's visit with his uncle. Since it represented a stellar point in Carter Davis's career as an art dealer, his uncle would never have sold the print, no matter how much money was offered.

Besides, as Lynwood added, his uncle didn't need the money. He'd made tons dealing in art, which immediately raised the eyebrows of the sergeant. I knew what the cop was thinking. If this death turned out to be murder, Lynwood would probably head to the top of the suspect list. After all, didn't they say most murders were family affairs, particularly when large inheritances were involved? And since Lynwood was Carter's only family, he no doubt was the sole heir.

While Carter's nephew traipsed through the house with another policeman in tow, searching for other items that might be missing, I provided an immaculately uniformed cop by the name of Sergeant Hue with the salient details about myself, such as my relationship with the victim and the reason for my visits. The only points I failed to mention were the two pale grey envelopes securely zipped into my fleece jacket pocket. I did ask if I could look around for my mother's print, but citing the need to keep the crime scene undisturbed until they were finished with their investigation, Sergeant Hue, the officer-in-charge, took the particulars down with a promise to notify me when it was located.

A short while later, Lynwood and the other officer returned with the news that nothing else had been taken despite the presence of other valuable pieces of art, not to mention the silver in full display in the dining room. This prompted Hue to ask, "Why was just the one item stolen?"

I glanced at Lynwood to see if he was going to answer, and when he didn't, I told the two cops about the significance of the missing *Mystical Owl*. I finished by saying, "So you see, given the importance of this print, it probably means that the person who stole it knew something about Inuit art. Even though there are many valuable pieces here, I doubt any of them come close to the $70,000 value of the *Mystical Owl*."

Hue nodded while the constable in the rumpled uniform wrote frantically in his notebook.

"However, it's probably safe to say that the thief didn't know it was a fake. Otherwise why would he take it, since he'd probably find himself arrested for trying to sell a forgery?"

The constable taking the notes said, "Could you go through this fraud thing again?"

So I repeated once more the information the retired art dealer had given me and followed it with, "But I'm no expert. I suggest you talk to someone like Mary Goresky at the McConnell Art Gallery."

"Gosh," Lynwood piped up. "Uncle Carter never told me it was a fake. I just thought it was important, 'cause it was worth a lot. But you know, it's not the only pricy thing here. Uncle told me that carving over there is worth more than a hundred grand." He pointed to a stunning prancing caribou with ivory antlers standing on the central place of honour on top of the buffet. "So why didn't the guy steal that one too?" he asked.

The Chinese cop raised his eyebrows. "Yes, why not?"

"Maybe he didn't know it was as valuable," I hazarded.

"Possibly," Sergeant Hue replied noncommittally.

For me there was one last burning question. "Do you think it possible Carter Davis could've been pushed down the stairs by this thief?"

"At this stage in our investigation it's too early to draw conclusions, but it will be one of several possibilities we'll be investigating."

I left shortly afterwards, leaving my contact information, but with the letters safely hidden in my pocket. I walked down the front stairs to the street just as another police vehicle arrived. A man and woman climbed out carrying heavy cases and camera equipment. I wondered if the greater expertise of forensics had been called in, now that the possibility of murder had raised its ugly head.

For some crazy reason I wanted to get a safe distance between the police and myself so I didn't stop to read the letters until I'd reached the first service centre on Highway 401, a good forty-minute drive away. Even then I waited until I was safely installed in the ladies washroom, blocked from view in my cubicle. I had no idea why I was going through these silly manoeuvres other than a vague sense that there might be a connection between these letters and Carter's death, but more realistically that I could be guilty of taking away possible evidence if the police proved Carter's death was murder. I didn't want any potential witnesses watching me reading them.

I decided to start with the envelope with the earlier cancellation date. Printed in red on the back flap was the name of a hotel, Frobisher Inn, and its address, Frobisher Bay, Northwest Territories. As I pulled out a single sheet of paper in the same pale grey colour, I couldn't help but feel not only a thrill that my father's hands had once touched this page, but also a sadness that it could very well be one of the last letters he'd written.

It started simply.

Carter
Remember that business you told me about the Mystical Owl? *Well, I think I've found something. In conversing with the Crazy Russkie last night, he mentioned something that started me thinking. I plan to pursue it and will let you know, once I learn more.*
Sutton

Short and sweet, it raised all sorts of intriguing questions, but contained nothing tangible other than a name, Crazy Russkie, and even that name wasn't exactly tangible.

As I opened the other pale grey envelope sent ten days later, I wondered if Father was writing Carter about what he'd discovered. It too was a Frobisher Inn envelope, which I assumed was the hotel where father was staying. But…it was empty.

Damn. The letter must've been lying underneath the other magazines, and I'd missed it.

Unfortunately, the first letter was of little value on its own, which must mean the second letter was the reason for Carter's call. "Might shed some light," he'd said, which made me think it likely this second letter contained what Father had discovered about "that business you told me about the *Mystical Owl*." I assumed "business" related to Carter's *Mystical Owl* being a forgery. But beyond that I couldn't begin to conjecture what more father might have learned, if anything. I also reasoned it couldn't have been all that startling, otherwise Carter would've brought it to the police's attention years ago when he first received it.

I thought of asking Sergeant Hue to look for the missing letter but decided against it. He would want to know how I came to know of its existence.

*　*　*

I reached Three Deer Point as the sun's red ball was sliding behind the hills on the far shore of Echo Lake. An excited Sergei, glad to be home, thumped his tail on the seat beside me. With little regard for the cast on his lower back leg, he jumped out of the truck and was immediately greeted by a joyous Jid.

I breathed in the fresh forest air, an elixir to chase the city dirt from my lungs. I opened my arms to embrace the solitude, the peace that had settled on this sleeping land, and felt the tension of the past days slowly seep away. It was good to be home, back in my own house, back to where I was in control, not my mother, and back to where there were no lurking demons.

The windows of my Victorian cottage winked in the setting sun, almost as if to say, "Good to have you back." Yes, I was glad, very glad to be back in my own space.

I lingered for a few minutes longer, watching Jid and Sergei reconnect and listening to the rising flute-like song of a recent summer arrival, a hermit thrush. I heard a faint rustle and turned to see a deer, a young buck with antler nubs, emerge from the darkness of the woods into the growing twilight. He stepped deftly up to the salt lick at the far side of the cleared grounds. So engrossed was he in this tasty treat that he failed to notice my presence. I stood immobile for several minutes admiring his beauty, but when Jid and the dog suddenly scampered around the corner of the house, he vanished back into the safety of his forest.

"Well, guys, you're both probably hungry," I said to the two playmates. "Let's go inside to see what we can find to eat."

A frozen pizza did the trick for Jid and me while the dog wolfed down his organic lamb-and-brown-rice kibble before settling down for a gnaw on his moose bone. After we'd done the dishes, I washing, while Jid dried, I got down to the task of going through the mail, mostly bills, that had collected during my absence and the voice mail. Most messages were from friends, but there were two messages that caught my immediate attention. One was from Corporal Reilly in Iqaluit and the other from my mother.

A quick glance at the clock told me I would have to wait until tomorrow to talk to the corporal, while my mother's message really didn't require a response, and I wouldn't have responded anyway.

It was crisp and succinct. "I'm so sorry, dear, you had to leave in such a rush without saying a proper goodbye. Please don't wait so long for your next visit." I heard rustling as if she were about to hang up, then as if she'd changed her mind, her voice came back on the line, "Hope your dear dog is not too seriously hurt." The message beeped to a close.

Nothing about Father, the man she betrayed, or about finally seeking the answers to what happened to him. And nothing about my visit, being glad to see me, or even a thank-you for driving all that way.

But no, I was letting my hurt feelings get away with me. It had been a good visit. I'd enjoyed talking with Shelley, even seeing Jean and her family again. And though Mother'd had her moments, she had in the end agreed to my following the trail of the prints and the letters.

And yet as I settled myself into Aunt Aggie's old rocker on the screened porch, I couldn't help but wish I had some of Shelley's twelve-year-old single malt to help keep the demons at bay.

Eighteen

When I called the Iqaluit detachment first thing in the morning, I was told that Corporal Reilly wouldn't be back in the office until late in the afternoon. I was more fortunate in reaching Frankie Ashoona, the contact for Suula that Carter had mentioned. We agreed to meet at his place in Ottawa any time after eleven a.m., which would give me enough time to prepare breakfast, drop Jid off at school and make the two-hour drive to the city.

Deciding Sergei and I had been parted long enough, I brought him with me. I figured Frankie wouldn't mind another visitor. And if not, the day was cool enough for the dog to stay in the truck with the windows down.

We had a pleasant drive into Ottawa with Sergei either intently scanning the roadside for glimpses of four-legged critters or resting contentedly curled up on the passenger seat as best he could with his broken leg. Once or twice he licked the paw below the cast, but for the most part he ignored it. Fortunately for him, I hadn't needed to put on the awkward Elizabethan collar the vet had given me to prevent him worrying the cast.

We reached the MacDonald/Cartier Bridge that traverses the broad expanse of the Ottawa River into the city from the Quebec side of the river with a good fifteen minutes to spare. But this was quickly consumed by stop-and-go jerking through road construction that had reduced the three lanes of King Edward to a narrow defile of bumps, dirt and stalled transport trailers. Thankfully, I only had to stay on this section until the first major light, where I turned east and eventually crossed the narrower Rideau River into Vanier, where the Inuit artist lived.

Vanier, one of Ottawa's poorer neighbourhoods, was a riddle of streets that curved off in odd directions with no one road seeming to run parallel to another. It required a couple of stops for directions at barred-window corner stores before I finally parked outside the artist's building, or I should say collection of buildings.

Narrow, two-storey, vinyl-sided structures lined the two sides and back of what was probably once a single dwelling lot. They surrounded an open space of asphalt, possibly meant for parking, except it seemed to have become more a dumping ground for unwanted items and recycling bins. A bike in relatively good condition was chained to the iron railing of a set of stairs leading to the second storey of the back building, stairs which I realized the dog and I would have to climb to get to Frankie's place, 37D.

I was a bit leery about taking Sergei up these steep metal stairs, so I left him behind in the truck. His mournful howl was enough to convince me that he was going to overcome his injury no matter what. As if to emphasize the point, he jumped and hobbled to the top with ease.

After several unanswered knocks, I was beginning to feel annoyed that I'd come all this way only to have him cancel on me, but as I turned to leave, the scratched metal door sprang open, and out stepped a short burly man. His almost circular face was framed by long straggly black hair and a wispy goatee. Round wire-rimmed glasses perched on his button nose. He appeared to be in his late forties.

"Nice dog," he said and let Sergei sniff his hand before giving him a hearty pat.

"Excuse me, I fell asleep." He smiled apologetically and ushered us into a sparsely furnished room whose walls were covered with a myriad of Inuit figures enacting scenes from traditional Inuit life. Except in most cases, the incursion of the modern western world was evident. In one, a movie star face peered out of a traditional hand-held drum, while in another what looked to be a satellite dish ranged over an igloo. I noticed one in particular, a black and white drawing of an Inuk woman with a child in the oversized hood of her traditional parka. Halos framed the heads of the mother and child.

"That's beautiful," I said. "I assume you have called it *Mother and Child*."

"That's my girlfriend." His face creased into another shy smile. "With our child. I named the picture after the baby—Elisapee, Inuktitut for Elizabeth."

"You must've been very happy over her birth."

He shrugged. "I suppose, except it was a long time ago. A long time since I see Elisapee. A long time since I been up north too."

"Yet you still hang her picture on your wall." I was a bit taken aback by his seeming lack of concern for his own flesh and blood.

"I like the picture," he replied simply.

"Yes, I like it too." Not knowing what else to say, I changed the topic. "I'm curious to know the name of the garment the mother is wearing."

"*Amauti*." He smiled again.

In the days to come, when I would get to know more Inuit words, I would discover that the shy smiles came frequently, either through a desire to be friendly or as a defense mechanism.

"It's very good for carrying young children," he continued. "Very warm and comfortable for the child and lets the mother do her work. When the baby's hungry, the mother moves the hood around to feed it. This way the baby isn't exposed to the cold. Practical, eh?" He said this last with a certain degree of smugness, almost as if to say, "See, we Inuit aren't so backward, are we?"

"Yes, very practical."

At this point Sergei caught our attention as he slumped

down onto the bare linoleum floor with a deep sigh. Frankie gave his head another playful rub.

"As I said on the phone, I'm looking for a woman by the name of Suula. I gather you knew her or know of her."

"She was my girlfriend." He laughed.

As my eyes shifted to the woman in the Elisapee drawing, he laughed again. "No, not that one, another one. Had many girlfriends, but no wives. Better that way, eh?"

"I couldn't agree with you more," I said, thinking back to Eric's unwanted offer of marriage. If only he thought the same way as Frankie. "Do you know where Suula is living now?"

"Before we talk about her, can I get you some tea, coffee or a beer?" He snapped open a beer bottle standing on the counter next to a plump, white 1950s fridge, the kind with rounded edges and chrome handles.

The kitchen occupied an alcove at one end of the long, narrow room, beside a door that opened onto a tiny bathroom. I didn't see any other doors. At the other end of the room stood a large table with a jumble of art supplies. An easel with nothing on it was shoved into the corner. It didn't appear as if he were currently working on anything.

"A beer would be nice, thank you." I'd drunk enough tea this morning. Besides, one beer surely wouldn't hurt.

I sat in the only seat possible, a partially collapsed Lazee Boy, its tweed covering splattered with liberal applications of duct tape. The only other possible spot had been the sofa bed, but it was still in bed mode.

Frankie handed me a bottle of Canadian. "Guess I'd better put this thing up." He flipped the bed back, sheets and all, into sofa mode and sat down. He raised his bottle in toast. "Cheers." I toasted him back.

"Great lady, Suula. What do you want to know about her?"

"I suppose I should ensure we're talking about the same woman. Her father's name was Nanuqtuaq. It might've been her last name too."

"Yeah, it was Nanuqtuaq."

"And she was an artist. I gather quite a good one."

"Really? Sure didn't draw when I was around."

"She made some stonecut prints. I have three of them, at least my mother does." I left it at that. I didn't want to get into the story behind them.

"That right? Funny, she never told me. But she liked art. Liked to watch me drawing."

"You said Suula was your girlfriend. Was that here in Ottawa or up north?"

"Up north. Tasilik." He took a long swig of beer. "For a while, then she left." He smiled. "Didn't like my sleeping with other women."

"Do you know where she went?"

"Back home to her kids."

"And do you know where that was?"

"Naujalik. Her family's camp."

It sounded like it might just be… "Does that mean 'the place of seagulls'?" I asked hopefully.

"Yeah. She said there were lots of them on the other side of the island."

Great. I'd finally found her. "Do you know where this camp was?"

"Nope. Never there. But I think it was on an island near the mouth of the sound."

"By sound, you mean Cumberland Sound, the one Tasilik is on?"

"Yup. She talked about Naujalik a lot. Where she lived with her husband and kids."

He must've sensed my surprise, for he quickly added, "He was dead. I think he'd been dead awhile. Think the guy was *qallunaat*."

"And when did you two link up?"

"Not long before I came south. Let's see…" He upended the beer bottle and drained it. "I left Tasilik in 1993 or thereabouts. So guess last time I saw her was a few months before that."

"That's more than fifteen years ago. Do you think she might still be at this camp?"

"Nope, she's dead."

"Oh," was all I could think to say. Shit. There went any chance of finding out where Father died.

"Yeah, heard she killed herself a few years back."

"Oh," was again my feeble reply. "Sorry to hear that."

He shrugged. "Nothing to be sorry about. Happens a lot up north. Something goes wrong, like your man or woman leaving you, you call it quits. Or you just get tired of living. It's no big deal."

"But it is. You're dead." As soon as I said these last words, I realized how silly they sounded. "What I mean is, committing suicide is so final. It doesn't solve anything. Besides, most problems can be dealt with. It's just a matter of having the energy to deal with them or the patience to wait out the tough times. Things don't remain down forever."

His dark eyes took on a thoughtful look. "Bit of a philosopher, eh?"

"No, I guess you could say I've been there myself."

Raising his empty beer bottle to me, he said, "Cheers." And left me with the impression he'd been there too.

"Well, I guess this is as far as I can go. I had really wanted to speak to her." I stood up. "I should be on my way. Many thanks for answering my questions."

He got up too. "You could always talk to her kids."

"I doubt they could help, but I suppose it wouldn't hurt. Do you know where I could find them?"

"Maybe Naujalik. But probably not. Not likely they're still living there. She had three, two girls and a boy. The older girl was away at school when I knew her. The other two, a boy and a girl were at the camp being looked after by her mother. Still young. Probably gone to school after that."

"Do you know their names?"

He started to shake his head, then stopped. "Don't remember the boy's or the oldest girl's, but think the youngest was Apphia."

"Would they have the same last name as their mother? Or do you know their father's last name?"

"I'd go with Nanuqtuaq. Never heard Suula use any other name."

As I stood at his door I ran my eyes over the artwork covering his walls for one last time. "I really like your pictures, especially the one of Elisapee. Would you be interested in selling it?"

"Nope. It's not for sale. But you know, I do have a drawing of Suula. I'll give you that one."

"I'd love to see it."

He leafed through a large cardboard box filled with various size drawings and prints and pulled out one of a woman sitting on the ground. Dressed in traditional clothing, she appeared to be cleaning a piece of sealskin. And any doubts I might've still harboured over this Suula not being the woman I was searching for were completely erased when I saw the plane in a spiral freefall that Frankie had depicted above her head.

"So you know about the plane," I said.

"Yeah. Suula talked about it a lot."

"Did she say what happened to the people inside?"

"Nope, never mentioned them. Just said there was this plane crash near her father's camp. Happened a long time ago, when she was young."

"Was it near Naujalik?"

"Yeah, I guess. She never said."

"My father was in that plane." And I told him about the missing plane and the desire to find out where my father died.

"Tough. I mean about your dad. Not a nice way to die. Wish I could help you more. I'm afraid that's all I know. But keep the picture. It means more to you than me."

"No, I'll buy it from you. Just tell me how much."

"Ain't worth much. Not one of my better ones. How about we saw off on a case of beer?"

So I gave him enough for a case of twenty-four, and when he wasn't looking, slipped a hundred dollars under his empty beer bottle.

As I helped Sergei down the steep outside stairs, I couldn't help but ask myself a question that had been nagging me since learning Suula was dead. Since she couldn't have mailed the pictures to Mother, who had?

Nineteen

Although Corporal Reilly didn't return my call until late in the afternoon of the following day, I was visited much earlier by another policeman, one from the Sûreté du Québec police station in Somerset, the closest town to Three Deer Point. He'd been asked by the Toronto police to obtain a formal statement from me regarding the murder of Carter Davis.

"So they have determined that Carter was murdered," I said in French, out of respect for Sergeant Beauchamps' first language. "Do they have any suspects?"

"I don't know," he replied in the same language. "But you know, Mme Harris, I'm not allowed to divulge such information." An expansive smile spread across his boyish face. His blue eyes twinkled beneath the brown rim of his cap.

I'd had previous dealings with this cop and liked him. He was sympathetic and open-minded. Even Sergei liked him, as evidenced by his butting his muzzle against the man's thigh, his way of requesting a pat. And Beauchamps replied with vigorous rubbing of the dog's black curly head.

"And do they think the motive is the theft of the *Mystical Owl?*"

"I've no idea, madame." He shrugged with his hands out in true Gallic fashion. Then he pulled an envelope from his uniform pocket. "The Toronto police would like you to read and sign this statement."

A quick read assured me that the answers I'd provided in Carter's kitchen were accurately reflected. I signed and passed it pack to Beauchamps.

"They would also like me to tell you that they were unable to locate your picture."

"Oh, dear. That probably means he gave it to someone. He said he was going to have a colleague look at it, but I have no idea who that person could be."

"Was it valuable?"

"No, other than perhaps a sentimental value. It was just a picture of an Inuk hunting seal." What was I going to tell my mother now, particularly since I'd forgotten to tell her that I'd left it with the dead man? "I can only hope that the man he gave it to will return it when he finds out Carter's dead."

"I'll let the Toronto police know." He pulled a small spiral notebook and a felt pen from his jacket pocket. "They have some follow-up questions they would like me to ask you."

I tensed for a second over worry that they'd found out about my removal of Father's letters, but even if they had found the missing letter, I doubted they would realize that there had been another one. Unless of course, Father had mentioned something about it in this later letter. But chances were they would assume it no longer existed.

I invited him into the front room, where he'd be able to use the coffee table to write on, and offered him a cup of freshly brewed coffee, which he readily accepted, along with one of Shelley's chocolate chip cookies.

"Since this information is for the Toronto police, I think it best we continue this interview in English. I hope you don't mind. It saves me from having to translate your answers." His mouth twisted into a crooked smile as if to say, "the poor unilingual slobs", then he turned serious. "You said in your statement that your father was a former client of Carter Davis."

"My father was a collector of Inuit art. He bought a lot of it from Carter."

The SQ cop scribbled into his notebook, then asked his next question. "Were you aware that he was also a business partner of Mr. Davis?"

I raised my eyebrows in surprise. "First I've heard of

this. But I was only ten when he disappeared, so it's not likely I would know. The Toronto police should be asking my mother about it."

"I believe they'll do this."

"So why ask me?"

He shrugged. "I was asked to obtain the answers to these questions. You said in your earlier statement that the reason for your visit to Mr. Davis was to find out information about your father."

"Yes. As it says right there in the statement I just signed, I'm looking into my father's missing plane. I was hoping Carter could provide some answers."

"And there was no other reason for your visit?"

"No, why should there be?" Surely they weren't thinking I'd stolen the print and killed the retired art dealer in the process.

"Are you aware that Carter Davis owed your father, or should I say his estate a significant amount of money?"

My antenna went up in alarm. "No, of course I wasn't. But Father disappeared more than thirty-five years ago. Surely this debt would've been resolved when his estate was settled after he was declared legally dead in 1980. But again, only my mother will know the answer."

I tried to read from his face what was behind this line of questioning, but his normally friendly face had taken on a certain opaque coldness.

I asked, "How much money is involved?"

"I believe about $250,000. You are certain you know nothing of this debt?"

"Very certain. Besides, what has this got to do with Carter's death? Surely the person who stole the *Mystical Owl* killed him."

"And he did not mention this debt when you were talking to him on…" he flipped his notebook back several pages, "on May 12th."

I tried to shove my rising annoyance aside. "No, he

didn't. Look, if you are trying to tie this money to a possible motive for murder, it doesn't make sense. This money has been owed since 1973. If it were really needed, my Mother would've gone after it years ago. Besides, I doubt she needs the money. Her home in Rosedale must be worth at least $10 million, plus there is the Harris trust fund which has many millions in investments. So you see, $250,000 is pretty small change."

"But what about yourself, *madame?* Have you need of such money?"

His eyes passed over the antique furniture crowding the pine panelled room with its expanse of windows overlooking the lake. I watched his eyes rest on the wall where I'd hung Frankie's portrait of Suula with the burning plane in the background amidst a collection of landscape oil paintings, which included a couple of Group of Seven cigar box paintings. But although I'd inherited all this valuable furniture and art in addition to Three Deer Point, I'd hardly be called flush with cash.

Still, I wasn't about to tell him that. "Does this place look like I'm hard up for money?"

He nodded in acknowledgement then concentrated on writing in his notebook. The strained silence was filled with the scratching sound of his pen.

As if sensing the tension in the air, Sergei rose awkwardly from his lying position on the carpet in front of the unlit stone fireplace and gave the sergeant a long questioning stare before turning around and around then flopping back down onto the floor. He rested for a minute, then got up again and repeated the process twice more until he finally found a position that was comfortable.

I took our two empty mugs into the kitchen to refill them. When I returned, Beauchamps had set his pen down on the coffee table beside his notebook and was patting the dog.

"Madame Harris, I have a couple more questions then I think we are finished."

"Okay." I wasn't sure what more he could ask that would be relevant; after all, I'd only just met Carter Davis and knew almost nothing about the man.

"You indicated that the work of art that was stolen was fraudulent. Are you aware of any other fraudulent pieces of art in Mr. Davis's possession?"

"No…Wait a minute, he did mention something about another illegal print that he'd come across. But I think he said he refused to buy it."

"Did he indicate to you whether he knew who was behind this fraudulent activity?"

"No, not at all. Are you saying that this was why he was killed?" I asked, tensing. Did this mean there really was a link to Father's letters?

"I understand the Toronto police are following a number of different leads. This is just one of them."

"But if so, why would the person steal the print?"

He shrugged. "Unless there was something in this print that would point to the counterfeiter."

"But I saw it. I don't recall seeing anything, but then I know very little about Inuit art or any kind of art for that matter."

"This pertains to the last question Toronto would like me to ask. Was there anything about this print that was unusual?"

"Like I said, I know nothing about Inuit art. The only thing I remember was that the edition number was supposed to be a duplicate and that the lines of the image weren't as sharp as they should be given the low edition number. Oh yes, and there was the tiny nick in one of the owl's eyes that apparently is not in the real version. But these are things Carter told me. I would never have noticed them myself. I thought it was an original. It looked just like the one hanging in my mother's living room."

Beauchamps uncapped his pen and resumed writing in his notepad.

When he'd finished, I felt the time had come to speak

up about the letters, but fearing the consequences, I was economical with the truth. "You know, I didn't mention it when I was speaking to Sergeant Hue, because I didn't think it important, but I gather from Carter Davis that the letter he was going to pass onto me might've had something to do with the fake *Mystical Owl*. The Toronto police didn't happen to find it, did they?"

"Do you know what it said?"

At least I could answer truthfully. "Nope, no idea."

He searched my face for a few seconds as if trying to satisfy himself that I wasn't hiding anything, then said, "I will pass this information over to Sergeant Hue."

After writing a few more words, he flipped his notebook closed and placed it along with the pen back in the breast pocket of his uniform. "I think that is everything, *madame*. You aren't planning on travelling in the next while, are you?"

"Not immediately. But I will probably be going to Iqaluit in a few weeks. Why?"

"In case there are more questions. When you do, could you please notify Sergeant Hue at this number."

After bidding me *adieu* and giving Sergei one last hearty pat, he departed, leaving me feeling slightly uneasy. I was very much a minor player in this murder. In fact, it was only happenstance that I was at Carter's house when his body was discovered. Why would they think that I could provide them with any worthwhile information? And why were they asking these questions about my father and my family. Surely they didn't think there was a link to Carter's death. But then there was my father's missing letter. How I wished I knew what was in it.

I debated calling my mother to ask her about Carter's debt and to warn her, if it hadn't already happened, about a pending visit from Sergeant Hue but thought perhaps it wouldn't be wise. If it looked as though we'd been talking, the police might become suspicious for the wrong reasons. Better for Mother to show real surprise. After all, we had nothing to hide. Besides, I couldn't quite get up the nerve to talk to her, not yet.

I spent the rest of the day doing chores, the kind I detested, like dusting, vacuuming, washing floors, doing laundry, tossing out piles of old magazines and newspapers, putting clothes back where they belonged and so on. In the early days at Three Deer Point, I'd had a cleaning lady, a woman who'd become my friend, but after her tragic death, I couldn't bring myself to hire someone to replace her. So I muddled along, letting the dirt, dust, dirty clothes and old reading matter pile up until I finally couldn't take it any longer, then in a spurt of energy would have the house gleaming and in perfect order. Unfortunately, this would only last a day or two, as the effort to maintain order gradually dissipated.

Afterwards, as a reward for being so conscientious, Sergei and I ambled along a trail skirting the shoreline. The late May day was bright but cool. Echo Lake sparkled. The waves lapped against the shore, while overhead powder puff clouds scudded beyond the forest canopy. I was glad I'd worn my fleece jacket. I zipped it up tightly and placed my hands in the warm pockets.

Sergei's leg cast gave him little difficulty as he scrambled up and down the rocks lining the shoreline. Occasionally he'd surprise a frog resting in the weeds and attempt to follow it as it leapt into the water. Thankfully I didn't have to worry about his damaging the cast in the water. The dog hated water; the most he'd get wet was his snout. Still, I kept him on his leash, just in case the chase got the better of his distaste, and he rushed headlong into the lake after a frog.

I hadn't bargained on the moose. We rounded a point and there, about twenty metres away, stood the most massive moose I'd ever seen, knee deep in water, blissfully gobbling up waterweed shoots. He raised his monstrous shelf of antlers still covered in the fuzzy velvet of spring, his molting spring coat a patchwork of long and short fur. He peered at us through small shortsighted eyes, his long pendulous dewlap undulating as he continued to chew. With an ah-ha yelp, Sergei lunged forward. The leash slid through my hand. Barking wildly, the dog careened to a stop a good ten metres from the moose, no doubt when he realized this animal, way bigger than any deer, was considerably more threatening.

Eric had often said to be careful around moose, they were too unpredictable. Fearful of triggering a charge, I remained frozen, afraid to call the dog, waiting to see what the two animals would do. The moose raised his enormous ugly head higher, stopped chewing and stared intently at the dog, who stupidly continued to bark, although I thought with less confidence. At any moment I expected to see the moose's ears flatten in preparation for a charge. Then the dog, still barking, started to back up.

I hazarded a quiet, "Come!"

He turned around and scampered back to me. I grabbed the leash.

Poised to make a dash behind the nearest tree, I waited to see what the moose would do next. His skin twitched from the biting bugs. He stepped forward, shook his mammoth head, sending water and bits of water grass flying. Then with one last glance at us, he bent his head down to get on with the business of eating. I slowly turned around and walked gingerly back along the trail with the dog firmly clenched to my side.

Only when I had rounded the point did I let out a sigh of relief. He might have been one gorgeous moose, but I sure would've preferred meeting up with him with considerably more distance between us.

The phone was ringing as I headed up the back porch stairs.

Twenty

I answered the phone in time to hear a familiar deep masculine voice say "Corporal Reilly returning your call, ma'am."

I must admit when I heard his voice, I couldn't help but conjure up the classic image of a tall, muscular Mountie standing ramrod straight in red serge with the signature broad brim, brown hat and the canary yellow strip running down the sides of black jodhpurs. No doubt when I finally met him, he would turn out to be short with a weak chin and a beer belly trying to break out of his uniform.

"Actually, I was returning a call you made while I was away."

"That's right, ma'am. We talked a few weeks ago about a submerged plane sighting near Resolution Island. I just wanted to let you know that we have a better handle on its location based on a couple of other sightings, so we plan to send the salvage boat out after it once the ice frees up."

"When do you expect that to be?"

"Normally, I'd say end of July, sometimes even into August, but lately ice break-up has been happening earlier." He paused. "Global warming, I guess."

"Once you have an exact date, could you let me know? My family wants me to be there. I think you realize this is very important to us. We want to know our father's final resting place."

"As I said earlier, ma'am, it's highly improbable this is your father's plane. And it's not likely to be a pretty sight."

"That's a chance I'm prepared to take. And seeing bones

119

won't bother me. The most important thing will be knowing they belong to my father."

"Okay, ma'am. Divers are lined up for week of July 15th. We plan to leave Iqaluit on the sixteenth. I suggest you come a day early and come see me at the detachment. And bring warm clothes. It'll be pretty cold on the water."

"Sounds good to me. What's the address?"

"Just ask. Everyone knows where our detachment is. Besides, we're an easy walk from Frobisher Inn, if you plan to stay there."

My ears perked up at the mention of the inn's name. It would be a fitting place to stay.

I also realized while I was talking to him that there was one thing I hadn't done. "By the way, you mentioned in our last phone call that you would be happy to look into finding the sender of some letters. I just—"

"Letters, ma'am?"

"Letters that were recently sent anonymously to my mother from Iqaluit. They seemed to suggest that my father is still alive."

"Yeah…right. I remember now."

"I'm afraid I haven't had a chance to ask her about sending copies to you. But I'll try to get them to you as soon as I can." Given how touchy Mother was about the subject, I'd been reluctant to ask her.

"No rush. My case load is pretty full right now. But if you're in a hurry to find out who sent them, I can assign them to one of the constables."

I hung up thinking I might leave it for the moment. I didn't feel confident that the police would be able to identify the sender. And asking Mother might prompt her to change her mind again about my going to Iqaluit. Best to leave it alone for the moment.

Still, I couldn't avoid talking to her altogether. She would need an update on the plane. But I wasn't sure I could pretend I hadn't seen that damning love letter. There was no way I wanted to bring it up. The affair happened so long ago. Even if she had eventually married Harold, it took place only after Father had been declared legally dead. And as Shelley suggested, perhaps Mother'd had her reasons. After all, Father had been frequently away from home. No, there would be nothing to gain by accusing her of betraying Father other than a venting of my own sense of betrayal.

But I needed to calm my nerves and bolster my courage. Too bad I didn't have a wee dram of Shelley's medicine. After picking Sergei up at the vet, I'd almost stopped at the Somerset liquor store to buy some, but at the last moment my conscience got the better of me. Now I wished I had. Instead I'd have to rely on a mug of extra-strong coffee to give me strength.

With a steaming mug in hand, I headed out to the porch to Aunt Aggie's old rocker. As my eyes soaked in the dark waters of Echo Lake spreading out to the distant hills, I sipped my coffee and rocked back and forth, back and forth.

Sergei lay exhausted beside me. The stress of his accident and the moose confrontation had been just a little too much. He didn't even have the energy to cock an eyebrow when one of his nemeses, a red squirrel, chattered at us from a safe perch on a nearby branch.

Even though the mid-May air still carried a hint of winter, I was comfortable in my layers of fleece and sheepskin slippers. Fortunately a stand of massive white pine on the north side of the house protected me from the wind, which had increased since our walk, judging by the roar rising from its canopy. The wind was also whipping the lake into a whitecap frenzy. I rocked back and forth to the sound of the waves crashing on the rocks below and tried to banish all thoughts of that betraying letter from my mind.

By the time I finished the coffee, I felt more fired up with nervous energy than with cool, calm, collected courage. Nonetheless, I felt I couldn't put off calling Mother any longer.

I hoped Shelley would answer the phone. A few words with her might help to steady my nerves. Instead I got Jean.

"What do you mean by leaving so suddenly?" she said without so much as a cursory greeting. "You really upset Mother."

She wasn't the only one upset, I thought, but there was no way I was going to tell my sister about the love letter. "I don't know why she's upset. She knows I had to leave because Sergei was in an accident."

"Then you have to get involved in a murder. The police have been here all day bothering her, as if she had anything to do with it. She didn't even know the man."

"Yes, she did. He was the art dealer Father dealt with years ago."

"But she herself had nothing to do with the man."

"Let me talk to her."

"And to top it off, the media has linked me to you. They even had the nerve to mention I was a judge. Meg, I can't have this."

Ah, now we were at the heart of the matter. "I'm happy to tell them you're not my sister. Now would you please get Mother."

I heard the phone rattle as she dropped it.

Finally after what seemed like interminable minutes, my mother's voice, sounding somewhat weak and groggy, came on the line. "Is that you, Margaret?"

"Sorry I woke you, Mother, but I felt we should talk."

"I'm so glad you called. I was so worried."

"But I told you in my note I had to leave suddenly. Sergei was hit by a car."

"But dear, you could've come into my room to say goodbye."

"I didn't want to wake you," I said and left it at that, although I really wanted to shout back, "You betrayed Father!"

122

"That's very thoughtful of you, dear. But you have quite upset me, you know." She paused as if waiting for an apology from me, something I wasn't about to do. She continued. "This dreadful murder. How could you involve your family?"

"What? You think I did it?"

"Of course not, but you were there."

"Coincidence. That's all it was."

"But why are the police questioning me? I didn't know the man." She stopped for a moment as if to catch her breath. "Did you tell them to?"

"Oh, Mother, how can you think that? I had no idea they were talking to you until the Quebec cop sent to question me mentioned it. But don't say you didn't know Carter Davis. You did. In fact, you brought up his name last week."

"But I never met him, dear. Only your father had dealings with him."

"I gather from the cops that it was more than a buyer/seller relationship. Apparently he had some business relationship with Carter. Did you know that?"

"I did. The poor man got into financial difficulties, and your father, bless his soul, helped him out."

"Is this what that $250,000 debt is all about?"

I heard a deep sigh, then she spoke up. "Yes, I suppose so. I don't really know. Your father felt business matters were better left to him, so he never told me much. That's what I told the nice Chinese policeman."

"So you don't know if it was ever paid back?"

"No. After your father disappeared, I let Harold handle Sutton's financial affairs."

"So you had no idea that this money was owing?"

"No, I didn't. That's what I told the policeman."

"Well, regardless, I don't see what this has to do with Carter's death."

"Nor I, dear. But Margaret, what were you doing at this poor man's house?"

"I was trying to find out if he knew the artist of those prints you received."

I heard Mother suck in her breath. "But I thought I told you not to bother any more."

"You did, but you changed your mind, remember?"

It took a few seconds for her to answer. "I suppose you're right. I'm so forgetful these days."

"I also wanted to tell you that the police in Iqaluit have located the plane. They will be raising it in July. I plan to be there."

"Do they say where it is?"

"Corporal Reilly said something about it being near Resolution Island, wherever that is."

"I'm afraid my knowledge of the Arctic isn't very good. Do you think it's near Cumberland Sound? I recall Harold mentioning that the town your father flew from was on that body of water."

"No idea, but I can check."

With portable phone in hand, I searched for an atlas on the shelves that lined the walls of the den. Not being especially organized, I'd never arranged my books, and the ones I'd inherited from Aunt Aggie in any order other than to consign the big books to the bottom shelves and the smaller ones to the shorter top shelves. Fortunately, the atlas was a large book with World Atlas clearly marked on the spine.

"You're right about James Lake being on Cumberland Sound. Resolution Island is much further away. It lies in Davis Strait at the mouth of Frobisher Bay, which is south of the mouth of Cumberland Sound by a couple of hundred kilometres."

"Frobisher Bay. The same name as the town where your father's plane was supposed to land. It must lie on that body of water. Is this island far from the town?"

"Quite far. The town is at the head of the bay. Resolution Island lies a good couple of hundred kilometres or more to the southeast."

"Strange that Sutton's plane would fly so far off course."

"That's why the police don't think it's his plane."

"Perhaps you shouldn't go to Iqaluit."

"But it doesn't explain why someone would send you a copy of the article about this plane and the pictures of a plane crashing. *They* seem to think it's Father's plane. No, I think I should still go."

"It's up to you, dear. Let me know when you need money. If you don't mind, I'm feeling rather weary. So if we have nothing further to discuss, I'd like to hang up."

I was about to disconnect when I heard her voice come back on the line. "Margaret, I do wish you would think of your sister's position. Your being involved in this, this murder, makes it very awkward for her."

I pretended I hadn't heard and clicked the phone off. It was only then that I remembered I hadn't told Mother about the missing picture.

Twenty-One

The next two months passed by in a flurry of activity. My hundred-year-old cottage needed some major repairs. I found myself caught up with roofers and well drillers. I'd been putting off replacing the deteriorating cedar shake roof for the past several years until the leak in my bedroom ceiling during this past spring's glacial melt had finally forced me into action. But it was no easy matter to find a roofer experienced and daring enough to re-shingle the numerous steep roofs of the two-storey timber building, let alone be willing to make the half-hour drive from Somerset. But find one I did, at a premium cost.

I did, however, opt for asphalt shingles instead of cedar shake in the interests of not only keeping costs down but also forest fires at bay. After my close encounter with one last summer, I had developed a deep appreciation of their destructive might. If asphalt shingles would prevent sparks from igniting, I was all for diverging from the traditional use of cedar shakes with their tinder box quality.

While I nervously watched the roofer and his workers cling mountain goat-style to the steep roof, I set about contracting a well driller. I didn't want to find myself this summer having to filter out brown sludge, as I had during last summer's drought, when the original artesian well had almost gone dry. Fortunately, there was a well driller who serviced the area, but he had several jobs to do beforehand, so he didn't arrive until two weeks before I was to leave for the north.

And like the roof, it turned out that drilling a well

through a couple of hundred feet of solid Precambrian granite was neither cheap nor easy. And of course the new well, located no less by the driller using his old fashion divining rod, was in the opposite direction from the old well, so I had to bring a contractor in to lay a new pipe connection to the house.

Meanwhile, I had an Arctic trip to prepare for, so I made several trips into Ottawa to buy the latest in "guaranteed to keep you warm at minus 40ºC" kind of clothing. I will admit, I did get caught up in all the permutations and combinations of outdoor technical clothing Mountain Equipment Co-op sold. It was all I could do to keep myself from buying more than I needed. Still, I kept reasoning, it wouldn't be wasted money. It was the kind of clothing I could always use at Three Deer Point when the thermometer plunged to arctic-like temperatures, something that happened most winters.

The bed in the room next to mine was soon covered with capilene long john tops and bottoms, or base layers, as I was corrected by the sales clerk; several pairs of thick wool socks; micro-fibre underpants and bras guaranteed to wick the sweat away from the skin; a down vest and a down jacket with a hood rimmed with wolf fur; several washable merino wool tops that didn't retain odours; a couple of pairs of heavy micro-fibre pants; a soft shell jacket to be used either on its own or as a middle layer; a rain/wind jacket and accompanying pants; Gore-tex lined hiking boots, and so on. I even bought a sixty-litre backpack, thinking a suitcase wasn't quite suitable for taking on board the kind of rugged ship the Mounties would no doubt be using.

I felt I was preparing for a major expedition. When I finally checked the average temperatures for Iqaluit in mid-July, I realized the temperatures wouldn't be quite as frigid as I was anticipating. Still, Corporal Reilly had said to dress warmly, and we would be out on Davis Strait with icebergs drifting by. So warmly dressed I would be.

I also had to make plans for Sergei. Fortunately, his

cast had been removed at the end of June with no residual effect on his gait. Though I knew Jid would be upset, I made arrangements with Teht'aa for the dog to stay with her at Eric's place. It wasn't Jid I was concerned about; he was very responsible, and he'd made considerable progress in training Sergei to pay attention to moving vehicles. No, it was his aunt I didn't trust. She didn't view the care of pets in the same way I did.

Teht'aa would ensure Sergei was safe and wouldn't leave him out all night to fend for himself, as I discovered Jid's aunt had done on more than one occasion. Teht'aa would feed him regularly and provide a regular supply of water. But to help assuage any hurt feelings Jid might have, I gave him the responsibility of walking Sergei a couple of times a day, at lunch and after school, when Teht'aa was at work. Teht'aa also said the boy could come visit any evening if he wanted to.

On one of the occasions I'd called Teht'aa, I got her father instead. After brusquely telling me she wasn't at home, Eric had stayed on the line as if wanting to say something else. For several agonizing seconds, I'd waited half hopeful, half fearful of what he might have to say. But when he said, "Meg, look, I want…" I chickened out and clicked the phone off.

I couldn't go back there. Too much time had passed. Too many tears had flowed. Although I deeply regretted my kneejerk reaction to his offer of marriage, if Eric were to ask me again, the answer would still be the same. I couldn't. Not then. Not now. Not ever. And he would insist on knowing the reason, something I could never tell. I wouldn't be able to bear the disgust that would spring into his eyes. But enough. I had to get over him and get on with my life.

During this time I gave little thought to the sender of the pictures, nor was there any action apart from some follow-up by people I'd contacted earlier. Not surprisingly, the minister's wife in Broughton Island called to say she was unable to find any mention of a girl by the name of

Suula in their church records. But given what I'd learned from Frankie, it didn't matter. The nurse in Tasilik was able to confirm that the dying man she'd attended to years ago was in all likelihood Suula's father. A search through the nursing station records had revealed that his last name was the same as his first name, Nanuqtuaq.

The information I received from Chief Superintendent Dan Bouchard, the case officer for the Nanuqtuaq shooting, on the location of their camp only served to confuse me. Apparently the camp they'd investigated was not at the mouth of Cumberland Sound, but in the opposite direction at the end of the sound and had been located not on an island, but on one of its many inlets. Still he said it was possible that this seagull island I mentioned was also one of their camps, since it wasn't unheard of for an Inuit family to have more than one camp. They were a nomadic people, after all.

I heard no further word from the police regarding Carter's murder, which made me hopeful that my father's connection to the art dealer had nothing to do with the old man's death. Although I checked the news daily, I saw no mention of arrests. In fact, his murder had been replaced by a more newsworthy drive-by shooting in downtown Toronto and a triple killing in the suburbs.

Mother and I chatted a couple of times, both at her instigation, not mine. Perhaps she was feeling guilty, or she just wanted to show she really did have some motherly concern for her daughter. She wanted to make sure that I had enough warm clothing for the arctic cold. She even offered to pay the bill, which I thankfully agreed to in light of my other major expenses. She also wanted to assure herself that Sergei was all right, something she'd failed to inquire about during our previous conversations. In her last call, she mentioned she'd had no more visits from the police, which gave me another reason to assume the Harris family had moved off the radar screen of Carter's murder.

Finally, two days before I was to fly out, with the roofers finished, the new well and pipe installed and the dog scampering around as if he'd never had a broken leg, I was able to focus on my trip to Iqaluit. I was in the midst of trying to figure out how I was going to cram all my new clothes in my new backpack when I got a call.

It was from my brother-in-law. Mother had been rushed to the hospital a few hours before. They had her in intensive care where they were closely monitoring her. It seemed she'd had some kind of heart failure. Although Leslie thought there was no need for me to go to Toronto, I decided to. I would never forgive myself if she died without my seeing her again.

Shoving all plans for my trip aside, I drove to Ottawa and grabbed the next flight to Pearson Airport. Fortunately, with arrangements already made for Sergei, it had been an easy matter to drop him off with Teht'aa. Throughout the short flight, I worried about Mother dying before I got there and chastized myself for not being a better daughter. But I also promised myself I would make up for it in the time remaining.

I expected to find her on her deathbed, but when I arrived in the intensive care unit, she was propped up in bed, smiling, albeit wanly. Although her vitals appeared on the high side on the monitors, I thought, given her seventy-eight years, they probably weren't far from normal. Jean, her eyes red from crying, sat in a chair by her side, clasping her hand.

"Oh, Margaret, you shouldn't have come. I told Leslie to tell you not to." Mother's voice was little more than a whisper.

"You're my mother. I had to come."

She held out her other hand. "I'm so glad you did."

For once I felt her words were genuine. I leaned over to kiss her fully on the lips, not the usual non-committal peck on the cheek.

For the rest of the afternoon, Jean and I sat on either side of her, while she drifted in and out of sleep. Leslie joined us for a little while but left to pick the girls up at school. Other than sharing our concerns for Mother, there was little Jean and I had to say to each other. We'd grown too far apart. Nor did I think it opportune to take my sister aside and tell her about Mother's love letter to Uncle Harold. In fact, I really had almost forgotten about it. It was amazing how the importance of such transgressions faded when faced with the possible death of the transgressor.

Occasionally our vigil was broken by the arrival of a nurse to check on Mother's vitals and once by a technician wheeling in an EKG machine. But when asked, both refused to comment on her condition. We'd have to wait for the doctor, who finally appeared close to dinner time with a couple of young interns in tow.

After many minutes behind Mother's closed bedcurtains, the slim, fair-haired woman emerged to say that Mother had not had a heart attack. Though her heartbeat was now regular, the paramedics had noted an irregular heartbeat when they'd brought her in. It might have been the arrhythmia that had caused her to faint. They would know more after a series of tests on her heart. In the meantime, they would continue to monitor her.

Jean and I wrapped our arms around each other with relief. We laughed. Our mother was going to be okay. Leslie arrived with their two children, and after a brief visit so as not to tire their grandmother, they left *en famille* with Jean promising to return first thing in the morning. I stayed for another hour or so, but once Mother was comfortably set for the night left with the intention of returning the next morning also.

Although Jean had invited me to spend the night with them at their Queen's Quay penthouse overlooking Lake Ontario, I decided I'd rather spend the night in my old bed. Anxious for news, Shelley and Hannah both rushed to answer the doorbell. I was able to allay their fears, and in answer to their entreaties, reassured them that Mother would be very happy to see them both the following afternoon.

I was ensconced in my usual place in the kitchen, eating a bowl of Shelley's scrumptious wild mushroom ravioli topped with fresh basil and plum tomatoes when Hannah approached me.

"I thought you might be interested in seeing this." She held out several ripped pieces of paper. "I found this on the ground near where your mother fainted."

She smoothed out the jagged pieces on the table and placed them together like pieces of a jigsaw puzzle. It took me a second or two to understand what I was looking at and when I did, almost choked on my food. No wonder Mother had fainted.

Another Suula print, similar to the earlier ones, with Hannah confirming that a largish envelope had arrived in yesterday's mail. It was clearly the next frame in the story of Father's plane crash. Like the others, this one showed an Inuk male out on the land with his dog team. And like the others, the plane was in the sky, continuing the flaming downward spiral begun in the last print. There was, however, one major difference which sent my blood running cold, the distinct shape of a parachute with a man dangling from its end.

Twenty-Two

The next morning when I arrived at the hospital, Mother was asleep and still attached to the various monitors and the IV machine. But Jean was fully awake sitting next to her, nervously sipping a large cup of Second Cup latte.

Without saying a word, I thrust the picture, the pieces scotched tape together, into her hand.

It took several minutes for the parachutist's significance to register, but when it did, her reaction was much as mine had been: shock, pure and simple.

"Does this mean he's...?" she stopped almost as if she was afraid to say the word "alive".

"Your guess is as good as mine." I whispered back, afraid to wake Mother. I pointed in the direction of the door, and Jean followed me into the hallway.

"Did you find this at Mother's?" she asked the minute the door was safely closed behind us.

I nodded and moved out of the way as a hospital bed complete with patient, IV paraphernalia and oxygen tanks whisked past us and into the intensive care unit.

"And I guess Mother was the one who tore it up?"

"I'm assuming so. Hannah found it on the floor near where she fell when she fainted."

"I imagine this brought on the arrhythmia." Jean squashed herself against the wall as another bed trundled down the hall. This one contained not only the patient but also several plastic bags of belongings piled at the foot of the bed.

"I'd like to ask her about it, but I'm a bit worried it might trigger something again."

"Yes, it might," Jean agreed. "The other pictures had notes with them. Did this one?"

"I don't know. I forgot to ask Hannah." I thought back to the content of the notes. "I guess the words 'Your man okay' means literally that. He's okay, he's alive."

Jean shrugged with the same perplexity that I was feeling, then asked the question I'd been asking myself since seeing that parachute drifting down to the ice. "Why has he never let us know?"

"Maybe he hit his head and ended up with amnesia," I hazarded. "It can happen. You read about people suffering from it for years, then one day the memory comes back. Maybe that's what's happened to Father?"

"But why not contact us directly, instead of sending us these drawings?"

She had a good point. Maybe there had been another reason he hadn't wanted to return home.

I told my sister about the love letter, but she didn't show the shock I'd felt on first reading it.

"I'd suspected something was going on," she said. "Remember those anonymously-sent roses that Mother would get every year on her birthday? Well, one time I overheard Uncle Harold ordering them on the phone. But I thought he was just being a secret admirer. I never knew she reciprocated. At least not back then. She always acted as if she didn't like him. Remember?"

I did. In fact, it had come as a surprise when Mother had taken up with our uncle a few years after Father's disappearance. "I guess she wanted to fool us…and she did."

For the first time, I noticed my heart was beating wildly, as if I'd just climbed a mountain. And perhaps I had. "Maybe Father found out about the affair and decided if his wife didn't want him, it was better to pretend he was dead?"

"But even if Father wanted nothing to do with Mother, what about us? We weren't a part of this love affair." Her eyes, the same azure blue as Mother's, betrayed the hurt she was feeling. "Surely he could've contacted us, especially after we'd left home."

There was nothing I could say in response. I was feeling the same sense of betrayal. Without thinking, I reached out to hug my sister, just as she extended her arms towards me. We clung to each other as if clinging to a lifeline. For once we shared a common bond. It felt good. Another hospital bed being pushed into ICU finally forced us apart.

"So what do we do now?" Jean asked.

"We can't ask Mother about it."

"I agree. It might kill her. Besides, I doubt she knows anymore than we do."

"I guess we now have an even greater reason for trying to find out who is sending these pictures."

"Hopefully they know where Father is living," Jean added. "Even if he did abandon us, I would still like to see him. I want to know why."

"Me too. So even though this submerged plane no longer concerns us, I think I should still go to Iqaluit, since the letters came from there. But I think it best to postpone my trip until Mother is better."

"Yes, I suppose it can wait. It's waited this long. But when you go, I'd like to come with you."

Her request took me by complete surprise. I scanned her fine porcelain features, so like Mother's and saw genuine feeling. "Yes, I would like that."

But our plans were immediately changed when we returned to Mother's bedside. She was fully awake, sipping tea. The nurse had removed the IV, but she was still hooked up to the heart and oxygen monitors. The readings appeared normal to me. Thank goodness.

"I'm glad you are both here." While she paused to catch her breath, I could see with alarm that her heart rate was increasing. "Sit down both of you. I have something quite shocking to tell you."

Much to our astonishment, she proceeded to tell us in a very calm and steady voice about the parachute picture and her suspicion that Sutton was still alive.

Jean reached over and hugged her. "Shsh…you don't have to say anything more. Meg and I know. She found the picture."

I noticed the monitor's heart beatline had taken on a certain jagged appearance as tears began to trickle down Mother's cheeks. "It's all my fault."

Before either of us could come up with a fitting response, the monitor suddenly gonged, and nurses came running. They shooed us away and whisked the curtain around her bed, but not before Mother cried out. "Meg, you must go to Iqaluit. I want you to find him. I want to see him one last time."

For many anxious minutes, Jean and I waited on the other side of the closed curtain, listening to the sounds of the medical world doing its job. At one point, the pretty cardiologist walked behind the curtain, and minutes later flipped it aside. Mother appeared to be resting. Her heart rate seemed to be down, her heartbeat less spiky, her oxygen levels higher.

The doctor approached us. "I'm afraid your mother has had another attack of arrhythmia. The nurses seem to think it was brought on by stress. They noticed she was quite upset during your visit."

Jean and I both mumbled something in guilty acknowledgement.

The doctor continued, "She's resting comfortably now. She's been given a sedative. We'll be doing an echocardiogram later today and other tests to find out what's behind the arrhythmia. In the meantime, I would request that you refrain from upsetting her. Until her condition is stabilized, I will be imposing visitor restrictions. Only one visitor at a time and twenty minutes maximum per visit. I don't like to do this with family members, but you must appreciate that keeping my patient alive is my primary concern."

Without another word, she turned on her spiked heels and clicked away to another patient.

One of the nurses came up to us with a hint of a sympathetic smile. "I know you girls didn't mean any harm. She's sleeping nicely now. Why don't the both of you go have a cup of coffee in the cafeteria and in a hour or so come back one at a time for your visit?"

Despite Mother's plea, I was reluctant to go to Iqaluit. It was such a long way. Although she and I'd had little to do with each other over the past several years and we fought more than we supported each other, she was still my mother. At any moment she could die. I should and wanted to stay by her bedside. But over coffee, Jean convinced me to go.

"You have to find Father," she said. "You know how some people want to tie up loose ends before they die. I believe Mother wants to seek Father's forgiveness now that she knows he's alive."

So I agreed, and knowing every minute counted, I phoned the airline to book the next available flight back to Ottawa and to confirm tomorrow morning's flight to Iqaluit. I left the hospital only after I'd spent my allotted twenty minutes with Mother. In fact, it was twenty-seven minutes before the nurse shooed me out. As I kissed Mother goodbye, I prayed it wouldn't be the last time.

Twenty-Three

Next morning, I was still in a state of shock. Even after endless hours spent agonizing over the implications of the parachute, I still couldn't believe that Father could be alive. I didn't know whether to feel joy that he had survived the plane crash or anger that he had forsaken us, his family, his children.

As the swirl of conflicting emotions continued throughout the morning's drive to the Ottawa airport, I knew it would only be resolved when I confronted him. And confront him I would, no matter how difficult it might be to find him. Since the letters had been sent from the Arctic, Jean and I assumed that he was living, if not in Iqaluit, at least somewhere in the far north.

On the plus side, I could at least rest more easily over Mother. An early morning call from Jean confirmed that she'd had a good night and was showing signs of modest improvement. Yesterday's test had revealed the beginnings of congestive heart failure, which could be managed with the appropriate medication. The doctor had continued to caution Jean not to unduly upset her, so we had agreed that we'd say nothing further to Mother about Father until I had located him and learned why he'd wanted his wife and his children to believe he was dead.

If I had thought for one moment that I was travelling to a typical Canadian city—after all, Iqaluit was Nunavut's capital—my expectations were soon corrected the minute I arrived at the InuitAir check-in counter. Yes, there was the usual collection of business passengers, complete with pinstripe suits, trench coats and leather briefcases that one would expect on a weekday morning. But they were clearly in the minority. In fact, their professional formality looked decidedly out of place amidst the friendly casualness of the rest of the passengers, which I realized could be easily split into two groups; visitors and residents.

The visitors were immediately recognizable because they were dressed as I was, in brightly coloured Gore-tex jackets with gloves and toques jammed into pockets, bulky down vests, heavy-duty safari pants and thick-soled hiking boots. Like myself they were prepared for the cold, despite the temperature outside the airport being in the low twenties of a typical Ottawa morning in mid-July.

Although one or two of these passengers were pulling the standard wheeled suitcase, for the most part they were carrying or dragging fully loaded backpacks, many the large towering seventy to eighty litre variety with tents and rolled mats strapped on. I noticed one smallish woman about my age struggling with one such monster pack and wondered how she was going to deal with it once we arrived in Iqaluit. It seemed to be almost as tall as her.

When a slim, athletic-looking young woman arrived and summoned many of this group around her with an Arctic Adventures sign, I realized they were a group of hikers and she their guide. From the hesitancy lurking under the forced joviality of several of the grey-haired hikers, I wondered if they weren't wondering what they'd gotten themselves into.

The Nunavut residents were equally obvious, not only by their physical features, for many were Inuit, but also by the boxes of Tim Hortons donuts that most were carrying. And like the visitors, there seemed to be a uniform of sorts; jeans, T-shirt, windbreaker and running shoes. Although none of the men wore traditional garb, several of the women wore the large hooded parka I'd seen in the picture at Frankie's place. One young pig-tailed woman even had

139

a baby, its dark eyes wide with wonder, nestled within the confines of the fur-trimmed hood. These multi-coloured parkas, some made from cotton, others duffle, added a certain festive air to the check-in line, along with the chatter and smiles, and of course the children. That was another aspect that distinguished the InuitAir check-in from other airlines—lots of children, cavorting about and laughing.

I had hoped the forty-odd passengers waiting in the departure lounge meant it would be a mostly empty plane, with plenty of free seats to spread out in. But I hadn't realized that InuitAir was more than just a passenger airline. When we finally boarded, rather than my seat in row sixteen being in the middle of the 737, I found myself facing a partition that divided the plane in half. I could hear the thumping and banging of cargo being loaded on the other side. It turns out InuitAir, in fact any plane flying north, served both as a passenger and a cargo plane. It was the only way goods could be brought into the far-flung island communities of Nunavut, apart from the annual sealifts, which brought the heavier supplies in during the two months of the summer when the seas were ice-free.

Aside from these idiosyncrasies, the flight was like any other flight I'd travelled on. Passengers crammed sardine-like into seats with minimal leg and arm room. I was glad to have a window seat, one I'd specifically selected to enable me to spend much of the three hour flight peering out the window at the passing terrain below. My father had often talked about watching the land change on his flights north. I wanted to see for myself this transformation from the endless expanse of the boreal forest, with its limitless rivers and lakes, into the equally vast expanse of frozen tundra and its ice-clogged waterways and seas.

As the flight attendants prepared for departure, the seat between myself and the aisle seat remained empty. I smiled and gestured the good news to my seatmate, a tiny wisp of an elderly Inuk lady. When I'd taken my place, her bronze face had crinkled into a thousand wrinkles as she smiled her greeting. But a few short words between us told me that would probably be the extent of our conversation. My Inuktitut was nonexistent and her English almost as minimal. Still, with the occasional exchange of smiles, we managed to convey our desire to be friendly.

However, just as I was about to claim the empty seat by placing my newspaper on it, I heard footsteps coming up the aisle, accompanied by a variety of greetings in Inuktitut and English. Then a youngish Inuk man stood in the aisle facing our row. Of a slightly stocky build, with his glossy black hair trimmed short, he was dressed like the other Nunavut residents in the *de rigueur* windbreaker, jeans and T-shirt. Except in his case, the buttery leather of his orange and black jacket, the crisp newness of his designer jeans and the silky cotton of his Boss T-shirt spoke of a shopping trip to a high-end clothing store. They were in stark contrast to the more plebian Sears or Zellers origins of the other residents' clothes. And if I had any doubts about the depth of his wallet, his heavy gold bracelet, diamond ring and gold necklace quashed them. Moreover, unlike many of the other Inuit passengers, he had a certain aura of confidence about him.

A baseball-capped man across the aisle grabbed his attention for a moment, before he turned back to my elderly seatmate and spoke a few words to her in Inuktitut. She twittered and sank further into her seat to allow him to slide into the seat between us. I hastily crammed the newspaper under my seat.

He turned a pearly white grin towards me. "I bet you thought you had a free seat, eh?" He laughed.

Actually it was more like a chuckle, which made my heart skip. It reminded me of Eric.

"Oh well, can't win them all," I replied, trying to shove Eric's laughing face from my mind.

"I'm John. Friends call me Johnnie." He held out his hand. "Your first trip north?"

I grasped his hand, which felt firm and warm. "My name's Meg, Meg Harris. And yes, it is my first trip."

"Harris, eh?"

He mulled the name over, almost as if it meant something, so I asked on the off-chance, "You don't happen to know anyone with that name, do you?"

The twinkle in his dark brown eyes vanished before he laughed. "Yeah, I suppose I've come across a Harris or two. You from Toronto?"

"No, from Quebec. But I was wondering whether you knew any Harrises living in Nunavut. I'm looking for someone of that name."

His gaze hardened. "They live on Baffin?"

The musical timbre of his voice reminded me of someone, but I couldn't recall whom. "I think so, but I'm not sure."

"Sorry, can't help you. Try the RCMP in Iqaluit." Without waiting for a further response from me, he plugged his earphones into his ears and turned his iPod up so loud, I was listening to the blaring music whether I wanted to or not.

The plane started down the runway, and within minutes we were flying over Ottawa, heading northward across the Ottawa River. As the plane rose higher, the sprawl of Gatineau was quickly replaced by cottage-lined lakes and villages scattered amongst the all-encompassing forest. I recognized Somerset by the dam that spans the Rouge River, and a short while later thought I spied Echo Lake and the distinctive finger like intrusion of Three Deer Point. But before I had a chance to verify it by sighting the more distinctive buildings of my neighbour, the Forgotten Bay Hunting and Fishing Camp, the wilderness below was obliterated by the opaque grey of cloud.

The minute the seatbelt sign went out, Johnnie jumped out of his seat and began visiting other passengers. That, I realized, was another characteristic that distinguished this northern flight from its southern sisters. Many of the passengers knew each other. In the check-in line, it had almost been like old home week as they greeted each other and got caught up on each other's affairs. I supposed since the population of Nunavut was only around thirty thousand, people were bound to know each other.

While I sipped a cup of tea, I glanced through the Ottawa paper I'd jammed under the seat. Little interested me. I was tired of reading about Iraqis killing Iraqis, of Afghanis doing likewise and of Israelis killing Palestinians and vice versa. Even the latest report on cancer-causing foods no longer sparked interest. If I followed all the recommended strictures, I'd be left drinking water and eating celery, as long as it wasn't genetically modified.

I was about to put the newspaper down and start on an old issue of *Maclean's* magazine, when a headline caught my eye. "INUIT ART FORGERIES DISCOVERED."

It proved to be a lengthy article, but the gist of it was that the Toronto police had uncovered a storage facility filled with several hundred forged works of Inuit art, ranging from prints to stone carvings. Some forgeries were believed to have been done fairly recently, while others were considered to have been made as long ago as the 1970s.

Needless to say, I immediately thought of Carter Davis's forged *Mystical Owl*, so when I saw that a recent murder investigation had led the police to the discovery, I was fairly confident which murder investigation they were talking about. Unfortunately, the article didn't provide specifics about the link, so I was left wondering if these forgeries were behind Carter's murder or if something in his art collection or papers had led the police to this illegal hoard. I didn't want to believe he'd been behind the forgery. He'd been too honest and open with me.

No mention was made of arrests or possible suspects in Carter's murder other than a brief mention that the police were currently questioning Lynwood Greenberg. I hoped this didn't mean that they suspected Carter's nephew, for

I'd rather liked the guy. Still, a rich inheritance had incited many a nice person into murder.

There was however one small reference that made me sit up. Apparently this storage facility had once housed the Inuit art collection of the late Sutton Harris.

Although there was no explicit suggestion in the article of a link between my father and the forgeries, the fact that his name was mentioned made me nervous. When I reached Iqaluit, I would have to call my sister to alert her. Perhaps with her connections, she might be able to learn if the police were trying to link our father to the forgeries.

Twenty-Four

My socializing seatmate returned to his place in time for the free lunch of Arctic char and wild rice, which was a considerable step up from the cardboard sandwiches offered for a price by other airlines. Still, given the considerably higher cost of the airfare, I'd probably paid for it thrice over. If I was hoping to chat more with Johnnie, the iPod earphones complete with head beating to the rhythm prevented me from even considering it. Instead I read every article in *Maclean's*. I tried to catch up on lost sleep, but found I was too excited to keep my eyes closed for longer than a few minutes.

Finally the clouds dispersed, and I was able to pass the time by watching the endless maze of lakes, rivers and forest pass underneath, except its mile-after-mile of unrelenting sameness soon lost my interest. Even the gradual shrinking of the dense forest into treeless tundra only managed to interest me for a short time. The only bits of excitement were the clouds of smoke rising from a number of scattered forest fires, which from this high altitude appeared as unthreatening as camp fires, but no doubt were consuming hundreds of square kilometres of forest. For a short while we followed a string of transmission lines snaking their way southward, lines that were probably carrying electricity generated at Quebec's enormous James Bay hydro-electric complex. But apart from this and the odd road that led nowhere, man had made no indentation on this vast empty land, easily the size of Texas, if not larger.

Bored, I turned to another outdated magazine. By this

time, my neighbour had unplugged his ears and gone off to hang out with friends, while the tiny Inuk lady softly snored.

A trip to the washroom, however, proved that Johnnie wasn't the only one with acquaintances on the plane. At first glance, the shock of white hair of the woman sitting at the back of the plane didn't register, but then I spied the familiar rhinestone glasses.

"Mary Goresky," I said, leaning over the empty aisle seat beside her. "What a small world. Are you going to Iqaluit to check out the latest in Inuit art?"

The brown eyes behind the glasses arched in surprised recognition. "Meg, isn't it? Meg Harris, Leslie's sister-in-law. How nice to see you again. Yes, I'm travelling on to Cape Dorset to do research for a new book. And what brings you to the Arctic? Your father?"

Thinking it was too soon to tell her he might still be alive, I stuck to the official line. "I'm not sure if I mentioned to you when we met that the Mounties have found a submerged plane that might be my father's. I want to be there when they raise it."

She nodded sympathetically. "Not a happy trip then, but at least you and your family will finally have closure."

She paused for a moment to sip what looked to be red wine in her plastic glass. "I'm sorry I wasn't able to get back to you with information on the artist of your prints. It's proving a most difficult task, but rest assured, my grad student is still looking into it."

"Oh, don't worry, I was able to get some information from other sources."

"Suula, that was the artist's name, wasn't it?"

"Yes, Suula, and I've since learned that her last name is Nanuqtuaq."

At that point a voice behind me said, "Suula. Did you say Suula Nanuqtuaq?"

I turned around to see Johnnie standing behind me in

the line for the washroom.

"Did you know her?"

"She's dead."

"I know. But if you knew her, maybe you could tell me where I could find her children."

His black eyes seemed to mist over. For a second, I thought he was going to say he knew them, but then a look of alarm flashed across his face, and he lunged past, pushing me into the empty seat and into Mary, causing her wine glass to tip over. Fortunately little wine remained.

"Sorry." I straightened up. "Wonder what that was all about?"

Mary's hand twitched near her mouth, almost as if it was lost without a cigarillo to hang onto. An amused smile passed over her lips. "Probably couldn't hold it any longer."

I laughed too but stopped when I realized it was the second time he had abruptly terminated our conversation. However, any thought of pursuing it further was shoved aside after I closed the door on the toilet and saw the young man chatting up a stewardess in the galley. She was one of those tall, willowy Swedish princesses that tended to make me grit my teeth in envy.

I returned to my seat in time to see the transition from frozen land to frozen water. We had reached Hudson Strait, a large body of water that separates Baffin Island from northern Quebec. The shimmering white expanse of shore ice soon broke up into thousands of jostling ice pans. With the break-up had come a curious change in colour. The edges of many of the floes and the surrounding water had taken on a translucent blue colour, almost a turquoise, not unlike that of tropical seas, but rather than emitting warmth, it spoke of the chilling arctic cold.

The snowbound mountains of Baffin Island were fast approaching when the plane began its descent into Iqaluit, and Johnnie returned to his seat, making every effort to ignore me.

Before he had a chance to plug back into his iPod, I asked, "Do you live in Iqaluit?"

At first I thought he wasn't going to answer, but then he shrugged and said, "Yeah. Also got a place in Tasilik."

"Is that where you knew Suula Nanuqtuaq?"

He paused before answering, "Yeah."

"Did you know her children?"

Snow streaked tundra passed beneath us.

He turned his face towards me. "Look, why do you want to know about Suula? She was just a simple Inuk woman. She had nothing to do with the south."

"I think she might have known my father, whose plane went missing in 1973 after it took off from Tasilik."

"And who's your father?" His voice had taken on an almost belligerent tone.

"Sutton Harris."

I thought I saw startled amazement on his face before he wrenched his head away from me. "Never heard of the guy," he muttered.

"I think you have."

Ignoring my accusation, his eyes remained glued to the partition directly in front of us. The wheels of the plane rumbled into place as the plane descended towards the runway.

"Please, I'm trying to find my father. If you know anything about him, tell me." Splashes of vibrant magenta passed underneath, which I realized came from thousands upon thousands of tiny flowers scattered across the tundra.

He remained silent. With a jolt the plane landed, and we both lurched forward with the force of the brakes. An oddly shaped saffron-coloured building filled the view from my window.

"Maybe you don't want to tell me now, but if you change your mind, I'm staying at the Frobisher Inn."

But I wasn't certain he'd heard me, for by then he'd plugged himself back into his iPod.

Damn, what was I going to do? I was convinced he knew something about my father. But why wouldn't he tell me?

Before the plane had barely come to a full stop, he was up and pushing his way to the back of the plane, acting as if he wanted to get as far away from me as possible. I tried to shove my way through the passengers now filling the aisle but found it impassable. I was left to watch him leap from the last stair onto the tarmac and bound towards the frosted doors of the yellow airport.

By the time I entered the warmth of the airport lounge, his distinctive orange and black jacket was nowhere to be seen among the milling passengers. He hadn't even waited to collect his baggage that was still being unloaded from the plane.

My only consolation was that in a town of less than seven thousand people, perhaps the number of Johnnies were few in number, especially ones with money. Hopefully someone, even the police, might be able to point me in his direction.

While I waited for my luggage to appear on the airport's sole luggage carrousel, which looked more like a grocery store conveyor belt, I chatted with Mary. It turned out she was also staying at the Frobisher Inn before heading off to Cape Dorset. Although I shouldn't have been surprised, since the choice was limited to three hotels plus a handful of B&Bs. We agreed to share a cab.

"But you would have to share anyway," she said. "Besides, it doesn't make any difference in the fare. No matter the destination, the fare is six dollars per person, and as long as there is room in the cab, the cabbie will pick up passengers. You sometimes find yourself getting an unexpected tour of Iqaluit as the cabbie drops off other passengers before reaching your destination."

"I wouldn't mind that. A tour of Iqaluit for six bucks would be cheap in my books."

"Wait until you see the town. You might change your mind. This time of year, just after the snow melts, it looks pretty godforsaken." She thrust herself towards the carrousel and pulled off a black and red leather suitcase, then reached for a matching bag. My luggage was still not in sight, even though the amount of luggage was fast dwindling to a trickle.

"Oh dear, I hope my bags aren't lost. I packed Suula's prints in them, plus all my warm clothes." I shivered at the thought of going back outside, where the airport workers on the tarmac were bent almost in half as they walked into the wind. The Canadian flag flew straight out at a right angle from the pole.

"Surely you didn't pack the prints in a suitcase? They could be damaged."

"What else was I going to do with them? I don't have a special art carrying case like yours." I pointed to the large, flat, zippered case she was carrying. "Besides, I've carefully wrapped them in bubble wrap with a hard piece of cardboard to keep them from getting bent."

"Well, I suppose that should work." She paused for a minute before continuing. "I hope seeing your father's airplane doesn't prove too stressful for you. It won't be easy seeing your father's remains."

"The police are saying chances are it's not his plane, so it may be no problem at all. And I do want to find out what Suula's children might know if anything about him."

"You mentioned that Suula's last name was Nanuqtuaq, didn't you?"

"Yes, do you know that name?"

"Not as it relates to her, but you know that young man you were talking to. His last name is Nanuqtuaq. Johnnie Nanuqtuaq. He's one of Nunavut's most successful stone carvers. Maybe he's her son."

"Damn" was my only response. Why wouldn't he tell me such a simple thing?

Twenty-Five

I must admit, it felt a bit surreal staying in the hotel where my father had spent his last days. I even wondered if by some lucky fluke I was occupying the same room. Although the letterhead on the notepaper appeared similar to the one on his letter to Carter, I doubted much else would be the same thirty-six years later. Even though the furniture in my room was ageless hotel style, it looked relatively new, and the closet-size bathroom appeared to have been recently updated. I doubt even the view of Iqaluit from my fourth floor window would have remained the same. Its population was reported to have skyrocketed since becoming the capital of Nunavut, and along with it had no doubt come the growth in buildings, housing and roads.

Still, the natural situation of the town wouldn't have changed. But at this time of year, it could hardly be considered attractive. Bleak and inhospitable was all I could think as I looked out over the dirty sprawl to the tidal mudflats that not only filled the narrow bay upon which Iqaluit sat, but also extended far out to where the inlet met the much larger Frobisher Bay. All signs of winter's cleansing white were gone, except for a rim of white along part of the shore. Across the inlet stood a clump of rust-streaked oil tanks and several flat-roofed warehouses. Not exactly the pristine Arctic beauty of my imaginings nor the exotic grandeur I'd always believed had enticed my father to spend so much time away from his family. However, across the glittering blue expanse of Frobisher Bay, a distant ridge of snow-streaked mountains hinted at such beauty. Perhaps that promise was what had lured him.

Beneath me a most bizarre building straddled a mound of sand. Like something out of *Star Trek*, it consisted of two rows of white, oddly shaped cubes attached Lego-like to each other. Instead of windows, portholes peeked out from various angled projections. I felt the black yawning gap of an entranceway would be enough to deter anyone from entering out of fear of being swallowed whole, but watching the kids scamper so nonchalantly over the play equipment standing in one corner of the building's large sandy yard made me realize it was just my southern prejudices taking over. These kids were very accustomed to such futuristic architecture. In fact, they probably spent a considerable amount of time inside it, since it was likely a school.

Then suddenly, out of the corner of my eye, I caught a glimpse of a familiar orange and black jacket before it vanished behind a house on a street bordering the schoolyard. A few seconds later, the man appeared again on the other side of the house and disappeared behind the next house before I could focus my binoculars on him. I waited for him to walk into the next gap, but when he didn't, I decided he must've stopped at the last house. I debated racing off to the house in case it was Johnnie but decided against it when I realized the most direct route would require me to clamber down a steep rocky slope. Moreover, without a street map, an easier road route wasn't readily apparent. Besides I felt I could pursue this later. Either Johnnie lived there or someone who knew his whereabouts did.

However, as an added precaution, I checked the local phonebook, which turned out to be for all of Nunavut. But although a J. Nanuqtuaq was listed for Iqaluit, no address was provided. In fact few addresses were associated with any of the names. I guessed in a town this small, it was assumed everyone knew where everyone lived.

At least I had a phone number, but when I dialed, I got

only voice mail. Figuring he would probably ignore it, I didn't bother to leave a message.

I also noted that there were no other Nanuqtuaqs listed in the directory's Iqaluit section, which meant if he had relatives, they didn't live here. Nor did I find any listings for Nanuqtuaq in the Tasilik section, not even a listing for Johnnie, even though he'd mentioned having a house there. I would have to rely on finding him in Iqaluit. And when I did, hopefully I'd be able to prevent him from escaping before I had a chance to find out if he was the person sending the drawings to my mother and if so, why.

My next task was to meet with Corporal Reilly before he left for the day. Unfortunately, my missing backpack wouldn't arrive until the next day, so I was forced to brave the cold without fleece and long johns. But fortunately, as the policeman had promised, the detachment was only a short walk from the hotel. By the time I reached the squat, single storey, grey and brown building, the bone-chilling wind had barely penetrated my Gore-tex outer layer, but it had left my cheeks feeling like blocks of ice. Hard to believe it was mid-July.

But Corporal Reilly was out. In fact, I was told by the clerk at the front window that he wouldn't be returning for at least another couple of days.

"But I was supposed to go on a boat with him tomorrow. Do you know where he is?" I asked.

The walls of the vestibule were hung with posters of Canada's most wanted, as if any of them would end up in this deep freeze, and photographs of what I assumed were past heads of the detachment wearing their best red serge uniforms and smiles.

"You must be Margaret Harris," said the young Inuk woman. "Wait here." And she disappeared from the window.

Within minutes, she returned with a flustered young female constable in tow, who introduced herself as Constable Curran. With her dark navy Kevlar vest barely able to contain her ample breasts, her silky blond hair clamped into a ponytail and lush eyelashes framing violet-blue eyes, she didn't exactly fit my image of an officer of the law. But one could not call her pretty, for a jagged scar puckered one side of her freckled face into an ugly grimace. It would be difficult for a once-pretty woman to live with such a scar.

"Oh, dear, didn't you get Corporal Reilly's message?" The lilt in her voice spoke of Newfoundland outports.

"Where? At the hotel?" I wasn't sure I'd told Corporal Reilly where I would be staying.

"No, at your home. He left it a couple of days ago."

Damn. I was so caught up with Mother and my trip that I'd forgotten to check my messages before leaving. "Sorry. What did he want to tell me?"

"The salvage boat and the divers arrived early, so they left yesterday. He told me to tell you he's sorry he couldn't wait, but they wanted to take advantage of the good weather window forecasted for the next few days. He figures barring any trouble, they'll be back with the plane by Friday."

"Well, it doesn't matter now. Even if the plane is my father's, his body won't be on it."

Her demeanour suddenly took on a more cop-like tone. "What do you mean? Do you know something we don't?"

At that point a man entered the vestibule behind me, so Constable Curran suggested we continue our conversation at her desk.

I soon found myself squeezing into a chair beside a cluttered desk of a small workstation, one of several crammed into a not very large squad room, while she took up her seat in a rigid desk chair.

As the young Mountie hastily covered-up some papers on her desk, she asked, "How do you know his body won't be on the plane?"

"My mother recently received some new information that suggests my father survived the plane crash."

"Why didn't you tell Corporal Reilly?"

"I haven't had a chance. We just learned about it a couple of days ago."

She opened up her notebook. "What kind of inform-ation?"

"Actually it was conveyed in a series of pictures."

She raised her brow in disbelief. "What do you mean?"

"Someone, we don't know who, has been sending my mother a series of Inuit drawings that depict a plane crashing. I told Corporal Reilly about the anonymous letters, but hadn't yet had a chance to tell him that they also included pictures. Maybe you know about the letters?"

She shook her strawberry blonde ponytail, a colour I wished I'd been born with instead of the fiery red I'd been saddled with. "Nope, Corporal Reilly didn't pass this info onto me. Best you wait until he returns."

"Anyway, the latest drawing shows a man in a parachute. We assume it's supposed to be my father."

"Do you have the pictures with you?"

"Not yet. They're in my backpack, which the airline lost, but I'll bring them in when they arrive tomorrow."

"Do you know who sent them?"

"As I mentioned already, there was no name or return address."

"Right."

"However, we believe the artist is a person by the name of Suula Nanuqtuaq." And while Constable Curran wrote furiously in her notebook, I explained what I knew about Suula and finished by saying, "I believe Johnnie Nanuqtuaq might be her son."

"You don't say." She cast a wistful eye towards her computer screen, which showed a mélange of photographs of Arctic places and people, one of which I recognized as Johnnie. "I'll check the records."

She'll probably ask Johnnie instead, I thought, which would solve my problem. "And while you're at it, perhaps you can find out about Suula's other children. I believe there was a daughter by the name of Apphia and one other daughter, whose name I don't know."

"I'll pass this onto Corporal Reilly, since this is his missing persons case."

"But he won't be able to get to it until he gets back and that might not be for several days. Is there any way you could look up the information at the same time as you're checking on Johnnie?"

She sighed and glanced at her computer screen again. "I'll see what I can do, but I can't promise anything. I'm busy myself on a couple of cases."

"Thanks, I'd appreciate any information you can provide," I said without any real expectations. I would just have to find Johnnie myself.

She returned to her notebook. Finished writing, she mused, "If your dad did survive, funny he never turned up, eh?"

"I'm sure he had his reasons. Perhaps while you're at it, you can check to see if his name appears in recent records."

She nodded. "You know, if a person doesn't want to be found, it's pretty easy to keep out of sight in the north. Just have to hide out in some isolated camp and live off the land. No one would ever know, apart from the Inuit, that is, and they wouldn't tell."

She paused. "I've never been able to understand why a white person would want to live a traditional Inuit life. All that raw meat." Her lips curled in distaste. "You know that's what the word 'Eskimo' means. It's Cree for 'eaters of raw meat'. That's why the Inuit hate the word."

"I'm also wondering if you've ever heard of an Inuit camp by the name of Naujalik? It's supposed to be the name of Suula's camp. I've been told it's somewhere on Cumberland Sound, that is if it still exists. Suula's dead now, so there may not be anyone living there any more."

"Nope, but Corporal Reilly can check up on that too. But you know, Ms Harris, it's pretty near impossible that your father is alive. Even if he survived the crash, he wouldn't have survived afterwards especially since he would've been hundreds of miles from help."

I expressed a theory that I'd been mulling over since learning of the possibility of his survival. "What if some Inuit found him, specifically Suula or her family. Perhaps that's what the pictures are trying to tell us."

"Yeah, I suppose, but he was probably badly injured. No way he would've survived without proper medical attention. Still, I've learned in my short time here that anything's possible in the north. So yeah, we can follow up on this." She closed her notebook to bring the interview to a close.

"When do you think you'll be able to get back to me? I'm not sure how long I'll be staying here."

"I'm pretty busy myself. Will probably have to wait until Reilly gets back."

"You said that would be in a couple of days?"

"Yeah, maybe. But could take up to a week to get that plane up, especially if they get into a patch of bad weather. I tell you, it can sure get rough out on the sea this time of year. Storms come up sudden like, just like back home, eh?"

"Newfoundland?"

"Yeah, the Rock, how'd you guess?"

She laughed when I mentioned her accent. But any further conversation was cut short by her ringing phone.

By the time I walked back out into the blustery cold, I'd made up my mind to continue my own search. I had no idea how long it would be before Corporal Reilly would follow up, and by then it could be too late for Mother.

Besides, I was here. I knew of one location where Johnnie might be found. I also knew his phone number, even if he never answered. Besides, I was sure a lot of people in town would know where he lived. After all, he was supposed to be one of Iqaluit's most successful artists. And when I did find his house, I would stay on his doorstep, sleep there if I had to, until he answered my questions.

Twenty-Six

On leaving the RCMP detachment, I noticed a couple of kids skipping down the embankment to the right. I scrambled after them, hoping this would take me to the lower part of town, to the house Johnnie had entered.

The dirt path skirted a rocky ditch that a month or more ago would've been filled with fast-flowing snowmelt. Today the stream was little more than a trickle, and the ditch was filled with the detritus of winter; plastic pop bottles and cans, the odd baseball hat, a couple of squashed soccer balls and a kid's twisted tricycle. I even saw animal bones, one with a splayed hoof at the end which couldn't belong to a deer. Deer didn't roam the Arctic, but caribou did.

Once beyond the embankment, I headed towards the hovering bulk of the school through a housing complex of white, faceless town houses. With only a smattering of greenery, the all-pervasive dirt only served to compound their boxlike unattractiveness. But then again, my southern sensibilities were taking over. For of course in this barren land, hundreds of kilometers north of the treeline, green vegetation, especially lawn-like grass, would be a rarity, if not altogether non-existent.

But when a couple of young women, one with a baby peeking over her shoulder, smiled shyly at me as they passed by, I realized the Arctic had something else to offer, friendliness, a rare commodity in the south. An elderly man sitting on the wooden stairs of one of the units waved as I walked by and beamed a gap-filled grin. Even the kids playing in the schoolyard noted my passage, with a couple running up to find out where I came from. When I mentioned Quebec, one pig-tailed girl laughingly displayed her knowledge by replying in a few words of French. She even asked me if I knew the song "Frère Jacques", which I obligingly sang and was joined by her and her friends. Yes, this open warmth more than made up for the town's stark sterility.

The drab grey house stood at the far end of the short street bordering the school, but the peeling paint and matchbox appearance didn't strike me as the kind of house Johnnie would live in, with his designer clothing and gold jewellery. I could see him living in the large two-storey house next to where I stood at the beginning of the street. A tarp-covered skidoo occupied a corner of the front yard, while a dusty Xterra was parked before the street's only garage. Yet I'd lost sight of him at the shabbier house, which at the moment was showing considerably more life.

As I approached, a couple tramped down the front stairs while a man brushed past them and went inside without bothering to knock. I, on the other hand, couldn't just walk into a strange house, so I knocked. No one answered. Several more knocks were likewise ignored, but I could hear raucous laughter and chatter inside. Pushing aside my southern inhibitions, I entered a small vestibule and almost tripped over a motley assortment of boots and shoes scattered over the worn plywood floor.

Unfortunately, I didn't see Johnnie's leather jacket among the jackets hanging on the walls, but I did see something that reminded me that the capital of Nunavut was only a street away from the wilderness. A couple of rifles were propped barrel-up in a corner, while above them hung several dead birds, what I took to be ptarmigan, an Arctic version of the ruffled grouse I was used to seeing around Three Deer Point. Their brown and white feathers looked so soft, I couldn't resist running my hands over their plump bodies.

Despite the hollow clunking my boots made on the vestibule floor, no one came to check, so I gently pushed open the inside door and found myself peering into a large room which seemed to occupy most of the house. Directly across from me was a kitchen area with a linoleum-covered counter and stainless steel sink. On the floor by the fridge lay a flattened piece of cardboard covered with bloodied chunks of raw meat. And in the middle of the room sprawled a circle of people, men and women, slapping cards onto the floor in front of them. In the centre lay a growing pile of loonies and toonies, every denomination of dollar bill, in addition to a variety of brass bullets. I even thought I spied a government cheque buried under the pile. The sight of a couple of almost empty liquor bottles reminded me that I wanted to buy some scotch before returning to my hotel.

So intent were they on their play that no one noticed me, not even the old woman sitting on a chesterfield shoved against the front window. She was too focused on sewing baby clothes. Beside her lay the recipient of these clothes, a tiny baby, its eyes tightly closed, its chest rising and falling with the steady rhythm of sleep.

Since it was obvious Johnnie wasn't among the gamblers, I decided to slip away unannounced when a voice behind me suddenly rumbled. "Are you going or stayin'?"

He so startled me that I almost fell into the room. Several players, likewise startled, looked up, but only for a second before turning their attention back to the game.

"If you're staying, you'd better take your boots off. Geela doesn't like us tracking in dirt."

His finger pointed to the old woman. In the other hand he carried a couple of full plastic grocery bags. Although his voice hinted at annoyance, the twinkle in his black eyes said otherwise.

A cap of straight black hair framed his perfectly round face. He held out his hand and smiled. "I'm Pete Pitsiulak. Not from around here, are ya?"

Shaking his hand, I introduced myself.

"Guess you've never seen Inuit playing *patiik*. Come on in and join us for a hand. It's not too different from gin rummy."

At this point, a thin wiry man, his hair tugged back into a scraggly ponytail and a grin stretching from ear to ear, slapped his wrist, shouted in Inuktitut and hauled the pile of money towards him.

"Given the size of that pot, I'm not sure I can afford it."

For a moment he seemed distracted, then he laughed. "Amazing, a southerner who thinks she can't beat us Eskimos."

"Now, if that isn't a challenge, I've never heard one." I laughed. "But I'm dreadful at cards. I can never remember what's been played. Thanks for the offer, but I'll give it a miss."

"At least come on in and have a drink."

Afraid of intruding, I was about to decline, but the welcoming smiles on many of the players' faces made me change my mind. Besides, a bit of liquor would go down well about now.

After dutifully removing my boots, I followed Pete to the kitchen, where he poured me a good measure from a fresh bottle of Canadian Club.

While I mixed in some ginger ale, he bent down to pick up the bloodied cardboard. "I don't suppose I could interest you in some fresh seal meat."

I glanced at the raw chunks but decided that as much as I loved sushi and steak tartar, I wasn't about to try this Arctic delicacy, not yet.

On the other hand, the rye and ginger went down very smoothly, almost too smoothly. It took me back to my university days, when my hand was rarely without an ice-filled glass of the bubbly sweet mixture. In fact, my mother would probably insist it was a contributing factor to my failure to graduate.

While he motioned me to sit in one of the chairs at a nearby table, he downed his scotch and soda, "Boy I needed that," he said, pouring himself another. "It's been a rough day."

Without his bulky down jacket, he seemed taller and leaner than my first impression. He placed opened bags of chips on the floor amongst the players and took a chair across from me.

For a few minutes he silently watched the players, then turned to me, "What brings you to Iqaluit?"

I was about to tell him some inconsequential story, but his look of genuine interest dissuaded me, so I told him about my father's missing plane.

"No kidding. I remember when that plane went missing. I was twelve or thirteen. My dad was guiding for the RCMP back then. He made several trips with them to check out possible sightings, but they never found it."

"Do you know where they were looking?"

"Yeah, it was when we were living in Qikiqtarjuaq, or Broughton Island as it was called back then. The search plane thought they saw some wreckage on the ice near Cape Dyer before bad weather set in. Coast is pretty rough up there. Lots of mountains and fjords. Plus it was close to spring break-up. They almost lost a team of dogs when the ice gave way. Plenty of polar bears too. Boy, we feasted for a month on the one Dad brought home. Mom still has that skin. It was one big bugger."

Remembering my initial inquiries about Suula, I said, "Broughton Island is north of Tasilik, isn't it?"

"I see you're not such a northern neophyte, after all." His eyes twinkled.

"I'm afraid I don't know much about Baffin Island, but I recently talked to a couple people from there. I'm surprised, though, that the search party would be looking that far north of Tasilik, since my father's plane was supposed to be heading south to Iqaluit."

"I'm afraid I can't help you there. Could be they thought the pilot might've gone way off course. I remember the weather was pretty stormy about that time. Anyways, Dad musta been gone a month before they finally came home."

He paused to take a drink. "So that was your dad, eh? Sorry to hear that."

"Actually, we've recently learned that he might've survived the crash."

"That right? But even if he had, no way he could've survived for long. Too damn cold and with no gun, he would've starved."

"But what if he was rescued by some local people?"

"Yeah, I guess. But I remember Dad saying they checked out the camps in the area. No one saw anything. He was pretty sure the plane didn't come down near there. He figured who ever saw the plane wreckage was wrong."

"We believe a woman by the name of Suula Nanuqtuaq might have witnessed the plane crash."

"You don't say. Must be Johnnie's *anaana*?"

The pony-tailed player called out again and, smacking his lips with glee, added to his growing pile of winnings. Pete leaned over and gave him a congratulatory slap on the back.

"If that means 'mother', yes. That's why I'm here," I said as he continued to watch the gamblers. "I thought I saw Johnnie come to this house an hour or so ago."

Pete kept his focus on the game for so long that I thought he hadn't heard me. As I was about to repeat the question, he shifted his gaze back to me and said, "Yeah, he was here. But didn't stay long. What do you want with him?"

I explained about the drawings.

"They sound interesting. Did you bring them with you? I'd like to see some of Suula's work."

"I did, but unfortunately they're with my baggage which the airlines lost."

"Don't worry. It happens frequently. They'll be on tomorrow's flight. You know Suula's dead, don't you?"

"That's why I want to see her son. I'm hoping he knows something about them and can tell me why they were sent to my mother."

Pete's eyes turned thoughtful as he mulled over my

words. While I took a last sip of my rye and ginger. Finally he said, "I can take you to him, if you like."

"Thanks. I'd really appreciate it."

"But it'll have to wait until the game's over. I can't leave Geela alone with this drunken lot."

"How long do you think that'll be? I can come back later."

"Won't be long now. This game's been going on since yesterday morning. I think most of the players are pretty well cleaned out. Only one who's made any money is Mala."

Chortling, he pointed to the lucky gambler whose pile of winnings towered over everyone else's. A youngish woman in form fitting jeans and a black sweatshirt with a polar bear outlined in white sat quietly crying in a corner.

Pete sat down beside her and placed an arm around her shoulders. "You've done it again, haven't you, Lucy? You've lost your government cheque."

She nodded as another flood of tears cascaded down her cheeks. "What am I gonna do? I was supposed to buy some of that special formula she needs." She pointed to the baby who was beginning to cry.

"How much you need?" Pete asked pulling out his wallet. He extracted a wad of twenties and counted five. "Will this do?"

She slipped it into her pocket. "Pete, what'd I ever do without you?"

"You gotta stop doing this. You have this new baby to look after. She needs you more than you need the drinking and the gambling. Promise me you'll stop."

She nodded meekly, but as she lifted the baby up to her bare breast, I knew that the next time temptation presented itself, she would give in. I should know. But at least I could not count gambling as one of my vices, my skinflint Scottish blood no doubt coming through.

Twenty-Seven

It turned out that the two-storey home I'd admired belonged to Pete. Johnnie, he informed me, lived in Apex, a short drive away.

"In fact," he said, starting up the Xterra, "it's the only place you can drive to around here. There are only two other roads that go beyond Iqaluit. One is to a park and the other is the Road to Nowhere."

"To Nowhere? You can't be serious."

"You bet. It was originally built for a new dump, which never materialized, so the road just stops in the middle of the tundra. Some of you white folk like to jog along it when the weather's good."

"And not you Inuit?"

"Nah. We get our exercise from pushing the start buttons on our skidoos and ATVs." He chortled.

I laughed with him. I liked his free and easy manner. So much like…no, I wouldn't go there.

"But it looks to me as if the only people I see walking around here are Inuit."

We were passing a straggle of young men tramping along the side of the dirt road towards Apex with their windbreaker collars up to ward off the icy wind and their bare hands stuffed into their pockets.

"I guess most white folks get their exercise from turning the steering wheels of their cars," I quipped.

"Right on." He fired a mock gun back at me. "Can make you crazy, all this driving around in circles with no place to go."

We climbed up onto the heights surrounding Iqaluit, past several new housing developments. The dirt landscaping and skidoos parked in the front yards might not conform to *House and Garden* standards, but these houses sure had spectacular views of Frobisher Bay and the snow-streaked mountains of the far shore. "I guess there's a housing boom going on."

"You better believe it. Since Iqaluit became the capital, it's been a boomtown. But it's also brought its share of problems."

He suddenly swerved to avoid a tanker truck without any markings that had turned onto the road in front of us. "Damn trucks think they own the roads." Another nameless tanker truck lumbered past.

Cursing under his breath, he focused on his driving as we passed a sprawling single-storey building that looked much like a typical southern school. In the yard a group of children cavorted on the play equipment.

A few minutes later, we drove by the last house in Iqaluit, a green roofed A-frame surrounded by rock and tundra with probably the best view in town. By this time we were a good hundred metres or more above the water. Beyond a string of islands, the broad expanse of Frobisher Bay glimmered in the afternoon sun. I thought afternoon until I checked my watch and realized it was well past seven o'clock. No wonder my stomach was beginning to feel empty.

"The angle of the sun has confused me. I didn't realize it was so late. I hope I'm not keeping you from your dinner."

"No problem. It's easy enough to get confused this close to the Arctic Circle. While the sun does set for an hour or two in Iqaluit, if you go further north, say to Tasilik, you'll find yourself in continuous daylight."

"Doubt I'll have a chance to experience that. If Johnnie can answer most of my questions, I won't need to go to Tasilik. You're sure he'll be there?"

"Yup. He said he wanted to finish polishing a sculpture he was working on."

"Good." I watched a couple of small white and black birds flit amongst some lichen-covered rocks. "You mentioned something about the Iqaluit boom bringing its share of problems."

"Yeah, that's right. You see, thirty-forty years ago when most of us still lived on the land, there were almost no economic divisions. The ability to hunt was essentially the determining factor, with some hunters being more successful than others. Still a good hunter would share his kill with those in need. As long as hunting was good, no one in the camp went hungry. Not so today." He waved at another group of young men walking along the edge of the road, this time in the opposite direction towards Iqaluit.

Rolling hills of rock and tundra spread out on either side of the road. While the pervasive colours were brown and grey with a touch of dull green, a sudden splash of magenta had me exclaiming, "Wow, what a gorgeous colour. I saw that same flower as the plane came into the airport."

"That's Nunavut's territorial flower, the purple saxifrage. And that's arctic poppy over there." He pointed to several clumps of nodding yellow flowers. "We may not have many flowers here, but the ones we have pack a powerful lot of colour for their tiny size."

Through a break in the hills I could see further inland. The same undulating terrain continued, with its share of magenta and yellow and the occasional white clump of snow that had not yet melted in the summer sun. Several ravens circled overhead, while one craggy oldster, feathers ruffled in the wind, guarded his domain atop one of the highest rock outcroppings.

"Today we have a middle class, courtesy of employment, mostly government employment," Pete continued.

"But I would think that would be a good thing."

"It is, but not all Inuit have jobs; in fact, many don't. But

167

the old ways of sharing have disappeared. The middle class Inuit keep their money to themselves and their extended families and let the unemployed Inuit rely on welfare and other government handouts."

"Sounds much like what happens in the rest of Canadian society."

"Yeah, I suppose. But we're not used to it. It creates divisions in our society that aren't good. It also means you have a lot of people with nothing to do. They can't go out on the land because they don't have the money for gas, bullets or rifles, let alone for a skidoo or boat. So without country food, they're forced to buy food from stores. And since everything has to be shipped in by air, you can imagine the exorbitant prices. Some white folks have even started up a food bank, something that would've been unheard of a few years back. And when people have nothing to do, you know what happens."

"I can guess, drinking, gambling... What I saw at Geela's house."

"Yeah. Some are even into drugs. And of course, there's the petty crime that goes with these addictions. It's a bad situation, and we're struggling to cope with it."

"But you seemed to do your part of the sharing. You're obviously a part of this middle class, yet I saw you being very generous to that young woman who'd gambled away her monthly cheque."

He shrugged. "I try, but I'm just one person. Let's talk about something else. Tell me about your father. His name was Sutton Harris, wasn't it?"

I concurred, surprised he remembered.

"Coincidentally, his name was mentioned recently."

"Probably in connection with the submerged plane discovered last fall."

"No, had to do with art. I gather he helped one or two of the Baffin Island art co-operatives get off the ground in the early days by finding southern buyers for their art."

"I don't know anything about that. I was only told he was a collector of Inuit art. He was on one of his art-buying trips when his plane went missing."

"But he also sold Inuit art, didn't he?"

"Maybe he did, but as far as I know, he kept most of what he bought. You have to remember, I was only ten when he disappeared. Who told you this?"

He glanced sideways at me. "A Toronto policeman's in town. He's investigating a possible Iqaluit connection to a crime committed there."

"You must mean Carter Davis's murder," I said, realizing that I'd forgotten to let the Toronto police know I was coming here.

"You know about the murder?"

"I happened to go to his house just after his body was found. It left me feeling quite sad. I rather liked the old man."

His eyes flicked in my direction then turned back to the road. "He was a good friend to many of our early artists."

"I don't understand why the cop would think there is a connection between my father and Carter's death. Any dealings my father had with him stopped thirty-six years ago."

"So your father was involved with Carter Davis?"

"I gather from my mother that he bought much of his art from Carter's gallery. But what does it matter to you? Are you a policeman?"

"No, I'm an elected official with the Nunavut Government. Among my many hats, I'm the Minister of Culture."

"Oh. You don't look or act like one to me," I blurted out without thinking. "Sorry, that didn't come out right. I meant you don't look like the puffed-up, full-of-their-own-self-importance politicians I'm used to seeing on the news."

"Thanks. I'll take that as a compliment." He laughed.

We rounded a curve and began our descent beside a cascading river towards a bridge that crossed onto a narrow peninsula. Assorted coloured bungalows and one or two larger buildings, including a church, huddled amongst the rocks. I even spied a patch or two of green in the yards of some of the houses.

"Is that Apex?"

"Yes, but Johnnie doesn't live there. He lives on this side of the river where the old Hudson Bay Company store used to be."

"If you don't mind my asking, what is the policeman saying about my father?"

"I'm afraid I can't tell you. In fact, I shouldn't have mentioned it at all."

But I wasn't going to give up. "I read something in the paper about Inuit art forgeries being found in a warehouse that once belonged to my father. Does this have anything to do with that? Is this cop trying to say my father was involved?"

"Sergeant Hue is still in town. Perhaps you should ask him."

I glanced at Pete and wondered what he wasn't telling me. "Thanks, I will."

At this point, the politician turned his suv onto a road that led down a sharp decline to several red-roofed houses strung out along a sandy beach, an empty beach, I might add, devoid of any activity, not even the all-pervasive group of playing children that I'd come to expect as an integral part of the Iqaluit scene. Mind you, it did have its share of ravens and one or two soaring sea gulls. Further out into the small bay, I spied a flash of movement. Someone wearing a bright blue almost turquoise jacket was navigating an aluminum motorboat through some ice pans. When they reached open water, they revved up the engine and streaked beyond a rocky point in the direction of Iqaluit.

Rather than stopping at what I thought might be Johnnie's house, a prosperous looking storey-and-a-half with crisp white vinyl siding and a shiny red metallic roof, Pete drove past it and a couple of other less prosperous-looking bungalows to where a red BMW SUV was parked beside the least prosperous house, a more grey than white clapboard house that had clearly seen too many winters.

My initial assumption, however, was proven correct, when Pete said, "Johnnie lives in that first house. But he uses the old HBC building as his workshop and gallery. This's his car, so he's gotta be here."

I followed Pete around the side of the house and found myself stepping through a thick layer of greyish-green dust and stone shards.

"Good, he's here." Pete pointed at a wooden table likewise covered in stone dust and shards. "Must've just gone inside for something."

On the table lay a variety of chisels, hammers and other carving tools, including a power cutter, an uncut block of grayish-green rock and a facemask thick with dust. The sculpture Johnnie had been working on was no longer in sight, although I could see an outline in the dust where it had stood.

Pete pushed open the side door. "Johnnie, it's me, Pete. You decent? I have company with me." He stepped inside with me following close on his heels.

The large square room was lined with shelves, on which stood a variety of bears, seals and whales at various stages of carving. Although one or two of the more finished ones looked to be fairly good, for the most part they appeared rather amateurish. Not what I would've expected from one of Nunavut's master carvers.

Noticing my reaction, Pete said. "Johnnie teaches carving to a number of young aspiring carvers. These are probably their efforts. If you want to see perfection, come into the next room, where he keeps his gallery."

Although I noticed footprints in the dusty floor heading towards the door we were approaching, we'd not yet heard an answering response from Johnnie. I was beginning to worry that he'd escaped me again.

"Where's Johnnie?" I asked.

"Probably stepped outside or gone back to his house. I'll show you the gallery and then we'll go back to his house."

Pete opened the door to a smaller but considerably cleaner room, although the polished wooden floor did have its share of tracked-in stone dust. Soft direct lighting bathed a variety of carvings perched on pedestals. Several more were encased in glass. About half of the carvings were of traditional subjects, bears, walruses and the like created out of a variety of stone ranging from speckled grey to mottled green with a few carved out of a white streaked black stone. But unlike the students' attempts, these ones came alive. One almost expected the polar bear rising on its hind legs to pounce after its quarry.

The rest of his carvings were of more contemporary subjects. In fact, several explored the theme of Inuit addictions, which made me wonder if Johnnie was the sculptor of the one my brother-in-law had bought.

But nowhere did we see Johnnie.

"It looks as if he might have left," I said, pointing to another line of dusty footprints leading to an outside door. The tracks however vanished into the coarse sand beyond the door.

Worried Johnnie would get away again, I suggested Pete take the road back to his house, while I went along the beach. That way we would hopefully have all exit routes covered.

For the first time since arriving in Nunavut, I realized I was smelling something other than man-made odours. Salty sea air. It smelt good.

But the land was still, almost too still. Waves lapped languidly onto the coarse brown sand. The cold air wafting off the water was barely a breath. Clouds drifted imperceptibly over the water. However, the ravens were restless. One voiced his displeasure from atop Johnnie's roof, while a couple of others hopped around an object lying in the sand in front of his house.

I moved off the beach to the road side of Johnnie's house and reached his door at the same time as Pete without seeing any signs of Suula's son.

"If he's not here, I don't know where he's gone," Pete said, once more pushing open a house door without knocking.

My hopes rose when I noticed Johnnie's orange and black leather jacket hanging inside the door. But when we entered the kitchen, the house felt as silent and still as his workshop, although a half full mug of tea had been left on the counter beside an opened package of chocolate chip cookies. The tea looked cold, and even though my stomach growled from hunger, I resisted the temptation to help myself to a cookie.

"Johnnie, you here?" shouted Pete. He swung the kitchen door open and walked into the next room. "Nope not here, either." I then heard a door click open, immediately followed by, "Hell! Not again!"

I rushed towards the sound to see Pete bending over someone lying outside on the sand. He shook the still figure and cried, "Johnnie! Johnnie! Don't die on me, you bastard!"

The ravens scattered.

Twenty-Eight

Pete's jacket dripped with blood, as did his hands. "I think I feel a pulse. Quick, call the operator for an ambulance. I'm gonna try to stop the blood." As Pete wrenched off his jacket, I raced inside in search of a phone.

Unfortunately, Johnnie hadn't put his portable phone back in its base in the kitchen, an annoying habit I too was guilty of, so I found myself frantically pushing the pager button and scrambling towards the beeping before it stopped. I had to do it twice before I finally found the handset lying under a book on his night table.

But as I reached for it, I caught sight of something else, something I hadn't seen in thirty-six years, not since my father had pulled it out of his pocket the night before his final trip to the Arctic. Great-grandpa Joe's gold pocket watch with its distinctive engraving of "JEH" on the cover. It took all my willpower to focus my attention on the emergency call, but as soon as I was satisfied the paramedics were on their way, I returned to the watch.

Not wanting to believe my eyes, I picked it up carefully and ran my trembling fingers over its smooth surface, the way I liked to as a child. And yes, there was the scratch, the jagged scratch on the back where Mother's diamond ring had accidentally nicked it during one of their arguments. Father had been terribly upset and Mother equally apologetic, but I remember noticing the faint hint of satisfaction in her eyes. She'd resented the influence the long dead Joseph Ernest Harris still had on his family.

Finally, concrete proof of a connection between Johnnie

174

and Father. But how had the artist come by it? Had it come from a living man or from his dead body lying on the snow? I prayed even harder that Johnnie would live to tell me what he knew. I slipped the watch into my pocket before heading back out to Pete. I doubted anyone knew of its existence. Besides, by rights the watch was mine.

Pete, his top completely bare, bent over Johnnie, who was quiet, too quiet. Blood soaked the sand where he lay. I couldn't see any wounds on his head, arms or legs, but the cloth Pete held against the injured man's throat was soaked in blood. I looked for a possible weapon, a gun, a knife, whatever, but I didn't see anything that could cause such blood lose.

I thought I saw Johnnie's eyelid twitch. "Keep holding it, Pete. I think you're stopping the blood flow," I cried.

My ears pricked up at the faint sound of a siren.

There was that slight twitch again. "It's working. The ambulance is almost here."

The siren reverberated off the surrounding hills. A crunch of tires on the sand, doors opening. A scurry of feet and the clanging of equipment as it fell to the ground. A uniformed paramedic brushed Pete aside and continued clamping down on the blood-soaked cloth while another paramedic prepared a bandage. Blood spurted from the wound while the paramedic quickly assessed the damage before securing the bandage over it. The other paramedic checked Johnnie's vital signs and pierced a vein for an IV drip.

She looked up. "It's going to be touch and go, Pete. He has a pulse, but it's very faint. Do you know how he was injured?"

"It's obvious, isn't it? He cut his own throat." Pete flung back in anger and despair.

She nodded solemnly and began readying Johnnie for removal. Blood seeped through the bandage.

"Pete, I'm not so sure," I interjected. "I don't see any knife. Look for yourself. If he did try to commit suicide, it would be near him."

175

Pete lurched to his feet and began searching the surrounding sand.

"Why would you automatically assume he tried to kill himself?" I continued.

"Because, it's the popular way to die around here, didn't you know?" His voice filled with bitterness. "Nunavut has the highest suicide rate in Canada."

The paramedics carefully lifted Johnnie onto the stretcher and half-pushed, half-wheeled it through the sand to the ambulance.

"But I don't think Johnnie took that route. Have you found a weapon yet?"

"Nope."

"Nor have I. And if there isn't one, you know what that means." I finished just as a marked RCMP pick-up truck stopped beside the ambulance. Out strode Constable Curran and her partner.

While the male Mountie stopped to speak to the paramedics, Curran approached us. "What's happened here?" she asked.

Pete told her about finding Johnnie bleeding on the ground. I watched the paramedics. They didn't seem to be in too big a rush to leave. Poor Johnnie, I thought. And poor Pete. He was going to be very upset when he learned that his friend had died.

Curran's partner walked over and began taking pictures. At the sound of the ambulance leaving, Pete looked up, and I watched his shoulders slump as the significance of its slow pace registered. Tears seeped from his eyes. I put my arm around him in sympathy.

"What a waste," he said.

Both cops seemed shaken. I guessed Johnnie had been a well-liked member of the community.

Curran's partner began stringing up yellow security tape around what was now a murder scene. While the sand had soaked up much of Johnnie's blood, the red stain was still very evident. The blood-drenched cloth Pete had used lay caked in sand on the ground. I glanced at Pete's bare chest and decided that the cloth was his T-shirt.

"You're shivering," I said. "Better put your jacket back on."

Ignoring his bloodied hands, he reached down to where his jacket had landed, and without bothering to shake the sand out, he put it back on.

Tapping his shoe against the filthy shirt, he said to Curran, "You can throw this in the garbage. I don't ever want to see it again."

She nodded grimly.

"Do you think he was trying to defend himself?" I asked, pointing to an area of disturbed sand from which a line of blood led to the spot where Pete had found his dying friend. Not far from the scuffed sand was a strange indentation, as if some heavy object had been placed there.

"Hard to tell," Curran's partner replied. "But we'll know more after forensics has done their investigation."

Curran asked, "And both of you are certain you didn't see any knife or other sharp object?"

We shook our heads. And then I remembered. "I did see a motorboat out in the bay. It could've been coming from this beach. I couldn't tell if the person in it was a man or a woman."

While Curran wrote in her notebook, I tried to provide as many details as I could, including the turquoise jacket.

"Aluminum boats are pretty common around here," she said when I'd finished. "But maybe someone else saw it, too."

For the first time I noticed a number of people watching from the other side of the yellow tape.

"We might be able to find someone in Iqaluit who saw the boat arriving. It couldn't have gone anywhere else."

"Unless it went to one of the camps on the Bay," Pete interjected. "There are a couple not that far from here."

"Right. Do you know of anyone who would want to kill Johnnie?" Constable Curran's voice almost cracked.

"Nope. Everyone liked him."

The young Mountie nodded. "What about a possible motive?"

Pete glanced around as if trying to find one amongst the empty rocks and waves. A raven squawked overhead. The tide had receded by several feet, leaving a strip of dark wet sand sprinkled liberally with rocks. Curran's partner walked beside it, searching for possible signs of the departing boater or anything else that could be evidence. A short distance in front of him, I spied another strange indentation, except in the wet sand this one appeared almost squarish, as if it had been made by a small but heavy box.

"What about theft?" the politician said turning back to the constable. "As you know, some of his carvings go for as high as $10,000. You should check his gallery to see if any are missing."

"We'll do that next. Why don't you come with me?" Curran turned to leave.

"First, I'd like to get cleaned up," Pete held up his blood-stained hands, before heading towards the water.

"If you don't mind," I joined in, "I'll come with you. I noticed some footprints that might not be Johnnie's."

Twenty-Nine

From the door to Johnnie's workshop, I pointed out the tracks I'd noticed on the floor leading to the gallery. Unfortunately, many had been obliterated by the ones Pete and I had made, but there was a clear set where neither of us had walked. Because of their smooth tread, they were easily distinguished from the rippled treads made by my hiking boots and Pete's Nikes.

"They're probably Johnnie's, but they could also belong to his killer," I said. "I also noticed others in the gallery."

"Our forensic investigator will determine that. He'll also want to take imprints of your shoes. Could you two wait here while I take some pictures? But stay put, don't move. There's probably evidence out here, too."

When she'd finished taking her photos, I pointed to the outdoor workbench. "I'm not sure if it's important, but earlier I noticed an outline where a carving Johnnie was working on might've stood. I don't remember seeing any unfinished works on the shelves that could've been his."

After taking pictures of the table and surrounding ground, Curran suggested we go inside. "But step exactly where I step, okay? I want you to check for missing items."

Pete followed the young police officer into the workshop with me pulling up the rear. So intent was I on staying exactly in their tracks that I almost forgot to look around, but then I wouldn't be able to tell if anything was missing anyway. I did scan the shelves for Johnnie's partially-finished carving but failed to see any candidates amongst the crude efforts of the students. Most likely he'd taken it to his house.

After several long minutes standing in an almost hunter-like stillness, Pete likewise indicated that he thought there was nothing missing. "But," he said in an apologetic tone, "I haven't been here that much lately, what with Johnnie being away so much, so it's difficult for me to identify anything missing. Besides, the only things worth stealing in this room are Johnnie's tools, but with all the kids coming and going, they get misplaced or lost all the time. Nope, far as I'm concerned, the gallery has the only stuff worth stealing."

"Boy, lots more tracks in here." Curran stood in the doorframe looking into the gallery. "Forensics will kill us if we mess them up. Can you guys tell me where you went in here and if you touched anything?"

Pete answered. "Once I realized Johnnie wasn't here, we just walked straight through to the outside door."

"Almost," I interjected. "I wanted to see his carvings, so I stopped at one or two as we passed by. I think I might've touched the one of the bears too."

From the door, my dimpled tracks were clearly evident on the floor beside the carving, but I also noticed the smoother pair of tracks on the other side of the sculpture. From there they led to another pedestal holding one of the contemporary sculptures and then they disappeared behind the counter, whose wooden surface was clear but for a computer at the far end.

Curran asked, "Pete, do you know if Johnnie keeps his cashbox behind the counter?"

"I think so, but only when he's here. Otherwise he locks it up in his house. But I don't think there's much cash in it. Since his carvings sell for such high prices, I think most people pay by cheque or credit card. At least that's how I pay."

She cast a glance at Pete as if to say, "so you're a collector too". "Without going into the room, can you look carefully around and let me know if you think anything is missing?"

While Curran took more pictures, Pete scanned the room. After a few minutes, he pointed at one of the glass shelves, where a gap between a walrus carving and a hunter seemed unusually large. "I bought the snow goose that used to stand there. One of his best, with its wings spread out and neck arched ready to attack. But apart from that, things look pretty much how they looked when I was here last. I think it was just after my trip to Toronto in mid May."

Turning to me, Curran said, "Miss Harris, I want you to stay here. Pete, could you come with me? I want you to tell me if there is anything missing behind the counter."

The constable took a route that skirted as far away from the various tracks as was possible with Pete keeping within her tracks. When they reached the other side of the counter, Pete showed where Johnnie kept the cash box.

With her hands encased in plastic gloves, Curran opened the drawer. "Not locked and nothing inside but some credit card receipts. I'll check his house. Anything else missing?"

"Yeah," Pete replied, nodding his head towards the floor underneath where the large flat computer screen stood, to where some wires dangled. "The computer's gone."

Before Curran could warn him not to, he'd pulled up one of the cables that was attached to the back of the overly large computer screen. "See."

"Please, don't touch anything else," Curran said, gritting her teeth. "Can you describe it for me?"

He shrugged. "Just a big rectangular box, grey, I think, with a big apple on the side."

"Sounds like a Mac, which makes sense, since this screen is also a Mac. Okay, anything else missing?" she asked, taking photos of the counter and behind it.

My thoughts turned to the beach in front of Johnnie's house. "You know, there was a strange mark in the sand where Johnnie was attacked and another down by the water. They could've been made by something heavy like a processor?"

The young Mountie shot me a querying glance. "Run that by me again."

As she furiously wrote in her notebook, I described the squarish indentation I'd seen.

"Right. I'll let my partner know."

At that point, the outside door banged open, and a man encased in white peered inside. "*Tabernac*! Curran, how many times do I have to tell you not to enter a crime scene until it's been processed."

Curran blushed. "Sorry, sir, I was real careful. But I thought while Pete was here, it'd be a good idea to determine if anything was missing. And he has found a couple of things. Looks like the cashbox is gone, though I'll check his house to make sure. And the CPU is gone too."

The forensic investigator shrugged. "It's probably at the repair shop. It happens to mine all the time."

"Yeah, but, sir, a set of recent tracks leads right up to where it was, and you can see a smudge mark in the dust where it was moved before being lifted."

"Okay, noted. Unless Pete notices anything else gone, get out of there now. You'd better come this way."

"Sorry, sir, I think it best we go back the way we came. Lots of tracks near you."

"That's what I meant, constable." This time his face took on a pinkish glow. "I'll need imprints of Pete's and the other witness's boots. Go back to Johnnie's house. I'll do it there." He ducked back outside and slammed the door shut.

The four of us met at Johnnie's back door, where the stiff and unsmiling forensics cop introduced himself as Sergeant Boudreau before saying to Pete, "Too bad about Johnnie. He was a wonderful carver. I have some of his work."

I was beginning to wonder who didn't own a Johnnie Nanuqtuaq carving.

Indicating a police truck parked next to the house, he ordered, "Please sit in the front while I do the imprints."

Then, as if finally remembering Pete's political importance, he said, "I am sorry about the inconvenience, sir. But this won't take long, then you can go. Could you please take off your shoes?"

"No problem. You've got a job to do, Michel. Any idea yet on how or why Johnnie died?"

Boudreau shook his head. "It's too early to tell. But we're fairly certain he was killed close to where you found him. It looks like he tried to defend himself. I'm hoping we'll be able to pick up some of the killer's DNA on the body. Since his body was lying near the door, he was either going into or out of the house. But it's hard to tell whether he knew his killer or not. "

"Do you think someone saw the murder?" I asked.

"You know, *madame*, I can't tell you anything about an ongoing case. But perhaps you saw something." I guessed I didn't have the same status as Pete.

"Nope, nothing as I've already told Constable Curran, except of course the man in the boat."

At his request I explained once more about the motorboat, but this time I remembered something else. "There was a bulky object in the bow of that boat. It might've been that computer processor."

"You got that, Constable Curran?" he said.

"Yes, sir," came back the quick reply.

While Sergeant Boudreau was making the imprints, another Mountie arrived. He acknowledged his acquaintance with Pete with a handshake then introduced himself to me as being with the General Investigation Section. After Curran brought him up-to-date on our involvement, he cautioned both of us not to say anything to the media and reminded Curran to take my home contact info. Motioning the forensic cop aside, he continued talking for a few more minutes before going inside Johnnie's house.

A few minutes later, Boudreau was finished with a perfect set of imprints from both our footwear. I was putting my boots back on when a voice startled me, and a man I associated with Toronto, not Iqaluit, appeared on the opposite side of the truck.

Sergeant Hue, dressed in a black leather jacket and blue jeans with a wool toque firmly pulled down over his ears, walked up to Curran and said, "May I speak to you for a minute, Constable?"

I ducked, hoping he hadn't recognized me. I didn't really want to have to explain my presence at yet another crime scene.

"Sorry to bother you," Hue continued, "but I've just learned that Johnnie Nanuqtuaq has been murdered, and as you know, he was a person of interest in—" The rest of his words were cut off as the two of them walked further from the truck.

But I didn't need a police badge to guess that he was linking Johnnie to Carter's death, which surprised me. Sure, they might have known each other, since one was an Inuit art dealer and the other an Inuit artist, but Carter had probably retired from the business before Johnnie's sculptures had begun appearing on the scene. What would Johnnie, a highly successful carver, as evinced by this fancy kitchen and his BMW, have to gain by the death of an old man who lived thousands of kilometres away?

Thirty

The last task the forensic investigator performed before allowing Pete and me to leave was to take our fingerprints, which didn't really bother me, since I had nothing to hide. Well, almost nothing.

When he asked if we'd touched anything in Johnnie's house, I felt a vague twinge of guilt when mentioning only the phone used to call the ambulance. I didn't tell him about my father's gold watch lying concealed in my jacket pocket. It was mine. Not Johnnie's. It wouldn't help them solve Johnnie's murder, but it might help me to find my father.

Hue nodded grimly in acknowledgment when I passed him still talking to Curran outside Johnnie's house. Hoping to avoid a grilling, I continued walking. But I'd barely gone a few steps when he called out, "So that *was* you, Ms Harris. Fancy meeting you here…at another crime scene." He paused as if to emphasize this last point. "And what may I ask brings you to this one…and to Iqaluit?"

I felt another twinge of guilt at not having informed him of my trip. "I've come on private business that has nothing to do with Johnnie's murder. Now if you don't mind, I'm keeping the Minister of Culture waiting."

I started back along the dirt road, to where Pete's Xterra still stood parked next to the dead carver's workshop at the end of the road.

"Just a moment, Ms Harris," Hue called out. "I have some further questions to ask you with respect to Carter Davis's murder. When I'm finished here, I would like to drop by your hotel. I understand you're staying at the Frobisher Inn."

"Sure," I muttered, somewhat annoyed that Curran had passed on my hotel information. "I'll be in the dining room." I wasn't about to give up my dinner to please him.

I glanced at my watch. 8:45. No wonder I was starving. But the sun was still far from setting. It was going to take me some time to get used to these endless days.

When I reached Pete's SUV, I found him leaning against the door in conversation with a silver-haired man with a pronounced paunch, who, aside from a skimpy ponytail, looked as if he'd just stepped out of a *Town and Country* magazine, from his tweed jacket and paisley ascot to slightly scuffed brown leather brogues.

At the sound of my footsteps, he stepped away from Pete and turned to me. "Miss Harris, a pleasure to meet you," he said with a slight burr of a Scottish accent while griping my hand in a firm shake. "Angus McLeod. Pete was just tellin' me about you. Good man, your father. I knew him well."

"That's nice. May I ask when?" The moment I asked this question, I realized it was a bit abrupt. But his words had so taken me aback that all I could think was he'd known my father after the plane crash.

But he didn't appear to be the least perturbed by the question. "I believe we first met in the late 1960s, when he began comin' up here. I was workin' at the Hudson Bay Company store in James Lake at the time. Wonderful chap. He did so much for the Inuit art community."

"When was the last time you saw him?"

"Sadly, I was probably the last person he saw before his plane went missin'. He'd been at my house in James Lake. Such a terrible tragedy. The community was very upset by his loss. As it was doubtless a dreadful loss for you and your mother."

I mumbled some appropriate words while he continued. "He'd come to look at the latest collection of carvings and prints at the James Lake Co-op. By 1973, I'd taken over as director. When the Inuit started it in the late '60s, HBC was quite upset. Intrudin' on their monopoly, they said. I myself thought it was a grand idea, so when I refused to use intimidatin' tactics to scare off the Co-op, HBC fired me and the Co-op hired me." He chuckled.

"I'm wondering if you've ever heard of any rumours that suggest my father might have survived the crash?"

"I understand from Pete that you believe this to be so. I might be able to help you. Why don't you come to my house tomorrow, and I can tell you what I know."

At last someone who could help me. "Is tomorrow morning too soon?"

"Sorry, I'm tied up, but late afternoon would work, say around four p.m. You'll find me at house 342."

"And the street name?"

"My apologies. I forget, this is a curiosity of the north. For the longest while, Iqaluit had no street names, so houses were simply numbered. If you're comin' by cab, the driver will know where to find me. But if you're walking, the house is on the road that runs along the ridge. It's not hard to find. It's the only house in that part of town with a greenhouse."

Pete spoke a few minutes longer with Angus then the two of us climbed into the Xterra and headed back past Johnnie's house with its ring of yellow tape flapping in the wind. Most of the onlookers had gone, although a couple of kids still played on the beach, which had grown considerably more expansive with the retreating tide. Since I saw no sign of the police other than their trucks, I assumed they were inside doing their job. Although I had only spoken·to the talented carver a couple of times, I couldn't help but feel sadness at a young life so quickly extinguished, particularly one that had shown such great promise.

As we headed up the hill to the main road, I said, "I'm very sorry about Johnnie. I think he's going to be sadly missed."

"You've got that right," Pete replied succinctly, waiting for a tanker truck to pass before he could turn onto the main road.

"How are you doing? It's not easy finding a friend in that condition."

"I'm okay. Thanks for asking."

"I only just met Johnnie. He was my seatmate on the plane. He seemed so friendly to everyone, it's hard to imagine that anyone hated him enough to kill him."

"That's why I think whoever killed him did it accidentally." He hesitated, as if trying to rein in his sorrow, then with a quick glance at me, he continued, "I think Johnnie must've caught the guy trying to steal something, and the guy felt he had no choice but to kill him."

"But for an unfinished carving and a computer?"

"People kill for less in the south. Besides Johnnie's got a lot of expensive stereo equipment and a flat screen TV in his house. The guy was probably after them when Johnnie surprised him."

It made sense. "Well, I sure hope they catch the guy."

"It's a small community. Johnnie had many friends. Someone knows who did it, and someone will turn the guy in."

We'd reached the heights, and I marvelled once again at the glorious view of Frobisher Bay. The distant mountains looked tantalizingly close while at the same time remote and untouched. Low, flat clouds scudded past them. The only sign of human intervention was an oil tanker chugging up the middle of the bay towards another that was moored at the far end of a peninsula on the other side of Iqaluit.

"Angus McLeod seems an interesting man," I said. "Sounds as if he has been in the north a long time."

"I suppose you could call him one of the old timers. I think Gus came to Baffin from Scotland with the Hudson Bay Company in the early sixties and never left. He's married to an Inuk, which is perhaps one reason why he never went south. Although several of his kids have moved south."

I had a sudden thought. "Is Ooleepeeka McLeod his daughter? I met her down south at the McConnell Art Gallery."

"Fancy you meeting up with her. I gather she's doing very well but plans to return north, once she has her degree. She wants to take over from her father. Gus made a big name for himself in the Inuit art business. Not only was he instrumental in getting the James Lake artist community up and going, but he also got involved with several other Baffin Island communities. He was key in setting up distribution links to southern markets."

"I guess you know a lot about the art community from being the Minister of Culture."

"Yeah, but I'm a carver myself. Used to do a fair bit before I got involved in the community. But I was never as good as Johnnie. He had that special spark." He sighed and banged his hand on the steering wheel. "Christ, what a shame."

I waited a few seconds before asking, "I guess Angus knows Johnnie from Tasilik? Johnnie must've sold through the Co-op."

"Yeah, used to. By the way it's now called the Tasilik Art Centre. Gus was pretty upset when Johnnie left. He was one of Gus's star artists. And I know Johnnie was pretty angry with Gus. Still, Angus gave Johnnie his start, and Johnnie respected that."

We'd reached the outskirts of Iqaluit. The collection of kids playing in the schoolyard had grown. It looked as if an impromptu soccer game was in progress.

"Do you know why Johnnie left?" I asked.

"He never said. I heard it was about a difference of opinion. It might have been over money, not sure. Anyways Johnnie has done well on his own. So I guess he didn't really need the marketing services of the Art Centre any more."

"Is that when he moved to Iqaluit?"

"Yeah, moved his workshop here. But he kept his house in Tasilik. Nice place."

"Is that where his sister Apphia lives?"

He turned a suspicious eye towards me. "So you know about Apphia?"

"Yes, an artist by the name of Frankie Ashoona told me about her. He was once Suula's boyfriend. He thought there was another older daughter, but he didn't know her name."

"Yeah, I remember Frankie. Used to be a good artist until drink got the better of him."

I didn't like his underlying tone of dismissal, so I said, "I saw some of his stuff. I think he's still good. He also said their father was white. Did you know that?"

He gave me a long, hard perusal before turning his eyes back onto the road. "Yeah, a lot of us with white blood. You see, our women were a warm diversion in the long dark winter nights. But when summer arrived, they took off, leaving their women and their kids to fend for themselves."

His bitter words left me feeling awkward, Unable to provide an adequate response, I asked instead, "You don't happen to know the name of Johnnie's other sister?"

"Was Margee."

"Was?"

"Yeah, she died a few years back. Another suicide, just like her mother."

"Oh, dear, I'm sorry to hear that. Is Apphia still alive, then?"

"Why do you want to know?" Again that tone of distrust.

"Like I told you, I think there's a link between the Nanuqtuaq family and my father. In fact, I know there's one, because I found something belonging to my father at Johnnie's house."

"You don't say."

I was about to show him the pocket watch when I realized I would be incriminating myself, so I returned to my question. "You didn't say whether Apphia was living in Tasilik or not."

"I didn't."

"But you know how to find her," I said more as a statement than a question. I took his silence as a yes. "Now that her brother is dead, I really want to talk to her. I would appreciate if you could tell me how to get hold of her."

At this point the front entrance to the Frobisher Inn came into view. "If you won't tell me, I'm sure I can find out from the police, or Angus McLeod, for that matter. He probably knows too." I clicked the door open and started to climb out of the car.

Pete finally spoke up. "I'd appreciate if you didn't do anything until I get back to you, okay?"

"Why?"

"She's had a difficult time. She's going to be very upset by her brother's death. And she might…" He stopped, not wanting to complete the sentence.

But I was fairly certain I knew what he intended to say. "You're worried she might follow in her mother's and sister's footsteps."

He nodded sadly. "So would you please wait until I have a chance to talk to her?"

But did I have the time this might take? I told him about my sick mother and her wish to finally know what had happened to her husband. Before we parted, he agreed to talk with Johnnie's only living sister as soon as he could.

"But it might be difficult to reach her," he said. "She doesn't spend much time in Tasilik any more."

Before I could ask him where she lived, he'd driven off. Nevertheless, I suspected it might be Naujalik. And if so, it would be almost impossible for me to speak to her without Pete's help, let alone try to find her on my own.

Thirty-One

Sergeant Hue found me in the Inn's still crowded restaurant just as my first course of smoked Arctic char was being placed in front of me. Even though they were suppose to stop taking orders after nine, I had managed to convince the maître'd that if I didn't immediately have some food in my very empty stomach, I might faint and cause a scene. Laughing, he'd acquiesced and advised me to have the caribou medallions with blueberry sauce, since it required minimal preparation time. I'd added a very fine and expensive bottle of Burgundy to the order as a way of thanking him. Besides, Mother could easily afford it.

"I know this is a bit irregular," the Toronto cop said, unzipping his leather jacket. "Do you mind if I join you? I haven't had dinner myself, and I'm starved."

I agreed, figuring if he was prepared to question me in the relaxed comfort of a restaurant, particularly while eating, his questions couldn't be all that threatening. However, since it was close to nine thirty, I wasn't sure if the policeman would be fed, but with a nod from my friend the maître'd, the waitress arrived with a smile and took his order of musk ox stew.

"Are you a collector like your father?" He pointed to the stone carving of an Inuk hunter I'd just bought.

"Not at all, but I couldn't resist his steely stare. If you wait along enough, you might be tempted to buy something yourself."

A petite woman standing next to our table shyly brought out a pair of embroidered felt boots complete with fur trim from a crumpled plastic bag and laid them on the table.

"Not bad." The sergeant's obsidian eyes creased with laughter. "My kid would love these. How much?"

She made a suggestion, and he countered. After a few more minutes of haggling, he was a proud owner of a pair of Inuit boots.

"See, what did I tell you?" I laughed. "These artists have been coming around since I sat down. I gather it's a nightly event. This way you don't pay the middleman's mark-up."

I needn't have been worried about his questioning. As the meal progressed, I realized he was learning more about my father and my family than he would've in the intimidating confines of a police station. He wasn't so dumb after all, particularly since the wine was loosening my tongue and not his. He'd turned down my offer of wine.

Still, it didn't matter. I had no reason to hide what little I knew about my father and his collecting or the fact that my mother had recently donated the entire collection to the Art Gallery of Ontario. But when he asked if I was aware that the AGO had discovered that some of the donated pieces were counterfeit, I felt the icy prick of apprehension.

"That's not possible," I shot back. "My father would never have bought counterfeit artwork."

"Mostly likely he didn't know. I gather the counterfeiting was very expertly done. Even had the gallery fooled until they decided to have all their Inuit artwork examined in light of the recent discovery of a large number of counterfeit pieces."

"Are you referring to the forgeries found in the warehouse that's supposed to be linked to Carter Davis's murder?"

"So you know about it?"

"I read about it in the paper." I paused, debating whether to bring the next point up, but figured if I didn't he would. "It also mentioned that this warehouse was once rented by my father."

"According to your mother, this was where his collection was housed before being given to the gallery. She never bothered to change the name."

"But someone else is renting it now." I took another bracing sip of wine. "I hope you haven't been bothering Mother about this. She's very ill."

"So I understand. I'm very sorry. But curiously enough, the current renter is, or should I say, was Johnnie Nanuqtuaq."

I tried to hide my amazement. It sounded a little too coincidental to me. No doubt Sergeant Hue thought the same thing.

"I was hoping to question him about it, so you can imagine my astonishment at discovering he'd just been murdered."

He leaned forward. "With you at the crime scene." He paused as if to let the significance sink in. "So I suggest you tell me about your family's connection to Johnnie Nanuqtuaq."

"There isn't one. I'd never met the guy, let alone known of his existence until today."

"Then why were you at his house?"

So I told him about the significance of the prints and Suula and my reason for going to see her son.

"Did you talk to him before he was killed?"

"Nope. I tried earlier on the plane, but I got the distinct impression he didn't want to talk to me."

"And you think your father might've survived the crash and that Johnnie's mother saved him?"

"I do, as incredible as it might seem. And I'm more convinced after finding something in his house that once belonged to my father."

I was in a quandary as to whether to actually show the watch to him, since I could be accused of stealing, then I realized that by having just mentioned it, I had already incriminated myself anyway. I shoved my wine glass away, thinking I'd better stop drinking before I really got myself into trouble.

"I'm afraid I might have done something wrong. But I

felt I was reclaiming what by rights belongs to my family."

I placed Great-grandpa Joe's pocket watch on the table between us. The table's candle glow glinted off its gold surface.

"You are certain it was your father's?"

I pointed out Great-grandpa Joe's entwined initials on the casing. "So you see, my father must've survived the crash."

Using a tissue from his pocket, he carefully looked it over. "It's a very valuable piece. Your mother can no doubt corroborate this?"

"Look, I know I shouldn't have taken it. But if you're thinking I stole it for its monetary value, no way. Besides, I wouldn't have told you about it, would I?"

His lips thinned into a smile as he clicked open the front case. "There's a picture inside. Do you know who she is?" He slid the open watch across the tablecloth to me.

I was about to say my mother, for Father had always kept a photo of her from the early years of their marriage inside the front case, but then Johnnie was the watch's current owner, so I wasn't surprised to see a drawing of a young Inuk woman. "Probably Johnnie's girlfriend."

Unlike the simple, stylized Inuit drawings I was used to, this one was a fairly life-like portrait. She looked quite pretty. Johnnie had been a good drawer too.

"I see the watch is still running slow. I could never figure out why Father used it. No matter how many times he had it fixed, it would always be running fifteen minutes late by the time he needed to wind it up again. And it looks as if it needs winding now." I flipped open the back case. "The key's probably in Johnnie's bedroom."

There was a piece of paper jammed inside this back case, and when I turned it over, I saw Mother staring back at me. "This doesn't make sense." I showed him my father's photo of Mother at the bottom of which was written the special name he always called her, Cessy, short for Cecilia.

The picture had been defaced with a heavy "X" across her face. "Why in the world would Johnnie do this? He didn't even know her."

"It's also curious that he would keep the photo instead of throwing it out," Hue added. "You better hand the watch and the photo back to me. I'll have to pass it on to GIS even though I doubt it has any bearing on the case."

"No, I suppose not. Though doesn't the fact it wasn't stolen point to the motive for Johnnie's murder being other than theft? This has to be worth several thousand dollars."

"You'd be surprised what some guys think is worth stealing. Anyway, this would be a lot more difficult to fence, particularly here in Iqaluit."

"I suppose you're right. Look, I'll want that watch back. Johnnie hasn't any use for it any more, and I doubt his sister would want it."

He slipped it into a Ziploc bag and tucked it into his jacket pocket. "I'm not familiar enough with family law to know what rights your family has, but I'll make sure the sergeant working on the case at GIS knows it belonged to your father."

"By the way, have you had any luck in finding my mother's print?"

"Print? Sorry, I'm not sure what you're referring to."

"The Inuit drawing that I left with Carter before he died. I told you about it in Toronto. I assume the reason it wasn't found in his house is because he'd passed it onto the friend he thought might be able to help in locating the artist. I was hoping you people would be able to track it down."

"Yes, right, sorry. I passed it onto someone on my team. I'll check with her tomorrow and get back to you, okay?" He chewed slowly on the last forkful of musk ox stew. "Boy, this was sure good."

"My caribou was good too." With my stomach feeling considerably more contented than it had when I arrived, I laid my knife and fork down on a very empty plate. "What about the letter from my father? Did you find it?"

"This I do remember. But sorry, my men didn't find it. I suggest you let Carter's heir know about it."

"You mean Lynwood Greenberg?"

"Yes, you know him?"

"No, but I met him at the crime scene. Is he free now? I'd understood you were holding him for questioning?"

"Where did you learn that from?" The policeman's eyes narrowed in suspicion.

"The paper again."

"Right. We were, but we had to let him go."

"Not enough evidence, I guess," I said.

Hue eyed me again. "Let's just say that even though a suspect is no longer in our custody, it doesn't mean he or she is no longer considered as such."

I nodded, as though I'd known this all along, and savoured the last sip of what had proven to be an exemplary wine.

By this time, the restaurant had pretty well cleared out, with only a few occupied tables remaining. With the two waitresses casting anxious glances in our direction, we decided it was time to leave, just as another couple made the same decision. We met at the exit. I noticed Mary Goresky first, with her distinctive white hair, before I recognized with surprise the tweed jacket of her companion. But then perhaps I shouldn't have been surprised. After all, his daughter worked for the gallery director.

"Hi, Mary, Angus, I hope you enjoyed your meal as much as I did."

"Yes, Angus and I are old friends," Mary said. Her rhinestone glasses glinted in the overhead lights of the lobby.

"Mary is one of my longest-standing clients," Angus added. "I've introduced her to many an emergin' artist, who later became a name in the Inuit art world. That's right, eh, Mary?"

"Indeed. You have certainly contributed to making the

McConnell's Inuit art collection one of the pre-eminent collections in Canada."

"I'm surprised you're still here," I commented. "I thought you were travelling straight on to Cape Dorset."

"I was supposed to, but had to make a last minute change. I'm flying to Tasilik instead."

"Some hot new find?" I asked jokingly.

Mary lit up one of her signature cigarillos. "As a matter of fact, you're right. Angus wants me to see some of the latest work of a young woman. So I decided to go there first before going to Cape Dorset."

It was at that point that I realized I'd forgotten to introduce Hue. But before I could, the Toronto cop held his hand out to Mary and said, "Ms Goresky, I'm not sure if you remember me, but I was talking to you recently about that collection of forgeries we found in Toronto."

"Why Sergeant Hue, yes of course. I do hope I was able to be of assistance in your investigation."

"Yes, your expert advice and that from the Art Gallery of Ontario helped us to identify all the fraudulent pieces."

"Thank goodness," Mary replied. "It was most fortunate you were able to confiscate them before they entered the market. You can't imagine the damage that number of pieces would've done to the credibility of Inuit art. Have you arrested the people behind it yet?"

"Not yet, but we're working on it. In fact, that is my reason for coming to Iqaluit."

"Oh, do you suspect it's someone from here?"

"I had someone in mind, but unfortunately he's turned up dead."

"Mary, it was Johnnie Nanuqtuaq, remember, the guy on the plane," I broke in.

Before Mary had a chance to reply, Angus cut in. "Yes, I was tellin' Mary the sad news over dinner. Such a tragedy. A carver of his magnitude only happens once in a generation, although of late, his work had declined somewhat. But there must be some mistake. I find it very hard to believe that you would suspect him of forgery. His name commanded high prices. He had no need to pretend he was someone else."

"Let's just say we're not sure what his role was, just that there was a possible link," Hue replied.

"I do hope you apprehend them, for we canna have those bloody bastards—" He glanced sheepishly from Mary to me. "Please pardon my language, lassies. We canna have them floodin' the market with forgeries. As Mary said, it will do irreparable damage to Inuit art."

"Before you go, Mr. McLeod, your name has been passed to me as an expert in the art business here in Nunavut. I would like to meet with you to get a better idea of how it works."

After arranging to meet the policeman at his house the following day at a time that didn't conflict with my afternoon meeting, Angus left us, while the three of us headed up the elevator to our separate rooms. Although Mary got out on an earlier floor, Hue stepped out with me.

As he followed me down the hall, I wondered if he had more questions to ask me, but it turned out that his room was only two doors down from mine, which proved almost immediately to be a good thing.

When I inserted my keycard into the slot, the door swung open. Startled, I must've said something, for Hue called out, "Anything wrong?"

"My door's open," I called back.

"Don't go inside!"

He pulled out his gun and in the classic TV police show stance, stepped into the room. Within seconds it was obvious no one was inside, but it was also equally obvious that someone had been, for the daypack I'd brought on the plane with me lay upside down with its contents dumped onto the bed. Fortunately I had my wallet with me, so all that'd remained in the pack were a couple of crime novels, a Nunavut travel guide, my make-up case, an extra pair of mittens, eye-shades, some chocolate bars and a water bottle, nothing worth stealing. And nothing had been.

"At least my backpack wasn't here," I said, watching Hue replace his gun in his holster. "Not too smart a thief to pick my room. Hope he had better luck elsewhere."

"I suggest you report this to Constable Curran. But since you're probably tired, it can wait till morning. I'll let hotel security know. It's likely not an isolated case."

It was only later when I opened my book to read a few pages before going to sleep that I realized something had been stolen. The letter my father had written from this very hotel to Carter Davis the day before he disappeared.

I'd been using it as a bookmark, in part to keep it from going astray. Despite a thorough search of my daypack, I failed to find it. Curious. Why would someone take a letter written over thirty-six years ago?

Thirty-Two

Next morning, when Curran asked me if anything had been stolen, I hesitated, unsure if I should mention the letter. I had after all taken it from Carter Davis's house while he lay dead on the basement floor. But since I didn't need to reveal exactly how I'd got it, I told her about it.

"I brought this letter to Iqaluit," I said, trying to get comfortable in one of the detachment's hard metal chairs, "because I was hoping to find the man my father mentioned by the name of the Crazy Russkie. You don't happen to know who he is, do you?"

She shook her blonde ponytail. "Maybe someone in the detachment does. Can you tell me what the letter said?"

"There wasn't much to it. It just mentioned wanting to follow-up on something this Crazy Russkie guy had told him about the *Mystical Owl*."

"*Mystical Owl*?"

I told her about the print's significant value and the fact that the copy hanging on Carter's wall had been a forgery. "Carter's copy was probably stolen by the person who killed him."

"Do you think there's a connection between the Toronto robbery and yours?" She asked, looking up from her notebook.

"I suppose it's possible, since the letter does mention the *Mystical Owl*. But they would have to know of the existence of this letter, and I haven't told anyone about it." I paused. "Though it's possible Carter could have mentioned it to someone."

"Do you know who this person might be?"

"Nope." Then a sudden thought sent a chill down my spine. "I sure hope the thief isn't the person who killed Carter." I glanced at Curran, who didn't react as if this was a new thought for her. "I guess I'd better pass this information onto Sergeant Hue."

A helmet of black hair rose above the partition separating Curran's desk from her neighbour. "Did I hear my name mentioned?"

"Good morning, Sergeant Hue. It turns out something was stolen from my room after all." I repeated what I'd just told the Iqaluit policewoman. "So Constable Curran and I are wondering if there might be a link to Carter's murder. What do you think?"

He nodded. "Constable, we'd better get forensics checking for fingerprints. See if we have a match with any at the Toronto scene."

"I take it, sir, you don't yet have a solid suspect for the Toronto murder," Curran said.

"Not yet."

"Is that really what brought you to Iqaluit?" I asked.

He glanced briefly at Curran then back to me. "Let's just say that I'm following up on leads for both cases."

"Do you have any suspects at all?"

"Ms Harris, you know I can't comment. But I will admit the theft of your father's letter is just a little too coincidental. Are you sure you told no one about it?"

"Defin—no, wait a minute, I think I told my sister. I suppose she could've told someone, who in turn told someone, etc. But I find this very hard to believe. She's as reluctant as I am to discuss our father's disappearance with outsiders. In fact, even as a family we never talked about it. It was just one of those forbidden topics. So I really think it unlikely she would mention this letter to anyone other than her husband."

"Did you tell your mother about it?"

"No. She was upset enough by the drawings. I was afraid to upset her further."

"Would your sister mention it to her?"

"Perhaps. But if she had, Mother would've demanded to see the letter. But she never asked for it or even hinted she knew of its existence. No, you're way off base if you think someone in my family might be behind this theft. Besides, if they wanted the letter, it would've been a lot easier to take it when I was in Toronto."

I felt as I watched him write in his notebook, that he hadn't really believed me, so I added, "Sergeant Hue, let's be realistic about this. What motive would any member of my family have? In fact, why would anyone want to steal it? The letter doesn't say much of anything. Unless, this guy, Crazy Russkie, is important."

Turning to the young Mountie, he asked, "Do you know of this man?"

"I was gonna ask the older members in the detachment. And I can get Anna to look through our files," she replied.

"Good, the sooner the better. And you'd better get forensics over to Miss Harris's hotel room before the cleaning staff arrive."

"I will, but before I do, sir, I want to show Ms Harris a drawing we found in Johnnie Nanuqtuaq's house. Sergeant Hue, you might be interested in this, too."

At the mention of the word "drawing", I wasn't the least surprised when the Mountie placed another print by Suula on top of the clutter on her desk. Of the same size and artistic style as the previous drawings, this one portrayed an Inuit family of two smiling adults and two small children, a girl in pigtails and a young boy, who just might be Johnnie, while the girl could be his older sister Margee, the one who'd died. Like the other prints, black ink had been used, except for the colour of the man's hair. It was brilliant orange.

I tried to quell my rising excitement. Could it be? Surely not? But then it could explain a lot.

Fingering my own flaming locks, I said. "It's possible this could be my father. He had red hair, just like mine."

"Many men have red hair," replied Curran.

"True, but this picture has to be the next installment in the series of prints I told you about. I found another print like this one in my step-father's belongings that depicts this same family but with just the little girl. And like this picture, the man has orange hair. I doubt there are many red-haired Inuit. I don't know about you, but it makes a lot of sense to me."

I could tell she still didn't believe me. "I'm not sure, Constable Curran, if you are aware that Johnnie's father was white. Well…I think we share the same father."

Curran glanced at Hue, before saying, "Ms Harris, like I told you yesterday, the chances of your father surviving a plane crash on the frozen tundra hundreds of kilometres from help are almost nil. And the likelihood of him being Johnnie's father is even less."

"But how do you explain Johnnie having my father's watch, a family heirloom that is traditionally passed down from first born boy to first born boy? And since there are no boys in my family, if Johnnie is indeed my father's son, then he would've been the first born boy."

At that point, the constable's phone rang. "Curran here," she said curtly, before smiling as the other party spoke. With the scarred side of her face turned away, she looked quite pretty.

"Morning, sir. How's it going?… I see." Her eyes shifted to me as her face became sombre.

There were several more minutes of "I see", "That's right, sir" and so on, all the while keeping her gaze fully on me.

So when she finally put the phone aside and said, "It's Corporal Reilly," I wasn't surprised. "He would like to talk to you."

"Have you found the plane?" I said the minute I heard his deep-voiced greeting.

"Yes, ma'am, we have. We raised it early this morning."

"And is it my father's?"

Curran motioned Hue away from her cubicle to another part of the squad room, out of earshot from me, where she started speaking intently to him.

"The registration matches that of the plane your father chartered, ma'am."

I felt my hopes rise, although I was a bit taken aback by the brusqueness of his tone. "And was my father aboard?"

"There are the remains of two persons, ma'am."

"Did you say *two* people?"

"That's right, ma'am."

"Are you sure?" I'd really wanted Father to have survived.

"We will need to do a DNA analysis to confirm identification, ma'am. But since there were only two people on the flight, it is safe to assume that one set of remains belongs to your father."

Even though it was good to know his body had finally been found, I couldn't help but feel disappointed. "My mother will be glad the uncertainty is over."

"There's one further thing you should know, ma'am."

Curran and Hue returned to the cubicle. Both wore solemn expressions.

"Yes?"

"We found a bullet in the skull of one of the victims."

"Are you saying someone shot my father?"

The two policemen exchanged glances.

"Did your father know how to fly?" Reilly asked.

"No...I don't think so. Why are you asking?"

"Ah....well, ma'am, the victim with the bullet was sitting in the pilot's seat."

Its full significance took a second to register, and when it did, I exclaimed in horror. "Are you suggesting that my father shot the pilot?"

"We won't know what happened until we identify the remains and conduct an investigation. Now, ma'am, if you don't mind, I have to go. We should be back in Iqaluit in a couple of days. You can follow up with us then."

I hung up feeling as if the bottom had just come out of my world. Surely Corporal Reilly couldn't be thinking that my father was a murderer. But as I noticed the expressions on both Constable Curran's and Sergeant Hue's faces, I knew this was exactly what they were thinking.

"But Johnnie had his watch. Where would he have got it from, if not from my father?"

Curran glanced at Hue, who said, "Your father might've left it behind or given it away before he left Iqaluit."

"Nope, never. It meant too much to him."

"The plane went missing in late April before summer break-up," Curran said. "It might've crashed on the ice. This woman Suula could've come across the plane and taken the watch."

I shoved aside the repugnant image of the woman going through my dead father's clothes. "But how do you explain her drawings of the man parachuting and the two with the man with the red hair?"

"They're just pictures, ma'am. It's likely Johnnie's mother made them up."

For several agonizing seconds, the three of us kept our thoughts to ourselves, glancing anywhere but at each other, until I said, "You believe my father killed the pilot."

Curran's eyes flicked towards Hue, who answered. "Miss Harris, it's too early to draw any conclusions without further investigation."

"He didn't do it," I almost shouted, rising from my chair. "No way. They'll need the gun to prove it. And Reilly didn't mention finding a gun."

I didn't wait for an answer. I stormed out of the detachment, intent on proving them wrong.

Thirty-Three

How dare they accuse my father of murder? He'd never held a gun, let alone fired one. Sure, his father and grandfather had been avid hunters, but Father had never shared their thirst for blood. Instead he'd helped Great-aunt Aggie make Three Deer Point a haven for the wildlife that roamed its forests.

No. There was no way Father would've killed the pilot. There had to be another explanation. Maybe the shooting was an accident. Maybe Father, for whatever reason, had been doing something with a gun, and it had accidentally gone off. Or maybe the pilot had pointed the gun at Father and forced him to fly the plane. Maybe…a very weak maybe…

Too upset to return to my room, I headed away from the detachment, away from the hotel into the frigid, damp wind rising from the bay. Fortunately, my missing backpack had arrived that morning just as I was about to leave, so I was sufficiently encased in three layers of clothing, mitts and a wool toque.

Winter! Did I say winter? This was mid-July, for heaven's sakes. Summer! I should be in shorts and T-shirt. I zipped my Gore-tex jacket up until it was tight against my chin, rubbed my cheeks against the icy cold and stuck my mittened hands back into my pockets.

Unfortunately, the wind also brought with it a bone-chilling drizzle that seemed to be doing its best to penetrate the warmth of my jacket. Nonetheless, I continued to wander the streets of Iqaluit, whose monochromatic drabness only served to contribute to my low spirits.

I tried to put reason to the confusion swirling around about my father. On the one side, I had the drawings and the pocket watch telling me he had survived the crash. On the other, the stark evidence of his remains lying in the cockpit of the downed plane. Evidence that was hard to refute. And now the police were accusing him of murder.

So why had Johnnie, for who else could it have been, sent the drawings to my mother? What possible motive could he have for upsetting our lives with the glimmer of hope they had brought? For thirty-six years, we had lived with the belief that Father was dead. Why open the door now, knowing that the plane holding his remains would soon be raised from its burial ground? What could Johnnie have possibly hoped to gain from it?

I was so lost in my thoughts that I stumbled into a large boulder suddenly blocking my path. Annoyed at it, at everything, I kicked it, only to receive a sore foot. Finally, my thoughts cleared enough for me to notice a neighbouring boulder. I skirted around it and the others.

They were strung out in fence-like fashion alongside a blue two-storey house. As an ATV whizzed past behind me, I realized they were probably the best defense in keeping drivers from straying off the dirt roads onto the dirt yards. A few hundred yards later, I followed a line of waist-high posts bordering the road that must be serving the same purpose, for there really was no other way to distinguish the roadway from the surrounding ground.

The drizzle was becoming more insistent and the wind colder. I shivered, thinking a cup of hot coffee laced with a wee dram would go down well about now. A nearby massive box-like building with "North Mart" emblazoned across the front looked like just the place to buy a bottle. If not, no doubt someone inside would be able to direct me to the nearest liquor store. But after roaming aisles as orderly and well-stocked as any southern grocery store, although I was aghast at the prices, easily double what I paid at home,

I failed to find anything remotely alcoholic.

My question about the nearest liquor store was greeted with a snicker. "Sorry, you can't buy alcohol in Iqaluit, in fact anywhere in Nunavut." Apparently only hotels and private clubs sold liquor. Remembering yesterday's gamblers and their array of empty bottles, I added bootleggers to the list. But of course, I had no idea where to find a bootlegger. Besides, at ten thirty in the morning, it really was too early to be drinking, let alone thinking about it, so I decided to concentrate on finding ordinary coffee.

By this time the rain was slanting harder and the wind becoming more penetrating. Despite my warm clothes, I was beginning to shiver. The sooner I could escape inside the better. I passed a collection of wooden two-storey buildings housing a variety of businesses. None looked as if they sold coffee. However, a short distance further I came across an intriguing igloo-like structure that announced itself a restaurant. Not caring if the coffee was good or not, I fled up the stairs.

I entered the warmth of a dark, dome-shaped room and ran smack into my Samaritan of yesterday, Pete Pitsiulak, leaning over a table in deep discussion with Mary Goresky. The politician was jamming his finger into the table as if trying to make a point with the art director, who seemed to be resisting. Feeling I wouldn't be welcome, I took a seat at an empty table on the other side of room and breathed in the inviting smell of percolating coffee. Neither one noticed me.

Because of the shape of the ceiling, their voices slid up the dome and back down to me, sounding as close as the next table. They were speaking in hushed tones, so I was only able to grasp snippets of their conversation, but it was enough for me to realize they were talking about the Toronto art forgeries. Curious, I strained to hear more, but all I could glean was that Pete was very angry, while Mary's voice carried a more placating tone, although the expression on her face seemed to suggest she was more shocked by what Pete was telling her than accepting.

Pete must have felt my intent gaze, for he abruptly stopped talking and turned in my direction. For a moment I thought I saw him frown, then his face broke into an expansive welcoming smile, and he invited me to join them. As I sat down at their table, I sensed Mary's feelings weren't entirely as welcoming.

"Just finalizing some details for an exhibition of Nunavut art at Mary's gallery next year," the Minister of Culture said. "Hope you were able to sleep last night. Many southerners find it difficult with the lack of any real darkness."

Although I was dying to ask him about what they'd really been talking about, I thought they wouldn't appreciate knowing I'd been eavesdropping, so I said, "The blackout curtains helped."

"I hear you had a robbery last night," Pete said.

"Boy, news travels fast around here."

Pete chuckled then grew serious. "I hope nothing of value was taken."

I shook my head. "Nope, nothing of importance."

I thought it prudent to keep the detail of the missing letter quiet, but it did raise a question to which Pete might know the answer.

"You don't happen to know if a man by the name of Crazy Russkie lives in Iqaluit, do you?"

"What a curious name," Mary said. "But I'm afraid I don't recall ever meeting anyone called Crazy Russkie either up here or at home."

"You know, the name Crazy Russkie rings a bell with me," Pete said. "But not from here. From a long time ago, when I lived in Broughton Island. But before I begin, can I get you a coffee, Meg? You look like you can do with some warming up."

After placing the order, with more coffee for Mary and himself along with a plate of donuts, he continued, "Now where was I? Oh yes, Crazy Russkie, Well, one day, this *qallunaat* came out of a blizzard, half frozen to death. If it hadn't been for his dog team, he wouldn't have made it. After recovering, he moved in with the teacher, a gal from Ontario. I guess she was feeling lonely." Pete grinned.

I gratefully took a sip of the surprisingly good and hot coffee, while Mary lit up another cigarillo.

"Anyway, he ended up spending the summer with us. He sure liked to paint. Even though he'd lost some fingers to frostbite, he could still hold a brush. We kids used to crowd around him and watch the colours grow on the paper. I suppose that's where I first got my interest in art. Then one day after winter freeze-up, he ups and leaves. Probably had a falling out with Miss Miller." Pete let out a chortle. "We never saw him again. Crazy Russkie, he called himself, because he was crazy and a Russian. And let's face it, he had to be crazy to travel Baffin on his own."

"And you've no idea where he went?" I was beginning to feel a little more human as the tingling warmth of the coffee spread through me.

"No, but there's not too many communities he could've gone to. The closest was Tasilik to the south. I suppose he could've gone north too, to Clyde River, but that route would've been too dangerous, particularly with the open water."

"Can you remember what year this was?"

"Not really. I was in school, one of the early grades, which means it would've been in the late 1960s."

"Well, I know he eventually ended up here in Iqaluit by the early 1970s. Have you ever run across him here?"

"No, and I've been living in Iqaluit since 1999. I've never heard his name mentioned. So if he ever lived here, I'd say it was some time ago."

"I guess the only people who would know are the RCMP, and I've already asked them to check."

"You might want to try Angus McLeod. He's a bit of

211

a Northern history buff and prides himself on knowing the name of pretty well every *qallunaat* who ever lived on Baffin."

"Thanks, I will. By the way, any word on Apphia?" I bit into a chocolate donut and felt the creaminess of its filling burst into my mouth.

"Like I told you, it's gonna take some time. I'll let you know as soon as I hear, okay?" The smile vanished from his eyes.

"You don't want me to see her, do you?"

"I'm worried you might upset her."

"Won't she be upset already with her brother's death?" I countered.

"Are you talking about Johnnie's sister?" Mary asked.

Her rhinestone glasses offered a spark of brightness in the otherwise dim light of the restaurant. A couple of middle-aged men a few tables away from us were flirting with the young, slightly plump waitress, who seemed to be enjoying the attention.

"Yes, do you know her?"

"I've never met her, but I've seen some of her work and it's very good. She's not a carver like her brother. Drawing is her medium. A number of her drawings have been made into prints and also used for a couple of tapestries at the Tasilik Art Centre."

"I guess artistic genes must run in the Nanuqtuaq family."

Mary blew out a stream of smoke in response, then said, "Remember when you were at my gallery, I mentioned that the style of those prints by Suula was similar to Joly Quliik? Well, that's one of his prints hanging on the wall over there."

She walked over to where several framed Inuit prints were hanging. They were small, like Suula's prints, and I made a comment to that effect.

"They're not originals," she countered. "Most likely from a calendar."

"Yeah," Pete joined in. "You won't find many original prints in Nunavut. They were all sent south. But we've changed that. We now have a fair size collection at the Legislative Assembly, just up the road. You should take a tour of the place."

Mary pointed to the man seal hunting in the Quliik print. "See how finely drawn the man is, almost three-dimensional, something rarely seen in traditional Inuit art. As I recall, the figures in Suula's prints were almost identical."

Even to my unpracticed eye, they did look remarkably similar. "Are you suggesting she copied him?"

"Well, it is curious. They must've worked at the same studio," she said.

"That would've been a long time ago. I gather Quliik died in the mid 1970s."

"That's right. His last print was part of the 1975 collection of James Lake prints. The Inuit art world suffered when he died."

"That's what Carter Davis said."

"Oh, you knew Carter?"

"Not really. I met him just before he was killed."

"Such a tragic death. And such a nice man. You know, I worked for him right after I graduated. Do you know if they've apprehended the murderer yet?"

The mug Pete was holding slipped out of his hand and landed with a clunk on the table. Fortunately he managed to steady it before it could create too much of a mess. "Woops, sorry about that. Pretty well empty anyways. What were you saying, Mary?"

"I was just wondering if they've caught the man that killed Carter."

"No, not as far as I know," I replied, watching Pete mop up the few splatters of coffee with a napkin and wondering if Mary's question had caused him to drop his mug.

Mary's cell suddenly rang. As she rummaged through

her pack, I continued watching Pete. After signalling for a refill, he settled back into his chair. Noticing my gaze, he smiled broadly and clicked a pretend gun at me, which left me even more curious to know what, if anything, he knew about Carter's murder.

Mary listened more than spoke to her caller. At one point she cast her eyes in my direction and said, "Yes, she happens to be sitting across the table from me." Holding her fingers over the receiver she asked, "Angus wants to know if he can move your meeting up to two o'clock."

The sooner the better, I thought. "That's fine by me."

While Pete and I mutely sipped our coffees and munched on donuts, she spoke for a few minutes longer. After clicking off, she said, "That Toronto cop can't see him until late this afternoon, so he felt he'd better move you up."

Thirty-Four

Curious to learn if there was anything behind Pete's strange behaviour in the restaurant, I tagged along as he walked back to his office. I used a desire to tour the new Legislative Assembly as my excuse for joining him, but when I brought up Carter's name or mentioned the forgeries in Toronto, he deflected me by commenting on some aspect of the Iqaluit landscape, such as the intersection of streets we'd just crossed. Known as the Four Corners, it apparently was Iqaluit's only true intersection, but I noticed it only warranted four-way stop signs instead of stoplights. Twice he'd interrupted my questions by stopping to talk to passersby. With frequent nods and waves, he seemed to know everyone in town. But I supposed that was to be expected from a politician.

Finally, as we arrived at the bottom of the bank of metal stairs leading up to the Legislature's entrance, I said in frustration, "I get the distinct feeling that you don't want to talk to me about what you know about the art forgeries in Toronto—or Carter's death."

He continued walking up a couple of the stairs before turning back to me. "Meg, you know as a politician, I can't discuss what I know."

"It didn't seem to stop you in the restaurant," I blurted out before realizing what I was revealing.

He raised his eyebrows in question. "I'm not sure what you're talking about. Mary and I were discussing the upcoming exhibit, nothing else."

"I'm afraid I overhead you mention something about the

215

forgeries to Mary. Since my family seems to be implicated, I want to learn as much as I can."

"Oh that." He laughed. "I was just telling her how worried I was at the damage these forgeries could do to our art industry. Now I want you to look at this entranceway. Notice the inverted runners of an Inuit sled on either side of the door. We designed this building to showcase Inuit culture and Nunavut's natural wealth. Now I want you to look at the—"

As I made admiring noises about the igloo-like lines of the navy siding and glass exterior, I couldn't help but think that the anger he had expressed in his conversation with Mary could hardly be interpreted as worry. But I didn't need to be a rocket scientist to know I was being given the brush-off, so I held my tongue. Nor was I given the opportunity to press him further, for when we stepped inside the front lobby, Pete was waylaid by his assistant, worried he was going to miss his noon appointment.

With many apologies, he escaped through a set of glass doors, but not before I overheard his assistant mentioning his upcoming trip to Toronto, which reminded me of his earlier mention of another trip to that city. And if I recalled correctly, it had occurred in mid-May, at about the time Carter was killed. Interesting. But just because he was there at the same time didn't mean he was connected to the former gallery owner's death. Still, maybe that possible link was behind Sergeant Hue's interview with the minister and not counterfeit art.

Since I had a couple of hours to kill before my meeting with Angus, I decided I might as well spend some of it exploring what this new building had to offer before seeking out lunch. I knew I should probably be using the time to update Mother on what I'd just learned about Father, but since arriving in Iqaluit, I'd managed to come up with enough excuses to avoid calling her. One more wouldn't matter.

Besides, I was more concerned about the impact this

latest news might have on her. Though Jean had told me that her health was improving with the doctors even saying she might be able to go home in a day or two, we were both nonetheless worried over the effect this nonsense about Father and the fake art might have on her fragile recovery. And who could know what would happen when she learned that one of the two people in the submerged plane had been shot?

The security guard at the front desk suggested I start with the Chamber, where the elected members of the Legislature ran the territory's business. He was quick to point out that the sealskin covering the members' chairs was Arctic ring seal, a staple of Inuit life for thousands of years, and not the North Atlantic harp seal, whose pups were killed each spring amidst worldwide controversy. Like the restaurant, the Chamber was also modelled after an igloo, except its domed ceiling was considerably more grand. And like the restaurant, its walls were covered in fine examples of Inuit art that were in all likelihood originals, not copies from a calendar.

In a glass case outside the Chamber lay Nunavut's mace, intriguingly different from most provincial maces. Made from an ivory narwhal tusk, it lay on the shoulders of four miniature Inuit carved out of soapstone. Given the realistic quality of the carvings, I wondered whether Johnnie Nanuqtuaq had been the carver.

I wandered back into the main hallway, where the walls were awash with the colourful subjects of tapestries, felt wall hangings and prints. There were several magnificent pictures of swirling feathered Arctic birds by the *Mystical Owl* artist. I even discovered a small drawing by Frankie Ashoona, the Ottawa artist I'd met, which surprised me given Pete's blunt dismissal of his talent. But I did notice the date was twenty years ago, perhaps before the bottle took over Frankie's life. And of course there were a couple of prints by Joly Quliik.

While I stood admiring his particularly riveting picture

of a narwhal hunt, a raspy voice suddenly spoke from behind me. "Beauty, eh?"

I turned around to see an elderly Inuk sporting a Blue Jays baseball cap over his wispy grey hair. His smile deepened the lines of a face that had spent more time out-of-doors than indoors.

"Great hunter," he emphasized with a nod of his head.

"Yes, it is a great hunting picture."

"No, no, Joly."

"You mean the artist was a great hunter?"

"Yes, yes."

"Did you know him?"

"No, picture tell Joly great hunter. See." He copied the way the hunter was holding the harpoon. "Only hunter know this."

He pointed to the hunter in the neighbouring Joly print, who was mimicking a caribou by raising his arms over his head as if they were antlers. "Caribou want know more. Come closer. Hunter shoot. Only hunter know this."

Perhaps this first-hand knowledge was indeed behind the artist's success. I thought of my mother's *Growling Bear* print and felt only an artist who'd come face-to-face with an attacking polar bear would've been able to capture so well the power of the animal and the fear it generated. Then I realized all the prints I'd seen so far by Joly Quliik, even those at the McConnell Art Gallery, depicted either hunting scenes or animals. So perhaps the old man was right: Joly was a hunter first and an artist second.

The old man and I continued along the hallway looking at the other works of art. Occasionally he would point out a key aspect of a picture or shake his head at something portrayed incorrectly. At the end he concluded that Joly was the best and returned to the Quliik prints, while I, after thanking him for his insights, headed back out into the frigid summer Arctic day. The wind had stopped, and the sun now shone. I shoved my wool toque into a pocket and unzipped my jacket a few inches. I did keep my mitts on. It had warmed up, but not that much.

Deciding I'd better call Mother before going to Angus's house, I headed first to a nearby café, where I picked up my lunch of a tuna sandwich on rye and a chocolate donut, then back outside to find a cab to return me to the hotel. Several full taxis whisked passed as I waited impatiently at the Four Corners. After a couple more equally laden drove by, I decided that walking might get me there faster.

As I was about to begin the trek, a dusty dark green SUV came to a halt at the stop sign. It was only happenstance that directed my eyes to the driver. Perhaps it was light glinting off her earrings or a flash of her hand that caused me to look at her, but the minute I saw her, I recognized the chubby face with the cap of short black hair. Ooleepeeka, Angus's daughter. I waved frantically, hoping I could get a lift. I thought for a moment that her gaze flicked in my direction, but when she continued on up the road, I decided she either hadn't seen me or failed to recognize me. Fortunately, the next car was a taxi with space for one more person. After a rather circuitous ride, in which I saw a bit more of Iqaluit, I ended up at the hotel.

Thankfully, the police were gone from my room, but they'd left a mess. After tossing my jacket, hat and mitts on top of the strewn contents of my backpack, I called my sister at her office, first to apprise her about the latest on Father and also to ascertain whether Mother was up to receiving the news.

Jean was in court and wouldn't be free for at least a couple of hours. A call to her husband Leslie proved just as fruitless, so I decided to chance the call to Mother and play it by ear. At the sound of her weak "hello", I felt telling her that her first husband might've been a murderer wouldn't be prudent. Instead, I mentioned only that the plane containing the two bodies had been found.

"I guess this means Sutton died in the crash, doesn't it,

dear?" Her voice sounded a bit stronger. "It was always a very faint hope that he had survived."

"I still think it's worth investigating the meaning of the picture with the parachute," I answered. "So I'm going to try to talk to the artist's daughter to see what she knows." I paused, debating, then decided she might as well know. "I've come across father's gold pocket watch, the one that belonged to Great-grandpa Joe."

"Sutton's watch. How curious! Does it still have my picture in it?"

To avoid mentioning the defacement, I only told her that it had been replaced by a picture of the girlfriend of the new owner.

"Does this man say how he came into possession of the watch? Did Sutton give it to him?"

"I didn't have a chance to ask him, but I don't think the man was old enough for Father to have given it to him directly. So maybe Father left it behind, which as you know isn't likely, or maybe someone in this man's family found it near the crash site."

I didn't bother to mention that the current owner had been murdered or that the most likely way someone could've found the watch was by going through the clothes on Father's dead body.

"Oh, I do hope Sutton didn't suffer." The sound through the phone line became muffled, but I could hear her telling someone that she was quite all right, but she wouldn't be much longer. When she returned she said, "Sorry, where was I, dear?"

"We were talking about Father."

"Oh yes, his body. At least we now know what happened. Did the police say when they would be releasing him for burial?"

"Sorry, I didn't think to ask. But I suppose it's something I'd better start arranging. Since there are two bodies, we have to assume father was the person sitting in the passenger's seat. I'm not sure how else to verify his identity without a DNA analysis."

"But dear, have you forgotten? It's very easy to identify Sutton. He had only two fingers on the left hand. Remember, he lost them as a child while trying to chop wood for Great-aunt Agatha?"

Of course. How could I have forgotten? But then his damaged hand was so much a part of him that I never really noticed it. "I'll let the police know. There is something else I should tell you. Mind you, you might know already. Have the police told you that some of the works of art in Father's collection were forgeries?"

"That can't be. Sutton was always so careful."

"I gather they were so well done, they even fooled the gallery experts."

"Just as well Sutton never learned of it. It would've killed him."

As she said these last words, I wondered if it had, but not in the way she meant. His letter to Carter alluded to something he wanted to investigate. Maybe he'd died as a result of what he'd learned from the Crazy Russkie. But how could this be tied into the killing of the pilot? Unless the pilot had somehow been involved. Maybe that was what had happened.

Still, for Father to shoot him made little sense, since killing the man flying the plane put his own life in jeopardy…which it obviously had. Unless it was the result of a dreadful accident. Maybe Father was forcing the pilot at gunpoint to change direction, which would explain why the plane was way off course, and the gun accidentally went off, which could make sense, since Father had little experience with firearms.

I promised to call Mother as soon as I learned more. After hanging up, I began trying to put my room to rights. As I picked up pieces of clothing strewn over the bed, I wondered why the police had felt the need to go into my backpack, let alone search through it since it was at the airport when the break-in occurred. While the chambermaid cleaned my room, removing the fingerprint dust on the furniture, I finished putting away my clothes.

It was only after I'd put everything away, that I remembered Suula's drawings. *They were missing!* I double-checked under the bedclothes, under the bed and other furniture, even the wastebasket, to make sure the brown envelope hadn't gone astray. It was nowhere to be found.

Annoyed, I immediately dialed Constable Curran and demanded to know why they had taken the pictures without my permission. She told me that they hadn't taken them or anything else from my room.

"Shit," I said. "Then someone has broken into my room a second time and stolen them."

"I'll be right over," she replied and hung up.

She arrived within minutes with her partner, who began dusting for prints yet again. "Since we just dusted your room, it'll be easy to isolate any new ones."

"When did you leave?" I asked.

He consulted his watch. "Two hours and ten minutes ago."

"That means the person had little more than an hour and a half in which to do it. Which means they were probably waiting for you to leave."

"Don't worry, Miss Harris," Curran broke in, "we'll be checking with the hotel staff to determine if any suspicious person or persons were hanging around the lobby or the entrance to the hotel."

"And how did this person get into my room? I didn't see any signs of forced entry."

"They most likely used a duplicate keycard."

"Does that mean it's someone from the hotel?"

"Look, Ms Harris, please leave the investigation up to us. We'll let you know as soon as we have apprehended the person. In the meantime, I advise you to change rooms."

"What's to prevent them from making another duplicate key?"

"We've already advised hotel security to be on the lookout. They have various security measures in place that will alert them if this happens."

"Well, it didn't seem to stop the person the second time," I replied, feeling very insecure. Mind you, they already had everything I had with me that pertained to Father, if that was what they were after, so there probably wasn't going to be another break-in.

But what reason could the thief have for taking an old letter and some pictures that only had meaning to my family? It wasn't as if any of these items had any real monetary value. Unless it pertained to their contents, but none of the items, even the letter, provided sufficient information that anyone could do anything with. Look at the difficulties I was having trying to make sense of them.

"I'll have the hotel post a guard on your floor," Curran said.

She and her partner spent several more minutes examining the room and taking down my statement. On her way out she said, "By the way, Corporal Reilly wanted me to let you know that the boat with your father's remains will be arriving tomorrow."

"My family wants to have them transported to Toronto for burial. When do you think this will be possible?"

"Once they've been identified. Hard to say when. We'll need to verify his remains through DNA."

"There is another, easier way to identify him. Check his left hand. He was missing two fingers."

"Good. I'll pass that on to Corporal Reilly."

Thirty-Five

Angus McLeod was right. The cab driver easily found house no. 342, which was perched on a ridge overlooking Iqaluit. The chalet-style A-frame was the last on a short cul-de-sac of an odd mix of houses, none of which bore the slightest resemblance to the other. It was almost as if each owner had gone out of their way to put their own particular stamp on their property. The only mark of similarity was the fuel tank on metal stilts attached to the side of every house and a curious light positioned on the front of the buildings, one that didn't seem geared towards providing illumination. In fact, on Angus's house it shone a bright red, hardly a colour to light up one's front door.

"I hope that doesn't mean what I usually associate with red lights," I joked when Angus answered my knock. Although his tweed jacket of yesterday had been replaced by a cable knit cardigan, he still sported an ascot, this one a muted maroon paisley.

For a second he appeared confused, then he grinned. "I doubt my wife would like having her home viewed as a brothel. No, it's indicatin' our tank is full." I heard the loud rumble of an approaching vehicle behind me. "And if I'm no mistaken, that bloody truck has finally arrived. It was meant to be here yesterday."

I turned to see one of the ubiquitous tanker trucks I'd become used to seeing turn into his driveway and stop right behind a familiar dusty green suv. The overweight driver lumbered out of the cab and dragged a heavy hose to a wooden box attached to the front of the house. He opened a trap door and inserted the hose into the gaping end of a large pipe. As he did so, my nose wrinkled at the foul stench of sewage coming from it.

After exchanging angry words with the driver, Angus turned back to me. "My apologies for speaking my mind, but Fred was supposed to be here yesterday." He held the door open. "Best we go inside. The smell can be a bit overwhelming."

With the sound of the truck's pump starting up behind us, he firmly shut the door and led me down a narrow hall. By now I was thoroughly confused. "What's he doing?"

"That's our 'honey' truck, something you don't have in the south." A smile spread across a surprisingly unlined face, considering that he must have been well into his seventies. Perhaps he spent more time indoors than out. Given the harsh Arctic climate, maybe this shouldn't be so surprising.

"A corollary of northern living," he continued. "Not all of us in Iqaluit have the luxury of being connected to public utilities, so our water is trucked in and the sewage out. Now I can offer you a proper cup of tea. You see, when the sewage tank is full, the water is automatically shut off."

"Must be annoying."

"Most times not. We generally keep an emergency water supply, but my wife forgot to refill one of the containers from our last episode, so we ran out this morning. I have some Murchies Queen Victoria tea. Hope you like that? Or would you prefer something milder, like a Darjeeling?"

"The Queen Victoria sounds good. I like strong tea. By the way, I see your daughter's here. It must be nice having her home."

"Daughter?" He stopped walking and turned around.

"Yes, Ooleepeeka. I met her at Mary's gallery. At least, I believe she's your daughter."

"Yes, she is, but she's out at the moment." His face was still, almost wary.

"Sorry, I thought she might be here, since I saw her earlier in the SUV parked outside."

"She was for a brief moment." He laughed but his eyes didn't. "You know daughters. They love to come home to see you, but they can't wait to escape to their friends. Come let me show you my Shangri-La."

Thinking the two of them must be having a father-daughter disagreement, I followed him into a sunroom overflowing with greenery and sunlight.

"Wow," I said, eying the multitude of plants. "I haven't seen this much greenery since I left home."

"I suspected you'd like my oasis. I call it my conservatory, although it doesn't approach anywhere near the size of a conservatory back home."

"You even have orchids! Look at the gorgeous cream-coloured blooms on that plant."

"That's a Princess Kaiulani 'flava' of the rare albino variety, *phal amboinensis 'flava'*. I'm fair proud of that beauty." He sprayed it with water from a tarnished brass spray bottle. "I like to say I'm the most northern orchid grower in the world. And this the most northern tropical garden. Mind you, there are some on Baffin that would beg to differ, but their gardens pale in comparison to the exotic nature of mine."

"I see you have lots of skylights, but they won't provide much light in winter, when the sun disappears. What do you do then?"

"See the line of floodlights along the ceiling? Those are special grow lights. I have to use them in summer too, because our light here isn't sufficiently intense. The long summer days also cause problems, since most tropical plants require a certain amount of darkness. So I've had blinds installed to plunge this room into night, even on the brightest of nights."

He flicked a wall switch, causing several thick black blinds to unravel over the glass portion of the slanted ceiling towards the outer wall, plunging the room into shade. I could see that by putting down the blinds on the glass walls, the room would indeed be almost as dark as night.

"The thickness of these blinds also helps to insulate the room against the intense cold we get in winter. Look, why don't you have a gambol around, while I see to our tea."

Although my knowledge of orchids was minimal, I did recognize many varieties that Mother grew, plus a few I'd never seen before, and I knew healthy orchids when I saw them, and these were real beauties, easily rivalling those grown by Mother's expert hand. But the fact that they were flourishing, when outside these thick glass walls, the harsh environment barely allowed a blade of grass to grow, could only attest to Angus's prowess as a gardener. I also couldn't help but wonder at the cost. This exquisite tropical garden wouldn't come cheaply in the Arctic. But then perhaps this was Angus's only interest, and he was frugal in all other aspects of his life.

This theory was partially dispelled when I entered the living room, where he'd placed a gleaming silver tea service on an antique inlaid mahogany coffee table, not too dissimilar from a table in the living room of the Harris mansion. But apart from a couple of other antique tables and a burled walnut sideboard, the rest of his furniture was modern and comfortable-looking, which I noted with no small degree of satisfaction. I gratefully collapsed into the soft cushions of a bulging armchair. However, unlike the sparkle of money which the tea service showed, the chair's faded chintz fabric suggested more meager means.

He poured some milk into a porcelain cup with a tiny crack running through one of its painted flowers. "Do you like your tea the English way or the European way?" He pointed to some lemon wedges on a small dish.

"English, but if you don't mind with the milk added afterwards. My great-aunt used to drink it like you do. Personally I'm not sure if it makes any difference."

He poured my tea into a delicate cup rimmed in faded gold before adding a dab of milk.

"You're probably right. All in what you're accustomed to." He sank back into the well-established hollows of his leather wingback chair. "I understand the RCMP have recovered your father's plane."

"Yes, along with his remains. Which pretty well kills any thoughts I had of his survival. I guess it was rather naïve of me to think it possible."

"Not at all." He offered me a shortbread cookie. "I thought it perfectly reasonable. There was a case a few years back where a *qallunaat* disappeared on his skidoo while traveling over sea ice. A week later, his damaged skidoo was found with no sign of him. The police assumed he'd fallen through the ice, until a few years later he reappeared, very much alive. Apparently a passing Inuk hunter took him in, and he decided to stay with the man for a while. Turns out the man had a willing daughter."

He let out a raucous laugh that seemed at odds with his demeanour of a cultured gentleman. But perhaps it went with his ponytail.

"I guess I'd been sort of hoping that my father had also been rescued by an Inuk, Suula's father. But since his body has now been recovered, that obviously didn't happen. Still, I think Suula might've known something about the crash. Perhaps she passed this knowledge onto her children. But with her son unfortunately dead, I'm now hoping to talk to her daughter. You don't happen to know her, do you?"

"Apphia. It's been several years since I've seen her. You know, she's a very good artist too. I have a couple of her works hanging in my study."

"Do you know where she's living?"

"I knew her when she was living in Tasilik with her brother. But about five or six years ago, she ran into a spot of trouble. Pour soul. She never really recovered from it. One day she packed up and left the community. She comes to Tasilik a couple of times a year to pick up supplies at the Northern store and to drop off her latest drawings at the art centre. But she's always been rather coy about where she's living, and the local Inuit community won't say. I suspect she's living at a camp somewhere along the coast of Cumberland Sound."

"Does the name Naujalik mean anything to you? This was the camp where her mother once lived. Maybe that's where Apphia is."

"Hmm…place of seagulls. There are a number of isolated islands that are breeding grounds for a variety of Arctic birds, but I've never seen them myself. I imagine they are pretty inhospitable places. All rock and not much else. Not exactly the kind of place where you'd want to set up camp. I think most are in Davis Strait and relatively far from the coast, which means having to cross many miles of fairly treacherous open water. I don't see a woman doing that."

"Maybe this particular island is closer to the mainland." I helped myself to another shortbread cookie. They were good. "You mentioned she'd had some trouble. Pete said the same thing. Do you know what happened to her?"

"Man trouble, what else. The man she was living with beat her up one night after downing a quart of scotch and a case of beer, this despite the fact Tasilik is a dry town. She had to be evacuated to Ottawa, where she spent over a month in hospital. She still had a limp when she got back. A week later, she was gone. I don't blame her. Johnnie helped her. He and one of his mates loaded her belongings into a couple of boats and took off. But he wouldna tell me where he took her. Naujalik, you say. May I ask how you learned of this?"

"From her mother's prints."

"Ah yes, the ones Pete mentioned. Apphia has always marked her location as Tasilik. If you don't mind, I'll ask around and see what I can come up with and get back to you, okay?"

"That would be perfect, thanks." Hopefully he wouldn't encounter the same resistance I was getting from Pete.

Thirty-Six

My mouth watered for another piece of shortbread, but I didn't dare take one. Today my jeans were feeling a little too tight. Too much good northern cooking.

Angus, as if reading my mind, pushed the plate towards me. "Go ahead, have one more, lass. I import them directly from Scotland."

I gave in. So much for self-restraint.

"By the way, those prints you mentioned," Angus said. "You didn't happen to bring them with you, did you? If so, I'd love to see them, if it's no too much trouble."

Believing it best not to reveal their recent theft, I lied. "Sorry, I left them at home."

He glanced at me over the brim of his cup. "I've never seen any examples of Suula's work. In fact, I wasna aware she was an artist. Perhaps when you return home, you might send me copies. I like to keep up with the northern artists."

"Sure," I muttered, burying myself deeper. I could feel my face heat up with a blush. Time to change the topic. "You said you knew my father."

"I count myself fortunate to have been numbered amongst his friends. We spent many a time discussin' art over a bottle of Glenlivet. He was fast becoming quite the expert. But I also had the wonderful pleasure of visiting your father at your Toronto home. A most remarkable house. Reminded me of Glencoe Castle near Edinburgh. I must say it surprised me. Your father was such an unassuming man."

Feeling somewhat embarrassed, I mumbled something in response. I never liked people knowing that I came from

230

money. Like father, like daughter, some people might say.

Angus continued. "I'd gone south to take samples of that year's collection to one of the galleries. I also had a couple of prints that weren't part of the collection, ones your father wanted to see, which, by the way, he bought."

"The gallery you mentioned, was that Carter Davis's gallery?"

"Why yes, it was. Did you know him?"

"Not really. I only met him once. But I guess you probably know that he's dead, murdered a few weeks ago."

He shook his head mournfully. "Mary told me the sad news. What a pity. Carter was a delight and his knowledge about Inuit art bottomless. Do the police know who did it?"

"I don't think so, but the police officer you met last night is also involved in this case."

"Surely he can't be thinking that someone in Iqaluit did it?"

My thoughts turned to Pete, but I knew it was an unreasonable suspicion. It was purely coincidence he happened to be in Toronto when Carter died. Besides, what reason would he have for killing the old man? "I've no idea. He only mentioned the forgeries to me."

"Forty years I've been in the Inuit art business, and I've never heard of such a travesty. Although I understand they're making knock-off carvings in China and passin' them off as Inuit made. But any fool can see they aren't originals." He spat these last words out in disgust.

Angus brought his cup to his lips, his pinky finger cocked above the handle in patrician British manner. But instead of a genteel sip, he slurped the hot tea, before asking, "Did this Sergeant Hue perchance mention names of anyone he was pursuin'?"

"As I said last night, only Johnnie Nanuqtuaq."

"Right, you did. But the man was far too successful an artist to be mixed up in such shenanigans. Though between you and me, I'm not surprised. I didna want to mention it last night, but lately he'd been flashin' a fair bit of money around, much more than his carvings would bring in. Forgeries would help to explain it. I suppose this Sergeant Hue didn't happen to mention what had been counterfeited, did he?"

"No, he didn't. But you can ask him when you meet with him later."

"I will. It'll help me to keep an eye out for any that might come my way in my own art dealings." His eyes took on a pensive gaze as he slurped more of his tea.

"Mr. McLeod, I—?"

"Please, lass, call me Angus."

"Okay. Angus… I was wondering if the name Crazy Russkie meant anything to you?"

His shaggy brows shot up. "Now, lass, wherever did you learn of that name? I haven't heard it mentioned in years."

"So you know him?"

"Knew him quite well, as well as any man could. A bit of a loner, he was. Now you haven't told me where you learned of his name."

Thinking I should also keep the letter to myself, I said, "It was a name that cropped up recently in relation to my father."

"I'm surprised your father would know the man. They didn't exactly run in the same circles, if you catch my drift. He was what you would call a loose cannon."

"I'd like to talk to the man. Do you know where I can find him?"

He shook his head. "I'm afraid it's quite impossible. The man left these parts nigh on thirty years ago. He was a bit of a wanderer. He couldn't stay still for more than a month or two before he'd be off with his dogs out on the land. No one would see hide nor hair of him for weeks, months at a time. But every couple of years, he'd make his way back to Tasilik. It took me a few years to realize he hadn't been around town in some time."

"Do you have any idea where he might've gone?"

"No, not really. Mind you, the nurse he was sweet on was transferred to Clyde River. So perhaps he turned up there. But if he did go there, he certainly wasn't living there when I visited the hamlet in the late '70s."

"And he didn't turn up anywhere else in the north?"

"Not that I've ever heard. And I like to pride myself on knowing pretty much all that goes on in our small white northern community."

"So he just vanished."

"I suppose he could've fallen through the ice or been killed by a polar bear. But I doubt it. The man was almost as knowledgeable on the land as the Inuit. More likely he finally got fed up with the north and returned south." Angus repositioned his ascot, which had twisted around his neck. "You know, the man really was a Russian. His parents were White Russians, fled the Crimean a few years after the revolution. They were members of the minor nobility. I believe his last name was Nabokov, but he never used it. First name was Sergei. I myself refused to call him Crazy Russkie. Although many did."

"Co-incidentally, my dog's name is Sergei." I laughed. "After a character in a Russian book I was reading at the time."

"You might try the RCMP in Tasilik. I know they sent out a missing person's report. Not certain if they ever found out anything."

"You don't happen to know the name of the nurse and if she's still at Clyde River?"

"'Fraid not. I heard she married a pastor and moved back south."

"Oh well, it was a long shot. I've already asked the police here if they can locate him, but from what you're saying, it's unlikely."

My spirits were sinking…fast. It seemed I was in the proverbial loop, for every two steps forward I was taking one back. Perhaps I should just take my father's body and leave. After all, finding him had been my reason for coming north.

"You know, Meg, your Uncle Harold might be able to help you."

I glanced up with surprise. "What do you mean?"

"I believe he knew Sergei."

"How could he? I don't think he ever came here."

"Oh, but he did. I met him a couple of times myself, right here in Iqaluit."

"I forgot. He did fly up when father's plane went missing."

"This happened earlier. On a couple of occasions. Once with your father and another time on his own. In fact, I think he was here about the time your father disappeared."

"Really? I don't remember that at all. But I was quite young and didn't always pay attention to family affairs. How do you know Uncle Harold knew this Sergei?"

"The man could never turn down a free drink. I saw him several times with your uncle at the Zoo."

"The Zoo?"

"Oh, sorry. That was the old bar at the Frobisher Inn. The actual name was Tulgaq, meaning raven. But I'm afraid the name Zoo was more fitting, particularly on a Saturday night." Grinning, he shook his head with the memories, then continued. "If I'm no mistaken, your uncle bought some of Sergei's watercolours. He was quite the artist, you know. Such a shame he didn't pursue it seriously."

"Now that you mention it, there are a couple of watercolours of blue ice and towering mountains hanging in one of the guest bedrooms of my mother's house. I think the artist's name is Sergei. But I'm afraid my uncle has been dead a few years, so even if he knew what happened to the Russian, he can't tell me now."

"I'm sorry to learn of this. I found your uncle a most congenial man. I believe he married your mother, didn't he?"

I acknowledged that with a nod and another cookie.

"A beautiful and very charmin' woman, your mother. I hope the passing years still find her prospering."

"As much as can be expected for a seventy-eight year old woman. She's having some heart problems at the moment, which we hope she'll overcome. Well, I've taken up enough of your time."

I reluctantly raised myself from the comfort of the chair. As I did so, I noticed the corner of a drawing peeking out from under a book on a nearby table. What I could see of it looked familiar.

Without thinking I walked over to the table to move the book aside and almost cried "thief!" before I realized it was not one of the prints that had been stolen from my room. But the style and the topic were almost identical.

"I see you have one of Suula's prints. You told me you didn't know she was an artist," I said, trying to appear nonchalant. "Where did you get it from?"

"Print?" Confusion passed over his face until he glanced at the table. "Right. I'd forgotten I left that there." He slid the artwork into a nearby folder. "No, it's not by Suula. It's one of Joly Quliik's prints. An old one my daughter chanced upon in a flea market near her university. She recognized his style."

"But it's exactly like Suula's. Are you sure it's not one of hers?" I tried to remember in my brief glimpse of the print, if the artist's syllabics were the same shape as those stamped on the four stolen prints and realized there hadn't been any.

"Quite sure. I handled all of Joly's work until he stopped producin'. I would recognize his style anywhere."

"But the scene is very similar to the ones sent to my Mother."

"I'm sure you've noticed that many Inuit artists draw the same scenes. Let's face it, there is only so much material one can draw upon in this barren land."

"May I look at it again?"

"If you don't mind, I'd just as soon you didn't." He kept his hand firmly on the cover of the folder. "You see, it wasn't meant to be seen. I want to keep this print under wraps until I have established its provenance to the satisfaction of the art world. Since Joly stopped producing, only a few pieces of his work have come up for sale. This unknown drawing could fetch a big price. So I would appreciate if you not mention seeing this to anyone, lass."

He took my arm by the elbow and began moving me towards the front door. "Now if you don't mind, I'm afraid I have another appointment, as you know. I'm so glad I had an opportunity to talk with you." The friendly warmth had gone from his voice.

With that the door clicked firmly in my face, leaving me feeling angry yet convinced this unsigned print was related to the signed prints sent to my mother. It depicted the next episode in the ongoing story of the plane crash. The red-haired man and his family standing in front of the igloo in this drawing had added another child, a little girl, a little *red-haired girl.*

So was this latest print really drawn by Suula? And if so, why had Angus pretended otherwise? Or were they all drawings by Joly Quliik but with Suula's name added to the ones sent to my mother. Again I had to ask the question "why"?

Regardless of the artist, I remained convinced these drawings connected Father to the Nanuqtuaq family and someone, for whatever reason, had wanted Mother to know. After the police had found the one in Johnnie's house, I'd assumed it had been him. But I supposed Angus could just as easily have been the sender. And if so, what could possibly be his reason for hiding it from me?

Either way, I was left with the answer to the question "Why send them in the first place?" still eluding me.

Thirty-Seven

The taxi had no sooner dropped me off at the entrance to the hotel than who should I run into but my brother-in-law as he was pushing open the glass door.

"Leslie, what are you doing here?" I cried out without so much as a sisterly greeting.

"Oh dear, I guess you didn't get my message," he replied, ignoring my rudeness, but then he was used to my unpolished ways.

"Did Mother send you?"

"You know your mother...hard to say no to." He nervously ran a hand through his thick brown curls then cleared his throat and continued, "But I think she has a point. This will be difficult for you, dealing with your father's ah... remains. She thought you would need some help."

He started to tug at the ends of his bow tie before realizing he wasn't wearing one. This was the first time I'd ever seen him not dressed in his standard garb; bow tie, oxford cloth shirt and grey flannels. Instead he was decked out in the latest outdoor wear, all of which rustled new. No doubt his concession to the purported rigours of Arctic travel.

"I can handle them perfectly well on my own, if you don't mind," I shot back, annoyed with my mother. "Bones are bones. It's not as if he died yesterday."

But as I watched a pained expression wash over my brother-in-law's boyish face, I hastily recanted, "Sorry, I didn't mean to take it out on you. You just took me by surprise. In fact, I'm surprised you got here so quickly. I only told Mother a few hours ago."

"Actually, the decision for me to come was made a couple of days ago. I guess I thought you knew. I didn't know his remains had been found until I phoned Jean after I landed."

I ran my eyes over his face to see what he wasn't telling me. But let's face it, how like Mother not to trust me to do the job. And how like her to keep Leslie's arrival a surprise. I wouldn't put him through the wringer for it.

I took his arm. "Let's go to the bar, and I'll bring you up-to-date. It'll be nice to talk it over with someone."

We snatched a quiet table close to the warmth of the fireplace, a gas one with fake logs and embers instead of the blazing wood one I'd always pictured as integral to any northern bar. But it wasn't as if logs were in plentiful supply around here.

By the time I'd finished telling him all that had happened since my arrival, I'd gulped down two glasses of single malt, and Leslie had finally stopped shaking his head in disbelief.

"So you see, there has to be some connection between father and the Nanuqtuaqs. I'm almost certain someone in the Nanuqtuaq family saw the plane crash. I think the red-haired man in the pictures could be Father and the red-haired girl his daughter. In fact he's probably the father of all three children. Yet the discovery of his body says this is impossible." I took another slurp of scotch. "I tell you, Leslie, I am one confused woman."

"The police are certain the remains are his?"

"Yeah. They found two bodies in a plane that was carrying two people." I paused at a sudden thought. "Mind you, I suppose it's possible that a third person could've been on the plane, someone the police didn't know about."

"Possibly, but that would mean there would've been another person going missing at the same time, and I would think the police would look into the possibility, don't you?"

"Yeah, you're right," I answered dejectedly.

Leslie lowered his glass of Perrier onto the table. He

didn't believe in drinking alcohol until close to sundown. But in this land of the endless sun, he might find himself getting a little thirsty.

"Perhaps there's a much simpler explanation for the pictures," he said. "The man depicted is just another red-haired man."

"It's certainly possible. But what would be the reason for sending the pictures to Mother?"

"Maybe they wanted her to believe the man is her missing husband so they could extort money from her."

I took another sip of scotch before responding. "There was no mention in the letters she showed us. But I suppose she could've received a separate request for money and decided not to tell us. Look at her reluctance to show us the pictures. We only found out they existed when we forced her to open that last envelope in front of us."

"She is quite protective of you girls, you know?"

As if we were still children, I groaned inwardly. "Still, it doesn't explain how Johnnie came to have Father's watch. Remember, this watch is a family heirloom. Father would never have given it away before he died."

"Maybe this Suula stole it from his body after the crash?" His hand reached again towards his missing bow tie, before he checked himself with an embarrassed smile.

"That's what Constable Curran suggested. But, for argument's sake, say Father did survive the crash, as the pictures suggest, and fathered Suula's three children, including Johnnie. People have told me that her other two children were girls. Father's other children are Jean and I—" My throat constricted as I reminded myself that this wasn't exactly true. I cleared it with another swig of scotch and continued, "Johnnie would've been his only son."

Leslie's worried brown eyes sought mine then turned away. "For what it's worth, I've read that Inuit name their children after dead relatives, and your grandfather's name was John, wasn't it."

239

"Yes…and you know something else? Pete told me that the sister who died also had a un-Inuit-like name, Margee, which could be a short form for Margaret."

"Just like 'Meg', eh?"

"And I was named after my grandmother."

For several minutes we each remained absorbed in our own separate thoughts. While Leslie ran his finger around the edge of his empty glass, I glanced glumly around the dimly-lit bar. Racks of dusty caribou antlers strung with lights hung from the ceiling in chandelier fashion. Hides of polar bear and arctic wolf were spread over the stone fireplace wall while a beady-eyed muskox peered at us from a neighbouring wall. Despite the rest of the hotel having a crisp urban veneer, the bar could've been a setting for a Jack London novel. The tired, ragged-at-the-edges appearance seemed to fit my mood exactly.

Finally Leslie said, "You really want your father to be alive, don't you?"

"Yes…yes, I do. I missed him terribly when he disappeared. You see…I was much closer to him. I was Maggie, his little magpie." While Leslie reached across the table to pat my hand, images flashed through my mind, images of Father comforting me after yet another run-in with Mother, of him showing me a tiny spotted fawn hidden by its mother in a clump of ferns, of us laughing together over the antics of an enterprising squirrel intent on stealing some birdseed, of him sitting on my bed reading…

"But enough of this nonsense." I released my hand. "Father's dead. So this Johnnie must've been running some kind of scam. I wonder if that's what killed him."

"Do you know if the police have arrested anyone yet?"

"Not as far as I know, but then I haven't been paying any attention to it. Maybe I should."

"You know, there might be another explanation." Leslie paused while he chewed a mouthful of bar nuts. "It's conceivable we've put the pictures in the wrong order.

Perhaps your father had these three children with Suula before the plane crash."

It could help to explain his many trips to the Arctic. But my father having an affair? It just seemed too impossible. But then look at Mother and Uncle Harold. Maybe Father had known. Perhaps Suula had offered the kind of support and solace that he couldn't get from his wife. But...

"Suula would've been very young. I think the artist in Ottawa said she was about forty when she died in 1997. Let me see...that would make her about sixteen when father died in 1973. And if your theory is correct, she would've had three children by then. Surely Father wouldn't have taken up with a girl barely into her teens."

In answer, Leslie's lips creased into a sad smile.

"But I'm forgetting, Johnnie wasn't old enough," I continued. "I understand he was in his early thirties when he died. And Apphia is even younger. No, like you said, it was probably an attempt to get money from Mother." I sipped my scotch. "I guess one of us should ask her. Probably you, since I doubt she'd tell me anything."

"What about this man, Angus McLeod? Where do you think he comes in, if at all?

"I don't know. The only connection appears to be this picture, even though he insists it's not by Suula. Though I do find it a bit curious how quickly he turned up at the murder scene of a man who no longer worked for him. Still, at the time I didn't have the impression Angus was trying to hide anything. Instead I felt he was genuinely upset by Johnnie's death."

"Nevertheless, he might know something. Do you plan to speak with him again?"

"I want to, but I'm not sure how successful I'll be. I had the feeling he didn't want to talk about that Quliik drawing or anything related to it."

"Why don't I go with you?"

"Thanks. It can't hurt. Maybe your blue-blood appearance

will loosen his tongue." I smiled. "You might want to throw on one of your bow ties. It'll match his ascot." I squeezed Leslie's hand. "And thanks for coming. I appreciate it. You're always so understanding."

His face took on the pinkish glow of a blush as he gently patted my hand in return. "I know it's been difficult for you, more so than Jean. Your father's disappearance, your mother's remarriage and that ah…unfortunate business with your brother."

At the mention of the word "brother", I felt my heart twist. I'd had no idea Leslie knew. But of course, Jean or Mother would've told him.

"And I must not forget your marriage. I know you were terribly upset by the way it ended, but you really are better off without him. Did you know—"

So Leslie had known all along about my brother Joey. But at no time had his manner been anything other than friendly and sympathetic. No hint of blame or censure. Maybe there was hope…

"Sorry my mind wandered. What were you saying?"

"Gareth, your ex, has been disbarred. Did you know that?"

"No, I didn't, but I'm not surprised."

"But as I was saying, you've had a tough go of it, and it's affected your life and how you live it. Jean, on the other hand, has a rather thick skin." He chuckled softly. "I suppose it's one reason why I married her. She's able to block out life's traumas and rise above them. But you and I on the other hand can't forget. We let them gnaw away until they become suppurating wounds. Meg, you need to find yourself a Jean, a rock to hold on to."

I took another sip of scotch. I hadn't told him about Eric…

While Leslie went to the washroom, I watched a forty-something man strut into the crowded bar. He had the hungry look of a man on the prowl, so I wasn't surprised when after a careful scan of the room, he sauntered up to a sweet young thing sitting very lonely at the bar and flashed her a come-on grin. I must admit, as his eyes passed over me, I couldn't resist patting my hair down in an attempt to tame it. But enough dreaming. No one ever picked me up. Besides, this hunk of muscle and pearly whites was definitely not my kind of man.

Leslie slumped back into the hard wooden chair and tossed back some peanuts. He wasn't my type either. Just as well.

"You mentioned these art forgeries," he said. "I hope you aren't worried that your father might be implicated."

"I don't know what to think. So far the police haven't actually said he was involved. But maybe you know differently. What have they been telling Mother? She didn't say much on the phone." I paused with a groan. "Oh dear, I forgot to ask how she's doing. What a terrible daughter I am. It should've been the first thing I asked. Sorry, Mother." I raised my glass to her, then emptied it and ordered another.

"Meg," Leslie intercepted, "why don't you switch to Perrier? I think you've had enough."

I glared back at him. Who was he to tell me what I could and could not drink? But when the waitress brought me the scotch, I returned it and asked for a Perrier instead. He was right. Alcohol and I were not a good combination.

"I'm afraid the police have brought the art experts in. They want to have every remaining piece of Inuit art in your family's collection analyzed and their provenance checked."

"Oh dear. Mother never mentioned this."

"She doesn't know. Your sister and I are keeping it from her as long as she's in the hospital."

"Probably a good idea. It could kill her. How's Jean taking it?"

"You know your sister."

He didn't need to say anything more. I knew Jean. She'd

243

be having a fit. After all, she had a position to maintain. And no doubt she was loudly proclaiming it was all my fault.

But I hadn't told Leslie the worst, mainly because I didn't want to believe it, let alone voice that it could be a possibility.

"Leslie, there's something else I should tell you about Father." I paused. Some scotch would be good about now. Instead I drank my Perrier. And it wasn't doing what I wanted it to do, numb my brain. "The police think Father killed the pilot."

The same shocked disbelief I felt crept over Leslie's face as I explained about the bullet hole found in the remains.

"And they're certain it was the pilot and not your father that was shot?" he asked the moment I finished.

"Only because the person sitting in the pilot's seat was the one with the hole." I paused. "But you know, a third person on that plane would change everything. The police wouldn't be able to so easily point the finger at Father."

Leslie cleared his throat. "You shouldn't get your hopes up, Meg. I think it unlikely another person could've been on that plane without the police eventually finding out. But we won't know for certain until they've done the DNA analysis. Have they mentioned when it's to be done?"

"No, just that they're going to do it. I'll ask Constable Curran."

I tried to shake the film that kept running though my mind of my father laughing and playing with three little children that didn't include Jean and me. "I tell you, Leslie, I'm sure not finding it easy discovering that the man I knew and loved as a child might not be the man I thought he was. I wonder what it'll do to Mother."

"Maybe she won't be that surprised. I remember Jean telling me that although they lived in the same house, it was as though your parents led two different lives. Your mother would be frequently off on one of her social events with your uncle as escort, while your father remained behind the closed door of his study."

"Or away on one of his many trips," I added. "You know, I don't remember the two of them ever taking a trip together. But regardless, I never thought him capable of betrayal. To me he was a kind and gentle soul who loved his family. On the other hand, my mother was the one, who... But no, I won't go there. I'm sure you've heard enough from Jean."

"Meg, you mustn't blame your mother too harshly. I think she's had a difficult life."

"With dear Uncle Harold by her side?" I quipped. "And speaking of Harold, I just learned that he was in Iqaluit shortly before Father's plane went missing. Which I find curious, because I remember him making a big deal about his first trip to the Arctic when he came here to follow up on the search for Father's plane. And what I find even more curious is the fact that he was seen talking to the very same man that Father was intending to speak to about some forgeries."

Leslie sighed. "Meg, you shouldn't be so suspicious. I'm sure he had his reasons. I knew your uncle well, and he was a good man. Come, let's go have dinner. I hear the caribou stew is very good."

Thirty-Eight

After a night spent hearing noises that weren't there and doorknobs turning when they hadn't, this despite having changed rooms, I took my brother-in-law early next morning down the road to the detachment. I wanted to introduce him to Constable Curran and find out when the boat with Father's remains would be arriving. And learn if they'd had any success in catching the thief.

An hour earlier, I'd met Leslie coming back into the hotel after a brisk morning walk in bright sun and near zero temperatures. The endless daylight had kept him from having a good night's rest, so he'd gone to explore Iqaluit before it woke up. He'd discovered, as I had, that the town never went to bed. No matter the hour, people could be seen outside on the streets, walking or chatting with friends. The light even drew the kids outside to play.

After a quick breakfast, we headed off to talk to the constable, who was just arriving with an extra large cup of Tim Hortons coffee and some donuts.

"Where'd you get that?" I asked in surprise. "I didn't know there was a Tim's in town."

"At the Four Corners. It opened up a month ago, and they've already had to double their supply of donuts, twice." Her smile revealed a missing molar in an otherwise perfect set of teeth.

As she led us to her cubicle, I made a mental note to go to the Four Corners once we'd finished and get some decent coffee. Although I'd only been drinking the hotel coffee for a couple of days, I was already tired of it.

246

After introducing my brother-in-law, I asked her about the salvage boat.

"Corporal Reilly radioed to say they're having engine problems. They're holed up in a small bay a couple of hours from here. He wasn't sure when it'd be fixed. He's worried they might need a new part, which could take a few days, especially if they have to bring it up from the south. I'll let you know."

"Thanks. If I'm not around, let Leslie know. He's staying at the Frobisher Inn too."

"Bob, I mean, Reilly wanted me to tell you they weren't able to identify your dad based on the missing two fingers you mentioned. The remains aren't…ah…totally intact. Sorry."

"I guess that means you'll have to rely on DNA."

"Yeah, we'll have to ship the bones…er, sorry, I mean remains south to our labs in Ottawa to run DNA tests and compare them to DNA samples from your family. Sergeant Boudreau says the analysis can only be done with DNA from your father's maternal relatives and not his children."

"Oh dear, I'm assuming you mean his mother, grand-mother, etc. I'm afraid they're all long dead. Are you sure you can't use DNA from my sister or me?"

"I'm told not when the remains are this old. The only DNA that remains is something called…" She glanced at a piece of paper on her desk. "Mito…mitochondrial. Apparently, this is only passed on through the mother's side. What about a sister of your father, even a maternal aunt? I think a brother would also work."

I shook my head. "Does this mean we would have to have my grandmother's body exhumed?"

"The staff sergeant was worried this might be the case. He said we should wait until the lab has fully examined the remains, just in case they find some of the other kind of DNA. Sorry, I don't know the name." She smiled apologetically. "If they do, they can compare it to a sample from you or your sister for identification purposes."

"But this could take weeks. And my mother might not have weeks. I think I told you, she's not well."

"I could see if I can get the staff sergeant to put an urgent flag on it."

"Would you do that?"

"I could also have Sergeant Boudreau get a DNA sample from you here in Iqaluit. It would save time."

"Good idea. I'm ready any time."

"He's out on a case, but when he comes back, I'll have him call you."

The mention of DNA testing gave me an idea. "I'm still not entirely convinced that Johnnie's father isn't also mine. Is there any way you could also do a comparison of his DNA with my father's remains, even mine? That way we'd know once and for all."

"Not sure if we can do it. It's a bit irregular. Probably would need his sister's consent. But I'll ask my staff sergeant, okay? You're lucky you mentioned it. We're shipping Johnnie's remains out tomorrow."

"To his sister?"

"Yeah, in Tasilik."

"Good, you've located her."

"I don't know. Our guys in Tasilik said just to send the body. They didn't mention the sister. I guess he's gonna be buried there."

As she said these last words, I made up my mind to follow the remains to Tasilik. Apphia was bound to be at her brother's funeral.

I hesitated, unsure if I should bring it up, but decided he was my father, after all. "I really don't like my father being considered a possible murder suspect. So I've been wondering, is it at all possible that a third person could have been aboard my father's plane?"

Curran shook her head. "Sorry, there were just two people. I radioed Corporal Reilly yesterday to make sure. I didn't want us drawing conclusions without checking. But he said there is nothing in the file to indicate that another person was on board."

"What about a missing person?" Leslie interjected. "Do you know if anyone else went missing from James Lake at about the same time? If so, they might've been on the plane without anyone knowing."

"I didn't think of that. I'll check with Bob."

I nodded my thanks to Leslie and turned back to the young policewoman. "Have you heard if the police investigating Johnnie's murder have arrested anyone yet?"

"No, not yet, although we're pretty sure the motive was theft. We found a couple of items taken from his house on a beach next to a boat. But so far we haven't found the hard drive or the sculpture he was supposed to be working on." She paused. "I'm helping GIS out. They're a bit short-staffed."

"Do you think that's the boat I saw?"

"We can't tell for sure, but it fits the description you gave us."

"So if you have the boat, you must have the killer."

"Nope. It was Harry Inookie's boat. He says he wasn't using it, but he knows someone was. It wasn't on Iqaluit beach by his shack where he always keeps it. It was left near the cemetery, a good kilometre or so from the main Iqaluit beach. He figured a bunch of kids must've taken it for a joy ride."

"And you believe Harry?"

"There's no reason not too. He and Johnnie were good friends. Besides, Harry spends most of his time out on the land. He wouldn't know the first thing about computers."

"So you don't have any suspects?"

"Someone who lives on the bluff overlooking the cemetery saw the boat coming in about an hour after the killing. Since the guy was wearing the turquoise jacket you mentioned, it's gotta be the same person. Although our witness was too far away to see the individual's face, they know it wasn't Harry. The person didn't limp like Harry does with his bad leg."

"Did anyone else see the guy?"

"Not that we know of. The beach is pretty isolated. Probably why the guy beached the boat there rather than on Iqaluit beach, which is a lot busier. Anyways, we're working on trying to identify the person. We're pretty sure they're Inuit, though."

"How can you be so sure? Lots of white people live in Iqaluit, don't they?"

"The weapon is telling us. The pathologist has determined that it was an *ulu* that killed him."

"Pardon my ignorance, but I'm not sure what an *ulu* is."

"It's an Inuit knife. They use them for skinning seals and other animals. Here, I have a picture of one."

From the cluttered shelf above her desk, she grabbed a well-thumbed copy of a book entitled *The R.C.M.P. Handbook on Inuit Culture.* The picture she showed us was of an oddly-shaped curved knife almost in a half-moon shape with the handle attached to the centre of this half-moon.

"Curious thing about an *ulu*," she continued, "the book says they're traditionally used by women. So when I read this, I thought great, we can narrow down the suspect to a woman. But I gather from Fred, our Inuit advisor, that in recent times men have started using them. I guess they make a pretty good knife. Besides, our witness is positive it was a man he saw in the turquoise jacket. What about you? Could you tell if the person in the boat was a male or female?"

"No, they were too far away. Besides they were hunkered down in the boat, so I don't have any idea whether they were short or tall, fat or thin, let alone identify their gender. But the colour of jacket is unusual. One could almost say it's a colour only a woman would wear."

"Yeah, I suppose. Except my boyfriend back home has a hockey jacket that colour that he wears all the time. Still, it's not a colour of jacket you see very often."

"That should help you to narrow in on a suspect, shouldn't it?"

"Yeah, we're working on it."

"And of course, finding the hard drive would help too."

"We think the suspect got rid of it. He wasn't carrying it when he walked away from the boat, which probably means he offloaded it onto another boat or left it somewhere else on the shore. The only trouble with this scenario is there aren't any good landing spots between the beach at Johnnie's place and the cemetery beach. The shore is pretty rocky and steep with no easy access."

"Maybe he tossed it into the water," I hazarded.

Leslie interjected again. "I don't mean to interrupt, but I just had a thought. Remember what a hard drive contains? Data. Maybe it was stolen in order to destroy the data. Immersion in saltwater would certainly do the trick."

"Yeah, Sergeant Hue suggested this." She glanced up as one of her colleagues walked into the room and sat in the cubicle opposite hers. Her face took on a more official stance. "Is there anything else I can help you with?"

"Yes, I'd like to know if you've caught my burglar yet."

"No, sorry, nothing yet."

"I think Sergeant Hue said he was going to see if he could match the fingerprints with those found at Carter Davis's crime scene."

"I'm afraid forensics wasn't able to get any good prints, it being a hotel room and all. Sorry." She shrugged. "But we're fairly certain you were targeted. There've been no other recent robberies in the hotel."

"Of course I was targeted," I shot back, feeling frustrated by the lack of progress. "Any fool can see that."

Curran blushed. "What I meant was…" She stopped, clearly at a loss for words.

Leslie's quiet voice broke the silence, "You mean, Constable, that you had to rule out all possibilities before you could focus in on potential suspects, don't you?"

Curran nodded gratefully at my brother-in-law.

"Do you still believe there is a connection to the Carter murder?" he asked.

"I'm afraid you will have to ask Sergeant Hue about that." She glanced apologetically at me, which made me feel guilty that I'd been so hard on her.

I turned to Leslie. "There has to be a connection. Carter was the only person who knew of the existence of both the letter and the prints. So it has to be either someone he told or the killer, if they're not one and the same."

Leslie nodded. "I understand, Constable, that Sergeant Hue was also investigating Johnnie Nanuqtuaq in connection with these art forgeries that seem to also be connected to Carter Davis. Is there any chance that the person who killed Johnnie is the same person who robbed Meg?"

As Curran gave the pat answer of following all leads, I couldn't help thinking about my suspicions regarding Pete Pitsiulak and a possible connection to Carter's murder. Maybe he had something to do with Johnnie's murder too. Although I felt he'd been genuinely upset by the discovery of his dying friend, he still could've killed him and used me to help establish his innocence. Maybe when he realized his friend was still alive, remorse took over, and that's why he'd tried so desperately to save him. When I met him at the house with the gamblers, he was coming back from somewhere, supposedly a shopping trip, but perhaps not. Maybe the boatman had nothing to do with Johnnie's death. Curran said they believed Johnnie's killer was an Inuk. And Pete would no doubt have ready access to an *ulu*. Moreover, he knew about the Suula prints. I'd told him, although I didn't think I'd mentioned the letter. Still he could've learned about it from Carter. Yet the time was very short, less than an hour between when we parted at the Legislative Assembly and my return to the hotel. Was it enough time to steal the prints?

I hesitated about raising my suspicions with Curran.

Pete, after all, was the Minister of Culture. When I raised my suspicions with Leslie on our way to Tim Hortons, he agreed it wouldn't be appropriate.

"You need something more definitive than conjecture," he said. "You need a motive. You need proof. I suggest you let the police do their job. If this man is guilty, they'll uncover it."

You have more faith in the cops than I have, I thought, opening the door to Tim's. Still, if I were wrong, Pete's reputation could be damaged. Besides I rather liked the man and didn't want to believe he could be guilty of murder, let alone of theft.

After satisfying our southern sensibilities with strong Tim Hortons coffee and chocolate cream-filled donuts, Leslie and I decided to visit Angus McLeod. Leslie thought it best we arrive unannounced, and since it was close to lunch time, chances were we would find him at home.

However, when we arrived at his front door, we were greeted by a shy, grandmotherly sort of woman, bearing a striking resemblance to Ooleepeeka, who informed us that her husband regrettably was not at home. In fact, he'd departed early that morning on a flight to Tasilik.

When asked if it was possible to have another look at a print her husband had shown me the previous day, one I was considering buying—this last bit added to make my request sound more plausible—she politely informed me that it best I wait for her husband's return, since she knew little about the business. She also didn't know when he would be returning. After wishing us a smiling good day, she gently closed the door in our faces.

The minute I returned to my hotel room, I booked my flight to Tasilik, while Leslie agreed to stay behind to look after the handling of my father's remains.

Thirty-Nine

The next day I was introduced to the vagaries of Arctic travel. I arrived early enough at the airport, the prescribed sixty minutes before my 11:35 a.m. departure to Tasilik, and checked in without so much as a hint that the flight might not be departing as planned. For an hour I waited amidst the growing number of passengers. I sipped insipid vending machine coffee while wishing I'd picked up a Tim's coffee on the way, all the while expecting to hear the boarding announcement at the appropriate interval before departure time.

I suppose the rain slanting across the tarmac should've warned me, but I'd flown in plenty of downpours, so I hadn't given it a second thought. I even watched a large jet from the south splash down and its passengers fling jackets or purses over their heads as they raced to the protection of the airport. I did happen to notice a much smaller plane standing unattended nearby but thought nothing of it.

Finally, at about thirty minutes after the scheduled departure, it was announced that the flight would be delayed for another hour. Since none of the other passengers seemed perturbed by this annoying delay, I sucked in a deep breath and tried not to fidget while I reminded myself that I had nothing pressing. After all, my only objective was finding Apphia in Tasilik, and for that I needed her brother's remains. But since I couldn't fly out, neither could he.

As I munched on a stale vending machine sandwich, several small Inuit kids cavorted around me, while their mothers, intent on their own conversation, blithely ignored them. Kids weren't exactly my thing, and I tended to remove myself as far from their high spirited antics as I could, although since befriending Jid, I'd become more used to their energetic ways. I supposed it was the shy smile of one little girl in pigtails that warmed me to their play, and before I knew it I was part of their game, a modified version of hide and seek.

I'd cover my eyes, count to ten, and the five of them would race off in separate directions to their respective hiding spots. Their giggling, however, invariably tipped me off to their locations behind pillars, other passengers, and in one case, a stack of camera equipment. I pretended to be mystified and spent several minutes scanning the small but crowded lounge, assiduously avoiding glancing at one little boy who kept jumping out from behind the central display case of Inuit art to see if I was looking in his direction. I would then advance towards the various hiding places and in the midst of giggles touch the hiding child. But I always returned to my seat scratching my head with one child still in hiding. After another minute or two, he or she would emerge beaming triumphantly from their hiding place.

Unfortunately, the room was just a little too crowded for such antics, so after one child accidentally ran into a passenger and another knocked a suitcase over, I suggested we play something a little less rambunctious. The shy girl with the pigtails pulled out a long piece of string with its ends tied together and invited me to join her in a game I recognized from my own childhood, cat's cradle. Several other children also drew out their loops of string and the contest began to see who could make the most intricate movements. I must admit my ingenuity was taxed to invent finger combinations as elaborate as these five kids managed to come up with. The one that most impressed me was called "dogs pulling a sled", which it seemed to mirror exactly.

Finally it was announced that all flights to Tasilik were

cancelled and to check with the clerk for a seat on one of the two flights the following day. It turned out the reason for the cancellation wasn't so much the rain but extremely high winds in Tasilik, so while my playmates dispersed with their mothers, I waited in line and eventually got one of the few remaining seats on the next day's afternoon flight.

It was after three before I was able to grab a cab and head back to the hotel. No rooms were available, no doubt because of other stranded passengers, so I went in search of Leslie to see if he minded my staying with him that night. He was nowhere to be found in the hotel, including the bar, and a call to Curran to see if he was with her also failed to locate him. I did learn from the Mountie that it would be at least two more days before the boat with Father's remains would arrive in Iqaluit.

The continuing icy torrent dispelled any ideas I might've had about wandering around town, so I hunkered down at the bar to wait for my brother-in-law. A couple of scotches later found me in conversation with one of the locals, no doubt a bar regular, given the speed with which the bartender refilled his empty beer glass without his asking.

Gordie was his name, and he'd been living on and off in the north since the late 1950s, when he'd come up from Missouri with the American military, who were running the airfield in Frobisher Bay at the time as part of the DEW line. After his fellow Americans left, he'd stayed on as an air mechanic working for the Canadian government until his retirement a number of years ago. He'd liked the northern life and had nothing to go back for. Besides, he'd found himself a nice little wife, a nurse from Newfoundland, who didn't want to return home either.

She'd passed away a few years back, and his children for the most part had scattered south, although one daughter was now a teacher a three-hour flight away in Pond Inlet. But flying was expensive, so he didn't see her and the grandchildren more than a couple of times a year. One of the highlights of his quiet life was his twice weekly visits to the bar for a couple of pints. Although it looked to me as if he'd already had more than a couple that day.

Gordie regaled me with many a tale of the early days of Frobisher Bay, when it was trying to establish itself as a permanent Arctic community. In fact, he was one of the town's first councilors, and although he'd run for mayor, he'd lost to a fellow who'd used booze to buy votes. He hadn't spoken to the man since, although the two of them had lived on the same road for more than thirty years.

He left Frobisher Bay in the late 1960s to help set up another airfield in James Lake but returned in 1973 to become airport manager. On the off chance, I asked if he'd ever met my father.

"Why, sure I knew Sutton." His red-rimmed eyes seemed to disappear into a trench of wrinkles as his smile broadened. "Great guy. Many a time the two of us spent hours discussing the affairs of the world in the Zoo, that's the old bar before they built this new one. It wasn't as gussied up with all these fool-dangled antlers. And the beer was sure a darn sight better back then. Strong enough to put hair on your chest." He smacked his lips. "Just imagine you being his daughter. I see you got his red hair. I was sure sorry when his plane went missing."

"I'm not sure if you know that they've finally found it, and in fact they'll soon be bringing it and his remains and the pilot's into Iqaluit."

"You don't say. Always knew they'd find it one day. Do you know where?"

"Not exactly, but I think it was out in Davis Strait, near the entrance to Frobisher Bay. A long way from where it was supposed to be."

"Yeah, but it stands to reason. Probably landed on pack ice on Cumberland Sound. The ice would've drifted out into Davis Strait then south till eventually it broke up, dropping the plane into the water. I suppose what's surprising is that

257

the plane didn't travel further before it sank. A lot of these ice floes end up along the coast of Labrador. I told the SAR guys at the time to check the ice in Davis Strait. But they were so sure the plane had gone down in the mountains between James Lake and here, they didn't bother. Guess I was right, eh?" Another smile revealed his yellowed teeth. He took a lingering sip of beer.

"Remember your uncle, too. Harold, wasn't it?"

"Yeah, I guess you met him when he came up here after the plane went missing."

"Yeah, and before too. Saw him a couple of times, sitting right here at this very counter talking to Sergei, that crazy Russian. A lot of strange people end up in the north, but that guy was one of the strangest."

"You aren't the only one who saw the two of them together. Like my father, my uncle was an art collector. I gather he was buying some of Crazy Russkie's paintings."

"Maybe, but it looked more like the two of them were hatching something. I remember seeing a lot of money changing hands, more than you'd pay for one of Sergei's stupid paintings."

"Do you know what it was for?"

"No idea, but I know Sergei didn't always travel the straight and narrow. He and Gus were thick as thieves."

"You mean Angus McLeod?"

"Right. You know him?"

"Only met him a couple of times. What was Angus involved in?"

"You gotta remember, in the early days it was hard to make ends meet, and the HBC didn't pay much. That's who Gus worked for at the time. Eskimo carvings were becoming a hot seller down south, and there weren't much in the way of regulations, not like today. So Gus set himself up as a dealer of sorts." He stopped to wet his lips with another long draft of beer.

"Hell, we all did it for a little extra cash. They were dirt cheap. The Eskimos had no idea how much they were worth. So for a bottle of whiskey, some smokes or a couple of boxes of bullets, you could make a tidy profit on them. But most of us only did it with the odd carving. Didn't like to take advantage of the Eskimos. Gus on the other hand, made a business out of it. I hear tell he had most of the carvers in James Lake beholden to him. He'd loan them money so they could buy items from his store. Then he'd demand they pay him back in carvings. Once a year he'd ship 'em down south and make a killing."

"And the carvers never saw any of this money."

"Not as far as I know."

"But he told me that the Inuit in Tasilik asked him to take over management of their art co-op. Surely they would've been very upset with him when they realized how he'd more or less stolen from them."

"Sure they were mad. But you see, the Eskimos are a very pragmatic people. They could see that he'd been successful in selling their carvings, so along with help from the Feds they established a few parameters that made sure they were recompensed appropriately."

"And that was the end of Angus's underhanded art dealings?"

"Not exactly. Although he liked to present a squeaky clean image, occasionally there'd be a bad odour coming from some of his art dealings."

"What kind of odour?"

"A number of years back now, a couple of dealers down south accused him of selling fake pieces. Said they weren't done by Eskimos. But Gus was able to talk himself out of it. Took a plane load of Eskimos down south who swore they were the artists."

I immediately thought of Carter's fake *Mystical Owl* and my father's forgeries. "How long ago did this happen?"

"Can't say for sure. Memory ain't what it used to be, but I'd say in the early '70s."

The timing fit, but it didn't explain the more recent discovery of fakes the police were trying to tie to my family. "How about anything recently?"

He shook his head. "Nope, Gus has been leading the life of a solid citizen of the north these past many years. Was Mayor of James Lake for many years. But you know… I always kinda wondered how he could afford to buy all them fancy orchids." He winked.

"You mentioned something about this crazy Russian, Sergei, being as thick as thieves with Gus. What did you mean?"

"Suppose it really wasn't anything, but whenever I was in James Lake, Sergei always seemed to be slinking out the back door of Gus's place. Know he used to go on errands for Gus to other communities on Baffin, but never knew what they were about."

"Could it have anything to do with Gus's art dealings? After all, Sergei was a painter."

"Maybe. I know Gus had a string of carvers in a number of Baffin communities. But pretty sure that was all legit. In fact, Gus still deals directly with a number of carvers, like that poor boy that got killed."

"You mean Johnnie Nanuqtuaq?"

He nodded sadly. "Great kid."

"I'd understood Johnnie handled his own distribution after he left the Tasilik Art Centre."

"Maybe so, but one day not too long ago, I seen Gus and Johnnie in a big argument. Johnnie sure looked mad. Kept shouting he wasn't going to do that shit for him any more."

"Do you know what he was referring to?"

"Nope, but figured it had to do with carving. That's about the only thing Johnnie did, besides drive that fancy car of his." Gordie upped the amber bottle and drained the last of his beer.

"Do you want another?"

"Thanks, but I gotta get going. Have to get back for *Coronation Street*. It comes on at seven."

I glanced at my watch. 6:40. I had no idea I'd been sitting here this long. I wondered where Leslie was.

Gordie started to slip his wiry but hunched over body off the high bar chair, then paused. "But before I go, I've got a question for you. You said something about your father and the pilot's remains being found."

"Yes, I gather they were still sitting in their seats, despite the length of time they'd been in the water." I wasn't, however, about to tell him about the bullet hole in the skull of the pilot.

"Any mention of a third body?" he asked.

Forty

Ah ha, I was right, I thought as I leaned back into the barstool with cautious relief.

"Are you saying there was a third man on the plane?" I asked, eying the old man for any indication he might be feeding me a line but saw only matter-of-fact open honesty.

"You bet." Gordie nodded eagerly. "I saw him climb in shortly before the plane taxied for take-off. I was in James Lake that day. They had a problem with some of their running lights. Asked me to look into it. I was outside at the time when I saw a man run up to the plane."

"Do you know who it was?"

He shook his grizzled head. "Guy jumped in too quick for me to tell. But from the clothes he was wearing, I'm pretty sure he was Eskimo."

"Did you mention this to the police at the time?"

"Yup. They said they checked through the Eskimo community to see if anyone was missing, but they never came up with anything. And they couldn't find anyone else who'd seen the guy. So they told me I musta been mistaken."

"And were you? After all, it sounds as if you only caught a quick glimpse of the man."

"Nope, I'm darn sure I saw him. Remember thinking it funny at the time, climbing in at the last minute like that. In fact, I kind of had the impression the people on board didn't want him. Seemed to be a bit of a tussle over the door, before the guy managed to yank it open and climb inside."

"Well, if there was a third guy, he wasn't in the wreckage. The police have only mentioned finding two bodies."

Suula's depiction of a man parachuting from a burning plane loomed large in my mind. I sure hoped Gordie was right and there had been a third man. If so, the identities of the two bodies were no longer certain. For who had been the man lucky enough to escape the burning plane? This third guy, the pilot or my father? Moreover, it also put the identity of the shooter into question, even the victim.

After convincing the old man to pass this information on to Constable Curran, I bid him goodbye. As I watched him totter out of the bar, I couldn't help but feel a renewed frisson of hope that my father was the man who had escaped. After all, a man with red hair had been depicted in Suula's pictures.

I also decided to let Curran know myself and called her from a hotel payphone. But she'd already gone for the day and wouldn't be back in the office for a couple of days since she'd been called off on another case. Needless to say, I asked who would be handling Father's remains when the salvage boat finally arrived. I was reminded that it was Corporal Reilly's case and he'd be handling everything when he and the boat got here.

My brother-in-law turned out to be equally elusive. Despite my being prepared to swear on a stack of Bibles that I was his relation, the hotel clerk refused to give me a key to his room. So I returned to the bar, where I sampled the buffet and several more scotches while I waited. I must admit, I didn't really remember Leslie coming to get me. I just have a hazy memory of being pushed into the elevator, along with my backpack, then force-marched down the hall to his room, where I toppled onto the sofa. In the morning, I woke stiff and sore, with a hundred woodpeckers hammering inside my head and Leslie bending over me, looking tragic.

"Oh, Meg, why did you do it?"

Freshly shaven and showered with his springy curls for once tamed and his body reeking of aftershave lotion and baby powder, he looked prim and proper like a reverend about to pour forgiveness on one of his stray lambs, which only served to make me squirm all the more.

My only defense was to retaliate. "It's all your fault. If you'd been here, I wouldn't have had to wait for you in the bar. Besides, where were you that it kept you out half the day and night?"

"I know you're angry with me, but most of all you're angry with yourself. Why don't you have a shower and change into a fresh set of clothes. You'll feel much better. Then I can tell you what I learned in my wanderings yesterday."

I grumbled something in response and wrenched myself off the couch and lurched towards the bathroom. I felt awful. I needed a drink. I wondered if Leslie had a bottle tucked away somewhere, but I couldn't look while he was in the room. Maybe I could convince him to leave.

"Les, do you have any Tylenol? I have a terrible headache." My brother-in-law shunned any sort of medication, so I was fairly certain he'd have to go to the lobby to buy some. But as he twisted the door handle to leave, my dry self took over. "No, don't bother. I'll get some later. I'll be finished in a jiff."

I closed the bathroom door behind me. That was close, too close. No way did I want to return to those mind-numbing, stomach-puking days of a drunk. I turned the shower on cold and stepped into it.

Leslie was right. I did feel considerably more human with my body clean and my clothes smelling fresh. I'd heard Tasilik was a dry town, and that was all the better for me.

The morning sun flooded through the windows of the dining room, yesterday's rain a distant memory. I was happy to see it gone, and the wind too, which meant my afternoon flight should leave as scheduled.

It was only after I'd injected sufficient caffeine into my

system that I felt lucid enough to find out what had kept my brother-in-law away from the hotel.

"Since we weren't altogether certain about this chap, Angus McLeod, and that politician you mentioned, I thought I'd do some checking on my own. Hope you don't mind."

He stopped to swallow a mouthful of brie and asparagus omelet. "Boy, this is delicious. Almost as good as Shelley's."

He sampled another forkful before continuing. "I'll start with the politician. I'm afraid he's got a lot of friends in town. Everyone I talked to from the bellhop to the cab driver had nothing but good words to say about the man and what he has done for his people and the new territory. This further supports the need for you to have some pretty solid proof before taking your suspicions to the police. But you may have already decided not to."

"Yeah, I've pretty much ruled it out. I'll just stay out of his way, which going to Tasilik will do."

"I did learn one thing, though." He stopped as the waitress arrived to deliver his side order of smoked arctic char.

Food, other than a piece of dried toast, was the last thing my stomach craved this morning, although the caffeine in the coffee was doing its job quite nicely of returning me to the land of the living, even if it wasn't Tim Hortons'.

When the server left, Leslie continued, "It seems he has killed a man."

"But how can he be an elected official?"

"It happened when he was a teenager. Apparently it was ruled an accidental death. I think it was a cousin or a friend he shot while hunting."

"Accidental, eh?"

"Unfortunately, I wasn't able to come up with any information that would connect him to Carter Davis or even suggest a reason why he might want to harm the man. The same goes for his friend Johnnie. Apparently Pete helped Johnnie out of a tricky situation a few years ago. But the person telling me about this wasn't able to say what the situation was. " He stopped to butter a muffin.

"So I guess it was a harebrained idea."

"I had much better luck in finding out more about Angus McLeod. I talked to an owner of a local gallery who directed me to a couple of carvers who once worked for Angus. I even found an old timer at the local newspaper, who told me a few stories about the man."

"My, you really were busy yesterday." I felt the twinge of a hunger pang. I reached for a croissant. Perhaps with a bit of cloudberry jam…

"I'd say I've learned more than I ever wanted to about the man. There does appear to be two sides to him. The journalist admitted that Angus McLeod was integral in getting Inuit art accepted as a genuine art form, but suggested that Angus didn't do it without taking the odd short cut, with some of them leading straight to his own pocket."

"That's more or less what I learned from my drinking buddy." And I passed on what Gordie had told me. "But he wasn't able to come up with any specific examples. Did you discover any?"

"One of the carvers I talked to, an old guy who'd spent some time in Tasilik in the 1960s, pretty much confirmed what you said about Angus's misuse of the early carvers. In fact, he admitted he'd been one. But at the time he'd been happy to get free bullets and liquor for something that had only taken him a few hours to carve. Besides as he said, or at least his grandson translating his words said, what would he have done with a lot of money when there was nothing to spend it on."

I thought of the endless kilometres of empty tundra and frozen sea with not a store in sight. He was right. It was just our southern sensibilities taking over.

"He said back then, pretty much everything he needed, apart from his rifle and ammunition, came from the land. And by the time he'd lost his dogs and was needing a snowmobile, he was getting good money for his carvings from the art co-op which Angus ran. So this carver really had nothing but praise for the man. Not so with the other carver."

Leslie stopped to order another cup of coffee, while I decided my stomach could take a little more food, so I ordered eggs benedict with lots of smoked arctic char and hollandaise.

"Leeno, the other carver, was much younger and a close friend of Johnnie's."

"Did he have anything to say about the killing, like who might've done it? Even why?"

"I had the impression he would love to see the ah... bastard, his words not mine, in jail for the murder of his friend. But unfortunately he saw Angus at Tim Hortons at about the same time as the murder."

"Did he say what he had against him?"

"It seems to have more to do with what Angus did to Johnnie, although the Scotsman did cheat Leeno on a couple of carvings. Apparently Leeno found out that a gallery had paid double the price Angus had told him, which meant he was paid half of what he was actually owed. But that wasn't why he was angry with the man. I gather Angus paid up when confronted."

"Makes you wonder how often the man's gotten away with it. I'd think it would be pretty near impossible for an artist to find out how much a southern gallery paid, don't you? Still, I would've thought the Inuit-owned Tasilik Art Centre would have to be more open in its dealings."

Leslie smiled in agreement. This morning he seemed more sure of himself. Not once had I noticed him reach for his missing bow tie. Sleuthing must have agreed with him.

He said, "It sounded as if Leeno was using Angus as an agent rather than going through the Art Centre. Apparently he was promised more money."

"I guess it's a case of taking your chances, isn't it? But

still, it does give us a good idea as to how Angus operates. Did Leeno say what Angus had done to Johnnie?"

"He didn't really know that much. Just knows that it's something that happened a while ago, when Johnnie first started out as a carver with the Tasilik Art Centre. Apparently he was asked to do various things that only much later did he discover were against the law."

"Did Leeno know what these were?" I thought of the warehouse in Johnnie's name.

"No, but he assumed it had something to do with carving. Anyway, it was one of the reasons why Johnnie left the Art Centre and moved to Iqaluit."

"I bet this is related to the forgeries found in Toronto, don't you?"

"Makes you wonder, given the Scotsman's history. Apparently Johnnie let slip one time when he was drunk that he took something of Angus's when he left, something that would get the man into big trouble."

"Any idea what it was?"

"Leeno said Johnnie clammed up the minute he asked and told Leeno if he ever mentioned it to anyone, he'd make damn sure Leeno never sold another carving again."

"Sounds like serious stuff. It also sounds like it could be a motive for murder."

"Except Angus was in Iqaluit."

"But he did turn up on the scene within an hour or so of Johnnie's murder, which given their falling out, could be viewed as highly unusual."

"Maybe he had gone to retrieve whatever Johnnie had taken before the police found it."

"That's what I'm wondering. However, when I saw Angus, he didn't act like a man desperate to retrieve something. In fact, he was pretty nonchalant. And I don't think it was a case of him having already found the item. He wasn't carrying anything, and he didn't act like he was anxious to get away from us and the police."

I placed my fork and knife on my empty plate. The eggs and smoked char had done the trick. I had returned to the land of the living.

After a final sip of coffee, I commented, "I find it curious that Angus went directly to Johnnie's workshop instead of the house where he'd been killed and where the police were."

"Perhaps he was checking to make sure the item was gone."

"Good point. And we know what the item was, the hard drive and all its data. So maybe what Johnnie had stolen was incriminating data about Angus. What do you think?"

"I think you might be on to something. I say we take a walk down to the detachment." Leslie signalled for the bill.

"But it still doesn't explain who killed Johnnie."

"We'll let the police figure out that one."

Forty-One

They were beginning to load the cargo onto the Tasilik plane when I took my seat once again in the airport lounge. Leslie and I had spent over two hours at the detachment, most of it waiting for someone to listen to our suspicions about Angus. With Constable Curran off on another case and Corporal Reilly still onboard the salvage boat, they had to scramble to find someone else. Even Sergeant Hue wasn't available. He'd flown to Tasilik two days earlier, so I made a mental note to track him down once I got there.

Finally a young constable, one could almost say a raw recruit, given his nervous stammering and apologetic politeness, took down our ideas. Other than to say that he'd pass the information onto the case officer, he offered no reaction to what we thought had been very able detective work, as good as any cop could do. We left feeling as if our time had been wasted and our efforts unappreciated, although we did learn that the parts for the boat had arrived, and they anticipated that it and its singular cargo would be reaching Iqaluit tomorrow.

So with a promise to ensure my father's remains were well taken care of and a warning for me to be careful, my brother-in-law put me and my backpack into a cab to the airport, where for the last hour I'd been waiting with more philosophical expectations than yesterday. Only now were they starting to load the cargo into the small turboprop plane I presumed was the one for Tasilik. Although it looked as if the flight would be delayed yet again, I was assured that we would be boarding, once all the cargo, two days worth given yesterday's flight cancellation, had been loaded. Unfortunately, my playmates of yesterday hadn't return, so I was forced to amuse myself.

Through the lounge window, I caught sight of a forklift ferrying an elongated wooden box towards the conveyor belt of the plane. It didn't take me long to realize that this box was large enough to contain a body, as in Johnnie's body. Although I didn't fancy riding on a plane with a corpse, I hoped it would draw out Apphia from her isolated camp, and if the gods were with me, she might even be at the airport when the plane landed.

It took another forty-five minutes for the crew to juggle loading the rest of the cargo into the plane and inviting the passengers to board. If I'd thought our small numbers would allow us to have plenty of seat space to spread out into, I was quickly proven wrong. The passenger area had been shortened to less than one third of the plane. As I took my seat at the front, with my feet pushing against the bulkhead separating us from the cargo area, I couldn't help but think that Johnnie's body might be on the other side.

The fifty-minute flight was uneventful, with skies clear enough to give me a full appreciation of the emptiness of this vast mountainous island. Miles and miles of endless rock, tundra and snow with only the occasional thread of a blue river cutting through the mosaic of browns, greys and white and the sporadic splatter of purple and yellow and even green. At one point we crossed a large stretch of white, which I thought could be an inland glacier, then the plane was descending towards an ice-rimmed shore and sparkling blue water. Once again I noticed the curious blue colour, similar to the turquoise of tropical waters, particularly where it mixed with the ice floes. The plane continued its descent across Cumberland Sound to the towering cliffs of the other shore.

I had a moment's alarm as we landed. Out of my window

I saw only water; out the opposite window, mountains with no sign of habitation, let alone an airport. Then we were taxiing along a gravel runway towards a diminutive single-storey wooden structure reminiscent of the Caribbean island airports I'd landed at. "Welcome to Tasilik" was emblazoned in French, English and Inuktitut across the front. I could just make out several roofs jutting above the water side of the runway, while on the other a cliff loomed.

I hoped that I would be able to readily pick out Johnnie's sister, but the hope left me when I saw the jumble of people, most of them Inuit, crowded into the narrow lounge. I assumed they were waiting to board the plane; however, when the keening started, I realized these were the dead man's friends and relations. With renewed hope, I scanned the tear-stained faces of the women for one who appeared the most upset.

The rising crescendos of wailing made me uneasy. I felt like a trespasser, an outsider. This was a very private and personal occasion, which didn't include me. My immediate response was to escape once my backpack was offloaded onto the middle of the floor, along with the other passengers' baggage. But I forced myself instead to stay and scan the mourners. My only reason for coming to Tasilik was to find Apphia, and this was my best opportunity.

Initially, all I could see was a sea of hats and black hair. In addition to the usual ball caps, several sported a distinctive style of woollen cap with a multi-coloured zigzag border and tassel. I craned my neck to peer around the heads, searching for the woman who might be Apphia. Influenced by Angus's picture of the Inuit family, I was looking for a hint of redness in the hair. At one point I thought I saw it, but when I gained a better view, I realized this streaked hair colour was courtesy of a bottle. Besides, the woman appeared too old to be Johnnie's younger sister.

Then the heads parted and I saw a woman, weeping, a baby peeking over her shoulder. Her hair was the exact same flaming red as mine, her skin almost as pale. My immediate reaction was to dismiss her as white, but I quickly shoved this bias aside when I realized she was wearing the traditional *amauti*. Moreover her facial features were more Inuit than Caucasian. I must admit the sight of her did cause me to pause. Was I looking at my father's child, my half-sister?

I tried making my way through the keening mourners towards her. At the same time, I noticed someone else was also trying to reach her, someone I couldn't fail to recognize with her designer cut white hair and flashing glasses.

Mary Goresky, however, wasn't having too much success either. The more she pushed, the more the circle of women tightened around the red-haired woman like a herd of muskox fending off a dangerous predator. At one point, Mary even called out Apphia's name, but one of the men approached her and suggested she leave the woman alone in her grief.

I took note and decided to return to where I'd been standing against an outside wall. When Mary finally took the hint and removed herself from the fray, I walked up beside her and said, "Hi. I'm surprised to see you here. You weren't on the plane."

She started and twisted her head in my direction. The rhinestones in her glasses sparked. "Why Meg Harris, whatever brings you to Tasilik? I thought your business was in Iqaluit."

"I came to talk to the same woman you want to talk to."

For a second I saw alarm behind her glasses, then she laughed, "But her friends sure don't want me talking to her, do they? What do you want with Apphia?"

"Just following up on my quest for more information about my father. And what about you?"

"Angus asked me to check up on her and see if there is anything she needs."

"I'm surprised Angus wouldn't want to do that himself? I gather he's here also."

"Yes, we came a couple of days ago. He thought she

might prefer a woman's touch." Her face was now a mask of self-control.

At that moment, a familiar voice rose above the noise, and I turned to see Pete Pitsiulak making his way through the crowd. Saying something in Inuktitut, he wrapped his arms around Apphia, who clung to him as if he were a lifesaver. This only served to unleash another crescendo of heart-rendering keening. One of the flight crew approached, and Johnnie's sister, still clinging to Pete, headed out the doors to the tarmac, to where I could see the end of the coffin sticking out from the back of a green pick-up. She and Pete climbed into the truck and drove off.

I must admit I had a momentary "what if". What if Pete had killed her brother, what would he do to her? But no one else seemed the least concerned by his offer of protection.

It also spelled the end of any probability of immediate conversation with Suula's daughter. But Tasilik looked to be a very small town. Someone would be able to tell me where she was staying. I turned back to Mary in time to see her purple coat disappearing over the brow of the road.

Forty-Two

My next challenge was to find a place to stay. In my rush to leave Iqaluit, I'd not bothered to book anything, thinking there was bound to be space in a local lodge. However, I quickly discovered the town had only one lodge, and the chances of getting a room without a reservation were next to nil. Like Iqaluit, Tasilik was in the midst of a building boom, and the lodge was supposed to be brimming with contractors and government workers. The only other possibility would be someone's home, but I couldn't be guaranteed a room to myself. So I decided to try my luck at the lodge.

Burdened only with my daypack, albeit an overstuffed one, I tramped down the airport road in the direction of the lodge. Not wanting to bother with excess weight, I'd left my large pack with most of my clothes and the sculpture at the Frobisher Inn with my brother-in-law. I headed towards the brown two-storey building that had been identified as the lodge. I must admit its drab, utilitarian appearance didn't shout comfort, but then my plan was to spend only one night, at the most two. I figured the funeral would be tomorrow, where I would meet up with Apphia and hopefully finally learn what her connection was to my father.

The lodge might have been standard issue, but its perch on an outcrop of rock overlooking a mountain-lined fjord would rival that of any of the best resorts in the world. Its view took my breath away. Picture postcard perfect. If it had been windy yesterday, it certainly wasn't today. Not a breath marred the jagged snow-streaked mountains mirrored in the flat expanse of water. Both sides of the fjord were rimmed by the towering heights until it vanished into the crowding peaks at the far end. And directly across was a cascading valley of amazingly green grass.

Then I spied a ripple. The tiny head of a seal popped up, stared at me and nodded almost as if it were welcoming me then it slid its sleek body beneath the surface. Several more sleek bodies broke through and disappeared again. Within minutes, a boat headed out after them, an immediate reminder that before modern society took over, seals had provided all the necessities of life.

With fingers crossed, I tramped up the metal stairs of the lodge and entered a dark, narrow foyer with a sign stating that all outdoor clothing and footwear must be left there. A couple of bulky work jackets hung from wall pegs while underneath them stood the owners' scuffed Kodiaks.

A single lamp provided some light in a tiny windowless office, where a blousy woman with fly-away bleached hair sat sorting through some papers. Smoke spiralled upwards from a cigarette lying on an ash-filled ashtray. Bracing myself for a "sorry we're full", I was gratefully proved wrong. One of the rotating doctors had just checked out and was taking the plane back to Iqaluit.

"And you're lucky," she continued in her throaty voice after introducing herself as Dorothy, the manager. "The room has one of the best views in the lodge. If you want some tea or coffee, just ask in the kitchen."

Dutifully leaving my jacket hanging from a peg and my hiking boots on the boot tray, I climbed the stairs to the second floor and was greeted by light streaming in through a wall of windows in a sitting area filled with a ragged assortment of chesterfields and chairs. It had a front row view of the fjord. Perhaps this place wouldn't be so bad.

Although my room was cramped, with two single beds, a couple of dressers, a rod for hanging clothes and not much else, it didn't matter. It was the view of the fjord that mattered.

After several minutes spent soaking up its tranquility and wondering whether those tiny specks moving in the valley across the water were caribou, I unpacked, found my way to the Ladies and returned to the sitting room to take up her offer of tea and wait for dinner.

Precisely at the promised hour, I along with the other lodgers, arrived in the dining room. I sandwiched myself at one of the communal tables between two burly men decked out in their stained construction clothes. At least their hands and faces had been washed. I fully expected to see Mary, but when I didn't, I assumed she was staying with Angus.

I wondered about the exact nature of their relationship. She seemed fairly chummy with the Scotsman, even going so far as to employ his daughter. If he really was involved in art forgery, did this mean she was too? But surely as a director of a fairly prestigious art gallery, she had a reputation to protect. Any hint, or perceived connection to counterfeit art would spell ruin not only to her gallery but also to her standing as one of the foremost experts of Inuit art in Canada, if not the world. Still, money can be as good a motivator as any, and from what I knew of the traditionally impoverished art world, I doubted her salary would be more than adequate.

I also thought back to the airport and her insistence on talking to Johnnie's sister. Was it really about ensuring Apphia was all right, or did she want something else? Regardless, I thought I might just pass on a word of caution to the red-haired Inuit woman when we finally met.

Eating was more important than conversing, so there was little opportunity for me to ask questions until my tablemates were relaxing with dessert. I will say that the meal of pork tenderloin more than surpassed my expectations. And the apple pie melted in my mouth. This chef would give even Shelley a run for her money.

But when I asked about Apphia and her brother, I received only blank stares. None of them even knew about a funeral, let alone that the body of a murdered man had just arrived on the plane. I should have expected it. Like most transients, these men were divorced from the goings-on of the surrounding community.

After dinner, as I was about to head off to my room, the manager waylaid me. "I heard you asking questions about the funeral."

"You don't happen to know when it will be held or where, do you?" I asked hopefully.

"The where is easy. Only one cemetery in Tasilik, and that's at the end of the runway. The funeral itself will probably be in a couple days, they usually are. But what's it got to do with you, if you don't mind my asking?" Dorothy plunked her tired body down with a sigh onto one of the sofas in the sitting area.

"Did you know Johnnie?" I took a chair across from her. "Or maybe you know his sister, Apphia?"

"You're clearly not from these parts, so I'm not sure why you care about these people." She lit up a cigarette and spewed out a stream of blue smoke. I coughed and backed out of her line of breath. Cigarette smoke and I didn't agree.

I provided her with the barest of details, feeling she had no need to know about the possible relationship between my father and these two people.

"Yeah, I heard about the missing plane. It happened long before I got here twenty years ago. So that was your dad, eh? And you think the Nanuqtuaqs might know something about it?" She blew out another stream of smoke, all the while staring intently at me. "I'd also heard tell that Johnnie and Apphia's father was white." Her eyes shifted to my hair. "Mind you, with Apphia it's pretty obvious."

I was a fool to think that the possible connection couldn't be hidden. "Do you know their father or at least know who he is?"

"From what I hear, no one knew the man Suula linked up with or where he came from. She just turned up here one day in her boat with her mother and three kids and the one a flaming redhead. The locals used to laugh and say the *Qalupaliq* got her. That's some kinda mythical monster. I never heard of anyone seeing the man. In fact, I had the impression people thought he was dead. Sorry."

She must've sensed my distress, but of course it was ridiculous for me to hope my father still lived. "So you can see my need to speak to Apphia. I saw her today, so I know she's in town. You don't happen to know where she's staying, do you?"

She shook her head. "Not at her brother's place. The police have that taped off."

"But the murder occurred in Iqaluit. It seems strange they'd search his house here, unless it's for something else. Do you know anything about it?" I asked, thinking of his apparent connection to the forgeries.

"Nope, nothing. The RCMP are being pretty close-lipped about it."

"Any ideas on where else his sister could be staying?"

"Nope, and not likely to find out either. When they want to, people here are pretty good at keeping us *qallunaat* outta their lives. But why don't you stay after breakfast tomorrow? My partner and I'll be selling some of the goods we ship in. Usually get a fair crowd. You can ask them. Once they take a look at you and hear your story, they'll pass it on to Apphia. If she wants to meet you, she'll find you."

"I saw her at the airport with Pete Pitsiulak. Could he have taken her to a place belonging to a friend of his, even a relative?"

"I suppose it's possible. He knows a lot of people here." She glanced out the window at a passing seagull. "Pete's a funny guy. Very protective of Apphia. I'm not sure why. He's already got a wife, eh? Mind you, that never stopped a man before."

She let out a peel of laughter that immediately turned into a coughing frenzy.

"If I can't find out where she lives, I'm hoping to catch her at the funeral," I said.

"Maybe, maybe not. When people around here don't want you to get close, they do their damnedest to make sure it don't happen, eh?"

I thought of the phalanx of women who'd done just that at the airport. After wishing the woman a good night, I headed outside. I decided to walk the streets of the small town to see if I could catch sight of the red-haired woman who might very well be my half-sister.

Forty-Three

Although it was past nine thirty, the sun was a good distance above the mountain ridge of the opposite shore. I wasn't the only one roaming the streets. I swore half of Tasilik was, which gave me hope of finding Apphia.

A group of teenage boys were playing golf along a grassy stretch of shore. I say grassy, even though it consisted mostly of rock and dirt. One boy accidentally sent his ball onto one of the chunks of ice still girding the shoreline. I watched him nimbly hop onto it and expertly hit the ball back onto some grass. Then I realized where he and the other golfers were heading. A patch of weathered carpet with a hole neatly dug in the centre, the Arctic version of a golf green. I laughed. Where there was a will, there was a way. I called out to see if they knew Apphia Nanuqtuaq, but they were too intent on their game and didn't even glance in my direction, let alone respond.

I followed the road bordering the shore, past a variety of matchbox bungalows. Each bungalow appeared to be anchored to the ground by thick steel cables running from one side of the house to the other. A passing walker laughingly told me it was to keep the houses from blowing away in the big winds, but when I asked him about Johnnie's sister, he turned his head away and kept walking.

I was nearly run over by an ATV overloaded with shrieking girls, one with her white *amauti* flapping in the wind. A group of younger children surrounded me, wanting to know where I was from, if I liked the Simpsons or which hamburgers did I like best, McDonald's or Harvey's. Again I received the same stony silence when I inquired about Apphia.

A number of houses I passed had dogs chained out front. Some barked, some snarled, all watched my passage intently. Most appeared to be a huskie mix. None would I want as a pet.

The whining sound of a power tool drew me to a house where a carver sat on a boulder polishing his latest stone carving. His face and clothes were caked in white dust, as was the surrounding ground. I figured he would know Johnnie and his sister, but he only smiled back uncomprehendingly, pointed at his carving and with his fingers suggested a price of a hundred dollars.

The street ended on a rocky knoll above the water in an enclave of newer houses, two-storey with some consideration for architectural design. An old woman stared impassively at me from her front stoop. A wooden frame with a sealskin stretched over it stood propped against the clapboard wall of a neighbouring house. A face disappeared from a window when I glanced in that direction. I thought of knocking on the door but knew it would prove useless. I was even beginning to wonder if persistent questioning might not hamper my chances of finding Apphia.

I continued walking. From an open second-storey window, a little boy sang at the top of his lungs. Although I didn't recognize the Inuktitut words, I did the melody. Our national anthem, "O Canada". Perhaps he was still celebrating Canada Day. Directly around the corner from the boy huddled a scraggly raven on the power line leading into the house. He seemed to be trying to cover up his ears with his wings to drown out the singing.

At one point I had the sense of being followed, but when I looked back, I didn't see an obvious candidate, although a number of people were walking behind me. They seemed more focused on their conversations than paying attention to me.

I approached a low building with the Canadian flag flying atop a metal pole and the RCMP insignia on the door. Although one of their trucks was parked out front, the door was locked. I would try tomorrow. Maybe they could tell me where Apphia was staying.

As I passed a tiny clapboard church with flaking paint, a small, rotund man with coke-bottle glasses and a shiny forehead was locking the front door. He introduced himself as the local minister, which immediately reminded me of his wife, the nurse who'd provided me with information about Suula and her father. In answer to my query, I was told she was in Iqaluit and wouldn't be back for a week. He too was unable to tell me where Apphia was staying, although he did know her and her little boy, even though she wasn't a parishioner. As he mentioned her, he glanced at my red hair, almost as if he too were making a mental comparison.

He would be conducting the funeral service, which was supposed to take place in a couple of days. He was certain she would be in attendance. She and her brother had been very close. And yes, it would be all right for me to attend, but he suggested that I stay at the back. Sometimes people got upset by the presence of whites who didn't belong, but then…and he glanced back up at my red hair again.

I passed more matchbox bungalows and more barking, growling dogs. Several children were playing on the swings of a play area. I glanced at my watch. 11:05. And not in bed, which would've had my mother shaking her head in disapproval. The sun had moved slightly lower and further along the ridge, almost as if it were making a line. Then I remembered my high school geography. Of course, in the land of the midnight sun, the sun inscribes a large circle in the sky, and this was the bottom arc of the circle.

I felt my back crawl again and turned quickly to see who was following me. I thought I saw a solitary man drop his head suddenly, but I wasn't entirely sure. I continued walking.

Suddenly I heard a shout. I turned around in time to see a dog racing towards me with the end of a chain dragging behind. I glanced quickly around, but any likely shelter was too far away. Besides, the dog would race me down long before I could reach it.

I decided the best defense was offense. So I began walking towards the dog saying, "Nice doggy."

It stopped. I stopped. We stared at each other. His upper lip curled in a snarl.

"Nice doggy."

I felt a prickle of fear as I realized he was about to pounce.

"Nice doggy," I said again in a louder voice.

Someone shouted. The dog looked back. Then Pete had him by the back of his collar. The dog twisted and snarled and snapped at him. But Pete held on and dragged the animal to where it had broken loose. Except it appeared it hadn't broken loose. The chain had been unsnapped from a large hook screwed into the side of the house.

"You okay, Meg?" Pete asked once the dog was safely secured.

I felt every nerve ending in my body quiver. "Just a bit shaken up. He didn't touch me. Thank you for saving me." I paused. "I'm very lucky you happened to be here at exactly the right moment." I thought of that feeling of being followed and wondered.

"You might want to stick to the main streets," Pete said, "Fewer dogs. As you saw, these dogs are pretty wild. Some might even have wolf in them."

"That dog was deliberately let loose, wasn't it?" But it wouldn't make sense for him to let the dog go then stop it. Unless he'd changed his mind at the last minute. I shivered.

"Possibly. But it could be the snap hadn't been totally closed, and the dog worked it open. How about I walk you back to the lodge?"

I glanced around. Several people were walking behind us while a group of children were playing further up the road. I wouldn't be completely alone. "Thanks."

We walked in silence for several minutes, before I said, "I saw you drive Apphia away from the airport. You must know where she's staying. I'd like to know."

"I haven't had a chance to tell her about you. She's still very upset about her brother. Can you hang on until after the funeral? I'll mention it then. If she wants to meet, I'll bring her to you."

"And if she doesn't, how do I find out about my father…" I paused "…who may also be her father?"

He didn't even blink at the words, which told me he'd suspected all along. But of course, he had the advantage of knowing both of us had red hair. "Meg, I know this is important for both of you. I'll do what I can to make it happen, okay?"

If I failed to talk to her at the funeral, he was probably my only means of reaching her. But could I trust him? "Okay. But tell me why you're so protective of her? If she lives on an island all by herself, she can't be that fragile."

"It's not just her I'm trying to protect. It's the child. You see, the boy is mine."

Forty-Four

For two days I waited and paced the busier streets of Tasilik for a glimpse of Apphia but saw no red head amongst the black ones. I had no word from Pete nor did I see his sturdy frame amongst the walkers, which would've given me a chance to follow him to where she was staying. Thankfully I had no more incidents with escaped dogs or suspected stalkers.

Despite Pete's warning to do nothing, I attended the lodge manager's sale in the hope that word would get back to Johnnie's sister of my desire to see her. But, although the women picking through the array of tax-free cigarettes, nail polish, handicraft sets and the like nodded when they heard my request, and some even smiled, no one owned up to knowing the red-haired woman, nor did anyone approach me afterwards with an address or a message from her.

The RCMP were similarly unhelpful. They only knew she was in town, not where she was staying. As I was leaving the detachment, I ran into Sergeant Hue, so I used the opportunity to pass on our suspicions about Angus. But apart from making a note in his notebook, the stony-faced Toronto cop gave no indication that Leslie and I were on the right track. However, as I was leaving, he advised me to have little to do with the Scotsman.

It wasn't difficult to avoid the art dealer. He never appeared at the lodge or along the streets where I roamed. Although I passed the clump of tent-like buildings of the Tasilik Art Centre several times, I refrained from going inside. In fact, I learned later the choice had been taken away from me. The entire hamlet had closed down because of the pending funeral. In addition to the art centre, the Northmart was locked tight, as were the school and health centre, except for emergencies.

I did see Angus from a distance. I'd noticed a large suburban-style two-storey house standing away from the other much smaller homes. It overlooked a lake, more like a large pond, that must've been the origin of the original "James Lake" name. I was walking along the ridge of a hill above this lake when I noticed a familiar figure get into an Explorer parked at the side of the house. While I watched Angus through my binoculars, Mary stepped out of the house and joined him, which made me ask myself if I was looking at two art forgers. I ducked behind a rock as they passed below me and headed towards the Art Centre.

On my return trip to the lodge for lunch, I noticed a couple of men digging a hole in the cemetery. For Johnnie, I realized with a sense of sadness. But it also meant the funeral would be soon, then hopefully I would finally be able to talk to his sister.

Leslie joined me on the second day of waiting. The salvage boat had arrived in Iqaluit on the previous day. He spared me the details of describing the remains other than to say they were to be sent to Ottawa for the DNA analysis sometime within the next few days. Now that I knew of the existence of the third man, I was half-hoping the results would prove they didn't belong to my father. Still, Leslie said it would be a good couple of weeks before we would know if my DNA could be used and considerably longer if my grandmother's body had to be exhumed. In light of my mother's fragile health, they had, however, promised to speed up the process as best they could.

Mother, so Leslie informed me, was in a holding pattern for the moment. She'd been sent home with twenty-four hour nursing care. Far from feeling happy about this good news, I felt only guilt. Once again, I'd forgotten to call her and find out how she was doing. And once again, it was Leslie, who wasn't even her own flesh and blood, who'd been concerned enough to make the call and also inform her of the status of her dead husband's remains. The minute dinner finished that night, I placed a call, and of course I was too late. She'd already been put to bed for the night. But I did talk to the nurse, who spoke optimistically about her recovery and promised to tell her I'd called.

The next morning, funeral day, I awoke to a true Arctic sight. A couple of caribou, their antlers high and wide, their molting brown coats patchy, were grazing on the grass below my window. Further along the shore, more caribou, several with young, also nibbled at the sparse grass. Then I heard a rifle bark. One of them dropped to the ground while the rest sprinted away. I threw on my clothes intending to race outside to catch a better view but was stopped at the door by Dorothy.

"Best stay inside. It's going to be a hunting free for all until the herd has left. I'm afraid not even a funeral can stop what's second nature to the Inuit. So chances are until the carcasses are carved up and the hides stretched, there'll be no funeral today."

I had breakfast with Leslie, who'd been fortunate enough to luck into another vacancy and tried to avoid looking at the carnage out the window. I kept reminding myself that the killing was natural, that these people had been doing this for thousands of years. But I found it hard to thrust my southern biases aside.

By the time I'd finished breakfast, the shooting had stopped, apart from the odd pop in the distance. What remained of the herd had escaped up the valley. Now the real work began. I saw several ATVs with a carcass tied on the back racing towards their homes. The manager was right. There'd be no funeral today. I did my daughterly duty and had a long talk with Mother.

The next day was blustery and cold. The wind swept

through the pass between the mountains and battered the town. It was all I could do to keep from being swept away as I walked outside the lodge. A sudden gust finally knocked me to the ground as it shattered the window of a nearby house. I could see now why they clamped the houses to the rock. I crawled back to the lodge, where I hunkered down with Leslie, convinced there would be no funeral today. But I was proved wrong.

Around noon, the wind dissipated, the sun came out and people returned to the streets. It took me a few minutes to realize they were all walking in the same direction.

"They're headed towards the church," Dorothy said. "To the funeral."

Leslie and I followed after them. But instead of going to the tiny Anglican church, they crowded into the school auditorium, where it looked as if the entire town had turned out. Following the minister's advice, we stood at the back against the gym wall and craned our necks to see around the people in front of us. A number gave us curious glances, while one or two smiled a greeting, almost as if we were expected. A break was made for us to move up closer.

Johnnie's plain pine coffin stood in front of a makeshift altar. Beside it stood the reverend decked out in his official vestments, including the black stole of death. In the front row of chairs, in the spot closest to her brother's coffin, sat Apphia, her bare red hair startling amongst the sea of black heads, baseball caps and scarves. She was wearing a pure white *amauti* with red and black braiding along the fur edging the hood. Next to her sat Pete.

People, from the youngest child to the eldest grandmother, paraded up to the open coffin and bent wailing to gaze and touch the face of the young man, who less than six days ago had been so very much alive. A group of singers, a couple of guitarists and a drummer provided a rowdier form of music, more country and western than the solemn funeral hymns I was used to hearing. In fact, the whole service was noisier and livelier than any funeral I'd ever attended, almost as if it were a celebration of a life rather than a lament. But the waves of intermittent keening quickly brought one back to reality.

The service, in Inuktitut and English, was short. The words of remembrance were equally short. The only longish one was from Pete, but that was perhaps because he gave it in both languages, unlike the other two men, who gave theirs in one language only. The Inuktitut speaker was wizened with the appearance of many years on the land. I took him to be a relative, maybe an uncle. The other man, speaking in English, was much younger, possibly Johnnie's age.

If I'd thought about it, I would've expected Angus to make a tribute too; after all the master carver had at one time been one of his most successful artists. But perhaps "at one time" were the operative words, and after their falling out, he was no longer counted amongst the favoured. Still, he had hurried to the murder scene. I didn't even see his grey ponytail among the mourners, which really was surprising given his stature within this community.

The guitars burst into the first strains of "Onward Christian Soldiers", and the pallbearers, including Pete, carried the now-closed coffin down the aisle. When they reached me, Pete nodded brusquely in my direction but kept his eyes forward as they headed out the door. Apphia, with her small son, and Pete's for that matter, sound asleep in her hood, walked with her eyes downcast, tears cascading down her cheeks. Beside her shuffled a gnarled and slightly hunched old woman, who when she saw me, whispered something into Apphia's ear. Her head jerked up, and she shot startled greyish-blue eyes in my direction. I thought she mouthed the words "You came" before the man behind her, the one I thought her uncle, pushed her forward, and out the front door she went.

Putting social niceties aside, I forced my way into the departing line but only reached the outdoors in time to watch the pick-up I'd seen at the airport race down the road carrying the coffin and the two old people in the back. The mourners followed, some riding their ATVS, one or two in cars, but most walking, like us.

Surprisingly, Angus was at the cemetery, surrounded by a number of people at the entrance. He wore a suitably sombre suit with a black ascot and a sombre demeanour. Mary, looking equally solemn, stood by his side. If he could make the effort to come here, why hadn't he come to the church?

My question was answered when Apphia ignored his proffered condolences by walking straight past him without any indication that she'd noticed his presence, let alone seen his arms outstretched to embrace her sorrow. As she approached the yawning hole where her brother's coffin waited to be buried, the keening started back up. Angus chose to ignore the rebuff and silently walked with the rest of the people towards the burial plot, although I did notice that the others kept a wide circle of space around him.

Leslie and I felt it best to remain at the back, but as had happened at the service, we found ourselves being eased forward with shy smiles and nods, almost as if it were understood we belonged. We ended up standing directly across the gaping hole from Apphia in time to watch them slowly lower the coffin. While Pete and the old man and woman noticed our presence, Apphia only had eyes for her brother's coffin. Beside them the minister spoke the words of the burial service. At the end Apphia fell wailing to the ground and threw what looked to be shards of soapstone, the fodder of her brother's life, onto the coffin. She then stood up with the help of Pete and dropped a shovelful of sand onto the coffin. She passed the shovel to the old man, who also added his shovelful, who in turn passed it onto the old woman.

Apphia's wailing ignited more. The rising crescendo seemed to take on a life of its own, almost as if it were attempting to summon the ancient gods. And perhaps it was, for I had no doubt that although their ancient religion had long since been supplanted by European religion, vestiges of their older faith still remained.

Throughout, people came up one by one and added more shovelfuls of sand. It was only when the shovel was placed in my hand that Apphia glanced in my direction. Again those shocking pale eyes. This time despite her Inuit features, I found she reminded me of my Great-aunt Agatha. Not that she looked like her, but that her expression was very like the one Aunt Aggie would put on when she was thinking.

Brushing Pete aside, she walked up to me. With the tears still wet on her cheeks, she hugged me closely. "You here," she whispered in my ear. "I come for you," then she broke loose and returned to Pete.

Without another glance in my direction, she left.

Forty-Five

I didn't have to wait long to hear from Apphia. Her messenger was waiting for me at the bottom of the stairs when I arrived back at the lodge after leaving the cemetery. We'd been invited to attend the funeral feast. Although Leslie accepted, I declined. I was tired and felt emotionally drained. I was also finding the continuous stares and comparisons with Apphia unsettling. Besides, I'd achieved what I'd set out to do, an opportunity to talk with Suula's daughter and find out if we really did share the same father.

The young boy handed me her note without so much as a query to ensure I was the right person, let alone an acknowledging smile and took off as fast as his legs could carry him. I guessed my identity was obvious.

The note was short and to the point.

Come to whale house. 9 o'clock tonight.
Apphia Nanuqtuaq

At last, I thought with a tremendous relief, although I couldn't help but feel disappointed that the neat handwriting of her note bore little resemblance to the childish writing of the letters sent to my mother. I'd begun to assume that if her brother wasn't the letter writer, she was.

I didn't have the foggiest idea where this Whale House was, but I figured Dorothy would know, that is if she returned in time from the funeral feast. Otherwise, I'd be forced to ask a passerby on the street, since it wasn't likely any of my fellow lodgers would know. But the lodge manager did return in time with twenty minutes to spare.

Her reaction to my question, however, took me completely by surprise.

"It's cursed," she said, not bothering to hide her distaste. "No one goes near it."

"What do you mean 'cursed'?"

"Exactly that. It's a death house. The Inuit call it *alianaqtuq*. Means it's haunted."

From what she knew, the abandoned building had been built in the early 1900s as a warehouse for whalers, who used the protected shore of what was then a nomadic Inuit camp as a whaling station. Later the Hudson Bay Company had converted it into a store, but as business increased, it was eventually replaced by a much larger store and became the manager's house. Unfortunately, it stank after years of housing whale oil, animal skins and the like, so when one of the managers finally refused to live in it, it became a guest house of sorts until it was given to the Inuit community for housing.

However, after the first Inuk resident went mad and killed his wife and his children, no one would live in it. But these weren't the only deaths the building had seen. One of the HBC managers hanged himself from the rafters after a particularly severe winter. Another was killed by an Inuk after stealing the man's wife. And the third man, a Russian, was presumed dead after vanishing into the tundra. It became clear that this man was Crazy Russkie, but since his disappearance happened many years before Dorothy's arrival, she knew little about him other than that the Inuit blamed him for the death of Joly Quliik.

"I'd just assumed that Joly had died from natural causes."

"That's what the Art Centre has always maintained. But the Inuit are convinced the artist was killed by Crazy Russkie while out on the land hunting.," replied Dorothy blowing a stream of smoke from her cigarette.

"Why are they so convinced? Did someone find the artist's body?"

"Not that I've heard. And there isn't any cross for Quliik in the cemetery. But that doesn't mean he's not buried somewheres out on the land. They also think the *qallunaat* never came back to Tasilik because he was afraid of what they'd do to him."

"Maybe Crazy Russkie never returned because they'd already done their revenge killing," I hazarded.

"Yeah, I suppose." She spewed out more smoke while keeping her eyes on me. "Are you sure you want to go to Whale House?"

"I'm meeting someone there." I decided I wouldn't tell her it was Apphia. Probably best to keep it quiet.

With a shrug that seemed to say "better you than me", she gave me the directions and finished by saying. "At least it will be light out, so you should be okay. I sure wouldn't go there in the dark."

Ten minutes later, trying to laugh off this nonsense of a haunted house, I set out for my rendezvous with Suula's daughter. As Dorothy said, it was broad daylight, and I'd never heard of ghosts carrying out their haunting in bright sunshine.

Her directions took me along the town beach, past boats in varying stages of peeling-paint aging to bright fiberglass newness lying on the beach's coarse sand. I passed a number of people playing what looked to be an Inuit version of the French game of *boule*, except they were using rocks instead of metal balls. As I walked past, I could feel their eyes for a moment turn to me, no doubt curious about my destination. It would be interesting to know what their reaction would be if I told them.

As I skirted a fenced-off area that contained a large number of stacked shipping containers and oil drums, I looked back and saw that several faces were still turned in my direction. Well, they would soon know.

I was heading towards the end of the beach, towards a rock outcrop atop which a derelict house perched, more like sagged. This was supposedly Whale House. The outcrop jutted out into the fjord, except at the moment instead of water, the mudflats of low tide surrounded it, although their expanse seemed to be narrowing quickly with the incoming tide.

I stopped when I reached the bottom of the outcrop and looked back to see if anyone was still watching. Unfortunately, the supply depot blocked the view, although I could hear the distant shouts of the *boule* players. I hesitated. It was pretty isolated, cut off from view by the cliffs bordering the beach. I didn't see any buildings nearby, except what looked to be the roof of a largish building peaking over the rise. I saw no one, but I heard the sound of a motorboat. It was out of sight and seemed to be moving away.

I had no choice. I had to talk to Apphia. Besides, the house, awash in sunlight, appeared more benign than threatening.

With my adrenaline on full alert, I clambered up the rocks to the dilapidated wood frame structure. Several boards were cracked or missing, while the foundation had collapsed at one end, causing it to tilt drunkenly towards the water. Rough, weathered planks barred the facing windows and door. I looked behind. The supply depot still blocked off the rest of the beach.

I wondered why Apphia would pick such an isolated location, but perhaps isolated was the operative word. Maybe she didn't want anyone to know we were talking. But this only made me ask myself why.

With an unsuccessful last glance to see if I could call on anyone should I run into trouble, I walked around to the other side of the house, where I discovered the planks had been removed from the door. On this side Whale House overlooked another beach, where two boats had been hauled up onto the narrow expanse of rock strewn gravel. One boat looked like a freighter canoe with an enclosed bow cabin and an ancient motor clamped onto a flattened stern, while the other was a much newer and sturdier brown fibreglass motorboat with massive twin outboard motors.

"Apphia, you there?" I called out as I knocked on the wooden door. A rusty piece of tin had been hammered over a gap at its base, while the hinges glistened from recent oiling.

Receiving no response, I gingerly pushed the door open and stepped onto the worn plywood floor of an empty room, except it wasn't completely empty. In the dim light filtering through the gaps in the boards, I could see that the castoffs of many occupants had been shoved aside to provide a cleared patch of floor. A pile of seal and polar bear skins had been neatly stacked to one side of this clearing, next to an open doorway that led to another room. Beside the skins stood what looked to be an Inuit stone seal-oil lamp, like the ones I'd seen in museums. And next to it lay a picture, which I recognized with a start. It was one of the prints stolen from my room. The one of the Inuit family with just the one child.

I could only shake my head in confusion. What earthly reason would Apphia have for stealing the pictures? In fact, how did she even know I had them, unless she really had been involved in sending them to Mother? But this reasoning made the stealing of the pictures all the more perplexing.

Apphia, however, wasn't here. Either she was delayed or she'd changed her mind. Regardless, she would have to return for her belongings. Reluctant to wait inside, I zipped up my jacket, pulled my toque over my ears and sat on the outside doorstep in the sun. I wouldn't leave until she came. As the minutes ticked by, I watched the tide seep across the mud flats until shallow waves jostled the sterns of the two boats. The fjord in front of me remained empty, with not so much as a bobbing seal head or a boat to break the reflected image of the mountains. A gull took up station on a rock and glowered at me for several minutes before taking flight with a squawk. I no longer heard the shouts of the *boule* players from the other side of the house.

Then I heard footsteps from inside the house.

"Apphia," I said turning around. "I didn't—"

A medicinal smelling cloth cut-off my words. For several long seconds, I strained to breath, then everything went black.

*   *   *

I awoke to the noise of racing engines and the realization that I was in a boat. I was lying on the floor, encased in something soft and bulky. My head ached, and the pounding motion of the boat only served to make it feel worse. I tried to sit up, but a wave of dizziness and a sudden lurch sent me back down.

"I see you've returned to the land of the living." The smugly grinning face of Angus McLeod loomed over me.

"Where are you taking me?" I struggled to sit up again and made it. It was then that I realized I was not wearing my own jacket, but a sealskin Inuit parka. Its hood covered my head. I climbed onto a vinyl-covered seat.

"I wouldn't sit there, lass. It can get wet." Angus laughed heartily.

Within seconds, my teeth were chattering from the bone-chilling spray. I moved forward to a more protected seat behind the windscreen and pushed the hood further over my head until its ring of fur covered much of my face. My feet, however, were another matter. I was beginning to feel a numbing cold through the soles of my boots.

An Inuk was piloting the boat, which I realized was the fiberglass boat I'd seen on the beach at Whale House. Like Angus, he was wearing traditional Inuit sealskin boots.

"Here, put these on your feet." The Scotsman flung me a pair of sealskin boots.

My feet quickly warmed in the thick inner fur of the boots.

"Where are you taking me?"

"Not much further." Angus turned to face forward into the wind. But before he did so, he said, "I wouldn't advise trying to escape overboard, lass. You wouldn't last two minutes in this water. It's barely a degree or two above the freezing level."

And even if I were to survive the frigid water, I could see there was no place to land. We were pounding through choppy waves along one of the most inhospitable shores I'd ever seen. Rough, jagged cliffs plunged straight down to the water, where breakers tossed ice blocks against stubs of broken rock. The mountains of the opposite shore were barely discernable across the vast expanse of whitecaps, which made me realize with a sinking feeling that we'd left the Tasilik fjord and were now in Cumberland Sound. Nowhere along the near shore did I see the potential for rescue. Not a single building, not even a tent watched our passage.

Although the sun was skirting the ridge of the distant shore, my watch indicated that it was a little after one in the morning. I'd been unconscious for almost three and a half hours. Enough time to travel a fair distance, particularly at the speed we were going. But surely in this light, someone had seen us leave Tasilik? What about those *boule* players? I could only hope that someone had seen me lying in the bottom of the boat and alerted the police.

But the softness of the sealskin against my face made me realize why Angus had replaced my own jacket with this Inuit garment, and it had nothing to do with warmth. No one would have paid attention to a prone Inuk woman, particularly after Johnnie's funeral feast, where despite being illegal, alcohol would've no doubt been available to the most determined.

I also realized I had another worry.

"Where's Apphia?" I called out above the noise of the wind and the engines.

Either he hadn't heard me or chose to ignore my question, for Angus continued to work on a piece of rope that had become entangled. Giving up in frustration, he pulled out a knife from his pocket and cut it. I froze when I realized what kind of knife it was. An *ulu!* Terrified that I was looking at the one that had killed Johnnie, I stepped backwards, wanting to put as much distance as possible between Angus and me.

At that point the boat suddenly veered towards shore, causing me to lose my balance. I managed to get myself upright in time to see us heading straight towards a wall of impenetrable rock. As we drew nearer, I realized there was a gap, partially concealed by a bulge in the wall and a rock fall. With the engines still on full throttle the pilot expertly drove the boat on a surge of water through the gap, narrowly missing several sharp rocks at the entrance, and immediately cut the engines.

Forty-Six

We entered a long, fjord-like bay, locked in by towering cliffs. At the far end, the cliffs gave way to a high valley, where I could make out the shimmer of a river cascading down a steep slope. While the rock face on the left side of the bay dropped straight to the water, on the right it stopped at a grassy plateau, which sloped down to a narrow stone beach, bordered by the mud flats of a low tide. A curious collection of low wooden buildings were scattered over the plateau. Below them a couple of white circular tents were anchored to large rocks on the near end of the beach. A short distance away, a group of children played beside several women, who were cutting up what looked to be seal carcasses. A piece of clothing fluttered on a tent guy line. A couple of ravens squabbled over a piece of meat. Despite the aura of innocence, I was afraid that this bay was about to become my prison.

The boat pulled up beside a rudimentary stone pier. While Angus held it steady with an oar, he ordered me to jump, and jump I did, almost turning my ankle as I scrambled up the rocks. I could hear Angus's grunts and heavy breathing as he stumbled up behind me. Not wanting to get within striking distance of the old man, I made no attempt to help as he struggled to maintain his balance.

Instead I held my breath and watched, hoping he'd fall into the frigid water. But when it looked as if it wasn't going to happen, I asked, "Why have you brought me here?"

"In due time," he rasped between pants and directed me to walk towards the beach.

A pack of dogs tied up beyond the tents suddenly howled as a man approached them with a bucket and starting flinging chunks of bloodied meat.

Worried he could use it against me, I tried to hide my growing fear as I watched these dogs pounce with the wild savagery of wolves

Feeding time," Angus laughed. "I advise you to stay well away from that end of the beach, otherwise…" He parodied a Frenchman's shrug.

"You don't need to threaten me. Just tell me why you've kidnapped me," I shot back. "If you're looking for money, tell me how much, and my mother will pay."

I said this last with more confidence than I felt. Although I was fairly certain Mother would part with a reasonable amount, I wasn't entirely sure that she would hand over a ransom in the millions.

"You honestly think I'm after your family's money?"

"I can't think of any other reason for taking me." I could think of another, but I wanted him to raise it, not me. Besides, it was hardly a reason for kidnapping me.

Rather than answering, he turned his head towards the echoing sound of a motorboat that had just come through the gap. As it drew closer, I recognized the freighter canoe that had been lying on the beach beside Angus's boat. I could make out three people. Although the boat was too far away for me to be sure, I thought the black-haired woman steering the boat might be Angus's daughter. But at the sight of the other two women, the shock of betrayal took over my fear. One had red hair, and so did the other.

"Apphia is involved, isn't she?" I thought of the drawings, the one in his house and the stolen one lying on the floor of Whale House. "This business with the drawings is one big con, isn't it? Apphia has no connection to my father. The two of you hatched this scheme to go after my family's money."

But even as I said it, I didn't want to believe that Apphia was a part of it. Her sisterly embrace had seemed too genuine. And I didn't want to let go of the hope that Father had survived.

The woman steering the boat was indeed Ooleepeeka. Another familiar figure sat in the middle of the boat, a woman I almost didn't recognize because of the red hair. But when her rhinestone glasses flashed in the light, I knew her—Mary Goresky, wearing a red wig with strands of white hair leaking out. Towards the bow sat Apphia wearing the white *amauti* from the funeral with her baby sound asleep in the hood and a very angry scowl on her face.

When I saw the way Mary forced Suula's daughter off the boat and up the side of the pier with a prodding rifle, I realized with relief that I was wrong. Apphia had nothing to do with Angus and his schemes. She'd been kidnapped too.

Apphia and her baby had no sooner been put ashore than Mary and Ooleepeeka took off in the freighter canoe, followed closely by the fiberglass motorboat. It was only as the two boats vanished through the gap that I realized the significance of the red jacket Mary was wearing. It was mine! It didn't take me long to jump to the next conclusion.

"You had the people in Tasilik think Apphia and I were leaving on the same boat. Since most know of our connection, no one would think it unusual."

"Most astute of you, lass."

"So maybe no one raised an alarm when they saw us leave, but when we don't come back, they will."

"No," Apphia said, her shoulders slumped in resignation. "They think we go to Naujalik, my camp."

"But I know my brother-in-law. He'll send the police out to check when I don't return in a day or two."

"And when they do, they'll find no one there," Angus replied smugly. "Instead they'll find Apphia's overturned boat caught in some rocks along the way."

"So that's what your daughter and Mary are doing. Making it look as if Apphia and I have drowned in a boating accident. But if I'm assumed dead, you won't get very far with your ransom demand."

"No, I won't, will I?" he replied succinctly, while the tone of his voice left me in little doubt as to our fate.

But surely neither of us could be a threat to him? What had we done to make him want to kill us?

"This about other kind of money," Apphia said more as a statement than a question. "Pictures."

"You're talking about the forgeries, aren't you, Apphia? The ones Angus is responsible for and your brother was involved in."

While Apphia's face expressed dejected agreement, Angus chose to ignore me, though I did notice he didn't deny the allegations either.

"Now, now lassies, enough talk. Let's go have a cuppa, shall we?"

Gripping each other's hand for encouragement, we followed the old man up a dirt path to the plateau, where a shack made from assorted wood planking leaned against a rusty oil tank. Further up the grassy slope stood two long, narrow structures made from what appeared to be canvas over plywood. They too had their requisite oil tanks.

"Excuse my bad manners," Angus said. "I forgot to welcome you lassies to Qamanaarjuaq, the summer camp of my wife's family." Angus flung out his arms as if to embrace the bay and its surrounding heights. "And for your benefit, Meg, it means 'the place where fish gather', for as Apphia well knows, that is an Arctic char river." He pointed to the river at the end of the bay.

"Like salmon, Arctic char spawn in the mouths of rivers. They like the near freezing waters of the Arctic and will spend the first years of their lives in the freshwater lakes that feed these rivers. Such a lake exists at the top of this valley. In late summer, the waters of this bay are thick with their red bodies. This is why my wife's family for countless generations has chosen this place for their camp."

He continued walking towards the shack's door, then

turned back towards us. "If you have any thoughts of being rescued, you can forget them. Apphia can tell you that the police will have no knowledge of this place. It is the kind of place that Inuit keep to themselves, much like Apphia's precious Naujalik, isn't that so, Apphia?"

She nodded bleakly.

"And as you have no doubt noticed, the entrance is somewhat hidden. So don't expect your Mounties to come chargin' through the gap to your rescue."

He started to push the door open, then stopped. "And if you are thinking of trying to escape, be my guest. You wouldn't survive a week on the land. In fact, it would save me having to do the dirty deed." He laughed and stepped across the threshold into the darkness beyond.

Forty-Seven

With the threat of death hanging over Apphia and me, I felt like I was in a time warp as we sat cross-legged on a polar bear skin in Angus's one-room shack genteelly sipping tea and eating Scottish oatmeal cookies. Despite light sifting through the only window in the room and the glow from two stone seal oil lamps, I could barely make out Apphia's worried features and Angus's self-satisfied grin. Amazingly, her baby still slept, not the least aroused by his mother's plight, and his for that matter. But surely Angus wouldn't harm a baby...

As my eyes adjusted to the darkness, I realized the sealskins covering the walls were the source of the room's gloominess. I took this to be an Inuit form of insulation, and it did seem to work for the room had a certain muffled coziness about it, despite an oil-burning stove standing cold in the corner.

Although it was close to four in the morning, I was too frightened to be tired. Nevertheless, I drank copious amounts of tea to ensure I stayed awake, fearful of what might happen if I did fall asleep.

Angus, sitting on the room's only chair, did all the talking, waxing eloquent on the many innovations he'd brought to his wife's family camp, while at the same time enabling them to retain much of their traditional lifestyle. In fact, while we'd waited for his sister-in-law to boil up the water for the tea on a Coleman stove, Angus had stepped behind a curtain at one end of the room. Within minutes he reappeared after replacing his jeans with sealskin trousers, but I did notice that he hadn't gone so far as to get rid of the ascot peaking out from the neck of his sealskin parka. Patting his round paunch, he said he liked the freedom of the relaxed fit of Inuit clothing.

Whenever I tried to broach the reason for our kidnapping, he deflected it with a "later". After several tries I gave up and concentrated on learning as much about our surroundings as I could. I noticed Apphia was doing likewise as she peered around the sparsely furnished room and out its only window. At one point I noticed several boats being hauled up onto the beach and wondered about them as a means of escape. But when a short while later the dogs were brought over and staked around them, I quickly dismissed that idea.

I also discovered the practicalities of the *amauti*'s large hood when Apphia's baby finally woke up and demanded his food. Without removing him from the warmth of the hood, she merely twisted the garment around her until he was able to comfortably nurse. Amidst the loud smacking of his feeding, we continued sipping our tea.

Finally I heard tramping outside and voices. The door swung open to reveal Mary and Ooleepeeka and the rifle.

"It's done," Mary announced while Ooleepeeka propped the gun against the wall.

Mary no longer wore the red wig or my jacket. However, the jacket she now wore sent my fear into free fall.

"We left the boat near the island you suggested, Dad. And watched it smash against the rocks." Ooleepeeka glanced hopefully at her father, as though seeking his approval.

And she received it with a gentle pat on the back as she dropped her plump body down onto the floor next to his chair.

"You hurt my boat!" Apphia cried out. "I need my boat."

"Not any more," quipped Mary, who'd remained standing.

"Why you do this?" Apphia turned pleading eyes towards Angus.

"You know why," he replied succinctly.

"I know nothing."

"Of course you do, lass. Your brother told you."

Her silence was answer enough.

"Shall we show you what Johnnie told you?"

She remained stonily still.

Angus hauled himself up from his chair. "Come, Meg, I want to show you our little operation."

"You kill my brother," Apphia whispered.

"I thought so too, but he didn't." I turned around to Mary. "You did!"

Mary pursed her lips, her eyes daring me to continue.

I pointed at her turquoise jacket, almost an exact shade of Arctic blue ice. "You were the person I saw in the boat leaving Johnnie's beach, weren't you?"

She lit a cigarillo.

"You killed him because he knew all about your forgery ring," I continued, with little thought for the consequences. I figured at this point it didn't matter.

"Business actually, quite a prosperous one, isna that right, Mary?" Angus answered.

"And you stole his computer because it contained information about your activities."

"My, my, you have been doing your homework, haven't you, lass?" he continued. "Actually, he stole the data from us, from Mary's computer to be precise. After he threatened to go to the police, we couldna let him live any longer."

"He had it with him on the plane, didn't he? Probably on a memory stick," I said.

Mary flicked a sculpted lock of white hair from her face.

"No wonder he left the airport so quickly, after seeing you on the plane."

"He forced me to do it. The stupid man wouldn't listen to reason."

I thought for a moment I saw regret in her eyes before they turned to ice.

"Come this way, lassies," Angus interjected. "I want to

show you our little operation. I'm quite proud of it."

At first Apphia refused to come, but when I held out my hand and whispered, "It might help us find a way to escape," she placed her small rough hand into mine and followed.

As she stepped onto the grass, her baby whimpered. She stopped and lifted her little boy out of her hood and held his squirming body above the ground. The poor child wore nothing on his bare bottom. But as he proceeded to let out a stream, I realized why. When he was finished, she neatly tucked him back into his warm furry bed.

With his daughter pulling up the rear with the rifle, Angus led us to one of the strange, almost tent-like structures made from plywood. With its white canvas covering held down by a line of large stones, it looked as if it would blow away with the first strong gust of wind. Although there were no windows, I could see a couple of skylights in the roof, on either side of a chimney pipe. As we drew closer, I thought I heard a low humming noise coming from beyond the building, its modern sound an intrusion into the weighted stillness of this prehistoric land.

At a rough wooden table near the entrance, a man was carving into a flat slab of greyish-green stone with what looked to be an artist's knife. He was carefully etching an outline of a picture that had been drawn onto the stone's smooth surface, a picture that seemed vaguely familiar.

"Recognize it?" Angus pointed to the drawing.

I tried to remember where I'd previously seen this drawing of quarrelling geese. Then bingo.

"I don't know the artist's name, but my father had a print just like this in his collection."

"You have a good memory."

"But that picture has to be almost forty years old, if not older."

"Forty-one years, to be precise. Now that the artist has been dead for a good ten years, its value has risen sufficiently to start spreading a few more onto the market. Come inside." He held the door open.

With Apphia following on my heels, I stepped inside and gasped. I'd expected a primitive interior, much like that of the shack. Instead, we'd entered into the world of a modern art studio.

Angus smiled broadly. "Fooled you, didn't I? For that very reason I decided to house my little business operation in these primitive Inuit buildings. If someone does happen to make their way into our bay, they'd just assume this is nothing but a traditional Inuit camp."

Although daylight was coming through the skylights, the majority of the light came from several bright overhead lights strung along the rafters.

Amazed, I asked, "Where do you get the electricity from?"

"We have a couple of generators concealed out back." The source of the humming noise. "We only run them for the lighting and our electric tools." He pointed to a large metal object with various arms and rollers. "The printing press, however, is manually powered."

At a table, a man was rolling green ink onto a stone slab with a drawing of an owl in full feather. Behind him hung several prints of this same bird, while a little further along on the wall behind another table hung prints of the quarrelling geese.

Noticing my gaze, Angus said, "Rejects. Not close enough to the original, so I'm having Iyola make another printing block. Here, judge for yourself."

From a shelf, he pulled out a print sandwiched between sheets of tissue paper. Carefully laying it on the table, he pulled back the tissue to reveal the geese, complete with artist syllabics, date and edition number. Then removing one of the prints from the wall, he laid it beside what was clearly the original.

Although I couldn't readily discern any differences other than perhaps a slight variation in the colour of the red ink,

Apphia immediately identified several lines in the feathers that were ever so slightly off from the original.

"Johnnie no do this," she exclaimed haughtily.

"Yes, you do have your family's artistic eye, don't you, lass? And you're right. He would've cut it perfectly the first time around. My best carver. Pity he had to go all righteous on me."

"It bad," she shot back. "Artist no get money."

"Yes, that did bother him, when he finally realized that the original artists or their families wouldna receive a penny. But as I tried to explain, they'd already been well paid for their efforts. Besides, chances were they'd gamble away their money or drink it."

Apphia shot him an angry glare. "Inuit buy many things. Boats, guns, bullets, snow machines."

Angus turned to me and shrugged as if to say, "See, what did I tell you?"

"As if your precious orchids are any better," I snapped back.

Angus's only response was a chuckle.

Running my eyes over the counterfeit geese, I thought of another forgery, just as expertly done. "You were behind the fake *Mystical Owl*, weren't you?"

"Yes, I was quite proud of that particular copy. It was my first attempt. Quite successful, wasn't it? But I'm afraid I made a mistake in the handlin' of that particular sale. I used Mary as my art expert for authenticity verification. You see, we'd gotten to know each other quite well when she did her doctoral research on Inuit art at the James Lake Co-op. I realized we were of like mind."

He glanced at the art director, who appeared more bored than interested in the recounting of their crimes.

"Unfortunately, this was early on in my art dealings. I hadn't appreciated how critical the term 'expert' was in the sale of such a valued piece of art. I thought Mary with her newly minted doctorate would do just fine. But the buyer wanted a more experienced opinion."

"And he went to Carter Davis, didn't he?"

"So that's how you know about the *Mystical Owl* fake. I was wonderin'."

"I saw it hanging on his wall."

"Pity he'd kept it. I hadna realized until he called me out of the blue a couple of months ago. We hadn't talked in years. He'd suddenly remembered something a mutual friend had told him about the fake. Although he didna connect me to it, I was worried he eventually would."

"You killed him. How could you?" I cried out in outrage.

He and Mary exchanged glances.

"No, you had him killed," I corrected. "Mary did it."

"It was an accident." Mary who'd been slouching against a wall, straightened up. "Gus sent me to see if I could point him in another direction, but like Johnnie, Carter also had a stubborn streak. He couldn't be persuaded. In fact, he started accusing me. I guess he'd finally connected all the dots. Anyway, when he threatened to expose my involvement, I knew I had to do something. I have too good a thing going for me at the museum. We happened to be standing in the hall at the time, right by the basement door. It was a simple matter of opening the door. And well…he slipped." She paused. "I didn't mean to kill him. I was sorry. I rather liked the old man."

"So you left him there to die all alone on the cold basement floor."

"He was already dead."

"And took the *Mystical Owl* with you."

"I was worried his heirs would have his collection evaluated and discover the forgery." She glanced back at her partner. "Besides, I thought we could make a good profit."

I turned to Angus. "You sold my father the forgeries that were found in his collection, didn't you?"

He shook his head. "No, he didn't buy them from me."

"Surely you're not suggesting that he was a part of your forgery dealings. That he was your distributor."

"You can rest easy. Your lilywhite father had nothing to do with it. It was your uncle who was my silent partner. He was the one that added the forgeries to your father's collection."

"Uncle Harold?"

"You sound surprised."

"I don't believe you. He had enough money of his own without getting involved in criminal activities."

"I think for him it was a lark, a titillating excursion into the dark side. He saw it as a way to get back at your father."

"What do you mean?"

"Why, your father was the eldest son, with all that it implies. Plus he had your mother, a most charming lady, a lady he didn't treat with the proper respect due her."

"You don't know what you're talking about."

"But I do. I was the one who introduced Sutton to his Inuit mistress."

"Are you talking about Suula Nanuqtuaq?" I asked.

At the mention of her mother's name, Apphia eyes sparked with interest.

"Not at all. I know nothing about this Suula. In fact, I'm hoping Apphia can enlighten us. No, I'm referrin' to my wife's niece, Geeta, a delightful little nymph. Pity their son died."

"I don't believe any of this," I said, even though I had a nagging suspicion that it could be true.

I remembered a Christmas Eve when I was about eight. We were putting the decorations on the tree when Father suddenly announced he had to fly up north next day, Christmas Day. Mother was so angry, she lost her normal self-control and began shouting that if he left, he might as well not return home. There were more angry words about sluts and wandering dicks, which at the time

I didn't understand. Even my older sister didn't know. It was only later, long after Father's plane disappeared, that I remembered the words and finally understood what they'd meant. As I recalled, Father stayed, but left early in the new year. On that occasion, he didn't return to Toronto until the tulips were in bloom.

"It doesn't really matter if you believe it or not, lass," Angus retorted. "Harold's dead, and I'm sure you wouldna want to sully your mother's memory of him. Besides, after the plane went missing, he wanted out, so I paid him the money he'd loaned me to help get the enterprise started and left those fakes with him to do with as he saw fit."

I had little choice but to agree. It was best to leave it alone. However, it disturbed me that a man I'd come to love almost like a father should have hated his brother so much that he'd wanted to ruin him.

Forty-Eight

I knew nothing about your forgeries." That wasn't exactly true, since I'd had my suspicions, but he wouldn't know that. "So why kidnap me, if not for money?"

"Simple. It's all about the pictures." Angus pulled the front of his parka down where it had bunched up over his stomach.

"What pictures?" I asked, although by now I had a fairly good idea.

"The ones Apphia sent you, of course."

I turned to the woman who I was coming to believe was my sister. "Is this true? You sent them?"

Her body tensed. "Yes. I want you come." She smiled. "And you here."

"But why didn't you include your name or address?"

A look of puzzlement passed over her face. "I put Naujalik on pictures. You come to camp."

I supposed in Apphia's small world, where her camp was the centre of her universe, she assumed everyone knew the location of Naujalik. "Did you tell your brother about the letters?"

"Johnnie say no. Say it bring trouble."

And it certainly had. In spades.

I took a deep breath. The time had finally arrived for me to learn the truth no matter how difficult. "Why did you want me to come?"

She glanced nervously at Angus. "Not here."

"Now is as good a time as any, lass," Angus answered. "Yes, let us know why you wanted Meg to come to Baffin."

She bit her lower lip but remained silent.

"It's about your father, isn't it?" he continued. "The one that gave you that marvellous red hair. Just like Meg's, eh?"

He had the nerve to brush his hand over my frizzy curls. Slapping his hand away, I moved beyond his reach.

I caught a flicker of anguish mixed with uncertainty in Apphia's eyes as she glanced at me before bowing her head in silence. I moved back beside her and put my arm around her to let her know it was okay. I'd be happy to have her as my sister.

"It doesna matter, lass, if you tell us or no. The pictures will. Ooleepeeka, get them, will you? I left them in the house."

While Apphia and I waited side-by-side in anxious silence, Angus sat down in a chair with a deep sigh. From a shelf Mary removed what looked to be a picture wrapped in tissue paper with a piece of tape holding it closed. She casually removed an *ulu* from her pocket and slit the tape. The minute she laid the half-moon shaped knife on the table I shivered with the realization that this was the weapon that had killed Johnnie.

She must've felt my eyes watching her, for she hastily slipped the knife back into her pocket before lapsing into studied indifference.

At that point Angus's daughter returned with a leather art portfolio.

"Lay them on the table," he said with a wave of his hand.

As Ooleepeeka proceeded to place the contents one after another in their order, I felt a growing outrage. The only print missing was the one the cops had. By the time she laid down the seventh and last one in the series, I couldn't keep quiet any longer.

"You stole the prints from my room!" I shouted at Angus.

"Sorry, you're wrong again, my dear. This time it was my daughter. She has a good friend at the hotel who gave her a duplicate keycard."

"Of course. How could I be so stupid to think you would deign to dirty to your fingers," I snapped back. "And needless to say, Mary stole this one." I pointed to the first picture in the series, the one with the hunter on his own without the plane, the one that I'd given Carter.

At that moment a loud thwumping noise suddenly reverberated through the walls. It took me less than a second to realize what it was. By that time, so had Angus.

"Hold them!" he shouted as I raced out the back door after the helicopter. Mary grabbed my arm and yanked me back inside, but I was in time to see Apphia standing poised on the front doorstep, while behind her Ooleepeeka held her baby in the air and shouted at her in Inuktitut. I didn't need a translator to know that Angus's daughter was threatening harm to the son if the mother dared go outside.

The baby started to whimper, a mournful sound that very quickly became a lusty cry of outrage. The sound of the helicopter faded. Casting a resigned look in my direction, Apphia returned to her baby and gently rocked him until he quieted. At the same time, Ooleepeeka retrieved the rifle from where it had been propped against the wall and pointed it at us as an extra incentive to ensure we behaved.

"Don't get your hopes up, lassies." Angus said, with a smug grin. "They won't be back. If the RCMP thought this quiet Inuit camp could help them, they would've landed."

I had a sinking feeling that he was right. Still it was encouraging to know that the search for us had begun. Hopefully it would continue along this section of Cumberland Sound. Perhaps if there was some dramatic way we could signal our presence…

I thought of the building's flimsy wooden walls. A blazing fire would certainly attract attention. This was the one time I wished I were a smoker and carried the means to

317

start one. Then I remembered the seal-oil lamp. There had to be matches in the main house.

"Now, lassies, back to the pictures. Apphia, I want you to tell me who drew them."

"*Anaana*. See name Suula here." She pointed to the syllabics along the edge of the four prints she'd sent Mother, including the one I'd scotch-taped together. She raised curious eyebrows at the drawing I'd found in Harold's belongings, no doubt anxious to know where that one had come from.

But she froze when she reached the last drawing, the one with the little girl with red hair that I'd seen at Angus's house. It was the only drawing without an artist chop.

She turned accusing eyes on Mary and said, "This Johnnie picture. You took it."

"I couldn't leave it behind." Mary shook her head. "When I saw it hanging in his workshop I knew it was a match to the pictures Meg had shown me at the gallery, pictures that were supposed to have been drawn by your mother. But I didn't believe it when I first saw them and I certainly don't now. So tell us, who's the real artist?"

With the six of them lying side-by-side, it was easy to see that the same artistic hand had drawn the simple but highly skilled lines.

"She's right, Apphia," Angus said. "Your mother was a good artist, but she couldna draw people as good as this. There is a three-dimensional quality about them. So who drew them? And don't tell us your brother did."

She hesitated, glancing at me as if seeking my approval. "*Ataataga*," she whispered.

"Your father," Angus said.

Apphia nodded. "*Anaana*." She paused as if searching for the right English word. "Mother tell me no tell."

"Why not?"

"Is bad."

"Why? Because he didna want anyone to know he had

survived the plane crash? That is him parachuting from the plane, isn't it?"

She nodded, her eyes wide with fear.

"What was his name?"

I braced myself.

She glanced in my direction and smiled, almost apologetically. "Sutton Harris."

At last I knew. My father had survived the plane crash. But…but instead of returning home to us, his family, he had stayed and fathered another family. As much as I wanted to rejoice in his survival, I found it difficult. I couldn't help but feel betrayed.

"Where is he?" I asked as nonchalantly as I could. "Is he still alive?"

She seemed to search for the words in English then spoke to Angus in Inuktitut.

"The man's dead. Apparently he died while she was a lass."

Casting an apologetic glance towards me, as though embarrassed by not being able to continue in English, she spoke again to Angus, and the two of them conversed for several minutes.

Finally, Angus turned to me. "She says that he was always sick. He couldna walk properly. Couldna go hunting. Her mother said it was from the injuries he received when he landed on the ice. Her mother and grandfather saw his fall from the plane and knew he was badly hurt. But he wouldna let them take him to the nurse in Tasilik. So her grandmother, who was familiar with traditional Inuit medicine, healed him as best she could. Apphia thinks she was about eight years old when he died."

Tears spilled from her eyes. He must have been a good father…as he'd been to me.

"She also says that her father was a great artist. He taught her mother how to draw and to make pictures from the supplies her grandfather would bring back from his trips to Tasilik."

Angus picked up the picture of the falling plane. "The minute my daughter showed me these pictures, I knew the artist could only be one person. And that man is not Sutton Harris."

"But he has to be," I insisted. "Apphia inherited her hair colour from him."

Apphia nodded vigorously. "He say his name Sutton Harris. He tell me he have two daughter in south, like me and Margee." She pointed to herself. "*Ataataga,* my father." And then pointed to me. "Your father."

"Sorry, lass, not the case. Your father wasn't the only red-haired man on that plane."

"Are you saying the pilot also had red hair?" I asked.

"No, it was the third man."

"But he was an Inuk." I thought of the missing artist. "That Inuk was Joly Quliik, wasn't it?"

"Not a bad guess. But I'm afraid you aren't entirely correct." Angus's smile took on the self-righteous satisfaction of the Cheshire Cat.

"No, the man was very much a *qallunaat.* I should know. I put him on that plane."

Forty-Nine

Crossing his arms over his chest, Angus settled back into his chair and gloated. His eyes flitted from me to Apphia and back again. Even Mary appeared surprised by his admission, as her cigarillo dropped forgotten from her lips. But his daughter had known. She leaned back on her heels, and like her father, watched for our reaction.

"Why?" I asked.

"Because your father had discovered our dirty little secret and was on his way to the Iqaluit police with some rather incriminating evidence I'd stupidly left on my desk."

"Father found out about your forgery operation from Crazy Russkie, didn't he?"

"That's what happens when you trust a drunk with your secrets. I'd foolishly sent the man to Iqaluit to pick up something for me. The fool hadn't seen a bar in so long, he almost drank it dry. Anyway, he became what all Russians become when they're in their cups, maudlin. Just my luck, your father happened to be sittin' next to him.

"I don't think Sergei gave away all my secrets, at least he insisted he hadn't, but put together with what your father already knew from Carter Davis, it was enough for Sutton to put two and two together and come up with me. After sniffing a bit more around Frobisher Bay, he found his way to James Lake and confronted me."

Like Father, like daughter, I thought. I wasn't sure how many times I'd put myself into a similar precarious situation with little thought to the danger it might bring. Like now. And all because I was too intent on seeking out the truth.

321

"I really thought I'd convinced him that I was an honourable man," Angus continued. "At least he acted all apologetic when he left my house. Fortunately for me, I discovered the missing papers before his plane took off. Papers, by the way, which itemized several of my less-than-legal transactions. I had no choice but to send my man after him to stop him."

"You sent this man to kill him, didn't you?" I said. "But he shot the pilot by mistake and in so doing endangered his own life."

"Ah, so that's what happened. I've always wondered…" Angus paused. "But perhaps killing the pilot wasn't a mistake. Remember, he parachuted out of the plane. I'd hazard once the plane began its downward spiral after the pilot's death, there wouldna been sufficient time to put on a parachute."

"Who was he?" I interjected, although I was certain I knew.

But ignoring my question, Angus continued his discourse. He appeared to be quite enjoying himself. "No, lass, I wouldna be at all surprised if he wasn't already wearing the parachute. Perhaps he tried to reason with your father to hand over the incriminatin' papers, but Sutton would refuse, as I knew he would. He did have this stubborn streak of a man of principle about him. My man would have no choice but to kill him and the pilot too."

"But it wouldn't make sense unless he knew how to fly," I said.

"Ah, but lass, remember the plane was off course. I'm willin' to wager he directed the pilot to fly to a place where he knew he could count on rescue. Perhaps he already knew Suula. Perhaps he knew where her family was likely to be found. So when he strapped on that parachute and jumped out of that plane, he knew he would be rescued."

It was all I could do not to try to wash the triumphant grin off the old man's face. From the look of outrage on

Apphia's face, I could tell she was having similar thoughts. But to make it doubly worse for her, she was having to deal with his accusation that her father had been a killer.

"You tell lies," she said. "My father no kill."

"Ah, but he did, my dear. Meg has already mentioned that the pilot was shot, so the police must've found a bullet in his remains. There was only one person on that plane who had reason to shoot him. The man I sent, your father."

"But it's all conjecture on your part," I said. "I don't believe he would intentionally shoot the pilot. No one would risk their own life like that. I think it's more likely that my father tried to get the gun away from the man, and it accidentally went off, killing the pilot. Afterwards the plane glided for a while. Maybe the man or my father attempted to fly it. That's why it ended so far off course.

"As for who parachuted out of the plane, it could just as easily have been my father. I'm sure there was more than one parachute on the plane." I glanced at Apphia, who looked at me through my father's grey-blue eyes. "I think the man who fathered Apphia was who he said he was, Sutton Harris."

Suddenly loud shouts erupted beyond the plywood walls. Ooleepeeka raced outside. Within seconds she returned, her face twisted in alarm. "The police are here!"

Through the open door, I could see at least five boats converging on the beach. All contained uniformed police with rifles pointing at the growing throng of people. And then I saw another sight that raised my hopes even further. A helicopter was breasting the ridge across the bay, followed by a floatplane with RCMP emblazoned along the side.

So much for this place being unknown to the police, I thought with no minimal amount of glee.

But before Apphia and I had a chance to race out through the open door, Mary had grabbed my arm and was dragging me kicking and yelling to the back of the building. Ooleepeeka clutched the screaming Apphia with one hand

and the rifle in the other. Angus no longer sat in his chair. Instead, he was snatching the counterfeit copies of art from the walls and throwing them into a concealed hole in the floor, while the printer smashed the stone block with a hammer. The last thing I saw before being dragged out the back door was Angus's sister-in-law placing Apphia's baby in the hood of a young Inuk woman.

Outside, I managed to wrestle my way free, but as I rounded the corner of the building intent on running to the beach, I ran smack into a man, who circled his arms around me and slung me over his shoulders as if I were a dead seal. That's all I remember, apart from a cloth being placed over my face with the same medicinal smell as the cloth that had started this nightmare.

*   *   *

I awoke shivering, feeling nauseous and as if my body had been sat on by a walrus. I couldn't move. My arms were wrenched behind my back and my feet tied together. I could barely breathe through the cloth tied around my mouth. I lay on my side on cold, hard stone. Beside me lay Apphia, still unconscious and similarly shackled.

We appeared to be inside a round stone building almost igloo-like with a low dome ceiling. A splash of brightness marked what must be the entrance, through which not even a tiny child could walk upright. Daylight seeped through the many cracks in the rows of irregular stone, providing enough light in the frigid prison.

Thank goodness I still wore the sealskin parka. At least my upper body felt warm, although my jean-covered legs could feel the dank coldness of the stone floor seeping through. With my watch behind my back, I had no idea how much time had passed since the police had come, but my throat was parched, my stomach very empty, so I must've lain here unconscious for several hours.

I strained to hear sounds that would tell me the police were still around, but I heard only a deathly silence. Nothing seemed to move. Not even the wind. It was almost as if Apphia and I were the only ones left alive in this nether world.

Apphia groaned. As I waited for her to wake up, I pondered our precarious situation. I debated making noise to let the police know where we were, but I decided against it. If the police had already left, my cries would only alert Angus. I didn't want to deal with him until I'd had a chance to figure out a way out of this mess.

But escape was purely wishful thinking. My hands were clamped so tightly behind my back, I couldn't move them. They were numb. Nor did it seem likely I would be able to work the bindings loose, not if I'd been tied up with the same plastic shackles that bound Apphia's wrists.

On the plus side, if there was one, at least the two of us were alive.

Apphia groaned again. I did the best I could to make noise through the gag to let her know I was there, but she continued to sleep.

After a number of painful gyrations, I managed to right myself into a sitting position and was able to inch my way over the freezing floor to a gap in the stone wall, but the view was discouraging. All I could see was the bottom of a lichen-covered rock wall about ten or so metres away. I did, however, catch a whiff of salty sea air, which meant we were still close to water.

Incredibly, Angus had managed to spirit us away, even though the camp was swarming with police. I assumed we were somewhere on the plateau but out of sight of Angus's camp, otherwise surely the police would've found us. But it was impossible to tell how far away we were. Were we far enough to avoid detection should we figure out a way to escape? Or, more worrisome, did Angus intend to leave us here to die?

Apphia groaned again and moved.

I made a muffled call to her again.

She twisted her body around to face me and opened her eyes. She struggled to speak through her gag. From the questioning fear in her eyes, I felt certain she was asking about her baby. I wished I could tell her that he was probably safe, although not with the police. I was fairly confident that Angus would've passed him off as the child of that young woman. Easy enough to do, since most babies look alike, particularly to less discerning men.

Instead, I could only grunt and nod my head in the hopes of transmitting the message that he was okay.

Apphia twisted herself into a sitting position and surveyed our stone jail. She shook her head as if to say that our situation was bad, with which I could only agree. Worse than bad.

At that point, I caught the sound of footsteps at the entrance. I tensed and waited for Angus to appear. Instead, his sister-in-law crawled through the low, tunnel entrance. I wasn't sure whether this was a good sign or a bad.

Speaking in Inuktitut to Apphia, she dropped a bag on the ground.

"Food," she said in English then removed our gags.

Perhaps a good sign. I took a great gulp of air as I felt life return to my lips, my jaw.

She spoke further to Apphia in Inuktitut, who translated. "She say RCMP go. We make lot of noise, no one hear. Hands and feet stay like this. We sleep. She bring food."

The woman brought out a container of what appeared to be two different types of raw meat and laid it on a large piece of brown paper. She placed two giant plastic pop bottles with straws on the ground beside them. "Tea, fish, seal."

She said a few last words to Apphia, before crawling back outside. Within seconds, she returned with some polar bear skins and sealskins and laid them on the floor. Then with a final nod of goodbye, she left.

"She say baby okay. *Ujuruk,* sister daughter, look after baby." Nonetheless, tears seeped from Apphia's eyes.

I tried to comfort her as best I could by saying that Angus had no reason to harm an innocent child. We were the threat, not her son.

She nodded and said, "She good woman. I die, she baby mother."

"But we're not going to die. We're going to get out of this mess, rescue your baby and live happily ever afterwards." Yeah, just like they do in fairy tales.

But Apphia seemed to take my words to heart, for she nodded again and said, "Eat. We go."

Fifty

I have *ulu*." Apphia's eyes sparked with triumph. "In pocket."

I glanced at the almost imperceptible bulge of her pocket and started to turn myself around so I could try to reach it with my tied hands. But before I could, Angus, breathing heavily, grunted his way on hands and knees through our prison door. A rifle was slung across his back.

"I thought so. She didn't untie your hands, did she? And you canna eat without them." He pulled out a straight-edged Inuit knife. not the *ulu* I'd seen on the boat. With its carved bone handle, I wondered if this was the knife men traditionally used.

"I have Maurie here as a deterrent for your escapin'." He unslung the rifle and laid it on the ground within easy reach. "Now Apphia, hold out your hands while I cut you free."

The knife sliced through the plastic tie, as if it were butter. As she rubbed her wrists and hands to get the circulation back, he cut my shackles.

"But you don't need feet to eat, so I'm keepin' those ankle bracelets on."

"I want baby," Apphia demanded.

"Now, lass, there's no need to worry your pretty red head about him. He's in good hands. I had Elisapee bring you some choice food, so no point in lettin' it go to waste." He winced as he dropped his bulk onto a polar bear skin and moved the rifle closer.

While Apphia scooped up the raw seal meat as if it were filet mignon, and for her it probably was, I had difficulties dealing with its overpowering oily fish odour,

328

let alone actually placing a piece in my mouth. And yet I was starving.

Angus must've noticed my reluctance, for he said, "It takes some gettin' used to, lass. That's why I had Elisapee include Arctic char. Consider it sushi." He pointed to the red salmon-like chunks.

I gingerly sampled one. As much as I hated to admit it, it was probably the best sushi I'd ever eaten. I devoured another. It was only when I'd almost had enough, that I started to wonder why Angus was being so generous, why he was bothering to feed us if he planned to kill us.

"Why are you keeping us?" I asked.

"You're mention of a ransom got me thinkin'. I figure your charming mother would be happy to provide a quantity of cash to see her dear daughter again."

"But I know all about your forgery operation."

"Them days are past. 'Tis only a matter of time before the police have enough evidence to charge me. So it wouldna really matter what you told them. No, it's time for me to leave the north and move onto another life, and for that I need cash."

"So what are you suggesting? Sending a ransom note to my mother?"

"Better yet. Send you. And to make sure you behave, I'll hold your sister and her child hostage."

I saw Apphia tense out of the corner of my eye. I tried to convey with a slight shake of my head that I wouldn't do anything to harm them. "Now you're calling her my sister. So you agree her father was Sutton Harris?"

"Let's face it, lass, we'll never know."

"But what about the pictures? You were so sure they were drawn by Joly Quliik."

"I still am, but your father knew enough of his style that I think he could've copied it."

"But why would he do that?"

"As a message to me."

"Why?"

"Because he knew the lie behind Joly Quliik."

"What do you mean?"

"Joly Quliik didn't exist. At least he didna exist as an Inuk. No, the real Joly Quliik was Sergei. That's what the bloody Russian revealed to your father. Our little scheme that had worked so beautifully. Not once did those art snobs suspect that their much-acclaimed Inuit artist was a white man. It was a magnificent deception that had brought me a nice tidy sum, and it all came to naught the second Sergei blurted it out to your father. You see why I had to stop Sutton."

"And the man you sent to stop him was Sergei himself?"

"Aye, lass. The damn fool came to me full of contrition. He knew he'd have to atone for his terrible mistake."

"And Sergei had red hair, just like my father." I tried to stifle a yawn and couldn't. My full stomach was making me sleepy.

"His colour wasn't quite as carroty red, but he was a redhead all the same. Perhaps it was that common bond that induced Sergei to confess."

I could see that Apphia was having difficulties in keeping awake too. "How do I know you will release Apphia and her child once you have the money?"

"I imagine the same way I know you'll get me the money without involving the police. Now I want you to put this plastic tie around Apphia's wrists, then I'll do yours. We'll finalize the details in the morning."

With his rifle pointed as an extra inducement, I snatched the long plastic tie from his hand and placed it around her wrists, trying to keep it as loose as possible without his noticing, but he pushed me aside and jerked it tight, which elicited a sharp cry from Apphia.

"Don't hurt her. If you do, I won't get you the money," I threatened hollowly, knowing if I didn't get the money, I'd be dealing with more than an injured Apphia.

I tried to position my wrists so that some space would

330

remain, but as he'd done with Apphia, he yanked the catch hard.

"Ouch," I cried as the sharp plastic bit into my skin.

"Sweet dreams, lassies." He chortled and lumbered back outside.

My last thought before I sank into sleep was that there was a very good reason why Angus had enticed us with food, and it wasn't because of our health. No, he had doctored it with a sleeping drug. But I was too dazed to worry about why.

* * *

When I awoke cramped and groaning, I was surprised to find myself still lying on the floor of the stone igloo. In my tortured dreams, I'd been convinced that the Scotsman had moved us far into the mountains to a hidden cave well out of range of the police. Instead I found myself burrowed into the pile of furs with Apphia's warmth beside me.

I also woke convinced that we needed to escape. The sooner the better.

It was obvious that Angus was just playing with me, like a killer whale with a seal. He might try to drug us again and this time move us elsewhere, like the cave of my dream, where he would leave us to die, someplace where it would be years if ever before anyone chanced upon our bones.

I nudged Apphia. "Wake up."

She groaned, speaking some words in Inuktitut, and struggled to get up.

"Apphia, we've gotta get out of here. But first we need to cut ourselves free."

Agreeing with a vigorous nod of her head, she answered. "*Ulu* very sharp. No touch."

Although I had to turn my back to her, she was able to direct my hands to her front pocket with little mishap. I reached my fingers in and was able to loop them around the cold bone of the handle and extract the knife with little difficulty. Unfortunately, with our backs towards each other the next step of cutting Apphia's tight shackle without slicing her wrist seemed pretty near impossible.

"I cut," Apphia volunteered, turning around and expertly grasping the *ulu* with her tied hands.

I gingerly presented my back to her and prayed that I'd only end up with cuts and not minus a finger or two, but before I had a chance to take a deep breath, my hands were free and I was shaking them to restore the circulation. I quickly cut the plastic tie from my ankles then freed Apphia.

But we'd barely had a chance to enjoy our newly won freedom when we heard footsteps at the entrance and Angus's sister-in-law thrust her head through. It happened so quickly that neither of us could pretend we were still tied. All we could do was smile innocently and hope she wouldn't notice. But she did.

"Good," she nodded, and much to our shocked amazement thrust Apphia's whimpering baby inside. While the young mother soothed and fed her child, the two women conversed in Inuktitut. With a last lingering look at the baby and words that sounded like "Good luck," Elisapee crawled back outside.

"We go," Apphia said. "She say Angus kill us. She no like."

I didn't feel any satisfaction learning my suspicions were correct, only heightened fear. We were locked in on all sides by unscalable cliff walls. The only possible exit from this bay was the river valley, and that hadn't looked an easy climb either. And even if we made it, how were two women and a baby without food going to walk the many kilometres over barren land to Tasilik and survive? We didn't even have a compass to point us in the right direction.

"Do you know of a nearby camp or community we can walk to instead of Tasilik?" I asked.

"We take boat."

"But someone will see us. And if they don't, the dogs guarding the boats will kill us."

332

"No problem. Elisapee say boat near river."

"But can we trust her? She might be leading us into a trap."

"Is okay. Nobody see."

She said these last words from outside our jail. When I crawled outside, I realized why. Our world had shrunk to less than a few metres before vanishing behind a wall of thick, impenetrable fog.

Fifty-One

Although I could hear voices and dogs barking, I thought they were far enough away for us to avoid detection, for the moment.

"We've got to get out of here before the fog clears," I whispered. "Which way to the boat?"

Apphia pointed in a direction away from the noise. Like blind men, we picked our way through the icy fog along a path of sorts that led up a fairly steep incline. Within seconds the mist closed around our prison, but not before I had a chance to notice that even if the police had come across it, they would've assumed it was only a pile of rocks and not an ancient stone igloo. They would never have thought for a moment that the women they sought lay drugged and shackled inside.

After several long, gasping minutes of climbing, we started traversing the incline, almost as if we were following a ridge. I found the opaqueness of the fog unnerving. I tried to follow as close behind Apphia as possible. If she moved beyond my line of sight, I knew I'd be lost. I had little sense of direction other than we were moving away from our prison, but it didn't seem to hamper Apphia. She seemed to be unerringly following a path.

"How do you know where you're going?" I whispered.

She pointed to a small pile of rocks. "Inukshuk."

I'd noticed them but had given them little thought, and while the rocks didn't exactly form the man-like shape I associated with the Inuit symbol, I could see there was a distinct shape to the rock pile. Within another few minutes, we came across another one.

By this time the sounds from the camp had been swallowed by an eerie muffled silence. Neither of us spoke, so intent were we on maintaining our footing on the rough, rock-strewn terrain. Occasionally our feet would sink ankle-deep into scattered patches of wet, mossy tundra, making walking even more precarious.

The land suddenly dipped. Unprepared, Apphia started sliding downwards on loose shale. I grabbed her sleeve. But her downward slide pulled me with her to the shattering sound of cascading rock. Within a few metres the slope levelled off and we came to a colliding stop that sent us sprawling to the ground with an even louder clatter. The baby began to cry. Apphia frantically tried to hush him as I peeled my ears for sounds of pursuit, but apart from the odd plunk of a stone landing and my pounding heart, the silence returned.

We rested a few anxious minutes to catch our breath, then resumed our journey, but where that journey headed, only Apphia knew.

At first I could only make out a low drone through the fog, but as we moved forward the sound increased, until I realized it was the noise of the river. Our path began to descend as the sound of rushing water grew louder, then I saw the river itself, cascading over the rocks as it made its way down the steep slope.

"I hope we don't have to cross this." I winced as a spray of freezing water hit my face.

Apphia shook her head. "Elisapee say boat down there." And she pointed below us.

We made our way carefully down the steep incline along the river's edge, stepping from rock to rock made slippery by the cold watery mist. It would've been a challenge in my hiking boots with their thick gripping tread. The smooth soles of the sealskin boots made it almost impossible. Without hiking poles or tree branches for support, Apphia and I had only each other to cling to. Using each other for stability, we picked our way downward.

Suddenly, Apphia stepped on a loose rock. She pitched sideways, and down she tumbled smacking her head on a rock.

Terrified, I knelt beside her. For a brief second she lay so still, I thought she was dead. Then she groaned.

"Apphia, are you okay?"

She moved her arm. "My baby?"

He lay nestled inside her hood against her body, which had protected him from the fall. He opened his eyes, smiled, then closed them again.

"He's still sleeping. Do you want me to take him out? It'll make it easier for you to get up."

"No. It okay."

Using my body for support, she struggled to stand up, but with a cry of pain sat down again. A trickle of blood seeped from the bump on the side of her brow where she'd struck the rock.

"Where does it hurt?"

She pointed to her ankle.

Shit. She must've sprained it, or worse, broken it.

"I'll take your boot off and check it out, okay?"

"Okay."

"It might hurt, so brace yourself."

She didn't flinch or make a sound as I pulled her sealskin boot off as gently as I could. But she did groan when I tried moving the swelling ankle.

Shit. If she can't walk…we're doomed.

"Look, Apphia, you should rest for a few minutes. Do you have anything we could wrap around it?"

I tried to think of anything I was wearing that could be used. But short of ripping a strip from my long johns, I had nothing. Apphia, however, thrust out a scarf, which I immediately immersed in the freezing cold river and wrapped it around her ankle to help keep down the swelling.

"I'm going to see how far away this boat is, then I'll be

back to get you, okay?"

She nodded. "Go to big water. If no find boat, go beside water." She pointed in the direction of where Angus's camp must lie.

Rather than risking a fall myself, I half-stepped, half-slid on my bottom as silently as I could down the remaining rocks. Fortunately it wasn't too much further down to the shore.

Worried Angus's sister-in-law had sent us into a trap, I waited at the water's edge, praying that the icy fog hid me from watching eyes. But it also blinded me, so I used my ears instead and strained to hear noises that didn't belong, but the river filled the fog with its roar.

The tide was in. It lapped against the high water mark. Although the mist still hung heavy and dense, I had the impression my visual world had grown by several metres, which prompted another worry. The fog was starting to lift. I had no time to waste.

I didn't see the promised boat. Hopefully that meant it lay only a few metres further along the shore. With my antenna on full alert, I inched my way very slowly in the direction Apphia had indicated, not knowing whether I'd stumble onto the boat or into an ambush. Every few metres, I stopped in an attempt to see what lay ahead and to listen. Once I felt confident enough that nothing menacing lurked beyond the fog, I would walk a few more metres. As I moved away from the sound of the river, I began to hear more distant noises, the cry of a seagull, the faint bark of a dog. I stiffened at a sudden shout, then relaxed a bit when I realized it came from somewhere far ahead of me.

I continued walking. Then I heard the thud of an oar against the side of a boat. I stopped. It sounded close, too close.

Someone was waiting!

I didn't know whether to keep walking and pray this wasn't an ambush or go back to Apphia and try to come up with another plan for getting us out of here alive. But with Apphia

337

unable to walk, we needed a boat. I had no choice. I had to put my trust in Angus's sister-in-law. I resumed walking.

Suddenly a loud screech exploded through the mist, the sound of a boat scraping rock. I froze. The boat was out there somewhere, just beyond my window of visibility. With no trees, no rocks to hide behind, I stood totally exposed, with only the mist to keep me invisible. At any moment it could lift, and when it did, I would be fully revealed.

I stepped backwards, away from the sound. But not soon enough. The mist parted. The boat appeared in all its frightening detail. An aluminum one with the motor raised drifted about five metres from shore, and sitting in it were two Inuk. I hastened to retreat back into the security of the fog, but not before someone had seen me.

"Apphia?" a quavering voice called out and said something more in Inuktitut.

Poised to escape back into the mist, I hesitated. I hadn't felt any threat in this man's voice. I called back. "It's me, Meg Harris."

"Thank god!" another voice called out. One that sounded familiar. And when the owner of that voice turned to face me, I saw Pete Pitsiulak, dressed as I was in sealskin.

"What are you doing here?" I whispered, somewhat warily. I still wasn't entirely certain about Pete. Could he be the trap?

"Come to get you," Pete said. "But we haven't got much time. This fog is going to lift soon. Where's Apphia?"

Knowing I had no option other than to trust him, I told him. Before I was finished, he'd already waded to shore and was now racing back along the way I'd come. I scrambled to keep up with him, but he reached Apphia before I even had a chance to show him her location. He almost ran into me on his way back down with Apphia and their son firmly gripped in his arms. When I saw the depth of loving relief in his eyes, I knew my fears had been misplaced. I slipped and slid behind him as I struggled to keep up. I didn't want to lose him in the fog.

We reached his boat without mishap. After gently lowering his mistress and child into the boat, he returned to carry me out.

"Too cold," he said. "You'll freeze your feet off."

"What about you?"

"Didn't you know? We Inuit have seal blood in our veins." He chuckled an all too familiar chuckle, which caused my thoughts to turn to painfully Eric before I thrust them aside.

As I settled myself on the seat beside Apphia, I recognized the other man. He was the same elderly man I'd seen at her brother's funeral. "My uncle," Apphia said. His eyes twinkled.

Using canoe paddles, the two men silently shoved the boat out into the deeper water. Within minutes, the fog blotted out the shore. Once again I felt eerily lost, my world reduced to this small aluminum boat and the people in it. I could barely see the water, although I could hear it lapping against the hull. I could hear dogs barking in the distance, no doubt from Angus's camp, but I didn't hear any other sounds, especially ones that would indicate our escape had been discovered.

Rather than using the boat's outboard motor, the men continued to push us silently through the mist with the paddles. I tried to remember where the location of the exit from the bay had been and couldn't, but I knew it was several kilometres away. Both men, however, seemed to be paddling with confidence, as if our escape route was firmly fixed in their minds. At one point, Apphia's uncle stopped and motioned Pete to stop paddling. For several long seconds he remained completely still before pointing in a slightly different direction from where we were heading. They resumed paddling, shifting the bow to this new direction.

"How do you know where to go?" I asked Pete.

"I don't, but the old man does. He's listening to the sound of the surf on the rocks near the gap."

I strained to hear, but picked up only muffled sounds.

The dogs had stopped barking. I caught no other sounds from Angus's camp, which by now we must be passing. It could be lying ten meters or a kilometre away. It was impossible to tell. Hopefully Apphia's uncle, with his supersonic hearing, was keeping us a safe distance away.

Then all hell broke loose. Hackneyed words, for sure, but it best described the sudden shouts and rifle shots that burst through the fog. Our escape had been discovered!

"Damn," Pete muttered. He spoke to the old man, who shook his head. Apphia added her words. But still the old man resisted.

"He doesn't want me to put on our motor. Says we're still too far from the exit. So start praying, Meg Harris, that they don't start coming out after us in the boats. They'll run into us for sure."

At that point we heard the sudden uproar of boat motors.

"Damn." Pete and the old man paddled harder.

"Do you have another paddle?" I asked.

Pete shook his head.

Apphia and I gripped hands as the boat silently slid through the water and the mist. Neither of us wanted to think what would happen if they found us. Apphia pulled out what looked to be a small religious painting from inside her *amauti* and began mouthing words in prayer.

The sound of the outboard motors grew louder. It was difficult to tell how many boats there were, but it was certainly more than one or two. I thought I remembered seeing at least five boats lying on the beach.

I peered ahead, straining to see anything through the opaque curtain. Suddenly I realized I was seeing water, something I hadn't been able to see a few minutes ago.

"Pete," I cried out, "I think the fog is lifting."

"I know. I'm hoping when it finally goes, we'll be close enough to the exit to get out of here alive."

The noise of the boats drew closer. It was almost as if they could see us through the mist, but more likely they were headed to the gap, hoping to stop our escape. In their haste, I hoped they didn't ram us and fling us into the frigid water, where our chance of survival was even less.

Then I could see the approaching black cliffs and the brightness of the gap less than fifty metres away. The mist had vanished. Our pursuers, all five boats, were still a good hundred metres away, but as Pete desperately tried to start the motor, they gained on us. I thought I saw Mary's white hair in the bow of the foremost boat and Ooleepeeka's grinning face in another, but in none of the boats did I see Angus's bulk.

After several more frantic pulls, the motor sprang to life, and the boat leapt forward. A rifle blasted.

"Get down!" Pete shouted. Apphia and I both dropped to the bottom of the boat. A bullet pinged off the metal hull. And another.

With the icon clasped tightly to her breast, Apphia resumed praying, while I prayed to whatever gods would listen.

More shots, but these I suddenly realized were coming from in front of us.

"Put your guns down!" a voice called out through a megaphone.

Another shot blasted from behind us. I heard it rip through the water beside our boat. Then I realized our pursuers were retreating. I looked up to see several police boats chasing after them.

"You guys okay?" a concerned Constable Curran shouted as her boat advanced towards us.

"What took you so long?" was Pete's reply.

As Apphia straightened up with relief, she forgot the tiny painting and dropped it. As I watched it fall to the floor of the boat, I realized she'd been praying over a stylized painting of a Virgin Mary, one that looked very much like an icon of the Russian Orthodox Church.

I picked it up and passing it to her said, "Where did you get this?"

"Our father."

Fifty-Two

The police rescue hadn't been a part of Pete's plan. When Apphia's uncle learned from a relative of Angus's wife that Apphia and I were being held prisoner at the family's camp, he went to the RCMP. But they dismissed his claim, insisting that the search planes had already flown over the camp without success. So he approached Pete, knowing of his relationship with his niece. The two of them decided to make their way to the camp and pretend they were a couple of lost Inuk, while at the same time hoping to catch sight of signs of our presence. Apparently my brother-in-law had wanted to join them, but since he didn't exactly look like a lost Inuk, it was decided he should continue to harass the RCMP.

Thankfully, the gods were with them, for as they'd approached the entrance to the bay, the fog had rolled in. It remained thin enough for them to find their way to the camp, where the first person they sighted was Elisapee, who did prove to be our guardian angel, after all.

She was very glad to see them. Upset by Angus's plan to kill us, she was trying to convince her son to help us escape in his boat, when she sighted Pete's boat. Pretending it belonged to distant relatives, she'd run down to the beach to intercept their arrival.

And so the three of them had proceeded to hatch a plan for our escape. By the time they'd finished, the fog had thickened, further increasing the chances of success. As an extra measure, Elisapee had spiked Angus's scotch with a secret Inuit remedy used to quiet disruptive children, no doubt the same ingredient used to put Apphia and me to sleep. When our police rescuers reached his camp, he was caught napping, literally.

Fortunately for us, the RCMP had eventually paid attention to Leslie, who'd brought to bear all the Harris influence he could muster, but by the time their flotilla of boats arrived at the gap, the fog had set in. Judging it too dangerous to proceed, they decided to remain at the entrance until it lifted. Thank goodness. Otherwise I'd hate to think what would've happened if their boats had been added to the blinding foggy mix.

We missed the arrest of Angus and his cohorts. I would've loved to have seen that Cheshire Cat grin erased from his face. Instead, Curran insisted on escorting us immediately back to Tasilik, which turned out to be a four-hour trip through turbulent windswept seas. The police boat was a considerably larger and sturdier affair than Apphia's uncle's small aluminum one, which made me wonder how four adults and one tiny baby would've made the risky trip if we had managed to escape on our own. Just as well the police had come to our rescue.

On reaching Tasilik, the three of us were immediately taken to the Health Centre, where we were thoroughly examined by one of the visiting doctors. Although Apphia's injury proved to be not a break but a serious sprain, it meant she wouldn't be able to return to her cherished Naujalik until she was more mobile. At least the family she'd been staying with was more than happy to accommodate her for as long as needed. It turned out they were Pete's cousins.

Apart from Apphia's ankle injury, none of us had suffered from our misadventure. In fact, the baby had thrived, for he'd gained a kilo since his last check-up. As for me, I was so ravenous now that the tension and fear had disappeared, any weight I might've lost during the day and a half of fasting would be gained back in no time. Not only did my body crave food, but once back on safe ground, it also demanded sleep. Unfortunately, I had to delay both until after Apphia and I gave our statements to the police.

Still wearing my sealskin jacket—I found it's warmth comforting—but changed into a relatively clean pair of jeans and a woollen top that hadn't been slept in, I sat beside Apphia in the cluttered office of the corporal, the only private room in the small Tasilik detachment, apart from the single jail cell. And that of course was occupied at the moment. The corporal very thoughtfully had one of his staff members bring us hamburgers and donuts to munch on during the interview.

In addition to the Tasilik corporal, Constable Curran and Sergeant Hue queried us about our kidnappings and what we'd seen and learned at Angus's isolated camp. That the art dealer had been involved in forgeries wasn't news to either the Tasilik or the Iqaluit police. They'd had their eye on his art dealings for sometime, but had never been able to prove anything, until now. The arrival of Hue and his suspicions had brought it into sharper focus. Apphia and I were able to fill in the gaps and tell them where to find the evidence.

The involvement of Mary Goresky came as a complete surprise to all three cops. At no time had her name appeared on any list of possible suspects. In fact, the art director had gained a reputation for squeaky-clean honesty amongst her art peers, especially after she'd brought several cases of counterfeiting to light. These cases, however, had involved not Inuit art, but Native American art. No doubt she'd used this to deflect attention away from her own fraudulent art dealings.

Both RCMP cops, however, had wondered about Angus's youngest daughter. Her graduate studies in Inuit art had smacked a little too much of the passing of the torch, particularly since she shared such a close relationship with her father. None of his other four children had shown the least interest in art, but they'd since learned from Ooleepeeka that this wasn't entirely the case. The eldest son, preferring to lead a traditional life style, essentially ran the camp at Qamanaarjuaq. He, along with Mary, had been the ones firing at us as we made our escape.

When Apphia and I told the police that Mary was Johnnie's killer, we raised police eyebrows even higher. Both Curran and Hue were speechless for several minutes, until Curran mentioned that there were several unidentifiable fingerprints in Johnnie's workshop, which if they matched Mary's would give them the evidence they needed to convict her. I also mentioned that if they hadn't found an *ulu* on Mary when they'd arrested her, they should check out the camp, where she'd probably left Johnnie's murder weapon.

"You can also charge her with the murder of Carter Davis," I said, turning to Sergeant Hue, "and the theft of the *Mystical Owl*. It's probably hidden somewhere at Angus's camp."

"My, my, you did learn a lot, didn't you?" The Toronto policeman beamed. "But it's good news. We have a witness who saw a woman leaving Carter's house the night before his body was discovered. She was carrying a tubular object, which could very well be the rolled-up print she'd removed from the frame found in the backyard. Apparently the woman's face sparkled in the headlights of a passing car. I'd say that sounds like Mary, wouldn't you?"

At the end of the interview, when we were about to leave, Curran asked me if I'd learned anything more about my father. I couldn't help but notice her eyes linger first on my hair then on Apphia's and back again. She of course had known my reasons for pursuing Johnnie's sister.

Turning my glance away from the blonde policewoman to Apphia, I said, "No, I'm afraid not."

Although I'd fully intended to reveal everything we'd learned from Angus, Apphia had expressed a wish for us to say nothing. The man who'd been her father had been a good man, good to his kids and good to his wife Suula. She didn't want his memory sullied by deeds he might or might not have done.

At the moment, we had no idea of the man's true identity.

Although the name he'd used, plus those he'd given his children and the fact he had my great-grandfather's watch pointed to Sutton Harris, his drawings, so like Joly Quliik's and the Russian icon he'd given his daughter, suggested it was Sergei Nabokov. But until the DNA analysis proved one way or the other, we wouldn't know.

On our way to the detachment we agreed that we would say nothing and would only bring up Crazy Russkie's name should the remains in the plane eventually prove not to be my father's. But we also agreed that regardless of the outcome, we would remain friends, if not sisters.

Curran rested her questioning eyes first on me, then on Apphia. I felt she wanted to say something more, but seeing our closed expressions, no doubt realized she'd learn nothing further.

Instead she said, "Your father's remains are scheduled to leave Iqaluit in a few days. My staff sergeant's put a rush on it, so you should get the results in a couple of weeks. The DNA unit will contact your mother directly."

Apphia and I spent the next couple of days learning about each other and each other's fathers. Like me, her father had disappeared from her life when she was a child, but at a considerably younger age, so her memories were hazier and more rose-coloured. Occasionally, when she was describing something her father had done, I would say to myself that it sounded like something my father would do. At other times, I felt the man she was describing was a stranger, no relation to me.

I did learn that her sister Margee had been the sender of the letters my mother received back in the 1980s. Apparently she'd sent these while she was at school in Churchill, Manitoba, shortly after their father died. Their father had told her sister that if the family ever needed money to contact a Mrs. Sutton Harris in Toronto. The family's dogs had died, and they needed to buy a snowmobile to survive. And contrary to what Mother had said, she had given them money. Not a lot. But enough to buy the snowmobile and the gas to operate it. Margee had sent a drawing of the family as a special thank-you. This was the picture Harold had hidden from my mother and I'd found in the attic. Over the years, additional amounts of money would come whenever they asked. Although it hadn't come directly from Mrs. Harris, but rather a Mr. Davis.

When I asked my mother about it, she didn't deny it. All she said was, "Now you know what I've had to live with since the first letter arrived ten years after his plane disappeared. I never wanted you girls to know that he might've survived, because that would mean he had forsaken you. I didn't want you to have to live with the same ache of betrayal I have lived with, knowing if he had survived, he wanted nothing more to do with us."

"But, Mother, chances are high the survivor of the plane crash was this Crazy Russkie I mentioned, who for some strange reason used Father's name. We'll know once they've finished the DNA analysis."

"Yes, I was never entirely certain that the girl who contacted me really was Sutton's daughter. But she did address those early letters with a name that only your father ever called me, Cessy. So that's why I decided to send her and her family the money. If they were indeed his children, I didn't want them in need."

She paused to catch her breath. Although her voice had sounded strong at the start of our call, I could tell she was tiring.

"Please, Mother, this is hard for you. I'm sorry I had to bring up these old memories. Why don't I let you go so you can rest?"

"Piffle. I'm fine. I might as well finish the story. I'm afraid I wasn't completely honest with you, dear, when you asked about the money Carter owed your father. I had Carter use that money for the family. I didn't want Harold to know about your father's betrayal, so felt it was the best way to handle the situation. But I never told Carter what the relationship of this family was to Sutton. Perhaps he guessed, but he never let on to me. And after our initial conversation, we never talked about the money again. I presumed he stayed in contact with this Margee and sent money whenever she asked."

We chatted for a few more minutes and ended our conversation with me suggesting that I stay with her in Toronto for as long as she needed me. Although she tried to dissuade me, saying I'd already been away from Three Deer Point too long, she didn't put up much of a fight. She even suggested I bring Sergei with me.

While I'd been busy with Apphia and talking to Mother, Leslie had spent his time shopping. He arrived at the Tasilik airport with several heavy cartons filled with carvings and other pieces of Inuit art, which resulted in many apologetic words at the check-in counter. Although the clerk initially insisted that they had to be shipped separately, she eventually relented and allowed them to travel on the same flight as cargo.

As we were about to board our plane, an RCMP truck drove onto the tarmac, and out jumped Constable Curran.

"I'm glad I caught you," she said. "They just called from Iqaluit. I'm afraid there was an explosion in the cargo bay at the Iqaluit airport. They were doing some repair work, and a propane tank exploded. Fortunately no one was seriously injured, but most of the cargo was destroyed in the fire, including the container holding your father's remains. There's nothing left for a DNA analysis." She paused. "Or for burial. I'm sorry."

So now I will never know if my father, Sutton Harris, was the man who parachuted from the burning plane on that frigid April day thirty-six years ago.

I don't care and neither does my mother, my sister, Jean or my sister, Apphia. Although we could probably establish through DNA if there is a blood link with Apphia, the four of us have decided we don't want it done. We know what happened to the plane. We know the role Apphia's mother and grandfather played in helping the survivor live. Each of us has our own memories, fond or otherwise, of the man we knew as Sutton Harris. Each of us has our own version of what happened on that fateful flight. We prefer to leave it that way. As for me, I like having another sister, even if Jean isn't keen on it.

ACKNOWLEDGMENTS

I have always had a keen interest in Canada's Far North and have longed to visit it. So I felt, what better way than to have Meg travel to Baffin Island? To do that, I had of course to scout it out for her. I spent a fabulous week in Iqaluit, Nunavut's capital and largest town, and Pangnirtung, noted not only for the world reknowned Uqqurmiut Centre for Arts and Crafts, but also for its picture postcard setting on the Pangnirtung Fjord.

I quickly discovered how friendly and helpful the people of Nunavut are and would like to thank a number for their valuable contributions in the writing of *Arctic Blue Death*. In particular, David Wilman, who not only spent several hours during my visit answering my many questions, but also proved invaluable during the writing of the book. And a special thanks to David's wife, Mary. Although she never answered my questions directly, she no doubt contributed to several of the answers. Others include, Deborah Merritt, Jolly Atagooyuk, Mick Mallan, Constable Pauline Melanson, Terry and Mehrun Forth, Donna Copeland and Ooleepeeka Arnaqaq. A special thanks to my editor Allister Thompson and publisher Sylvia McConnell.

And I'd like to thank my readers for their invaluable advice: Barbara Fradkin, Alex Brett, Judy Nasby and David Wilman. And as ever, I couldn't do this without the enduring support of my husband, Jim.

BIBLIOGRAPHY

Arctic Expressions: Inuit Art and the Canadian Eskimo Arts Council 1961-1989, Susan Gustavison, McMichael Canadian Art Collection, 1994

An Arctic Man, Ernie Lyall, Goodread Biographies, 1979

Cape Dorset Prints: A Retrospective: Fifty Years of Print Making at the Kinngait Studios, Leslie Boyd Ryan, Pomegranate Communications, 2007

Irene Avaalaqiaq: Myth and Reality, Judith Nasby, McGill-Queens University Press, 2002

Living on the Land: Change among the Inuit of Baffin Island, John S. Matthiasson, Broadview Press, 1992

Pitseolak: Pictures out of my life, from interviews by Dorothy Harley Eber, McGill-Queens University Press, 2003

Saqiyuq: Stories from the Lives of Three Inuit Women, Nancy Wachowich in collaboration with Apphia Agalakti Awa, Rhoda Kaukjak Katsak and Sandra Pikujak Katsak, McGill-Queens University Press, 1999

R. J. Harlick is an escapee from the high tech jungle and a lover of the outdoors. She can often be found roaming the forests of West Quebec or canoeing the waterways. She currently lives in Ottawa, Ontario.

Her first novel, *Death's Golden Whisper*, introduced Meg Harris and was followed by *Death's Golden Whisper*, *Red Ice for a Shroud* and *The River Runs Orange*.

She can be visited on line at rjharlick.com.